INCOMING FIRE

NATHAN BURROWS

Dedicated to those who serve, and to those who support them.

1

Corporal Barret had wanted to join the Royal Air Force since he was knee high to a grasshopper, but at no point in his career had he expected he would be occupying a coffin draped in a Union flag.

He was lying in a wooden coffin courtesy of a piece of shrapnel from an improvised explosive device. It had been adapted from an anti-tank mine that the Russians had somehow left behind when they were driven from Afghanistan at the end of the Soviet-Afghan war in early 1989, when Corporal Barret was still learning to walk. The device had exploded when he stepped on a pressure plate connected to the primary charge, both hidden under the surface of a small and well-trodden path in Helmand Province.

Robert Barret, or Rob to his mates, was unlucky on two fronts. The first and most obvious was stepping on the pressure plate. The first two RAF regiment gunners on the foot patrol had somehow passed unhindered. Not so Rob. The second piece of bad luck that sunny morning was that the IED wasn't intended to kill whoever activated it, but maim them because a casualty used up more resources than a body. This was something that the insurgents who had planted the device knew well.

The piece of shrapnel was smaller than Rob's little fingernail, but it didn't need to be large to be deadly. It had struck him in the groin, effortlessly ripping its way through the soft tissue of his upper leg and deep into his thigh where it transected his femoral artery. Despite the valiant attempts of the patrol medic to save him, Rob had bled to death in a corner of a foreign field like many before him. As he lay there looking at the sky, his vision slowly disappearing as his life ebbed away, Corporal Barret was defending Her Majesty, her heirs and successors in time-honoured tradition by dying for Queen and country.

Rob's coffin was laminated with an oak style veneer to hide the chipboard it was actually made from and it was covered with a hand sewn drape exactly two-and-a-half yards long. It was made from high-quality Ministry of Defence standard woven and knitted polyester by an elderly lady who worked for a flag company in Slough. The material had dried now, but as it was being sewn, it was damp with her tears for a serviceman she would never know. When the Hercules C130J transport plane that Rob was being transported in arrived home, the flag would be damp again with tears. His mother's. His father's. His girlfriend's, and his sister's. All of them mourning the loss of someone they loved, and to whom they'd never had the chance to say goodbye. So many things left unsaid, so many harsh words that could never be taken back, so many memories that would never be refreshed.

But Corporal Robert Barret, or Rob to his mates, knew none of this. He was dead.

2

Adams picked up the remote control and turned the television in the staff room on. He was starving and had been looking forward to his lunch break all morning. It was his own fault for almost oversleeping and not giving himself enough time for breakfast. He peeled back the cellophane wrapper of his sandwich and took a large bite, muttering to himself when a stray prawn, covered in some sort of pink sauce, fell out of the sandwich and onto his green hospital scrubs.

"Bugger," he said as he wiped it up with a napkin. Just as he was doing this, the door to the staff room flew open and one of the staff nurses stuck her head in. Her face was flushed, excited.

"Adams, I'm really sorry, but we need you back in Resus."

"Seriously, Hannah?" Adams said. "I've only just sat down, and I'm bloody starving."

"There's a trauma call on the way."

With a sigh, Adams re-wrapped the cellophane on his sandwich and got to his feet to put it in the fridge. He was the most experienced nurse on duty that morning in the emergency department of the Norfolk and Norwich hospital, and with a bunch of baby doctors starting at the same time, things were frantic out in the main Emergency Department.

"What is it? Anything interesting?" Adams asked Hannah.

"Man versus pig, apparently. Serious crush injuries to the chest. The man's, not the pig's."

"Okay, what else is in Resus?"

"We're just moving the chest pain back out into Majors to clear up some space in there."

"Good stuff."

Adams walked across the quadrangle between the staff room and the main department, deliberately taking his time. He knew that when he walked into the Resus room, it would be a hive of activity, most of it unnecessary, but it wasn't his place to say anything. He was only seconded to the department from his primary role in the Royal Air Force so he could keep his clinical skills up to date.

He dabbed his finger at the pink stain on the front of his scrubs, thinking about the sandwich back in the fridge. Since coming back from Afghanistan last year, he had put back on almost all the weight that he had lost while he was over there. Adams wasn't fat by a long stretch of the imagination, but he needed to make sure he didn't put on too much more or he would fail his fitness test, and the level he needed to reach wouldn't come down until he reached his thirtieth birthday, which was still a long two years away.

Adams laughed to himself as he imagined the civilian nurses he worked with having to do an annual fitness test.

Hannah would probably be about the only one who would pass it. There were several of them that would probably struggle to fit through the door of the gymnasium.

"How long, Hannah?" Adams called out. Hannah had already reached the door of the department.

"Ten minutes," she replied, looking back over her shoulder at him.

"Bloody hell," Adams said, turning on his heel to go back to the staff room. That was more than enough time to finish his sandwich.

When he got to the Resus room exactly seven minutes later, his stomach at least sated if not full, Adams cast a practised eye around the room. The bay they would use for this patient was in the centre of the five bays the department had. It faced the doors that the paramedics would bring him through. On one side of the bay was an intravenous drip stand, with a pressure infuser attached to it. The other side had an emergency trolley with a nervous looking anaesthetic Senior House Officer standing next to it.

"Where's the Registrar?" Adams said to him brusquely.

"Er, I'm not sure. He might be in theatre?"

"Well, he needs to be here. Go and have him fast bleeped." The doctor stared at him, open-mouthed, for a few seconds before doing as instructed. "Who's the senior on today?"

"It's Raj," someone replied. "He'll be here in a second."

Adams was pleased to hear Raj's name mentioned. Of all the Emergency Room registrars, Dr Pashanwar was the one Adams got on the best with. They had quickly built up a good working relationship, each of them naturally doing what they needed to without stepping on each other's toes. But most of all, Raj actually listened to Adams's opinion. Which, considering Adams had more trauma experience than all the other nurses in the Resus room that day put together, was just as well.

Just as Adams had finished tying his disposable apron behind his back, the ambulance doors opened and all hell broke loose.

"This is Mr Julian Hartley," the paramedic at the foot end of the stretcher said, his voice terse and breathless. "He's sixty four and approximately thirty minutes ago, he was crushed by a large pig in his farm out by Thetford. He's got—"

"It was a boar," the large man on the ambulance trolley said with a cough, "not a pig." That simple act told Adams a lot about Julian Hartley. He had a patent airway, or he wouldn't be able to speak. He was conscious and alert enough to correct the paramedic's mistake. But, as Adams looked at the farmer, he could see that the man was also in big trouble as the paramedic accompanying him confirmed with his next statements.

"He's got a significant crush injury to the chest with a potential flail segment on the left-hand side. Resps are thirty, sats on air are eighty-five per-cent. Blood pressure is low at ninety over forty, and he's tachycardic at one ten. He's got a line in there," the paramedic pointed at a cannula in the farmer's left forearm, "and he's had a litre of Hartmann's on the way in."

"Thanks," Adams said, looking around for Raj. "Mr Hartley? My name's Paul Adams, and I'm the senior nurse on duty today. You're in excellent hands, sir."

"Bloody hell," the farmer gasped as he looked at Adams's name badge. He attempted to smile. "A flight lieutenant, eh? Is the NHS that bad they've got the military in?"

Coordinated by Adams, the team slid the farmer onto the hospital trolley. Adams stood back for a few seconds, observing the nursing team as they bustled around the patient. There was still no sign of Raj. Adams took a couple of steps over to the paramedic. He knew him by sight, but didn't know him well.

"How big was this bloody pig?" Adams whispered.

"It was huge," the paramedic replied. "I don't know, maybe thirty stone?"

"I didn't know they grew that big. Any relatives?"

"Wife's in the family room. Lizzie's sitting with her."

"Lizzie Jarman?"

"Yeah." The paramedic glanced down at Adams's name badge. "Of course, she's one of your lot."

"I'll come and see her if I can before you have to clear."

"Sure, I'll let her know. It'll take us a while to clear up."

Adams crossed back to the trolley to have a proper look at the patient. He took a few seconds to look at the farmer's breathing pattern before he did anything else. He was just reaching for a stethoscope when Raj arrived.

"What've we got?" he said, his voice calm and melodious. Adams had yet to see the man flustered about anything.

"Man versus pig," Hannah said from the other side of the trolley.

"Dear me," Raj replied, looking down at the patient. "It rather looks like the pig won."

3

Sergeant Lizzie Jarman sat in the relative's room holding Mrs Hartley's hand. The farmer's wife was sobbing uncontrollably, and every time Lizzie tried to retrieve her hand she just grabbed it harder.

"He will be okay, won't he?" Mrs Hartley asked for what seemed to Lizzie like the tenth time.

"Your husband's in good hands, Mrs Hartley," Lizzie said, trying again to extricate her hand. She'd learnt the hard way not to tell people that everything would be fine. It didn't always turn out that way.

"I told him not to mix them pigs in together, but he wouldn't bloody listen." She smiled at Lizzie through her tears and tried to put on a brave face. "Bloody men, eh?"

Lizzie smiled back and finally managed to get her hand back. She got to her feet.

"Let me go and see if I can find someone to come and sit with you for a bit," Lizzie said, knowing that Patrick—her partner for the shift—would be moaning like anything at having to restock the ambulance on his own.

"Okay, thank you, dear," Mrs Hartley replied with a sniff.

Lizzie left the relative's room and made her way back out of the Emergency Department to the area where the ambulances drew up. Sure enough, Patrick was annoyed.

"You took your bloody time, Lizzie," he said as she stepped up into the back of the ambulance. "I've nearly finished in here now."

"Stop whinging, you old woman," Lizzie shot back, ignoring the look of annoyance on Patrick's face. "It's all your mess, anyway. I'm just the taxi driver. What still needs doing?"

"I might as well finish up," Patrick retorted, "seeing as I'm almost done. There was an army lad in there asking after you. Why don't you go and flutter your eyelashes at him?"

"Army or Air Force?" Lizzie asked.

"Don't know. Military, anyway. Buzz cut hair, thinner than most of them in there."

Lizzie left Patrick still grumbling under his breath about having to clean up and walked back into the Emergency Department. They had paired her up with Patrick all week, and he was beginning to get on her nerves. If it weren't for the fact that tomorrow was her last shift before she was back on teaching duties at RAF Honington, she would have asked the Paramedic Supervisor for another partner. Her clinical time was precious enough, and she didn't want to waste it squabbling with a civilian.

The doors to the Resus room were closed, but there was a round window in them she could look through. No-one would have said anything if she'd walked in—she was wearing a paramedic's uniform after all—but if the person who'd been asking after her was who she thought it was, she'd rather just stay put.

Her suspicions were proved right when she saw a familiar figure bending over the patient. Even though she couldn't see his face, she recognised him straight away from the small crescent-shaped scar on the back of his head visible through his short hair. She'd been with him when he got that scar. Lizzie subconsciously raised her hand to her cheek. Even though the metal plates holding it together were long gone, it still ached when it rained.

Lizzie watched as Adams put his hands on the patient's throat, pressing gently. She knew exactly what was running through his head as he did so. Was the trachea central? Were the neck veins flat or distended? Was there any crepitus? She could almost recite the drills as he was doing them, they had practised them so many times.

Next to Adams was an olive-skinned doctor whose face was a mask of concentration as he took some blood gases from the farmer's wrist. Lizzie watched him withdraw the needle and, without prompting, Adams reached down and pressed on the gauze covering the hole. Lizzie knew he would press hard to make sure that the farmer didn't start squirting arterial blood all over the place. As the doctor moved away from the patient and walked out of Lizzie's eyeline, Adams looked up and saw her peering through the window.

When Adams looked at her, Lizzie felt her heart lurch for a split second. She had been through so much with this man. But she didn't want to talk to him, just see him. His eyes lit up, and he grinned before holding his other hand up with his fingers and thumb extended and mouthing *five minutes*. She smiled back at him, remembering how he used to do the same thing in the back of the Chinook to let the medical team know they were five minutes away from landing.

Lizzie turned, suddenly not wanting to be in the Emergency Department any more. She had seen him. That was enough. She hustled back to the ambulance bay, hoping that Patrick had finished cleaning and restocking the vehicle. If he had, she could punch clear with control and they could get back on the road.

"Did you see your mate?" Patrick asked Lizzie as she approached the ambulance.

"Yeah, I saw him," she replied. "Are you done?"

"I am, no thanks to you."

Lizzie ignored him and climbed into the driver's seat before picking up the radio handset.

"Control, this is Charlie Three Zero One," she said.

"What, we're going clear already?" Patrick said. "I was going to grab a brew."

"Charlie Three Zero One, this is control. Go ahead, over," a distorted male voice came through the speakers of the radio.

"Control, we're now clear at the Norfolk and Norwich, over."

Patrick got into the passenger seat with a look of resignation on his face.

"Roger that, Charlie Three Zero One. You can return to base. Control out."

Lizzie started the engine and put the ambulance into gear.

"I'll buy you a Starbuck's on the way back to base if you're a good boy," she said to Patrick with a grin. "That'll be nicer than the crap from the machine in there."

4

There was nothing particularly technical about the timing mechanism attached to the rockets. Two wires, which when connected would complete the firing circuit, were separated by a block of ice. It dripped steadily in the early morning light of Kandahar province and, the moment the sun finally rose above the horizon, it would melt away in a matter of moments. The exact time it took didn't matter, as long as it was long enough for the insurgents who had placed the crude artillery barrage to be a long way from it when it finally launched.

The rockets were lined up in a row, all five of them leaning up against an earthen bank. Just over five kilometres in front of them, and a few hundred yards lower down, was the sprawling air base of Kandahar airfield. The insurgents didn't care where within the boundary of the base the rockets hit, although they prayed to their God that they would hit something. The tactic was not to destroy, but to terrify the foreigners within the wire below.

To let them know that at any moment, death could rain from above in an utterly random way.

The green tubes each weighed a few grams under twenty kilograms. Of this, just over eight kilograms was made up of a compound called trinitrotoluene, more commonly known as TNT. First invented in the late eighteen hundreds by a German chemist, it wasn't used as an explosive until before the First World War. Any contact between the explosive and the skin could cause it to turn a bright yellow-orange colour, and the munitions workers who handled it during the First World War were known as 'canaries' for that very reason. The insurgents knew none of this, however. They had simply bought them at an underground market in the foothills of the mountains that looked down on Kandahar. The TNT inside the shells was already safely encased by the metal of the warhead at the front of each rocket.

Behind the warhead was the largest part of the rocket: the motor. Sandwiched between two bourrelets, the metal bands which gave the rockets stability in flight, was the propulsion system. The propellant was made of a modern thermoplastic composite, unbounded to the walls of the combustion chamber just in case the owners wanted to overhaul the rocket at some point. The rear of the rocket had six canted nozzles which would rotate the rocket with high angular velocity. This, and the bourrelets either side of the motor, negated the need for fins.

In a tree a few yards away from the five rockets, an Afghan snow finch was singing to welcome the new day. As the ice melted away and the two wires in the crude timer touched, an electrical charge shot through the squib igniter in the base of the first rocket. The black powder magazine inside the igniter fired, passing a flame upward through a small hole in the centre of the propellant sticks. Once all seven propellant sticks had ignited—a process which took milliseconds—the gas they generated blew away the nozzle cover, and jets of flame shot out of the rear of the rocket. The roar this caused sent the small greyish-brown bird flying in the opposite direction as quickly as its wings would take it.

The first rocket launched into the air, wobbling from side to side for a few seconds before it started spinning. Then it stabilised and took flight properly, closely followed by its four companions.

A few kilometres away, in a technical truck parked next to an opium field, the insurgents who had planted the rockets in the pre-dawn light whooped and cheered as they watched the five smoke trails head towards the base below them.

5
———

Adams looked around, desperate to find someone to take over from him. Standing a few feet away from and watching what was going on was a student nurse. He beckoned to her and it took a couple of seconds before she realised that he wanted her to join him.

"Put some gloves on and press down here," Adams said, nodding to the farmer's arm. The student nurse's eyes widened, but she did as Adams told her. The girl was only supposed to be an observer, but she would have to get her hands dirty at some point, so why not now? "Hannah? You're in charge for a few minutes, okay?"

"Sure," Hannah replied, her attention focused on the monitor behind the patient's head. Adams made sure the student had a good hold of the patient's wrist—the farmer didn't need a huge haematoma from an arterial stab to add to his problems—and crossed to where Raj was standing next to the blood gas machine.

"Raj, I just need to nip out for a few moments," Adams

said. "You've got Hannah and I won't be long. Is that okay?"

"Um, well. If you have to," Raj replied with a look of concern on his face. "But don't be long. These gasses are pretty bad." He glanced at the farmer lying on the trolley.

"Five minutes, tops," Adams replied. "Look, radiology's here to do his chest. I'll be back before the images are ready."

Raj nodded and Adams stripped his gloves off, throwing them into a clinical waste bin before doing the same thing with his plastic apron. He left the Resus room and walked through the waiting room to the doors that led to the ambulance bay. When he got there, there were two ambulances parked in front of the Emergency Department. One of them was just unloading a patient, so he crossed to the other ambulance and walked up to the driver's window. When he looked in, there were two male paramedics sitting in the front. On seeing Adams, the one in the driver's seat wound down his window.

"You alright, mate?" the paramedic asked.

"Has the crew that brought that trauma call in gone already?"

"Yeah, they just left."

"Oh, okay," Adams replied, trying to hide his disappointment. "Did they get a job?"

"No," the driver replied. "It would have come to us first. We punched clear long before they did."

Adams paused for a second, not sure what to do. He thanked the paramedic and was walking back toward the hospital entrance when the student nurse who he'd left in charge of the farmer's arm came running out.

"Adams?" she said breathlessly. "Dr Raj needs you back in Resus."

Grateful for something else to concentrate on, Adams broke into a jog and followed the student nurse back into the building. When he got back to the Resus room, Raj was staring at a chest x-ray on a large computer monitor. The radiographers had been much quicker than Adams thought they would be.

"What's up, Raj?" Adams said as he joined him.

"This chap's in trouble, Adams. I've just bleeped the cardiothoracic registrar." Adams leaned forward to look at the x-ray. He pointed out a large whitened area on the screen.

"That's a huge haemothorax," Adams said. "Are you going to put a drain in?"

"I'm not sure. I'll probably wait for the cardiothoracic team. See the flail segment there?"

"Yep, that's going to hurt."

"Okay, so he's got classic hypoxia from the haemothorax. Gasses are rubbish on air, he's hypotensive and tachycardic. When we put a drain in and all that blood comes out, he's going to need a lot of support," Raj said, pushing his glasses further up his nose. It was the only tell that he was nervous about something.

"But?" Adams asked, knowing that there was something else.

"Can you see it?" Raj replied, pointing at the screen. Adams looked again, but he couldn't see anything that they'd not already discussed.

"You're going to have to talk me through it, Raj."

Raj lifted his finger and pointed at the screen.

"The mediastinum's wider than it should be, and look at the bronchi. The left mainstem is depressed, and the right one elevated."

An alarm bell started ringing in the back of Adams's

mind, but he couldn't put his finger on what it was. He was sure that during one of the courses he'd done in the past this sequence had been talked about, but he couldn't for the life of him remember what it meant.

"Which means what?" Adams asked, admitting defeat.

"I think he's got a traumatic aortic disruption. The only thing holding his aorta together is that." Raj pointed at the collection of blood in the lung. "If we release that haemothorax, his aorta could rupture."

"Bloody hell," Adams whispered. "If you're right, that's a great spot. So what next. CT?"

"I don't think he's stable enough. He probably needs to go straight to theatre. Can you sort some morphine out for the chap? Let's at least get his pain under control."

The second Raj said this, Adams felt awful. He'd gone running off after Lizzie instead of looking after his patient properly. He'd assumed that Hannah or one of the other nurses would have been drawing up some analgesia for the farmer while he was away, but they hadn't. It wasn't their fault—he was the senior nurse.

"Some bloody nurse you are, sunshine," Adams muttered to himself as he walked over to the controlled drugs cupboard on the wall. "Hannah?" he called out. "Can you check some CDs with me, please?"

6

Lizzie reversed the ambulance into its allocated parking bay and turned the engine off before turning to Patrick.

"How was the Starbucks?" she asked, receiving a wry grin in reply.

"Very nice, thank you."

"It should be for that price," Lizzie replied. "Listen, Patrick. I'm sorry if I was a bit snappy back at the hospital. That lad you mentioned. Well, I'd just not seen him for a while."

"Bit of history there, I take it?"

"Yeah, you could say that. Probably not the sort of history you're thinking, though." Lizzie stared through the windscreen for a few seconds, wondering how much to tell Patrick. She'd not spoken to anyone outside the military about her experiences and wasn't sure whether to speak to Patrick or not. "We served together in Afghanistan."

"Oh, okay," Patrick replied. He didn't say anything else, and Lizzie thought he was waiting to see if she would say anything else. She decided against it. He was a civilian, after all, and wouldn't understand. Not properly.

As she got out of the ambulance, her thoughts turned to Adams. She felt bad for running off when he'd seen her, but all she'd wanted to do was to see him. See how he was getting on. If he was okay, that sort of thing.

Lizzie hadn't seen him since the previous year when they'd both been in Cyprus for a Court Martial. In the end, neither of them had had to give evidence or even say anything, and it had left them with a week together before flying home. Their first—and last—night together had been memorable if only for the fact that nothing had happened. Not even a kiss. It wasn't that she hadn't wanted something to happen, but it was all too soon after the accident. She couldn't even say they'd slept together as she'd not slept a wink, spending the night wide awake and tearful while Adams snored like a baby beside her.

When they both came back to the United Kingdom, they'd made a vague arrangement to meet up at some point, but never had. Lizzie hadn't returned his calls, had ignored his e-mails and, when she changed her phone number after buying a new phone, she'd not given him the new one.

"Lizzie?" Patrick interrupted her train of thought. He was walking behind her and reached out an arm. When his hand touched her elbow, Lizzie flinched. "Sorry, didn't mean to make you jump. Are you okay?"

"Sure, I'm fine," she replied, forcing a laugh. "Just thinking, that's all."

"Listen, if you ever wanted to chat, you know, over a drink or something?"

"That's really nice of you, Patrick," Lizzie replied, "but

I'm kind of seeing someone." As she looked at his crestfallen face, she hoped he wouldn't see through the lie.

A COUPLE OF HOURS LATER, after the rest of the shift passed without any more jobs, Lizzie drove back to the RAF base in Honington where she had been working for the last month. It was a sprawling airfield in East Anglia, surrounded by pig farms and fields, and about as far away from civilisation as it was possible to get. Which, considering it was the home of the RAF Regiment, probably wasn't a bad thing. The regiment was about as close to an infantry regiment as it was possible to get without joining the army, and the men who made it up tended not to play nicely with other children.

Lizzie parked her car outside the Warrant Officer's and Sergeant's Mess and made her way into the foyer. All she wanted to do was to have something to eat followed by a hot bath and a glass of wine. It had been a long shift. She had another one tomorrow, and she would be back in the classroom the following week trying to teach regiment gunners combat first aid. Which, even on a good day, was like trying to nail jelly to the ceiling.

As she passed through the foyer, Lizzie saw Warrant Officer Tom Fowler, the Station Warrant Officer. He was talking to one of the mess staff, but when he saw Lizzie, he broke off the conversation and walked over to her.

"Lizzie, how are you doing?" Fowler asked. He was almost a stereotypical regiment Warrant Officer. Tall, broad-shouldered, and with a face like a man chewing a wasp. About the only thing that marked him out as different was the fact he walked with a stick, courtesy of an improvised explosive device that had taken his right leg off below the knee a couple of years ago. He was also the closest thing Lizzie had to a friend on the station. "Busy shift?"

"Pretty busy, yeah," Lizzie replied. "Went to a man crushed by a pig. I was driving, but my oppo said he was pretty well squashed."

"Jesus wept," Fowler replied. "Fancy a glass of wine? I'm buying, and you can tell me all about it." Lizzie thought for a second. Glass of wine, then food, then a bath. That worked.

"Sure, sounds like a plan."

They walked into the bar and Fowler ordered them both a drink. He nodded at a few of the other senior non-commissioned officers in the bar. As the Station Warrant Officer, he was pretty much the top dog on the station, and everyone knew that. Because there weren't any women serving in the RAF Regiment—although that was about to change—Lizzie was something of a rarity. Having a friend like Fowler ensured that Lizzie was treated properly although, as a medic, she would have been anyway. Given the number of casualties the regiment had suffered over the years, they had a great deal of respect for medics.

Lizzie and Fowler chatted for a while, him roaring with laughter as she recounted how she and Patrick had watched four policemen wrestling with a large boar so they could get to their casualty.

"Oh, that must have been a sight," Fowler said as he wiped a tear from the corner of his eye. "The most exciting thing that's happened to me today is that I got to shout at someone for walking on the grass."

Lizzie took a sip of her wine and looked around the bar. While she recognised one or two of the faces in there, there were a lot she didn't.

"Lot of new faces about," she said, raising an eyebrow in Fowler's direction.

"Pre-deployment training's being ramped up big time," he replied. One of the roles undertaken by the regiment was training RAF personnel in weapons drills, amongst other things. "The training squadron has had to put on a load of extra courses to get them all through." Lizzie didn't take too much notice of what Fowler had just said. It wasn't going to affect her, so she paid it no mind. "How is the pig farmer, anyway?"

Lizzie paused for a second before replying.

"I'm not sure," she said. "I'll ask control when I go in tomorrow." Her thoughts drifted back towards Adams, and the way he smiled when he saw her looking through the window in the door of the Resus room. "He was in good hands when I left him, though."

7

At the front of the five rockets that were currently making their way through the thin air above Kandahar air base were Chinese Jiàn-1 point detonating rocket fuzes. Their sole function was to ensure that when the rockets landed, the main TNT charge sitting behind the fuzes exploded.

As the rockets reached the top of their arc, they briefly entered an area of sky that was being constantly monitored by a COBRA unit located on the far edge of the airfield. The squat olive vehicle, with its large active electronically scanned array 3D radar, immediately located the rockets and tried to locate the position that they were fired from. It didn't bother trying to calculate the landing point of the rockets; that would be obvious enough in the next few seconds. But locating the firing point would mean that friendly forces from the base could examine the location to see if there was any valuable intelligence left behind. There wouldn't be—the insurgents were too clever to make such a basic mistake—and all it would do would be to place troops on the ground in danger from booby traps or secondary devices.

At the same time the computers inside the counter-battery radar system moved ones and noughts around at infinitesimal speed, the unit sent an alert to the Giant Voice system. A spilt second later, the network of large speakers spread about the base burst into life with an ear-piercing wail.

Behind the fuzes, the propellant in the motors was spent and, having reached the top of their arc of flight, the rockets started to lose altitude and make their way to the still unsuspecting base below. Any personnel up and moving about the base at that early hour would be looking around, trying to locate some cover to dive into. The vast majority of them, however, were still in bed. The only thing they would be able to do was roll out of their beds and get underneath them, for all the protection that would offer from the incoming rockets.

In the hills above Kandahar, the team of insurgents were watching the smoke trails of the rockets. When they petered out, they knew that their early morning gifts to the occupants of the base below them were only seconds away from being delivered.

8

Adams sighed as he looked up at the grey clouds that were scudding across the sky. One thing he'd forgotten in his rush to get to work earlier that day was a coat, and it looked as if it was about to start teeming down any second. This part of the country was one of the driest in the whole of the United Kingdom, but it still knew how to rain. He unlocked his bike from the rack outside the Emergency Department and looked around the ambulance bay. There was one crew he recognised, sitting in the front of their ambulance sipping from polystyrene cups. Adams walked up to the driver's window and tapped on it.

"You boys are from the Yarmouth station, aren't you?"

"Hey, Adams," the driver replied. "We are. Why?"

"I was wondering if I could grab a lift as far as Thorpe St Andrew if you're heading back that way? If you get a shout, I'll just hop out."

"And people wonder why we're known as big white taxis?" the driver said with a laugh. "Go on, shove your bike in the back."

"You're a star, thank you."

Adams opened the rear door of the ambulance and hefted his bicycle inside. Just as he did so, large drops of rain started to fall. Cycling back home in this weather would have been miserable at best, dangerous at worst. He climbed in and sat down, leaning through the hatch at the front to thank the paramedics for the favour.

As the ambulance pulled away from the hospital, Adams sat back in the crew seat and went over the shift he had just finished in his head. He still felt bad about not getting the analgesia ready for the farmer earlier, but Raj had told him to stop worrying about it when they'd discussed it. The doctor had been right about his diagnosis, and the farmer was in the operating theatre having his aorta repaired at that moment. If Raj hadn't spotted the abnormalities on the x-ray and gone ahead with a chest drain, the patient would almost certainly have bled to death in the Resus room.

In his pocket, Adams's mobile phone vibrated. He reached into his pocket, noting the *unknown number* on the screen, and answered it.

"Hello?"

"Is that Flight Lieutenant Adams?" a male voice replied.

"Yup, that's me." Adams sighed as he recognised the voice.

"Hi, mate, it's Wing Commander Daley from Air Command."

"Hi, sir."

Wing Commander Daley ran the manning desk at Air Command. If he was calling, then it could only be one of three things. To tell Adams he'd been promoted, but it was the wrong time of year for the promotion boards, so it couldn't be that. It could be to tell him about a posting, but Adams had been told he had at least a year of clinical secondment. The only other thing it could be was what Adams didn't want to hear.

"Got a job for you, old chap," the wing commander said. His voice had a forced joviality about it. Adams liked the man. He had an unenviable job, and it wasn't one that Adams could do.

"Seriously? It's not even been a year since my last deployment. It can't be my turn already, can it?"

"Strictly speaking, it's not," Daley replied, "but there's been a few people fall over, see?"

Adams sighed again. He knew he was an easy target for deployment. He wasn't married, didn't have children, and always said yes anyway. The two of them had done this dance before. Adams would complain, the wing commander would listen sympathetically, and then tell him he was going anyway.

"Where?" Adams asked, deciding to skip the complaining part. There wasn't any point.

"Kandahar. Got you a nice little desk job for a change."

"I didn't think there was a desk job out there," Adams replied. "The only post I know of is the one that Squadron Leader Swanson's in?"

"That's the badger," Daley replied. "Medical Advisor to the Base Commander. Cracking way to earn a medal."

"I've already got that medal," Adams replied frostily, "and the clasp."

"Well, just think of the extra cash then."

"I don't need the extra cash." Adams knew he was being petulant, but it didn't seem fair. Then a thought occurred to him. "So it's with acting rank then, is it?"

"Um, no."

"I'll happily do it if it is."

"Not my choice, old chap. That'll be up to the A1 Ops lot upstairs."

"Maybe you should ask them. If there genuinely isn't anyone else, then it shouldn't be an issue. Especially if there's a squadron leader in the post already."

"Let me get back to you."

Adams disconnected the call, grinning. He didn't need the money, but the chance to act up for an operational tour—desk job or no desk job—would do him no harm at all both in terms of actually being promoted at some point in the future and his bank balance.

The ambulance crew dropped Adams off outside his flat. He'd been expecting to be thrown out at the turnoff to the dual carriageway that lead back to Great Yarmouth, but the paramedic driver had taken pity on him given the weather. Adams thanked the two men in the front of the ambulance, promising them that the first pints were on him at the next leaving bash.

He carried his bike up the stairs and unlocked the door to his small two-bedroomed flat. It wasn't much, but it was his. One of the sweeteners for a year-long secondment to the NHS was the chance to live in his own place for a while.

Adams walked into his tiny kitchen and opened the fridge door. A cup of tea would be nice, but he wasn't sure about the milk. He was just sniffing it when his phone started ringing again. Adams grinned, hoping that the wing commander was calling back with some good news.

"Hi, sir," Adams said as he answered the phone. "How badly does the Queen need me, then?"

"I've got no idea, but I've never been called *sir* before."

It wasn't the wing commander. It was a female voice. A very familiar one.

"Hey, Lizzie Jarman if I'm not mistaken," Adams replied as he put the carton full of curdled milk on the counter. "It's been a while."

9

Lizzie sat on the edge of the sofa in her lounge, the phone clamped to her ear. She felt nervous, although the three glasses of wine she'd had in the bar with Fowler had helped, and a further one with her dinner. It had been the warrant officer who had persuaded her to call Adams.

"Life's too short to mess about, Lizzie," Fowler had said when she had told him that she'd seen Adams. Fowler knew pretty much everything about what had happened to her and Adams at the end of their last tour. There was a lot that was still classified, though, and always would be. Fowler had tapped his prosthetic leg with his walking stick. "You never know what's round the corner. Just live every day like it's your last."

"What, dance like no-one's watching kind of thing?"

"If you want to put it that way," Fowler had laughed, "why not?"

"How've you been?" Lizzie asked Adams. "Like you say, it's been a while."

"Well, you never write, you never call," Adams replied,

but she could hear the smile in his voice. "What can I say?"

"I'm sorry, Paul," Lizzie replied, only using his first name so he knew she was being serious. "It's been tough. When I saw you today, I…" Her voice tailed away, and she was suddenly unsure what to say.

"I really wanted to speak to you, Lizzie," Adams said. "I couldn't believe it when I saw you looking through the window. It's been what, almost six months since Cyprus?"

"About that, yes," Lizzie replied. "Like I said, sorry."

There was a silence between them that was threatening to become awkward when Adams spoke.

"I can't believe that the NHS is letting you drive an ambulance."

"Bugger off, you cheeky sod," Lizzie said with a smile. "I'm fully qualified on blue lights, thank you very much."

"What happens when it needs parking? Do you have to get out and let one of the lads park it for you?"

Lizzie started laughing. Adams could read her like a book, sensing when the mood needed to be lightened.

"I can't believe you're still a nurse," she countered.

"What do you mean?"

"Well, it's not really a man's job, is it?"

"Touché!" Adams replied, chuckling. There was another silence, this one much more comfortable.

"I've missed you, Adams," Lizzie said a moment later.

"You've got a funny way of showing it, mate." Adams's smile was back in his voice. "It shouldn't be this difficult, should it?"

"What shouldn't?"

"Look at us, Lizzie. After everything we've been through, every chance we've had, we're still just us. I always thought we would end up together. I even thought maybe in Cyprus that was going to change, and I totally get why it didn't, but you then just went radio silent on me."

Lizzie swallowed, feeling a lump start to form in her throat. She pushed it back, determined not to cry. She knew exactly what the problem was. It was that she loved this silly old sod, and was afraid that if they did get together, it wouldn't work out and then she would lose him as a friend. Fowler's words from the previous evening came back to her. Lizzie closed her eyes. It was time to stop messing about.

"What are you doing at the weekend?" she asked Adams, trying to inject some confidence into her voice.

"I'll be off. I'll have just finished a four-day stretch of twelve-hour days, so will probably be catching up on some sleep. Why?"

"I'm off as well. Can I come up to Norwich for the weekend? We can catch up properly." There was a silence on the other end of the line, and for a horrible moment, Lizzie thought the signal had died just as she had asked Adams that particular, very loaded, question. "Are you there?"

"Yeah, I'm here. I was just thinking about what you said."

"Right," Lizzie replied, crestfallen.

"When you say come up for the weekend, do you mean in the sense that I need to change the sheets in my spare room and put the toilet seat down? Or are you going to come up for the day on Saturday and then bugger off, leaving me watching *Match of the Day* on my tod?"

"No, I mean the whole weekend. Only if that's okay?"

"For God's sake, Lizzie, that's more than okay. I'd love to see you!"

"I don't know if you changing the sheets in the spare room is worth doing, though."

"Miss Jarman, are you suggesting something inappropriate with that statement?" Lizzie closed her eyes and smiled. She could picture the look on Adams's face as he said that. He would have one eyebrow raised and a cheeky smile on his face like a puppy waiting for a treat.

"No, it's just that you changing them is no guarantee that the new ones will be any cleaner."

Adams chuckled down the phone.

"You're so funny, you should be on the stage," he said. "Do you want to go out Saturday night, or stay in?"

"If you're threatening to cook, then let's go out."

"We could get a take out?"

"Or you could take me to a posh restaurant somewhere?"

"In Norwich?"

"Fair point. We'll think of something. So what time next Saturday then?"

"Lunchtime? I'm not really a morning person."

"No, you never were. Saturday lunchtime it is."

"Is this your new phone number?"

Lizzie paused before replying. The fact she'd not told him she'd changed it was potentially tricky.

"Yes, it is."

"Excellent." Adams didn't hesitate before replying. "I'll send you a series of increasingly erotic text messages over the next few days about what we could get up to next weekend."

She laughed, but it came out as more of a cackle than a laugh.

"Ew, no. Please don't do that."

Lizzie said goodbye to Adams and lay back on the sofa,

staring at the ceiling of her lounge. Fowler had been right last night. It was time to live every day like it was her last. Because one day it would be, and no-one knew when that would be. She just hoped that it wouldn't be before the weekend.

10

Mark Delaney was hot. Despite the fact that the sun had only just come up, the air was stifling already. He had been working at Kandahar for almost two weeks, so was supposed to be acclimatised to the heat by now, but he didn't feel like he was.

Delaney was a contractor working for Aeolus, a defence company based in Bristol with almost every other defence contractor in the United Kingdom. Originally from Hastings on the south coast, he had managed to land a job with Aeolus after being made redundant by one of their competitors. The company had landed the contract to defend the skies above Kandahar. It was the same contract that Delaney's original employer had failed to compete for. Aeolus's primary product—a counter rocket and mortar system called Steel Sky—was what he had been employed to install on the base.

On Delaney's left was an area known as the boardwalk. It was a haphazard collection of wooden buildings gathered around a running track and hockey rink. There was a TGI Friday restaurant, a Kentucky Fried Chicken, and a whole variety of other restaurants and shops all designed to keep the mostly American population of the airbase comfortable when they weren't fighting. The shops and restaurants were just beginning to come to life, and he watched as a group of locally employed civilians unloaded a truck full of God knew what into one of them. The guard with them looked as uncomfortable as Delaney felt, and for a moment he felt sorry for the man. At least Delaney only had to carry his body armour and helmet, and he didn't have to lug a weapon round everywhere he went.

Delaney had just passed the boardwalk and was a few hundred yards away from his offices when a deafening high-pitched warbling noise made him jump.

"Shit!" he said under his breath as he ran to the side of the road and threw himself into the ditch next to it. It was the Giant Voice telling everyone on the base to take cover, and he had been directly underneath one of the large speakers of the base-wide alert system when it sounded.

In the distance, Delaney heard a muffled *crump* as a rocket landed somewhere within the perimeter fence. He was struggling to get his heavy body armour on while at the same time lying down when there was another, much louder, explosion nearby.

"Shit, shit, shit," he repeated as he fastened the Velcro at the front of the body armour and jammed the blue Kevlar helmet on his head. There were more explosions, three altogether, and more distant.

Delaney lay in the ditch on his front, as he had been told to do in the event of incoming fire. When the alarm sounds, he had been instructed, get into cover, put your body armour and helmet on, and try not to shit yourself.

Above his head, he could hear vehicles on the road, and he risked lifting his head to see what they were. It was an ambulance speeding past, its red lights on the top flashing but no sirens. He looked in the direction it was going and saw a rising plume of smoke a few hundred yards away. For a few seconds, he thought it might have been his office, but he realised it was a bit further than the modular Portakabin complex he worked from.

11

Adams whistled tunelessly as he pushed the hoover around his flat. One of the advantages of having a small flat was that it was straightforward to keep clean. Adams was not a clean freak, but he wasn't a slob either. He just wanted the flat to be tidy for when Lizzie came round the next day.

After she'd called him and said she was coming over for the weekend, Adams had gone to a retail park on the outskirts of Norwich and bought a whole load of new bedding, both for his bed and the one in the spare room. It wasn't, he rationalised, just because she was coming round for the weekend. He needed it anyway, or at least that's what he told himself. He also bought some new towels, air fresheners, and cleaning stuff. All for the same reason.

When he had finished the hoovering, Adams turned the vacuum cleaner off and stood back to admire his handiwork. He didn't think the flat had been this clean since the day he'd moved in. His apartment was comprised of two bedrooms, although the smaller of the two wasn't much bigger than a box room, a bathroom, lounge and kitchen. He'd been careful when he moved in to not make it too much of a bachelor pad and had hung some prints on the walls as well as decorate the lounge with a selection of succulent plants. Taking pride of place in the lounge was a large flat screen television with a PlayStation nestled underneath it.

Adams glanced at his watch. It was almost seven in the evening, and he was starving. He couldn't really be bothered to go out and get anything from the supermarket, and besides, he'd just cleaned the cooker. He walked into his lounge and opened the drawer he kept takeout menus in.

"Indian or pizza?" Adams muttered to himself, holding one of each menu up as if he was weighing them. The smell of a curry would linger much longer than pizza would, and the shop he normally ordered pizzas from had a two for one deal on. One pizza for tonight, and one cold for breakfast. "Perfect," he said to himself as he fired up his laptop to place the order.

Less than ten minutes later, the doorbell rang.

"Bloody hell, that was quick," Adams said as he got to his feet, pausing the football on the television. Chelsea were one-nil up against Liverpool. Adams didn't really follow either team, but it was something to watch. He grabbed his wallet from the coffee table to give the delivery driver a tip for being so quick with his order—he had a theory that if he tipped them well, then they would be more likely to deliver future orders more quickly—and went to the door. But when he opened it, it wasn't the pizza.

Standing on his doorstep was a face he'd not seen for a while. Not since before he'd left for Afghanistan the previous year. He felt his jaw drop for a second before he recovered his composure.

"Sophie," Adams said to his ex-girlfriend. "What are you doing here?"

"Hi, Paul," Sophie replied, smiling at him. She was slightly shorter than Adams, around five foot seven, had fine blonde hair that cascaded over her shoulders, and an elfin face that had captivated him when they had started going out together. She had also unceremoniously dumped him while he was in Afghanistan. He had come back to the flat they had shared to find her gone, leaving only a note in her place.

"I was visiting a friend in the area, so thought I'd pop by." She inched up on her tiptoes to peer past Adams and into the lounge. "I'm not disturbing you, am I?"

"Er, no," Adams replied. "Not really. I'm just surprised to see you, that's all."

"Are you going to invite me in?"

"It's not really a good time, Sophie," Adams said. "I'm waiting for someone, in fact."

"Oh, right," Sophie replied, a look of disappointment on her face. "Okay. Maybe another time?"

Just as she said this, a figure appeared behind her. Adams saw over her shoulder a young man with a couple of pizza boxes balanced in his hands.

"Is this flat fourteen?" the deliveryman asked.

"Yep, that's me." Adams walked past Sophie, noticing the delicate smell of her perfume for a few seconds before it was overpowered by the smell of the pizzas. The fragrance of the perfume set off a whole raft of memories in Adams's head. Some of them were bad, like when he discovered she had gone. But some of them were good, and some of them were very good indeed. "Here you go, mate," Adams said as he handed the driver a crumpled five pound note by way of a tip for the pizzas he'd already paid for online.

"Thanks very much, fella," he replied, grinning broadly. "Very generous of you, cheers."

Sophie waited until the driver had gone before she said anything else. When she turned back to Adams, she was smiling.

"Is that who you were waiting for?" she asked him, her smile broadening. Sophie nodded past Adams at the television in the lounge. "Pizza, and footie on the telly? Doesn't sound like a particularly interesting Friday night to me, Paul."

Adams looked at her, and could feel his resolve weakening. She had hurt him a lot in the past, but it was in the past. That didn't mean he had to be rude, and she was right. Besides, he had more than enough pizza for two of them.

"The pepperoni one's mine," he said as he stepped back to let her into the flat. Sophie walked past him, turning as she did so.

"There, that wasn't so difficult, was it," she said, angling her head to one side and smiling just enough to reveal the dimple in her left cheek. "I won't bite." The smile turned into a playful giggle. "Unless you want me to."

12

Lizzie turned the shower up as hot as she could stand it and gasped when she stepped under the steaming jets of water. She lathered her hair, cursing when she got some shampoo in her eye, and washed the rest of her body with a particularly extravagant shower mousse that her mother had bought her for Christmas. Lizzie had been saving it for a special occasion, and this was definitely that.

After she had spoken to Adams the previous evening, Lizzie had called Emma Wardle, one of her friends in the Army. She was also one of the few people who had worked with Adams and Lizzie in Afghanistan. Emma was a nurse in the field hospital, so she'd had a different experience to Lizzie and Adams, but had become one of Lizzie's closest friends in the process.

"Are you serious?" Emma had screeched when Lizzie told her she'd invited herself round to Adams's flat for the weekend. "It's about bloody time, Lizzie Jarman."

Lizzie smiled to herself as she recalled the conversation she and Emma had had. Her friend's advice, for what it was worth, was to shag him until she cried God for Harry, England and St George.

"Won't he think that's a bit weird?" Lizzie had replied, "when his first name's not Harry?" Her reply had sent both of them into peals of laughter.

"Oh, Lizzie," Emma had said when they had both stopped laughing. "I'm so pleased for you."

"Nothing's happened yet."

"It will."

Lizzie got out of the shower, dried herself, and got dressed. Even though it was still spring, she had decided to wear a summer dress. It was one that she had worn in Cyprus when she and Adams had been on their rest and recuperation break, and she hoped he would remember it.

She flicked on the television in her lounge to put the news on. It was just before six in the morning, but she knew her neighbours in the Sergeants' Mess wouldn't be in, so her being up and about so early wouldn't disturb them. They were both bean stealers—slang for married personnel who lived in the mess during the week and went home to their families at the weekends. Even though they no longer got the free meals that people in that situation used to be entitled to, the derogatory phrase had stuck.

Lizzie hadn't slept much the previous night, if at all. She had tossed and turned, resisting the temptation to look at her alarm clock to see what time it was. When the dawn rose, she knew that she wouldn't be able to sleep anyway, so she had got up and gone for a run.

Adams had asked her to come over at lunchtime, but Lizzie was so excited to see him she couldn't wait. Her plan was to drive to Norwich and stop off at the McDonalds drive-through near Adams's flat for a couple of sausage and egg muffins. She knew they were his favourite food from the chain, so was going to surprise him with them and some decent coffee.

IT TOOK Lizzie just over an hour to drive from Honington to Norwich. It was a beautiful day, and she enjoyed the drive on almost empty roads. One thing she loved about Norfolk was the wide open skies. Some people called the landscape featureless, but it was far from it. She drove past a large pig farm similar to the one she and Patrick had been called to earlier in the week and smiled as she remembered how much Fowler had laughed when she'd told him the story about the policemen.

As she approached Norwich itself, the traffic started to get busier, but she still made good time. The closer she got to the area Adams lived in, the more nervous she got. She couldn't believe that she was actually doing this.

Lizzie strummed her fingers on the steering wheel of her Mini as she queued up in the drive-through. She was a grown woman, Lizzie told herself. She was doing something that she wanted to do. Something that she needed to do. Which was to be with the man that she needed to be with. It wasn't just about sex.

At the thought of sex, Lizzie's heart started thumping in her chest and she felt her cheeks starting to flush. Would it actually happen? If it does, when will it happen? It could even be minutes after she arrived.

Adams hadn't sent her a series of explicit text messages as he'd threatened to. He'd sent her just one.

I can't wait to see you. We should pick up where we left off, if you're ready.

Lizzie knew he was referring to Cyprus when they had almost, but not quite, got together after the Court Martial. She'd not been ready for anything then. At the time, everything had been so raw and fresh. She was still recovering from her injuries, both physically and mentally. But this was different now.

Absolutely xxx she had replied and got a smiley face in return.

"Two sausage and egg muffins, please, and two coffees," Lizzie asked the pock-faced teenager behind the drive-through counter. Her stomach grumbled as he handed the food to her, and she placed the coffees carefully into the cup holders of her Mini. As she drove off, she smiled at the thought of arriving with just one muffin, and telling Adams that she'd been so hungry she'd already eaten hers.

A FEW MOMENTS LATER, she pulled up outside the block of flats where Adams lived. She turned off the engine and took a few deep breaths, enjoying the aroma of the food but trying to calm her nerves at the same time. Lizzie looked up at the bay window of his lounge. She knew it was his flat because he'd told her that it was the only one with a bay window in the whole block.

Lizzie saw the curtains in the bay window twitching, and she smirked. Maybe he'd not been able to sleep either? Her smirk turned to fury when the curtains opened. It wasn't Adams who had opened them. It was a woman. Blonde hair, slim, very pretty. She had her hands wrapped around a mug and was talking to someone over her shoulder. And unless Lizzie was very much mistaken, the woman in the window was wearing a man's dressing gown.

"You bastard," Lizzie said as her heart sank in her chest. "You complete and utter bastard."

13

As soon as the Giant Voice sprung into life for the second time that morning, this time with a continuous tone to sound the *All Clear*, Delaney got to his feet and dusted himself down. He'd heard plenty about the rocket attacks on the base—that was the primary reason he was there, after all—but he'd never actually been subjected to one. The instructor who had told him to try not to shit himself was right, though. It was the thought of how random the impacts would be. He knew that the rockets wouldn't be aimed at anything in particular as the insurgents didn't have the capacity to do that yet. But at some point in the future, they probably would.

Delaney undid the strap on his Kevlar helmet and took it off before slipping out of his body armour. He looked towards his offices and at the large plume of smoke that was rising behind it. While he had been sheltering in the ditch, another ambulance and two fire engines had screamed past above his head, showering him in dust and pieces of gravel.

He started walking toward the area, wondering if he should go and offer to help. Not that there was a lot that he could do, but at least he would have asked. When he got to his offices, his question was answered when he saw a military policeman standing in the middle of the road, turning traffic away. Delaney walked up a short staircase, opened the door to his office and walked inside.

The inside of his second-storey Portakabin was full of computers and engineering equipment. The main shipment from the United Kingdom wasn't due in for another week or so, but that didn't mean there wasn't work to be done to prepare for its arrival. Delaney's boss, a sour-faced man called Mitch Rubenstein, was already in the office.

"You're late," Rubenstein said with his customary glare. Delaney couldn't stand the man. Rubenstein was in his late forties, overweight, sweated like a pig, and smoked like a chimney. Delaney didn't not like him for any of those reasons, though. He hated him because he was an absolute arsehole.

"There was a rocket attack," Delaney said, placing his helmet and body armour by his desk. He wouldn't put it past Rubenstein not to have noticed. "Did you get to cover? One of them landed not far away."

"I heard it, yes," Rubenstein replied, glancing toward the window. "Not much point getting under cover. If you get hit, you get hit." Delaney looked at him and saw excitement in the other man's eyes. "We've got some new data to work with, though."

"Was anyone hurt, do you know?" Delaney crossed to the window and looked again at the billowing smoke. From this height he could see that it was one of the accommodation blocks for the catering workers had been hit. One of the flimsy cabins had taken a direct hit to the roof, and a group of firefighters were trying to aim a jet of water through the window of the ruined building. Delaney knew the catering workers were mostly Indian and Bangladeshi men, working over here for next to nothing because it was relatively well paid. The poor bastards would have probably still been in bed.

"No idea," Rubenstein replied. Delaney looked at him. It was obvious that he didn't give a shit whether anyone had been hurt or not. "Stop gawping out of the bloody window and come and look at this data."

Delaney crossed the room to where Rubenstein was staring at a computer screen with digits scrolling down it.

"Is that the feed from the COBRA?" he asked Rubenstein.

"Yes," his boss replied, stabbing a fat finger at the screen. The rockets had only been in sight of the unit for a couple of seconds, but the radar had got a lot of information. Delaney stared at the scrolling numbers and groaned. He knew just what was coming. "It all needs crunching, of course. So the sooner you get started, the better. It's the radar cross section I'm most interested in. We need to see if Steel Sky can pick them up at a much lower altitude than the COBRA can."

"It should be able to," Delaney said, still watching the numbers.

"Best you get cracking then, as soon as the download's finished," Rubenstein replied. "I'm going for a smoke. You taken your meds this morning?"

"Not yet, no," Delaney replied, knowing that he was supposed to take them under Rubenstein's supervision.

"When I get back then, yeah? And no, you can't have one of my cans. Get some water."

"Take your time, you fat bastard," Delaney muttered as

soon as his boss was safely out of earshot. He walked back to the window to watch what was going on outside. He had all day to interpret the figures, but from the amount of them still scrolling down the screen, he would need more than a day.

Outside the accommodation block, there were two ambulances parked. Standing next to them with their arms folded were the ambulance technicians, all wearing bright red boiler suits. As Delaney watched, a firefighter wearing breathing apparatus emerged from the doorway of the cabin. He took a few steps forward, staggering slightly, and pulled the uncomfortable-looking mask from his face. Delaney was too far away to hear anything that was being said, but after a brief conversation, he saw the ambulance technicians shrugging at each other before returning to their vehicles.

A few moments later, both ambulances peeled away to return to their base, wherever that was. Delaney watched the firefighters damping down the cabin for a while, turning occasionally to see if the data download had completed. Then another vehicle arrived. It was a white van with stencilled lettering on the side. Delaney squinted to read what it said. According to the stencil, the van belonged to the Mortuary Services. He sighed as he realised why the ambulances had been turned away. There was no-one alive for them to treat.

14

"Sophie, please," Adams said with frustration. "Can you just go?"

"I will when I've finished my coffee," Sophie replied. Adams sighed, knowing that she would only leave when she was ready. If she knew, or even sensed, that he was trying to get rid of her, then she would stay even longer. And Adams had stuff to do.

He left Sophie looking out of the lounge window and returned to his bedroom. Adams had the beginnings of a headache right behind his eyes—a reminder why he rarely drank wine—so he grabbed some paracetamol from his bedside cabinet and went into the kitchen to get a glass of water. Frowning, he regarded the empty pizza boxes and bottles of wine stacked up on the counter.

Last night had started out amicably enough. They had eaten some pizza and drunk two of the bottles of wine that he'd bought for Lizzie's visit. Adams hadn't been planning on opening them, content with a can of beer with his dinner, but Sophie had disappeared at some point and returned with one of the bottles already open and a couple of glasses.

They had chatted for a while, both skirting round the reasons why they'd broken up. Or, more accurately, Adams had thought, why Sophie had broken it off with him. Eventually, when they were halfway through their second bottle of wine, she had brought it up.

"It was the thought of you being over there," she had said, fixing him with her aquamarine eyes that he'd looked into so many times. "If something happened to you, I don't know if I could have dealt with it."

Sophie knew none of what had actually happened in Helmand. She knew he was flying on the back of Chinook helicopters as a medic, but other than what she had seen on the news, she knew nothing else.

"That's a really twisted bit of logic, Soph," Adams had replied. Sophie had smiled when he used the diminutive version of her name.

"No-one else calls me Soph," she had said, looking wistfully into her wine and dropping her voice to a whisper. "We were good together, you and me. Weren't we?" Sophie had looked at Adams with doe-like eyes and twirled her finger through her hair.

"I think maybe you should go, Sophie," Adams had said.

"But I can't," she'd replied. "I've had too much wine to drive." Adams looked at the slow smile spreading across her face and finally worked it out. She had placed the wineglass on the coffee table and leant forward so that her face was only inches away from Adams's. "I was hoping maybe I could stay the night?"

Adams had known exactly what she wanted. She'd

wanted him to kiss her, and then what happened after that would have been inevitable.

"No, Sophie."

"What do you mean, no?"

"You can stay on the couch, but no to the rest of it." Adams had got to his feet, annoyed with himself for being such a sucker. "I'm not interested." He was interested, or at least one part of his anatomy was very interested, but he was also determined not to give in to the temptation.

"I'm not sleeping on the bloody couch," Sophie had said, a dark look on her face.

"Well, have the spare room then. But you'll have to leave early."

"Why?" Sophie had said. Her voice was belligerent. One thing she had never been very good at was not getting her own way, and Adams could see that she hadn't changed a bit.

"Because I bloody well said so," Adams had told her as he got to his feet. "I'm going to bed. See you in the morning."

About fifteen minutes later, just as Adams had turned off his light, his bedroom door swung open. Silhouetted against the light from the hallway was Sophie. She was wearing a negligee or something similar—it was too dark for Adams to see properly—that showed off her lithe figure to full effect.

"Are you sure, Paul?" Sophie had said, almost in a whisper. Her voice was low, sultry, and in Adams's opinion, pathetic. "Just for old time's sake?"

"Sophie, please just go to bed."

She had paused for a few seconds, obviously waiting for him to change his mind, before she wordlessly pulled the door closed.

. . .

"So, I guess I probably won't see you again for a while?" Sophie said as she put her empty coffee mug in the sink.

"Probably not," Adams said. "That's kind of how being an ex works." He was still annoyed with her for pulling that stunt last night, and also himself for not stopping it earlier.

"Paul, you really are a little boy still at heart, aren't you?"

"You hurt me, Sophie," Adams replied. "When I came back from Afghanistan and you'd gone, that really hurt."

"You hurt me last night." Sophie folded her arms across her chest and looked at him petulantly.

"No, I didn't," Adams said. "I turned you down, Sophie. That's nowhere near the same thing."

Eventually, Sophie got dressed and got her stuff together. Adams saw her to the door of his flat, and they said an awkward goodbye. He didn't know when—or indeed if—he would ever see her again. One thing he did know was that if it weren't for Lizzie, he probably would have ended up in bed with Sophie and regretting it.

"Bloody women," Adams muttered as he closed the door behind Sophie, not bothering to wait and see if she was going to turn and say goodbye. "Like London buses. Never around when you need them, and then two turn up at once."

It was just past eight o'clock in the morning. Adams went into his kitchen, grabbed the pizza boxes and empty bottles of wine before taking them outside and putting them into their respective bins. God forbid that the pizza boxes should go in the recycling. He'd already had one snotty note from the bin men about putting the wrong stuff in the wrong bin.

Adams went back into his flat and into the spare room.

He stripped the bed, bundling the linen together with his dressing gown before stuffing it all into the washing machine. He was going to have to nip out to get some more wine, but that could wait.

With a sigh, Adams got the hoover back out and started going round the flat again.

15

Lizzie shrank down in her seat and watched in her wing mirror as the blonde woman walked past her Mini. She heard the blip of a remote fob as a car a few behind hers was unlocked and, a moment later, a bright blue Audi TT roared past.

Whoever the woman in Adams's flat had been, she was beautiful. The moment Lizzie saw her up close, she immediately felt frumpy in comparison. For a bizarre second, Lizzie wondered if she was a prostitute, but even that thought didn't make her laugh. Lizzie sat in her car for a moment, wondering what to do. She wanted to storm over to Adams's flat, ring on the bell, and then punch him in the face when he answered.

"How could you, Adams?" she whispered, on the verge of tears. "How could you?"

Lizzie glanced down at the muffins on the seat next to her and felt sick. There was no way she would be eating one of them now. Even the thought of the coffee made her nauseated. She took a few deep breaths, wondering if she was actually going to vomit, but it soon passed. Lizzie was about to pick the food and the plastic cups up and put them in a bin somewhere when Adams's front door opened. She watched as he made his way down the steps leading up to his apartment with pizza boxes and a couple of empty bottles of wine before putting them in the bins.

Seeing him do that just made Lizzie feel worse. She waited until he was back inside his flat before she started the car and pulled out into the road. Lizzie didn't know where she was going to go. She wasn't going to go back to RAF Honington and sit in the pathetic couple of rooms in the mess that she called home.

Lizzie drove aimlessly for twenty minutes or so, her mind whirring with emotion. She didn't understand why Adams would have done that to her? If he had texted her to let her know that he was seeing someone, she would have been upset, but at the same time, she would have understood. But to not say anything at all?

When Lizzie saw the blue strip on the horizon, she realised that she'd reached the coast. She pulled into a lay-by and tapped at her sat-nav. When she was a child, her parents had brought her to the beach near Sea Palling a couple of times. Lizzie remembered those days fondly. The empty expanse of sand. It had been like having their own huge private beach. She punched in Sea Palling and followed the directions for the next twenty minutes. When she reached the village, Lizzie parked not far away from the holiday cottage she and her family had stayed in all those years before.

It took her nearly thirty minutes to find a stretch of beach with no-one else on it. In the distance, she could see a couple walking their dog with a child in tow. Even from this distance, she could hear the child shrieking with delight as he or she discovered something in the sand. A crab's pincer, perhaps? Lizzie felt a twinge of jealousy as she watched the family. They looked so carefree, so happy. Why couldn't her life be as simple as theirs?

In her pocket, Lizzie's mobile phone buzzed. She ignored it at first, figuring it was a text message, but when it continued, she realised it was an incoming call. Lizzie pulled her phone out and glanced at the screen. When she saw it was Adams calling, she pressed the button to turn her phone off. She thought for a few seconds about turning it back on so that she could block his number, but couldn't be bothered.

Lizzie spent the next hour or so just sitting on the beach, watching the waves rolling in and out on the empty sand. She wanted to cry, but couldn't. She wanted to scream and shout, but couldn't. She just felt empty inside. It was a feeling she recognised from before, from when she was recovering from her injuries. The nurse at the Department of Community Mental Health at RAF Brize Norton had told her that it was a warning sign. Her mind's way of trying to shut painful things out instead of dealing with them. Lizzie couldn't remember what she was supposed to do when she felt that way. She vaguely remembered some sort of coping strategy to get back on track, but she hadn't really been listening at the time.

"Well, bollocks to it anyway," Lizzie muttered as she got to her feet. She brushed the sand off her backside and started walking back toward her car. She might not be spending the weekend the way she'd hoped she would be, but that didn't mean she couldn't have some fun. She could call Emma, see what she was up to. They could perhaps have a girlie night in, or even better than that, a girly night out. Emma was the sort of woman who men crowded around, and if Lizzie was with her, then maybe she would get some attention as well?

Lizzie pressed the button on her phone to turn it back on and, ignoring the missed call from Adams, called her friend.

"Hey, Emma," Lizzie said when the call was answered. "Bit of a change of plan. What are you up to this weekend?"

16

"Can I get a car pass, please?" Adams said to the miserable-looking man behind the glass screen of the guardroom. He didn't blame him for looking miserable. If Adams spent his days dishing out car parking permits, he would be just as pissed off.

"You been here before?" the man asked. He was white-haired, probably in his early fifties, and was wearing a dark blue uniform with MPGS lettering on the epaulettes of his shirt. Military Provost Guard Services. Adams couldn't see him running after any intruders to the base any time soon.

"Yes, several times."

"Service number?"

Adams reeled off his service number, and the guard tapped away at his computer keyboard. If he worked out how to use more than just his index fingers, Adams thought, he would be a fair bit quicker. There was an interminable wait as he stared at the screen.

"Still got the MG?"

"Yes. MG ZR, green."

"How long do you need a pass for?"
"Today and tomorrow, please."
"Section?"
"Training. I'm here for pre-deployment training."
"Going anywhere nice?"
"No."

TEN MINUTES LATER, a laminated piece of paper in his hand with his car's details on it, Adams was finally good to go. He walked past the queue of servicemen and women who were waiting to get access to RAF Honington and wondered why they didn't have more than one person on the desk on a Monday morning.

The guard on the gate didn't even look at Adams's hard-won car pass as he waved him through. Adams drove into the base and tried to remember where the training section was. After a couple of false starts, he found it and parked a few hundred yards away. When he got to the building, there was a signpost pointing toward the students' tea room. There would be, Adams knew from experience, a Burco boiler in it with a pile of polystyrene cups and the cheapest tea and coffee that the instructors could find. He ignored the passive-aggressive price list next to the jar with a few coppers in it, and made himself a cup of what was, apparently, coffee.

"Morning, sir," a voice said behind him. Adams turned to see a warrant officer at the entrance to the room. "You here for PDT?"

"No," Adams replied with a grin. "I'd heard that this was the best coffee this side of Bury St Edmunds, so thought I'd pop in and see what all the fuss was about."

"I hope you've put your twenty pence in the jar, sir?"

the warrant officer replied, smiling and stepping forward with an extended hand. "I'm Mr Connolly. I know your face from somewhere."

The two men spent the next twenty minutes going through the standard military routine of trying to work out how they knew each other. They both reeled off the bases they'd worked at and the operational tours that they'd done before realising that for a brief period, they had both worked at RAF Lyneham before it had closed down. As they chatted, the students' tea room filled up with other service personnel, several of whom were brave enough to try the coffee.

"Ladies, gentlemen," a deep male voice boomed. Adams looked up to see one of the regiment instructors standing at the door, staring at the occupants of the room as if to see if any of them wanted a quick fight. "Kick off is in lecture room three. Through there to the left, toilets are on the right, but leave them clean. The last cubicle doesn't flush anything larger than a rabbit pellet, so don't use that one if you can help it."

Twenty minutes later, after the obligatory health and safety brief to make sure that they would all be safe sitting in a classroom, Adams was struggling to stay awake as a film played on the projector screen at the front of the room. The narrator was explaining why, according to the law of armed conflict, they weren't allowed to bomb churches. Adams had seen the film many times over the years. Finally the film ended, and the instructor came back into the room.

"Take a five-minute leg stretch, and then back in here sharpish, please," the instructor shouted as the occupants of the classroom stirred into life. Adams looked up to see him walking across to his desk. "You're a medic, aren't you, sir?"

"I am, yes," Adams replied.

"The next lecture's the first aid one, so feel free to skip it if you want?"

Adams knew that the main reason they didn't want medics in the first aid lectures was that every once in a while, they would start criticising the instructors over some minor point of first aid protocol.

"Okay, nice one. What time do you want me back?"

"This one will run until lunchtime, so can you be back for thirteen hundred?"

Adams looked at his watch. That gave him a break of almost three hours. He could get a decent coffee in the officers' mess, or grab a sandwich from the NAAFI and sit outside in the sun with his book. Deciding on the latter, he thanked the instructor and turned to the warrant officer he'd been talking to earlier.

"Enjoy the first aid lecture, Mr Connolly," Adams said with a wry smile.

"Thanks very much, sir," the warrant officer replied. "I'll do my best to." He lowered his voice. "You lucky bugger. I hate first aid."

17

Delaney looked at his computer screen with a real sense of satisfaction. Not only had he managed to analyse all the data from the COBRA system, but he had been able to do even more with it than he had thought. The software he had written to crunch the numbers was the main reason—possibly the only reason—that he had got the job with Aureos in the first place. It had taken him hours to do it, but he'd managed it without Rubenstein noticing. Delaney looked up from the screen to see what his boss was doing to see the fat bastard snoozing in a chair on the opposite side of the office.

He kept a close eye on Rubenstein as he reached into his pocket for the thumb drive he kept in there. It was tiny, the smallest one that Delaney had been able to find. He slipped it into one of the USB ports on the computer and transferred copies of the raw data and the analysis that he'd done onto it, watching Rubenstein all the while as the files were copied. Once done, he ejected the drive and slipped it back into his pocket.

"Do you want anything from the boardwalk?" Delaney asked Rubenstein just in case his boss wasn't actually asleep but just sitting there with his eyes closed. There was no response, so he scribbled a note on a yellow Post-it to let him know he'd gone for coffee. Delaney was tempted to stick it on Rubenstein's forehead, but it wouldn't stay there for long if he did. Even though he was asleep, Rubenstein was still sweating.

When he stepped out of the air-conditioned office, a wall of heat hit Delaney in the face. He grimaced and pulled his sunglasses out of his shirt pocket before slipping them on and hefting his body armour onto his shoulder. With a glance at the wreckage of the cabin that had been destroyed earlier that morning, Delaney walked down the steps and onto the road. As he walked the few hundred metres from the contractor's compound to the boardwalk, he wondered how many of the catering workers had been taken away by the mortuary services van.

Delaney queued up behind some soldiers to get himself a coffee in the Starbucks' concession before making his way to his destination. One of the wooden buildings housed an Internet cafe that was run by a Bangladeshi man called Darpak. It had four terminals and a ridiculously expensive satellite uplink to the rest of the world. It was a lot quicker after Delaney had reconfigured the routers that Darpak was using, which meant that he was able to use the terminals for nothing when he wanted to.

"Mister Delaney," Darpak greeted him as he walked into the stifling heat of the cabin. He was perhaps in his early sixties. Much too old, in Delaney's opinion, to be working in a war zone, but with six children back at home, he didn't have a choice as Darpak had explained to him one evening the previous week.

"Hey, Darpak," Delaney replied. "You mind if I use one of your computers just for a few minutes?"

"Sure, sure. You help yourself." Darpak waved a gnarled hand around the empty room.

Delaney slid into the chair in front of the computer and nudged the screen round by a few inches so that Darpak couldn't see the screen. He didn't think for a moment that the old man would be interested in what he was doing, but he wanted to be on the safe side. Delaney wiggled the mouse to wake up the screen and logged out of the guest account. When he logged back in, it was as a system administrator. He navigated to the BBC news website so he had a window to switch to if Darpak suddenly became interested in what he was doing, but the old man was paying him no attention at all. When he was absolutely sure that Darpak wasn't watching, Delaney reached around and slotted the USB drive into the back of the computer.

"Did you hear what happened this morning?" Delaney asked. "The rocket attack?"

"Terrible thing," Darpak replied as Delaney opened up a piece of software called *The Onion Router* on the thumb drive. When he had been helping Darpak upgrade his internet connection, he'd taken the opportunity to make sure he had admin rights to the entire network. This meant that he could install, and uninstall, software without leaving any trace.

"Were there many casualties, do you know?" Delaney asked, clicking on a couple of links on the BBC site in the other window he had open.

"Four dead, I heard," Darpak said. "All just boys from

the kitchens. Terrible thing."

Delaney opened up his secure Protonmail account and composed a new e-mail to an address that wasn't written down anywhere. He attached the encrypted data files from the COBRA system and his analysis and, with a furtive glance at Darpak, pressed *send*. He waited for a moment, idly clicking more links on the BBC site as he did so, but there was no response. It didn't matter. The files would reach their destination. Delaney wasn't sure what rules he'd just broken—the data were classified in every sense of the word—but he had no choice.

He uninstalled the software from the computer and logged himself out before signing back in as a guest. Then he brought the BBC site back up and randomly clicked through several pages so that there would be a browsing history before getting to his feet.

"All done, Darpak," Delaney said. "Thanks for that. It does seem much quicker now."

"Yes, yes," Darpak replied with a broad smile. "Is very quick, thank you again."

"No problem."

Delaney said goodbye to the man, leaving him to his oppressive little building, and stepped back outside into the heat of the day. He looked over at the Starbucks, wondering whether to get a couple of coffees for him and Rubenstein. It might deflect any snide comments about nipping out during the working day from his boss, even though he'd been fast asleep. Realising that it probably wouldn't hurt, he joined the queue.

As he ordered the coffees a few moments later, Delaney also bought a box of donuts. Maybe, he thought with a grin, he could feed Rubenstein up until his heart gave out.

18

Lizzie blinked in the bright light of the projector before moving to one side so she could see the classroom. Her eyes scanned the room quickly, noting rank slides before she spoke.

"Ladies, gentlemen," she said brightly. "Good morning. I'm Sergeant Lizzie Jarman, and I'll be going through first aid with you."

The phone call had come into her squadron boss first thing that morning. The regiment's regular first aid instructor had called in sick, and would they perhaps mind lending them their paramedic for a couple of hours? Lizzie was quite pleased to be asked, although she didn't let her boss know that. There was a fair amount of rivalry between the training squadron and Lizzie's squadron, so the favour would earn her some brownie points.

Lizzie settled into her stride, only referring to her presentation notes occasionally. As she spoke, she noticed that one of the younger students was busy playing with his phone.

"Excuse me?" Lizzie called out. "Do you mind paying

attention?" The young man looked up and leered at Lizzie. He had fabric patches on both shoulders, the so-called mudguards of the RAF Regiment, and a blue rank slide with a silver circle and propellor in the middle.

"Sorry, pet," he said, looking left and right and sniggering.

"What's your name?" Lizzie asked him.

"SAC Martin."

"Well, SAC Martin. Even here at RAF Honington we usually use rank when addressing seniors," Lizzie said, fixing him with a stare.

"Sorry, Sarge," the senior aircraftman replied, although his face showed he was far from sorry.

Lizzie continued with her lecture, giving the students a couple of minutes between the theory and practical sessions. When they returned, she had them arrange their chairs into a semi-circle. In the middle of the semi-circle was a resuscitation dummy. Lizzie took off her combat tunic, pleased that at least she had a decent t-shirt on underneath it. With the heat of the day outside and the number of people in the classroom, it was getting very warm.

"So, find the end of the breastbone where the ribs come together and then go up two fingers." She moved her hands into the correct position. "You should aim to compress the chest about five to six centimetres at about a hundred to a hundred and twenty times a minute. Singing *Nellie the Elephant* in your head will help you keep time. Now, watch."

Lizzie performed a series of compressions to show the group the correct technique, even though she was sure most of them had done this lecture a lot. It was part of their mandatory annual training. When she stopped, she looked up to see SAC Martin laughing and whispering something to the student next to him.

"Something to say, Martin?" Lizzie barked. The young man didn't reply, so she turned to the student next to him. "What did he say?" SAC Martin shot his colleague a filthy look, warning him not to say anything. But it didn't work.

"He said you've got a cracking set of tits, Sergeant," the student said, "and that he'd like to—"

"That's enough, thank you," Lizzie cut him off. "I'm guessing the last time you had your hands anywhere near a pair, they were your mother's, Martin?" A round of muted laughter rippled around the room. Lizzie looked at the other students, catching the eye of a warrant officer sitting at the back next to an empty chair. He was looking at her enquiringly, silently asking if she wanted him to use his rank and intervene. Lizzie shook her head at him imperceptibly. She didn't need any help with muppets like the young SAC.

Lizzie managed to get through the rest of the lesson without incident and dismissed the students for their lunch. She was tidying away her equipment when she heard the door to the classroom opening. Lizzie looked up, expecting to see one of the students returning for something, but it was the chief instructor, Flight Sergeant Hughes.

"Hey, Lizzie," the flight sergeant said, an easy smile on his face. "Thanks for helping out this morning." He was a good-looking man, early thirties, and had recently moved back into the sergeants' mess after his marriage broke up. It would be fair to say that he'd caught Lizzie's eye on more than one occasion.

"No problem, flight," Lizzie replied. "Happy to help out, you know that."

"I hear you had a spot of bother with one of the youngsters?" A frown crossed his face as he said this. "I'm sorry about that."

"It wasn't your fault," Lizzie said, "besides, it was nothing but a bit of nonsense."

"Well, we'll make sure he realises the error of his ways."

"How come your section's so busy?" Lizzie asked, keen to change the subject.

"There's a big push coming on Op Herrick to tie in with the opium harvest. Surprised your squadron's not in line for it, to be honest. Who's out there now?"

"Three four."

"They're up at Leeming, aren't they?"

"Think so, yeah."

"Ah, well. Happy days if we all get to go over to that shithole again."

Lizzie grimaced, knowing that if there was a big push back into Afghanistan, their squadron would probably be swept up in it at some point. Maybe that was what she needed? To get back in the saddle. She knew it would come at some point, so perhaps the sooner the better.

After having her lunch in the staff room with the instructors, Lizzie said goodbye to the flight sergeant who thanked her again for helping out and made her way out of the building. As she walked past the car park, she glanced across to see someone in uniform lying down on the grass, half-hidden behind a car. Curious, she approached the prostate figure to see it was someone lying on a camping blanket with a book over his face, fast asleep.

With a smile, she walked closer to the car park. Mr Fowler would have an absolute paddy if he found someone walking on his precious grass, let alone sleeping on it. When she got closer, she started laughing when she saw the officer's ranks slides. She nudged his foot with hers to wake him up.

"Excuse me, sir," Lizzie said. "The SWO will have a cow if he catches you sleeping there." The figure on the grass stirred, and the book slipped off his face.

"Bugger off, Sergeant Jarman," Adams said with a frown. "I'm trying to bloody well have a snooze." She looked at him, her mouth open for a few seconds before she saw a broad smile crossing his face.

19

Adams scrambled to his feet and put his hand over his eyes to shield them from the sun. He looked at Lizzie who was regarding him with a look of thunder on her face.

"What's that look for?" he said, surprised at her expression.

"Piss off, Adams," she barked, turning on her heel to walk away. He reached out and grabbed her arm, but she shook it loose. "Get your hands off me."

"Hey, what's going on? All I did was fall asleep on the bloody grass."

Lizzie span back round and glowered at him.

"Very funny, Adams." She reached out a finger and poked him in the sternum. "You, sir, are an absolute arsehole."

"Why?"

"You know full well why."

"Hang on a minute, Lizzie," Adams replied. He was starting to get annoyed. "If anything, it should be me being pissed off with you."

"Why would you be pissed off with me?" Her voice was high, and she had twin red spots of anger on her cheeks.

"Last weekend?"

He watched as she crossed her arms over her chest and took a deep breath.

"What about last weekend? Anything you want to tell me?" Lizzie said, her voice tight.

"I thought you were coming round. But no, not only did you not show up, but then you've been blanking me. Again." Adams crossed his own arms. "And then when we do meet, you're calling me an arsehole. That's not fair, Lizzie."

"I don't want to talk about it," Lizzie said. She turned again and Adams grabbed hold of her arm again. She shook him off. "I said get your hands off me."

Adams held out his hands in a placatory manner.

"Okay, okay. I'm sorry, but I do want to talk about it." He was trying not to plead with her. Out of the corner of his eye, he could see someone striding across the car park towards them. It was the regiment instructor from earlier. When he reached them, he saluted Adams but didn't look at him as he did.

"Everything okay, Lizzie?" the instructor said. Only then did he look at Adams, and from the look on his face, he was as pissed off as Lizzie was.

"It's fine, flight," Lizzie said. "Just a personal discussion, that's all."

"You sure?"

"I'm sure, thanks."

The instructor stared at Adams for a few seconds, leaving him with no doubt that if he touched Lizzie again, he would be flat on his back in seconds. He turned and walked away.

"Lizzie, please," Adams said when the instructor was out of earshot. "Can we just talk?"

"I saw her, Adams," Lizzie said, tightening her arms across her chest. Adams thought for a few seconds, wondering who she was talking about. "The woman leaving your flat on Saturday morning."

"Sophie?"

"I don't know who she was. Slim, blonde. Very pretty."

"That's Sophie. My ex-girlfriend."

"Your ex-girlfriend?" Lizzie said with a look of incredulity. "Nice of her to pop round so early."

"Lizzie, no, it's not like that."

"Don't lie to me, Adams," she replied, her face still like thunder. "I saw her in the window of your flat wearing your bloody dressing gown."

"Nothing happened, Lizzie. She came round and ended up drinking too much, so stayed over. In the spare room."

"I don't know why I'm even listening to this." Lizzie was tapping her foot on the ground.

"The spare room that I bought new sheets for. For you. I was hoping you wouldn't be sleeping in the spare room, but got them just in case you wanted to." Adams sighed. At least Lizzie hadn't walked off yet. She was still here, still talking to him. "Why would I lie to you about it?"

Lizzie looked at him, a frown creasing her forehead.

"What do you mean?"

"Why would I lie about it? If anything had happened between me and Sophie, so what? It's not as if you and I are a couple, is it?"

"I didn't think we were that far away from perhaps becoming one," Lizzie replied.

"She saw my Facebook update about going back to Afghanistan and came round unannounced. But nothing happened, Lizzie. I promise you."

"You're going back?" Lizzie asked him, her face falling. At least she was starting to look less angry.

"Yeah, Kandahar. I'm getting acting rank for it as well."

"You're going to be a squadron leader?" The ghost of a smile crossed her face.

"For a couple of months, at least."

"Bloody hell, they must be desperate."

"Thanks very much," Adams said, forcing a laugh. "I was chosen from a cast of thousands, apparently."

"Of course you were." Lizzie looked at her watch. "You'd better get cracking. Your next lesson starts in a few minutes."

"Lizzie, listen." Despite the fact that he could still see the flight sergeant staring at them out of the window of his office in the background, Adams reached out and took Lizzie's hand. "Come for a drink with me tonight. Let's talk properly. Work this out."

"I don't think that's a good idea, Adams," Lizzie replied, but to Adams's relief she made no effort to shake him loose.

"Please, Lizzie. Just a drink. Do you know the Red Lion in Thetford? Meet me there at seven."

"I don't know, Paul."

"Lizzie, please. Don't make me beg in front of your rock ape friend who's still giving me evils through the window. Let's meet for a drink and, if you want to walk away, then I won't stop you."

Adams looked at her, knowing that she was just about

to give in. The way she had just used his first name was a dead giveaway.

"Just one drink," she said eventually. "I'll be driving."

"I'll see you there." He squeezed her hand and let it go, turning to walk back to the classroom.

Adams walked into the training building, ignoring the pointed stare of the flight sergeant as he did so.

20

Lizzie parked her Mini in the car park of the Market Square in the middle of Thetford. She paused for a few seconds, checking her appearance in the rear-view mirror. Apart from bags under her eyes, which she'd tried her best to hide with concealer, she didn't think she looked too bad.

She looked over at the Red Lion pub, glancing around to see if Adams's car was parked close by. Lizzie couldn't see it, so she grabbed her phone and fired off a quick text message. The last thing she wanted to do was to walk into the pub on her own. A few seconds later, her phone vibrated.

I'm inside toward the back. Got you a glass of white.

Lizzie took a last look at herself in the mirror and got out of the car. She ran her hands over her hips to make sure that her dress wasn't crumpled and walked over to the pub.

The Red Lion was a grey brick building with large bay windows. Lizzie had been in it once before for a leaving do for one of the lads on her squadron. The interior was a combination of modern design with original features, which made it look a bit odd in Lizzie's opinion. It had a large interior courtyard with high-backed booths on either side. In the last booth on the right-hand side, Lizzie found Adams squirrelled away.

"Are you hiding from someone?" Lizzie asked as she slid into the seat opposite him. "Tucking yourself all the way back here?"

"I like it back here," he replied with a grin. "Nice and private." Lizzie looked around. He was right. Unless someone came back here deliberately, they couldn't be seen by anyone else in the place. Not that there were many other customers anyway on a Monday night.

"Where's your car?" Lizzie asked Adams.

"I walked."

"All the way from Honington? That's miles." Lizzie reached forward and picked up her drink. "Cheers."

"Chin chin," Adams replied, raising his own pint of lager. "Not from Honington, no. The officers' mess is full, so I'm in a Travelodge over the river. It's only a few minutes' walk from here."

"How's the pre-deployment training?"

"I heard the first aid training was a bit ropey."

"For those who actually bothered to attend it, maybe." Lizzie smiled, and Adams smiled back at her. Despite their argument earlier, the way they had slipped straight back into natural back-and-forth banter was one thing she liked so much about Adams. She couldn't stay angry with him for long, but she still wanted to know what had happened the other night. "So," Lizzie said, her smile slipping. "Tell me about Sophie."

For the next ten minutes, that was exactly what Adams did. Lizzie listened, not asking questions but just letting him speak. By the time he had finished, she hated the woman and the way she had treated Adams. Lizzie could tell the whole thing had hurt him. He didn't tell her that, but she could see it in his eyes.

"Why do you think she came round?" Lizzie asked Adams when he had told her the whole story.

"Because she could, I think. She wanted to snap her fingers and have me come running, so to speak."

"What a bitch," Lizzie said, sipping her wine.

"That's one way of putting it," Adams replied.

"When do you deploy?" she asked, partly because she wanted to know but mostly to let Adams know that she was done with talking about his ex-girlfriend.

"Wednesday."

"Wednesday?" Lizzie said with a frown. "But that's only two days away!"

"I know. Pre-deployment training finishes tomorrow, and then I'm straight to Brize. The flight's at stupid o'clock on Wednesday morning."

"That's a bit shit." Lizzie picked up her glass again to try to hide her disappointment.

Adams changed the subject, moving it to how she was getting on with the regiment. They chatted for a while, but they were just talking for the sake of it, and it wasn't the regiment that Lizzie wanted to talk about. Adams finished his pint and got to his feet to grab another, so Lizzie took the opportunity to nip to the loo.

Inside the bathroom, she examined herself in the mirror, wondering whether she needed any running repairs to her makeup. When Adams had told her he was flying back to Afghanistan so soon, Lizzie had wanted to cry. It wasn't fair, him going so soon.

Back in the booth, Lizzie sensed immediately that

Adams's mood had changed. He was quieter, for one thing, and almost brooding.

"Penny for your thoughts?" she asked him quietly. When he looked at her, there was a sadness in his eyes that hadn't been there before. But behind the sadness was something else. She swallowed, recognising the look. She had seen it before in Cyprus.

"Lizzie, I'm just going to throw something onto the table. And if you don't like it, then I apologise."

"Mind the drinks," she replied with a smile he didn't return.

"When you didn't come over the other weekend, I was really disappointed. More than disappointed. I was gutted. I'd been looking forward to seeing you for so long."

"Why?" Lizzie asked.

"The whole thing in Cyprus. When we were there for our R&R, when we were there for the Court Martial. It just feels like we've got... Shit, I don't know how to say it."

"Unfinished business?" Lizzie said.

"Yeah, that sounds about right," Adams replied, a smile finally drifting onto his face. Lizzie paused before replying, knowing what she wanted to say but not sure if she could bring herself to say it.

"What do you want to do about it?" she asked a few seconds later. The interior of the pub had got much warmer in the last few moments, and she knew her cheeks were flushing. Adams's smile broadened.

"That would get us barred from the pub, but it would be an interesting ten seconds," he replied. Lizzie tried to smile, but couldn't. Instead, she got to her feet and leaned forward to grab Adams's hands. He protested as she did so, but let her pull him to his feet until they were standing inches apart.

When he raised his hands to her face, Lizzie could see that his fingers were trembling. She closed her eyes when she felt them on her face and when she opened them again, he was just looking at her.

"Adams?" she said in a whisper. "Would you just bloody well kiss me?"

And he did, tentatively at first, but then with more confidence as she responded. Lizzie felt his hand slide down her sides to the small of her back. When he pulled her toward him, she realised why he had been reluctant to stand up. She pressed herself against him, the sensation sending a shiver down her spine.

Lizzie broke off the kiss and swallowed hard.

"How far away is this hotel?" she whispered in his ear.

21

"Bloody hell," Delaney muttered to himself as he looked at his watch. It was gone three in the morning, and he was wide awake. He turned in his bed, trying in vain to get comfortable on the thin, lumpy mattress.

The accommodation block was a stack of prefabricated buildings known as 'corimecs' after the Italian firm that made them. They were like shipping containers, but perhaps not as luxurious. Delaney had one to himself, which was a bonus, but he could still stretch out his hands and touch both sides. The interior was sparse; a bed, a small desk and chair, a steel cupboard and a struggling air-conditioning unit on the wall.

When he had finished work earlier that day, he had come back to his accommodation block exhausted. He wasn't sure why, although he'd had a busy day. After finishing the analysis in record time and sending it off to his contact back home, Delaney had gone back to the office and messed about on his computer for a while, pretending to still be crunching the numbers. Rubenstein had still been fast asleep when he had got back, and the only evidence that Delaney had left the office was the box of donuts on the table.

About half an hour after Delaney had got back, his boss woke himself up with a start. He had been snoring, each snore getting progressively deeper until he eventually stopped breathing for a few seconds. When he spluttered back into life, his eyes were bulging out of his head.

"Are you okay?" Delaney had asked him, not because he cared but because it seemed like the right thing to say.

"I'm fine," Rubenstein had replied with a dismissive wave of his hand. "Just nodded off for a couple of moments, that's all." *Two hours, more like,* Delaney had thought.

"There's coffee there, although it might be cold by now, and some donuts."

The two men had spent the rest of the afternoon poring over aerial photographs of Kandahar and the surrounding area. On the map were numerous small circular stickers. The red ones inside the wire were where rockets had landed and the yellow ones on the outside the predicted firing points. They both knew that the yellow stickers were a best guess, based on the limited information that the COBRA system was able to provide when the rockets reached a high enough altitude to enter their radar envelope. By the time they rolled the map away, they had identified a couple of potential locations for the Steel Sky system, when it finally arrived.

Delaney swung his legs out of his bed and sat on the edge, yawning. The United Kingdom was four and a half hours behind them, so it would be late evening over there. He stood up and reached up for the air conditioning unit on the wall, flicking the switch to turn it off. There were four screws on the back that took him a moment to undo, and he reached his hand into the casing. When he withdrew it, he had a small Nokia mobile phone with a charger in his hand. After it had powered up, Delaney composed a text message.

Did they come through??

Delaney waited for a few moments to see if there was a response, but he heard nothing back. With a sigh, he turned the phone off and replaced it in its hiding spot with the charger before returning to his bed.

THE NEXT THING DELANEY KNEW, it was just after eight in the morning.

"Shit, shit, shit," he said as he jumped out of bed. Either he had slept through his alarm or it hadn't gone off. It didn't matter either way. He was still late, and that would just give Rubenstein one more thing to complain about.

Delaney showered in record quick time, pleased that there wasn't a queue as there normally was for the communal showers. That wasn't something that he enjoyed at all, having to shower at the same time as other people in the accommodation block. As he was showering, he had a sudden thought about something that he'd forgotten the previous day. The files he had sent back home were encrypted, but he'd not included the password in the email.

He padded back to his small accommodation and hurried inside. Delaney swore to himself as he reached up for the screws on the back of the air-conditioning unit. He was late already, so being a bit later wouldn't make much difference, and he needed to get that password back home. The sooner they could look at that data, the better. He grabbed the phone, powered it up, and sent off a quick message with the random digits and letters that made up the password. He used a different one each time, just in case his e-mail got compromised, although it was unlikely.

Delaney waited for the message to send. When the phone *whooshed* to confirm it had gone, he reached up for the air-conditioning unit, already thinking about what he was going to say to Rubenstein when he eventually got to the office.

The pain in his hand was instantaneous. He felt the metal blade of the air-conditioning unit slicing deeply into the flesh of his palm, and Delaney gasped as he jerked his hand back. Spatters of blood were thrown onto his bedding as he did so.

"Fuck," Delaney muttered as he looked down at his hand. When he saw the damage that the blade had done, he instantly felt light-headed and nauseated at the same time. There was a deep laceration in his palm, so deep that he could see yellow stuff poking out of it. "Oh my God," he said, sitting down hard on the bed. Blood ran across his palm and dripped on the floor. At least it was oozing, not squirting. He'd seen an episode of *Casualty* where someone had cut open an artery and the blood had squirted out like a garden sprinkler.

Fighting back the nausea, Delaney reached into the drawer of his desk for a clean handkerchief. Gritting his teeth, he wrapped it around the wound, all thoughts of being late for work gone.

22

Sergeant David Miller—known as 'Windy' since the day he'd reported to RAF Halton for his basic training, was lying on his back in the sand. It was hot. Very hot. He was gasping for a drink of water, but he'd left his water bottle in the Jackal armoured vehicle that was burning furiously about ten metres away from him. It wasn't the only thing he'd left in the vehicle, although he didn't realise it at the time. Also in the 4x4 was most of his left leg and his right foot.

Thick black smoke billowed from the vehicle into the humid air above him. There was the noise of gunfire in the air as well, but Windy couldn't tell whether it was insurgents firing at what was left of his convoy, his colleagues returning fire, or rounds being cooked off in the intense heat of the burning vehicle. He rested his head back down on the sand and tried to remember what had just happened.

Windy's Jackal was the middle vehicle of a convoy of three. He had been the vehicle commander, standing in the back behind the .50 calibre heavy machine gun. His best friend, Robby, was in the front passenger seat with a new lad who Windy didn't know very well driving. The lead vehicle had just stopped near a hole in the road in front of them. There had been an improvised explosive device in the area a few days before. That was the reason for the patrol. To try to find, identify, and neutralise any others on the route.

What Windy and the other occupants of the vehicle hadn't known was that beneath their Jackal was a large mine, modified into an IED. There were two wires trailing just under the ground. One wire led forward to another IED, and the other one backward to the largest mine of the three in a daisy chain configuration.

As the lead vehicle rolled over the pressure plate hidden just underneath the surface of the road, the completion of the electrical circuit triggered the booster charge underneath it. This, in turn, triggered the main explosive charge. The consequences of this chemical reaction were almost instantaneous and catastrophic. The shockwave process converted the explosives to a hot, high pressure gas which travelled outwards at a speed of between three and four kilometres a second, violently pushing material out of the way.

In the case of the lead vehicle, the soil plug that the explosives ejected was diverted by the v-shaped hull of the Jackal, which was exactly what the floor was designed to do. The floor deformed, fracturing the ankles of the driver of the vehicle, but remained intact. The vehicle rose about eight feet into the air, driven by the huge explosion underneath it, and both the driver and the passenger had their heads smashed off the roof of the 4x4 as it slammed back down onto the ground. The rear gunner's femur snapped like a twig when it landed.

Behind Windy's Jackal, the rear vehicle was the most fortunate. When the driver had pulled to a halt, he had been about twenty feet further back from Windy's vehicle than he should have been; a fortunate error that would haunt the young driver for the rest of his life. He, and the other occupants of his vehicle, watched with horror as a mushroom of debris rose in front of them, obscuring their view of the first two vehicles in the convoy. Apart from being showered with earth and shrapnel, all three men were unharmed.

Underneath Windy's vehicle, the same process had ruptured the floor pan of his Jackal. This sent white hot shrapnel up through the floor, which sliced through everything inside it, including the driver and passenger. The fragmentation debris was preceded by a high pressure wave of detonation gasses that burned at around four thousand degrees centigrade, instantly turning the vehicle into a roaring inferno. Windy—who at that point was flying through the air—knew none of this.

Windy had been thrown clear of the vehicle, leaving a not insignificant part of his lower limbs behind. As he had impacted the ground, he had been mercifully knocked unconscious for a moment. It was only when he came to that he started to realise what had happened.

He struggled to sit up, but his right arm wasn't working properly. All Windy could do was to lift his head forward. As he did so, a shadow passed across the sun.

"Jesus Christ," a voice said. "Oh, Jesus Christ." It was the driver of the rear vehicle—Corporal Banks. "Windy? Can you hear me, mate?"

"Banks?" Windy said, his voice dry and rasping. "What's going on? I can't feel my legs." Windy saw Banks glance down at Windy's legs and back at him.

"They're gone, mate. Both of them."

"Fuck. They don't hurt, though. Why don't they hurt?" Windy scrabbled with his left hand, shoving down the front of his trousers to make sure that his genitals were uninjured. "Meat and two veg are all okay," Windy said, trying to smile. "I guess that's something."

Banks knelt next to Windy and started patting his pockets.

"That's going to slow you down in the fitness test, mate." Banks pulled a black tourniquet from a pocket and started applying it to what was left of Windy's left thigh. "Maybe I've got a chance of beating you in it for once?" He secured the Velcro strap and wound the plastic stick around itself a couple of times. "There's not much blood, mate. Do you want morphine?"

"It doesn't hurt, Banks," Windy replied. "It should, shouldn't it?"

"Dunno, fella. You'd better ask a medic."

Windy raised his left arm as much as he could to see if his white armband was still there.

"Banks," Windy said when he saw the Red Cross that was covered in soil. "I am the bloody medic."

23

Lizzie's eyes snapped open. For a few seconds, she was disorientated and unsure where she was. She blinked a couple of times, realising that she was with Adams in his hotel room. In the bed next to her, he was snoring softly.

She turned to look at him, remembering the previous evening. How nervous they had both been when they were finally alone together in the room. Adams had bought a bottle of wine in the pub for them to bring back, and they had taken their time drinking it. Delaying the inevitable.

Finally, Adams had put his empty glass on the table and leaned forward to take Lizzie's own empty glass from her hand.

"So," he had whispered. "What happens next?"

"Shall we get another bottle from room service?" she had replied.

"Sure." Before Lizzie could stop him, he had picked up the phone to order one. Knowing that nothing could happen until the wine had arrived, Lizzie took the opportunity to tell Adams something that she needed to let him know.

"Adams, can I tell you something?"

"Of course you can." He had taken her hands in his and was rubbing his thumb over the inside of her wrist. For such a simple movement, it had an unexpected effect on Lizzie and she felt her cheeks warm.

"I've not done this for a while."

"What, get pissed on cheap wine?"

"No, you know what I mean. I'm just not that, well, experienced."

Adams didn't reply, but continued to stroke the inside of her wrist. He was staring at her hands as if they were made of something incredibly fragile. Lizzie closed her eyes, enjoying the sensation.

"We don't have to do anything if you don't want to, Lizzie," Adams had said eventually. "We can just neck the wine, chat until we fall asleep. If you want?"

"What do you want?" Lizzie had asked him. When he looked up at her, she could see exactly what he wanted in his eyes, but his reply surprised her.

"I want you to be happy, Lizzie," Adams had said. "That's all I've ever wanted."

The wine arrived a few moments later, and Adams poured them both a glass. Then he picked up the remote control to the television and found the radio channels.

"Any preference?" he'd asked her as he scrolled through them. "How about this one?" He paused on a Christian rock channel. It sounded to her like any other rock channel except that all the songs were about Jesus.

Lizzie had smiled and taken the remote control from

his hand, settling instead on a channel called *Late Night Lovers*.

"I think this one," she said as a cover of The Chain by Kerala Dust started playing. They had sat and listened to it for a few moments, the tension increasing between them in conjunction with the tempo of the song.

When Adams had finally pulled Lizzie towards him, any fears she may have had dissipated within seconds.

Lizzie reached out for her phone to see what time it was. It wasn't even six in the morning. She looked at Adams, and remembering what they had done the previous evening, knew that she wouldn't be going back to sleep anytime soon.

She slipped out of the bed and padded toward the bathroom, picking up her knickers from the end of the bed. When she had finished in the bathroom, she put them back on and waited until the toilet had finished flushing before opening the door.

"Morning," Adams said sleepily from the bed, making her jump. Despite their intimacy the previous evening, Lizzie instinctively put her arms across her bare chest. She didn't need to, though, as Adams still had his eyes closed.

When she got back into bed, he snuggled in close and wrapped his arms around her.

"I thought you were going to do the walk of shame for a moment," he murmured. "Just get dressed and tiptoe out, leaving me here all alone in this bed."

"I prefer to call it the stride of pride," Lizzie replied. He smiled, still keeping his eyes closed, and beneath the duvet she felt his hand sliding down her hip.

"I prefer you without these," Adams said. Lizzie lifted her hips a couple of inches so he could slip them back off.

"What are you doing, Adams?" Lizzie said. "I'm now naked."

"I think you know full well what I'm doing, Lizzie," he whispered, and she could hear the smile in his voice.

24

Lieutenant Colonel Adèle Gautier looked at the broken body on the trolley in front of her. The entire resuscitation team had been working on the young man for almost an hour after he had been airlifted to their field hospital by an American Black Hawk.

"Je pense qu'il est parti," she said with a thick Québécois accent. *I think he's gone.* "Tout le monde est d'accord?" *Does everyone agree?*

Around her, the rest of the medical team nodded and murmured their assent.

"Il n'avait aucune chance de s'en sortir vivant," Adèle said to her second in command, Major Laurent. *He never had a chance to make it.*

"You're right," the major replied. "But we gave it our best shot."

The young man on the trolley was, according to his dog tags, Private First Class Tony Storey. The blood-spattered patch on his shoulder with two stylised letter 'A's identified him as a member of the 82nd Airborne Division, and as she removed the tags from around his neck, Adèle realised that he was only nineteen.

"He's only a child," she said as she looked at him. He was younger than her own son, but only by a couple of months.

"It's a desperate business out there," Major Laurent replied, shaking his head. According to the report from the paramedic who had delivered PFC Storey to the hospital, there had been a firefight up at a small village not that far away from Kandahar air base. His patrol had been out looking for a reported weapons factory hidden in one of the mud-walled buildings in the village when they had been ambushed. PFC Storey hadn't even managed to get a single shot off before he was raked by an AK-47.

Sighing, Adèle started cleaning up the resuscitation room while Major Laurent and a couple of the junior nurses started to roll the soldier into a body bag. As the senior nurse in the field hospital, she knew she could just get someone to do it for her, but she wanted to be busy and also to set the right example to the juniors. The alternative was to go back to her cot in the tent and be left with her thoughts, which she didn't want to do.

Adèle Gautier was in her early forties and had been working at the field hospital for almost six weeks since the Canadian Forces Health Services had been tasked with the command of the Multinational Medical Unit. It was fair to say that they'd had a rocky start when they assumed command, not helped by the language. Several of the nurses under her command spoke little English, and Adèle had to plan her teams carefully to make sure that they could actually communicate with each other. There had been an incident during the first week where a patient had almost died because the team members couldn't communicate quickly enough, and Adèle's Commanding Officer had almost been returned to his unit over it.

"Laurent, we'll do the hot wash-up in ten minutes, okay?" Adèle said as she filled up a bucket to mop the blood from the floor. He nodded and continued with his ministrations of the body. There would be a family somewhere in the United States whose day was about to change beyond all recognition. She tried not to think about the pain that a mother and father somewhere were about to suffer.

As she mopped the floor, Adèle's thoughts turned to her own family. Her son, William, was still at university studying engineering. To her relief, he had shown no interest at all in joining the military. Her husband, Samuel, was probably working, drinking, or sleeping. That had been all he had done for the last few years, anyway. When Adèle had heard that her unit was going to be deployed to Afghanistan for six months, she been quietly pleased, although she would never have said that to Samuel. It was, in her mind, a chance to make a real difference, but as she looked at the young body being zipped up into a body bag, it was difficult for her to see where it was being made.

A FEW MOMENTS LATER, Adèle and her team were sitting in canvas chairs in a loose circle. A hot wash-up where they discussed what went well, and what could have gone better, was crucial for Adèle, and she insisted that all of her team attend even if they didn't contribute.

"Before we begin," Adèle said in a quiet voice, "let us

all remember that a young life has been lost today. If you have a God, ask Him to look after his soul." She paused, her head bowed for a moment, with her fingertips touching the gold crucifix she wore around her neck. The last six weeks had pushed her faith almost to the limit, but at the same time she needed it more than ever before. "Okay, thank you. Now, let me tell you all what I think went particularly well this morning and then we'll go round the room."

Adèle was just in the middle of talking about the handover of the patient from the Black Hawk helicopter to the ambulance when the door to the resuscitation room opened. She looked up with a frown. There was a *Do Not Disturb* sign on the other side while they completed their wash-up, so whatever the interruption was would have to be good.

"Sorry to disturb you, Colonel Gautier." It was one of the young lieutenants from the ops room in the main hospital. "There's a major contact going on up country with the Brits. The TRT's just launching, but they're already reporting multiples."

Adèle crossed herself unconsciously, offering up a silent prayer for the soldiers involved.

"Right, thank you, lieutenant." The British Trauma Response Team deployed in Chinook helicopters with a full medical team on the back. The advantage was that they were able to stabilise casualties more easily than a single paramedic in the back of a Black Hawk. The disadvantage—from the hospital's perspective at least—was that the Chinooks could carry multiple patients who would all arrive at the hospital within minutes of each other. "Team, you know what to do."

Adèle got to her feet to go to the ops room to find out what she could. As she stood, she turned to Laurent.

"Laurent, get me a bed state and find out if there's any activity in theatres. Last I heard, the ICU was empty but can you check, please?"

"Yes, ma'am," Laurent replied, also getting to his feet. As he stood, he looked across at Adèle. "Are you okay?" he asked her under his breath so the rest of the team wouldn't hear.

"I'm fine," Adèle replied, hoping that he wouldn't see through the lie. "Come on, we've got work to do."

25

Sergeant 'Windy' Miller was lying in the shade of a small tree, surrounded by what was left of his patrol. He now had tourniquets on what was left of both legs, although neither was bleeding, and large field dressings on the stumps.

Corporal Banks was sitting next to him, and every few moments he shook Windy to make sure he stayed awake.

"Stay with me, Windy," Banks said for what seemed to Windy like the tenth time. "The TRT are coming, mate. They won't be long."

The only time Windy had actually been in pain, despite his horrendous injuries, was when Banks had carried him over his shoulder to the temporary helicopter landing site that they had identified a few hundred yards away from where Windy's Jackal was still smouldering. He was desperate for a drink, but Banks wouldn't give him anything. The Corporal was right not to, but it was still irritating Windy.

In the distance, there was a small black speck in the sky. It was high, perhaps five thousand feet or even higher, but as Windy watched it started spiralling downward. He could hear the faint 'wocka wocka' noise of the Chinook helicopter and, despite his situation, he managed to crack a smile.

"Queen of the sky, eh Banks?" Windy said.

"Damn right she is," Banks replied, putting a comforting hand on Windy's shoulder. "Won't be long now, mate."

The two men watched as the helicopter continued to spiral toward them. When it was close enough for them to see the blades rotating, Banks got to his feet and threw a green smoke grenade into the field in front of them. Windy watched with detached amusement as the smoke started billowing into the sky.

The Chinook flared, the pilot raising the nose and dipping the rear of the helicopter as he approached. The green smoke started blowing all over the place and was replaced by a brown cloud of soft dirt from the field.

The next thing Windy knew, all hell had broken loose. He could hear the sound of small arms fire over the noise of the rotor blades. Lots of small arms fire.

"Shit, shit!" Banks said, putting a protective arm over Windy and pressing him into the ground. The helicopter lurched to its left in front of them, the pilot throwing it into a sharp left-hand bank which brought the gun port on its starboard side around. Windy could see the flash of return fire from the small aperture in the window as the Chinook scrambled to safety and in the distance by the edge of the field, he saw a technical pickup truck moving. On the back of the truck was the distinctive silhouette of a heavy machine gun. Even in the confusion, Windy worked out that they must have been waiting for the reinforcements to arrive.

The small arms fire died away, only to be replaced by something much more frightening. Windy raised his head to see an Apache gunship appear over the top of the mud wall that separated the field they were sheltering in from the next one. On the front of the gunship, the chain gun was spinning rapidly, and the 'brrrrr' noise it made was the deadliest sound Windy had ever heard.

Both he and Banks jumped as another Apache helicopter flew directly over their heads, its own chain gun spitting death. Then there was an ear-splitting whoosh and a smoke trail shot out of one of the stubby wings of the black gunship. Seconds after that, there was a muffled crump and a smoke cloud where the technical had been.

It was only a few moments, but it seemed to Windy that the Apaches circled their location for ages before the Chinook returned. It came in low and hard, the pilot wasting no time at all in getting the heavy aircraft onto the ground.

Banks got to his feet and unceremoniously dragged Windy up until he was over his shoulder. As the rest of the survivors tried to help each other, Banks started running toward the helicopter. Soldiers poured out of the back of it and into an all-round defensive position. A group of four started sprinting toward them from the Chinook, two of them clutching stretchers.

Every footstep Banks took sent waves of agony through Windy's entire body. He couldn't locate where the pain was coming from, only that it was overwhelming.

When the group of four soldiers reached them, the lead just shouted at Banks and pointed at the ramp.

"Go, go, go!" Then they rushed past them to the other members of Windy's platoon.

"Close your eyes, mate!" Windy heard Banks shout. He

did as instructed, and a few seconds later he felt the searing heat of the Chinook's twin exhausts washing over him. Then there were more hands on him, dragging him into the relative safety of the helicopter. Windy felt himself being placed on a stretcher. There was more shouting, and he felt the stretcher being hauled further back into the helicopter. Someone pressed a mask to his face, and there was a cool breeze across his mouth and nose.

Windy opened his eyes, trying to see who was tending to him, but he didn't recognise the woman who was bending over his face. She leant in to his ear.

"We've got you, sergeant!" the woman shouted. "We've got you."

26

Delaney lay back on the hospital trolley and regarded his bandaged hand. He had managed to get dressed back in his accommodation without passing out and make his way to the medical facility, holding his injured hand close to his chest. When he had arrived at the entrance, a very pretty Canadian nurse had taken his details and had a quick look under his makeshift bandage.

"How did you do it?" she had asked him in a thick French accent that he struggled to understand. He had thought about what he was going to say as he was walking to the tented medical facility and had decided to say that he caught it on a sharp piece of metal. It wasn't that far from the truth.

The nurse, whose name was Isobel, had led him into the treatment area and got him to lie down on the trolley. She was slim, not much over five feet tall, and had a large brown bun on the back of her head. Delaney examined her face as she unwrapped a dressing pack. She was even more beautiful than he had originally realised. Dark brown eyes, high cheekbones, and a mouth with the sultriest lips he'd ever seen.

Isobel had unwrapped his hand for a proper look, cleaned the wound with saline, and applied a proper bandage. She was just telling him he needed to wait for one of the senior nurses, or maybe the doctor, when the inside of the hospital suddenly got a lot busier.

Delaney was lying in an elongated tent with three trolleys on either side. He was the only patient but, as Isobel had explained to him after another nurse interrupted her, there was an emergency coming in. Delaney had offered to leave—it was only a cut hand, after all—but he had been told to stay put. At some point, as soon as they could, someone would examine his hand properly and probably put some sutures into the wound. He wasn't looking forward to that one bit.

Delaney started laughing to himself as he imagined Rubenstein going bananas over the fact that he'd not turned up for work. He imagined the fat git thumping around the Portakabin, swearing to himself at the thought of actually having to do some work. With Steel Sky coming in at some point in the next few days, they were going to be busy, and they'd still not worked out the best place to deploy it. That was what they were supposed to be finalising today, but instead Delaney was lying on a hospital trolley. At least he would have a decent excuse for being late when he eventually arrived at the office with his sutured hand bandaged up.

In the distance, Delaney could hear the distinctive sound of a Chinook helicopter approaching. It got louder and louder, and when the thin canvas walls of the tent started shaking, he realised that it had passed directly over the top of the hospital. The sound receded slightly as the helicopter passed overhead, but it didn't fade into the distance as he was expecting it to do. Instead, it stayed at a constant level, much quieter than when the helicopter had been above the tents, but still very loud.

The public address system in the hospital burst into life, and a frantic female voice said something in French that Delaney didn't understand. He wondered for a few seconds if it was Isobel, but it continued in English a moment later and the accent was much less strong than hers.

"Major incident declared," the voice said, the fear in it obvious despite the distortion of the speakers. "All hospital personnel report to their stations. This is not a drill. I say again, major incident declared. All hospital personnel report to their stations. This is not a drill. End of broadcast."

Delaney sat slightly further upright on his trolley. He hadn't liked the sound of that broadcast over the public address system. Part of it was not wanting to be in the way if there were going to be wounded people about. He'd seen enough blood for one day and didn't relish the thought of seeing other people's. As he lay there, Isobel hurried back into the tent and over to his trolley.

"Mister Delaney, the head nurse has said you can go, but you must come back later." She was speaking so quickly that he struggled to understand her, her accent accentuated by the fact she was talking so fast. Delaney looked at Isobel's face, at the twin red patches on her cheeks. As he watched, she licked her lips and pressed them together so tightly that they almost disappeared. If it hadn't been for the fear he could see behind her dark brown eyes, Delaney would have found the gesture incredibly suggestive.

"When?" he asked as he swung his legs over the side of the trolley. "What time should I come back?"

Isobel looked flustered for a moment as she considered the question.

"Before this evening," she replied, "otherwise the wound will have started healing already."

"Will you be here?" he asked her.

"Yes, I will be here," Isobel said with a frown that was quickly followed by a nervous smile. "Now go. See you later."

Delaney got to his feet, grateful that the dizziness he'd felt earlier didn't return. He watched Isobel walking away from him and ran his eyes up and down her figure, focusing on the way her slim buttocks moved under the thin material of the scrubs she was wearing.

"Dirty bitch," he muttered to himself, grinning as he parked the memory along with the glance he'd managed down the front of her top when she had been examining his hand earlier.

He waited until Isobel had left the tent before taking a couple of tentative steps forward. No dizziness, which was a good sign. He walked through the same door and turned to watch Isobel hurrying down the corridor before he turned to leave the hospital. Delaney was only a few yards from the exit when the doors to the outside burst open. He pressed himself to the canvas wall of the corridor as a stretcher was pushed past by a couple of men in fatigues. On the stretcher was a soldier, one of his legs bent at the thigh at an impossible angle. The soldier was groaning softly, calling out a name that Delaney didn't catch. As the procession swept past him, Delaney caught a strong smell of cordite and something else underneath it. Something coppery, earthen almost.

"In there, mate!" a British voice shouted. It was one of the men pushing the trolley. "That's the ward. We'll get him in there."

Delaney took a deep breath and walked out of the hospital, grateful to be back in the fresh air. Whatever was going on in the hospital wasn't going to be pretty.

27

Lizzie had intended on staying in the hotel room for a while, but she wouldn't be able to get back to sleep, and besides, in the corridor outside she could hear the housekeeping team shuffling up and down. Hopefully, when he left, Adams had put a *Do Not Disturb* sign on the door like he said he was going to.

She got dressed and made herself a cup of coffee with the small plastic kettle in the room. While she was waiting for it to boil, Lizzie fired off a text message to Emma.

Can you talk?

A few seconds later, her phone buzzed with a reply.

Sure. Call me. Xxx

Lizzie swiped at her screen to find Emma's contact details. Her friend's phone only rang a couple of times before she answered it.

"Hey babes," Emma said. She sounded bright and chirpy, despite the fact it was only just gone eight in the morning. "How's things? You okay?"

"Yeah, I'm fine. Guess where I am?"

"Um, well, I'm guessing you're not in the mess?"

"Nope," Lizzie replied with a grin. "I'm in a Travelodge in Thetford." There was a pause on the other end of the line.

"Are you alone?"

"I am now."

"Oh my God, you haven't, have you?"

"Haven't what?"

"You've shagged him, haven't you?" Lizzie could see Emma's face in her mind's eye. She would have a look of mock horror on her face, but be smiling at the same time. "What about that woman you saw at his flat?"

The only person Lizzie had told about seeing Sophie had been Emma when they'd shared a bottle of wine the evening Lizzie was supposed to have been with Adams the previous weekend.

"That was just a misunderstanding. The stupid cow went round there, but he wasn't having any of it."

"And you believe him?"

"Yes, Emma," Lizzie said, determined not to let the question get to her. "I do."

"Cool. Anyhow, spill the beans. How was it?"

"Jesus, I tell you, Emma," Lizzie replied. "I was like a bloody virgin all over again. I was so nervous."

"Did you, er, *enjoy* it? If you know what I mean?"

"What do you mean, did I enjoy it? Of course I did."

"My God, Lizzie, you are such a nun sometimes. Do you want me to be blunt?"

"You might have to be."

"Did you come?"

Lizzie closed her eyes for a few seconds, feeling the heat rushing to her face.

"I *enjoyed* it several times, Emma," she said with a giggle. "He was very, what's the word, attentive?"

"Well, it's been a while, Lizzie," Emma said. "Bit like riding a bike, though."

"Nice analogy, Emma."

Emma cackled down the phone at Lizzie's comment and then spent the next few moments trying to extract as much information on the previous night as she could. Lizzie let her pry for a while until Emma gave up when she realised that she wasn't going to get any of what she called the gory details.

"I'm so pleased for you, babes," Emma said eventually. "I'm glad it all came together in the end." She started giggling and Lizzie felt her face flushing. "Sorry, maybe not the best term to use."

"He's going back to Afghan, though," Lizzie said.

"You're joking? When?"

"Tonight. Well, he's flying at stupid o'clock tomorrow. Desk job though, or at least that's what he said."

"That's bollocks, that is. But you're officially an item now, are you?"

"How d'you mean?"

"As opposed to a quick pump and dump before he goes away?"

Lizzie paused before replying, thinking for a few seconds. She and Adams hadn't really discussed anything like that. They'd both been otherwise engaged.

"We didn't really talk about that, Emma, to be honest." Lizzie sighed. What Emma had just said made her wish they had done, instead of just falling into bed together.

"It'll be fine, babes, don't worry," Emma said. "He doesn't strike me as the one-night stand type, anyway."

"He said he would call me when he got to Brize," Lizzie replied, "so I can ask him then, maybe?"

"You sure you want to ask him? You might come across

as being a bit needy. I mean, you are needy, that goes without saying. But you know what I mean?"

They talked for a few more moments before Emma told Lizzie that she had to go or she would be late for work. Lizzie finished her coffee and gathered her things together before deciding to have a shower before she left.

As she waited for the hot water to come through in the small bathroom, Lizzie thought about what Emma had just said. Were they an item, as it were? Or was it just sex? Now that their unfinished business had been completed, was that it? One thing that Lizzie did know was that she didn't want it to be just a one-night stand. But she didn't know what Adams wanted, and Emma had been right. If she brought the subject up, she would sound needy.

As Lizzie washed her hair, she thought back to the family she had seen on the beach the previous Saturday and how carefree they had seemed. That was what she wanted—the certainty of a committed relationship. She giggled to herself as she imagined herself asking Adams a question.

"So, Paul," Lizzie muttered. "Now that we have actually done the deed, I take it that means we're now in a committed relationship? For better and for worse and all that jazz?" She smiled to herself, but her smile faded as a thought started nagging at her. What if Adams didn't want the same thing?

Lizzie sighed, knowing that with hindsight maybe she should have thought about that before jumping into bed with him.

28

Adèle forced herself to pause for a few seconds and take stock of the carnage that was starting to emerge in her normally ordered resuscitation room. She had three bays, and only one of them was equipped for a full-on trauma resuscitation. The other two were designed for non-critically ill patients.

In the central bed was a young man with injuries the likes of which Adèle had never seen in over twenty years of working in an emergency department. He had lost both legs, one just below the knee and the other at the ankle. He also had a horribly damaged arm that he was probably going to lose as well. When they had been assessing his injuries earlier, Adèle hadn't been able to find a radial pulse. Despite his horrific injuries, before he'd been put into an artificial coma, he had been talking with the medical team. Joking with them even, as if he was trying to distract the younger medics from the awfulness of his injuries. The worst part of it was when she had seen the Red Cross on his arm.

"Il est l'un des nôtres," she had whispered to Laurent

as they had rolled the medic to check his back for any hidden injuries. *He's one of our own.*

"I know," Laurent had replied.

Adèle watched the medic for a moment, praying that he would get through the operation he was about to have to try to limit the damage that the blast had already caused. There was still so much to go wrong for him. His first challenge was to survive the forthcoming surgery. Then his ruined body would have to fight any infection in the wounds which, given the amount of soil and debris she had seen in them as they had dressed them, was highly likely.

If he survived and got back to the United Kingdom, he still had a long journey in front of him. He would have to learn to walk again. How to feed himself with only one arm. How to cope with the looks that he would be given. The stares of curious children who would ask their parents why that man had no legs and only one arm.

Adèle turned her attention to the other two patients in the resuscitation bay. One of them was a soldier with a fractured femur. He had a Thomas splint on it to keep the bone aligned, and as soon as the operating theatre had finished with the medic—whatever time of the day or night that was—he would be its next patient. She walked over to him.

"How are you doing?" Adèle asked. He looked at her, his eyes full of morphine.

"I've had better days," the soldier replied. Adèle had to concentrate to understand his thick local accent. "How's Windy getting on? Will he be okay?"

"Who?"

The soldier nodded toward the medic on the trolley who was surrounded by Adèle's colleagues.

"He's about to go to theatre. What did you call him?" According to his dog tags, the medic was called David Miller.

"He's called Windy. Windy Miller?"

"Okay," Adèle replied with a gentle smile as she picked up his chart to see how much morphine the soldier had had. To her surprise, he'd only had a couple of milligrams and that was when her team had been applying the Thomas splint. "How's the pain?" she asked him.

"It only hurts when I laugh," he replied.

"You soldiers are all the same," Adèle said, putting a hand on his forehead. "Always trying to be brave."

"I'm not a soldier," her patient replied. "I'm an airman. You never answered my question, though." He nodded again toward his injured colleague. "Will he be okay?"

Adèle sighed before replying. There was no easy way to answer it.

"He's very badly injured," she said a moment later as the medical team pushed Windy's trolley toward the door to the main hospital corridor. "Very badly injured indeed, but I think he'll survive."

"The others in his vehicle, Robby and the driver. They're dead, aren't they?" She felt tears pricking at her eyes as she nodded her head.

"Yes, I'm very sorry, but they are."

"I don't even know the driver's name," Adèle's patient said, looking past her with a vacant expression. "He only arrived a couple of days ago. I got introduced to him but never got his bloody name. Now he's dead." Adèle saw his eyes focus on the crucifix around her neck. "You believe in all that stuff, do you?"

Her hand unconsciously came up to touch the gold cross.

"Yes, I do," she replied. "Do you?"

He shook his head emphatically.

"Not a chance."

Adèle reached out for some gauze which she used to pat her patient's cheeks dry. His tears were leaving pink streaks through the mud and grime of the battlefield. Then she took his hand and squeezed it, offering up a silent prayer as she did so. For the man in front of her. For the medic on his way to the operating theatre. For the colleagues they had left behind, their bodies burned beyond all recognition.

She opened her eyes and saw that her patient was staring at her. He must have realised what she was doing. He licked his dry lips before asking her a question that she had asked herself numerous times since arriving in Afghanistan.

"Is He listening?"

29

Adams yawned as the regiment instructor went through the stoppage drills again. There were four of them with the instructor who was reeling off the various actions to take if a rifle failed to fire.

"So, sir," the instructor said, "what would you do if your weapon fails to fire, assuming you're still awake that is?"

"Sorry, flight," Adams replied. "Didn't sleep very well. I would tilt the weapon and observe the position of the cocking handle."

"Good. The cocking handle appears to be fully forward."

"Forward assist." Adams mimed the motion with the flat of his hand.

"Weapon still fails to fire."

"I would cock the weapon and apply the holding open catch before looking inside."

"Rounds in the magazine, but no round in the chamber." To Adams's relief, the instructor turned his attention to one of the other students. "What's the next drill?"

"Operate the bolt release catch, forward assist, and continue firing," the warrant officer to Adams's left said in a monotone voice.

Adams thought back to the previous night and suppressed a smile. He was exhausted, but it was a small price to pay. Lizzie had been so different to any of his previous girlfriends. She had been so nervous when they had got back to the hotel room. He was sure that she wasn't going to stay, but was going to make her apologies and leave. But she didn't. He thought back to the very start of the evening. Adams had been determined to make sure that Lizzie was satisfied and, without wanting to boast to himself, he thought he had achieved that before she had even touched him. He closed his eyes for a few seconds and remembered the way she had gasped softly as he touched her intimately for the first time.

"Just close your eyes and let me touch you," he had said. "Before we do anything else, just let me touch you."

And touch her he had. When he found her focal point, she had gasped again as her slim body tensed before a slow smile spread across her face as she encouraged him to continue.

"Just there," she had whispered in his ear.

Apart from those two words, Lizzie had remained absolutely silent at first, as if she was afraid to let go. But then her teeth had started to grind, and she started moaning softly, telling him not to stop. Then she was pleading with him not to stop. He hadn't and the look on her face, the noises that she made as Adams brought her gently to the edge and then over it, would stay with him for the rest of his life.

"Sir?"

Adams opened his eyes, blinked, and looked around.

"Yes?" he said to the instructor.

"The cocking handle is fully to the rear? What are you going to do?"

"Um, remove the empty magazine, check the rounds in the top of the fresh magazine, insert it and check that it's secure."

"And then?"

"Operate the bolt release catch, forward assist, continue firing."

"Very good, sir."

TWENTY MINUTES LATER, Adams had his green card signed and stamped to prove that he was competent to carry a weapon. There was one more lecture before lunch, which Adams was hoping he could snooze through in the back of the classroom, and then they were going to the firing ranges to zero their rifles and do their pistol training.

He and Lizzie had talked about meeting for lunch, but decided against it. He wasn't going to see her again for a few months, he had told her, and he wanted his last memory of her until then to be of her naked in bed with tousled hair and a flushed face. Lizzie had laughed and said she was going to stay in his bed for a couple of hours as she didn't have to be at the squadron until ten that morning.

Before he left, they hugged for ages.

"Just go, Adams," Lizzie had said eventually, tears in the corners of her eyes. "I'll see you soon, yeah?"

WHEN HE GOT BACK to his flat in Norwich, the first thing Adams did was to have a shower to try to wake himself up a bit and get rid of the smell of weapon oil and cordite. He'd completed all his qualifying shoots and the regiment instructor had congratulated him on his accuracy, particularly with the pistol. For a medic, the flight sergeant had said with a wry smile, Adams was a pretty good shot.

Adams didn't have too much to do in the flat—his next-door neighbour was going to water his plants and keep an eye on things while he was away—and he had a fairly long drive down to RAF Brize Norton. His flight was scheduled to leave at four o'clock the next morning, but he needed to be there at least two hours before that so he could hang around the terminal building with everyone else.

After doing a final check around the flat to make sure that everything was turned off that needed to be turned off, that the fridge was empty and the door open, and that the bins were empty, he knocked on his neighbour's door to give her the keys.

"You've got my e-mail if there're any problems, Mrs Higgins?"

"Yes, I have," she replied. Mrs Higgins was well into her sixties and lived alone with only a cat for company. Adams suspected that she was pleased to be trusted with his flat.

"No wild parties in there, you hear?" Adams said with a grin.

"Go on, off you go," Mrs Higgins said. "The male strippers I've booked will be here soon, so you need to make yourself scarce."

Adams got into his car and plugged his phone into the stereo system. He scrolled through his playlist, having downloaded a few new songs to it. He wondered what Lizzie would think of his new playlist—it was all the songs that he could remember from the television in the hotel room.

"Bit creepy, probably," Adams muttered to himself as the opening bars to 'The Chain' started up. He started the car and pulled out, turning the music up and smiling as he did so.

30

Lizzie looked at her phone for the tenth time in as many minutes. It still hadn't rung. She sighed, wanting to scroll to Adams's contact details and call him or text him. But if he was still driving down to Brize Norton, then he might try to answer the call or read the text message and crash the bloody thing. Plus, what Emma had said about Lizzie coming across as needy was still playing on her mind.

"Come on, Adams," Lizzie muttered, "just call, would you?"

She got to her feet and crossed the room to her small fridge, pulling out a half-empty bottle of wine. According to her phone, it was almost ten o'clock. Lizzie suddenly realised that the bar downstairs in the mess would be closing soon, and that she wanted more than a glass and half of white before going to bed. She put the bottle back and slipped the phone into her pocket. One of the advantages of living in the sergeants' mess was easy access to a bar. It was less than five minutes away. That was also one of the disadvantages. Access to alcohol was far too easy, and much cheaper than the local pubs. When she had first moved into her rooms at Honington, Lizzie had resolved that she wouldn't drink alone in her room. She would only, she had told herself, drink when she had some company. Later that first evening, as she sat on her bed and looked at the almost empty bottle on the floor, she had laughed at the fact her resolve hadn't even lasted a single day.

"A bottle of Pinot Grigio, please," Lizzie said to the barmaid a few moments later. The bar was empty, and the barmaid had been in the process of closing for the evening. Lizzie had cut it fine.

She paid for the wine and was just walking across the bar when she felt her phone buzzing in her pocket. Even though it was empty, using a mobile phone in a public area like the bar was a big no-no, so Lizzie hurried toward the patio doors to take the call outside. She peeked at the screen as she walked. It was him!

"Adams," Lizzie said excitedly when she reached the safety of the patio. "Are you okay?"

"Yeah, all good. I'm checked in, anyway. Now I just have to hang around pointlessly for hours and hope that the plane doesn't break while it's sitting on the pan." The RAF's transport fleet was notoriously unreliable, and Lizzie knew that it didn't take much for the crew to decide that they couldn't fly. It was more likely to happen somewhere hot and sunny like Cyprus than Brize Norton, though. "What are you up to?" he asked her.

"I've just got myself a bottle of vino from the bar," Lizzie replied. "I was going back to my room when you called."

"Do you want me to phone back in a few minutes when you're back in your room?"

"No, that's fine," Lizzie said.

"It's just I was going to ask you what you're wearing, and was hoping for something a bit more memorable than jogging bottoms, flip-flops, and a baggy t-shirt."

"That's not what I'm wearing," Lizzie said with a laugh. "It's not a baggy t-shirt, it's a baggy polo shirt."

"Of course, you can't wear a t-shirt in the mess." She could hear he was smiling. "I forgot."

"You were right about the jogging bottoms, though. Tell you what, give me five minutes and call me back."

"Are you going to get changed into something more comfortable?"

"What's more comfortable than baggy jogging bottoms? Maybe. Call me back."

Adams laughed down the line at her comment, and Lizzie grinned as she disconnected the call. A few seconds ago, she'd been tempted to take the screw top off the wine and have a slug from the bottle, but the barmaid was still messing about. Instead, Lizzie picked up the wine and hurried back to her room.

"So," Adams said when he called her back. He lowered his voice. "What are you wearing?" Lizzie grinned and sipped her wine, leaning back against her pillow.

"Hmm," she replied. "I'm wearing a Sakura bodysuit made by Coco de Mer. It's a wanton purple colour, and ever so silky. I'm stroking the material with my fingertips. Can you hear it?" There was a silence on the other end of the line, and her grin broadened as she imagined the look on Adams's face.

"Lizzie," he said a moment later. "You're still in those jogging bottoms, aren't you?" She giggled before replying.

"Spoilsport," she said. "Where's your imagination?"

"There's nothing wrong with my imagination, Lizzie Jarman."

"I took my flip-flops off for you," Lizzie replied. "Thought I'd better give my bunions an airing."

"What a lovely thought that is."

"I'm only joking. I haven't really got bunions."

"I know you haven't. I would have noticed them last night."

A silence developed between them for a few seconds when Adams mentioned last night. Lizzie took another sip of her wine, unsure how to broach the subject she wanted to talk about. Then she drained the glass in one large gulp.

"Paul, can I ask you something about last night?" she asked Adams as she topped up her wine.

"I don't really want to talk about it, Lizzie, if I'm honest."

Lizzie felt her heart sinking as he said this. Had Emma been right after all?

"Why not?" she said, trying to keep her voice as normal as she could.

"Hang on, let me move away from this bunch of lads."

Lizzie heard a few muffled noises on the end of the phone. When Adams next spoke, his voice was so quiet he was almost whispering.

"Lizzie, I can't talk about last night at the moment."

"But why not?"

"Because I'm in a terminal building with a bunch of squaddies, and if I so much as think about last night, I'll be wandering around with a hard-on the size of the Eiffel Tower."

"In your dreams," Lizzie said, her relief almost overwhelming. She laughed, slightly too hard. "I doubt they'd notice, to be honest. Your little trouser snake is more of an adder than a python."

"I didn't hear you complaining, Miss Jarman," Adams said quietly. "You were quite receptive to him, if I remember correctly." Lizzie could feel her cheeks colouring at his words. "What did you want to ask me, anyway?"

"Sorry, what?" Lizzie replied, her mind on other things for a few seconds.

"What did you want to ask me about last night? Whether I was faking my big Os?"

"No, I'm pretty sure you didn't," she said with a giggle. "Both of them seemed quite genuine to me, if a little rushed."

"Come on, spit it out." This time, they both laughed in unison. When Adams continued, though, his voice was serious. "What is it, Lizzie?"

"No, don't worry. It's just me being daft."

"What is it? Tell me."

"It's just, well, is that it?"

"Didn't you say that when I took my trousers off?"

"Paul, please. Stop joking around. It's just that we've not got unfinished business anymore, have we?" She topped up her glass of wine. "We've both scratched that particular itch, so to speak."

"Okay, sorry." His serious tone returned. "Are you asking if it was just a one-night stand?"

"Um, yes."

"Do you want it to have been one?"

Lizzie paused before replying. That was the last thing she wanted. Emma's words about being needy came back into her mind, but Lizzie pushed them away. She decided to be needy and take the consequences.

"That's the last thing I want, Paul." The silence on the other end of the line was excruciating and seemed to go on forever. "Are you there?"

"Yeah, I'm here," Adams said with a sigh. "I thought for a horrible moment there you were going to say yes." Lizzie let her breath out through her cheeks. She hadn't even realised she'd been holding it.

"You don't think I'm being needy by asking?"

"Yes, very." Adams started laughing. "But I like you being needy. It gives me a strange feeling in my underpants."

A FEW MOMENTS LATER, their goodbyes said, Lizzie ended the call. When she was sure it had disconnected, she took a large breath and started sobbing. It was partly sadness as the thought of not seeing Adams until his rest and recuperation, but it was mostly out of relief and happiness. Lizzie poured herself another glass of wine and composed herself.

"Just you stay safe over there, Adams," she whispered to herself as she took a large sip.

31

"Are you okay?" Delaney asked Isobel as she peeled the bandage away from his hand. "You look sad." She stopped what she was doing for a second and looked at him with a mournful expression. For a moment he thought she was about to burst into tears.

"Yes, I'm fine," she replied eventually. "Thank you for asking. It's been a long day." She returned her attention to the wound on his hand.

"So what happened earlier?" Delaney asked. "Were many people hurt?"

"I can't really say what happened," she replied, not pronouncing the 'h' properly, "but there were a few casualties and some died before they got to us."

"Oh," Delaney said, wishing that he hadn't asked.

Isobel spent a few moments cleaning the wound in his hand. Delaney leaned across to look at it before realising that it was a mistake. The edges of the cut had congealed, and she was trying to peel away the scabs that had formed with a piece of gauze soaked in saline.

"This might hurt a bit," she said, giving him a quick smile, "but I need to make sure that the edges are clean before I stitch it."

Delaney winced as Isobel continued to clean the wound.

"Where are you from?" she asked him, no doubt to take his mind off what she was doing to his hand.

"Hastings, in England. Do you know it?"

"No, I've never been to England."

"You're Canadian, right?"

Isobel looked at him and then at the fabric patch on her shoulder with a large Canadian flag. When she looked back at him, she was grinning.

"How did you guess? Is it my accent?"

He was just about to tell Isobel how much he liked her accent when she scraped again at the cut on his hand. Delaney gasped in response.

"Bloody hell, that hurt."

"I'm sorry," she replied with genuine tenderness in her voice. "I'm going to put some local anaesthetic in to numb it."

As Isobel got the equipment together to anaesthetise Delaney's hand, another female Canadian medic walked in. This one was older than Isobel and looked much more senior. The two women had a conversation in French for a moment and, as Delaney watched, the older woman reached out and put her hand on Isobel's arm. A few seconds later, Isobel was sobbing. When she left the tent, she didn't even look at Delaney.

"Mr Delaney, my name is Adèle," the woman said as she walked over to him. "I'm the senior nurse here and will be patching you up." She had a pulp tray in her hand that Isobel had been using to collect her equipment.

"Sure, no problem," Delaney replied. "What happened to Isobel?"

"She just had some bad news, that's all," Adèle replied. She sat down on a stool next to Delaney's trolly. He looked at her business-like expression and hoped that whatever she was about to do to him, it wouldn't hurt much. "One of her patients from earlier just died."

"That's not good," Delaney replied. There wasn't much else he could say to that.

As Adèle injected local anaesthetic into Delaney's hand, she took the same tack as Isobel had earlier and asked him questions. When he told her what he was in Kandahar to do, she paused and looked at him.

"A Steel Sky? What is that?"

Delaney smiled at her, pleased to have something to talk about other than where he was from or what he enjoyed doing in his spare time.

"It's a counter rocket and mortar system," he explained. "If it works, then it will destroy any incoming fire before it can land." Adèle's eyebrows went up a notch, and she muttered something in French.

"We could do with that," she said as she picked up a viciously sharp looking needle with blue thread dangling from it. Delaney tried not to look at the grey curved piece of metal. "One of the accommodation blocks took a direct hit this morning."

"I know," he replied. "I saw it, kind of."

Adèle's forehead creased as she leaned forward with the needle. To Delaney's relief, apart from some tugging as she sutured the edges of the wound together, he couldn't feel anything. A few moments later, she was done. Delaney looked down at the palm of his hand to see four neat stitches in a line. The edges of the wound still looked angry, but it didn't look anywhere near as bad as it had done.

"Thank you," he said, smiling at Adèle.

"It's my pleasure," she replied. "Now, keep those dry and come back in seven days to have them taken out."

"Will Isobel be here?" Delaney asked without thinking. A broad grin made its way over Adèle's face.

"You like her?"

"Um, no, I was just wondering."

"Sure you were," Adèle said. "Yes, she will be here. But if you ask for me when you get here, I'll make sure Isobel's free."

"Thank you. Could you thank her for me as well?"

"Of course I will," Adèle replied, nodding at his hand. "Now remember, keep that dry."

32

Warrant Officer Fowler stood outside the station commander's office door and glanced at his watch. It was exactly five minutes before eight on Wednesday morning and he was there for his regular weekly meeting with the group captain which was due to begin at eight o'clock sharp. Unusually, the station commander's door was closed. Fowler hesitated for a few moments, unsure whether to knock. It had never been shut before, at least not when he had a meeting with the station warrant officer.

Deciding against knocking on the door, Fowler sat down in one of the plush armchairs in the office that passed for an anteroom. It had a desk in one corner where the group captain's personal assistant normally sat and was decorated with prints on the walls that celebrated the RAF Regiment's battle honours. His stump was itching, and he was looking forward to being able to take his prosthetic leg off after the meeting for a while.

Fowler had just picked up a copy of the RAF News

from a small table when the station commander's door opened.

"SWO," the group captain said. Fowler got to his feet as quickly as he could and braced up in lieu of a salute.

"Sir," he said sharply.

"I'm sorry to have kept you. Come on in."

Group Captain Patrick Leeson was young for the rank he had managed to attain. He was in his mid-forties and would probably, in Fowler's estimation, get promoted at least twice more, if not higher, before his time was done. The station commander role at RAF Honington was a prestigious one, and often a stepping stone to higher things.

Fowler followed the station commander back into his office. To his surprise, the group captain closed the door behind him.

"Sit down, Tom," Leeson said. Fowler sat down with relief. His stump really was playing him up.

"No Sharon today then?" Fowler asked, referring to the group captain's personal assistant.

"I sent her home. She was a bit upset."

Fowler looked carefully at the station commander. Despite the difference in rank between them, their working relationship had led to a close friendship developing over the twelve months that they had worked together.

"What's the matter, Paddy?" Fowler asked. "You look exhausted. Is everything okay?"

"I was on the phone to Air Command when you got here. There's been an incident in Afghanistan. RAF Leeming have lost a couple of lads, and there're four injured. One seriously."

"Ours?"

"Yes. All from the regiment."

"Shit," Fowler whistled through his teeth. Even though the casualties were from another station, the regiment was small enough to consider itself a family. Whoever the casualties were would have been through RAF Honington at some point in the past. "Do you know names?"

"I do, but they've not been released."

The group captain checked his notepad and reeled off the names to Fowler.

"I don't recognise any of them," Fowler said. There was a soft knock at the door.

"Come in," Leeson called out. The door opened, and the padre walked in. "Padre Russell, thank you for coming."

"No bother at all," the padre replied. He wore the rank of squadron leader and a dog collar, but the rank slides weren't interpreted in the same way as usual. Padres always assumed the rank of the person they were talking to, no matter whether they were aircraftmen or the chief of the air staff.

"One of the lads who died, Corporal Russel, is from the patch. He was due to be posted here when he got back, but his wife and little one moved early to get settled."

Fowler sat back in his chair, desperate to itch at his stump. The wife's presence on the patch explained the padre's presence. At some point in the next hour or so, he was going to be needed.

"Have we got a notifying officer?" Fowler asked, referring to an officer from another station whose sole job was to break bad news. He or she would then go back to their original station, meaning that the family wouldn't see them again.

"Yes, there's a flight lieutenant coming down from Wittering. He should be here in an hour or so. Do you gents want some coffee?"

Fowler was about to get to his feet and offer to make it when the padre put his hand on his arm to keep him seated.

"I'll have tea, if you have it?" the padre said, squeezing Fowler's arm.

"Sure." The group captain got to his feet and walked into the anteroom.

"Jesus wept," Fowler said under his breath before immediately apologising. "Sorry, Padre. Wasn't thinking." The padre smiled in response.

"No bother, Tom." He raised his eyes to the ceiling. "He won't mind that one. I think Paddy just needs a moment."

"That's understandable, I guess. Do you know the family?"

"I met the wife once at the toddler group. She's ever so young. Corporal Russell was only twenty-two."

"That's no age at all. What a mess. Do you know what happened?"

"It was a mine strike." The station commander walked back into the room and handed Fowler a cup of coffee before passing a mug of tea to the padre. "A daisy chain that took two of the three vehicles in the convoy out. Then the medevac helicopter got shot up coming in, but went back in to get them out after a couple of Apaches had cleared up."

The three men sat in a contemplative silence for a while, each of them lost in their own thoughts. Fowler thought back to when he had been injured and remembered the sight of the Chinook helicopter with a medical team on the back thundering in to get him. He had never seen such a welcome sight in his life, having been convinced that he was going to bleed to death in a field. In Fowler's case, a field full of the empty casings of poppies.

"Tom," the padre said, interrupting his thoughts. "I wonder perhaps if Paddy and I could have a few moments?" Fowler looked at the group captain who was just staring at the wall. He was, Fowler remembered, a church goer.

"Of course," Fowler replied, getting to his feet. He adjusted his walking stick, trying to keep the weight off his stump. The padre smiled at him. "I'll go to the guard room to make sure the notifying officer doesn't get messed about."

"Call me when he gets here, Tom."

Notifying families was, unfortunately, a well-practised routine. The notifying officer and the padre would arrive on the doorstep, at which point the family and the neighbours would know exactly what was going on. Then the officer would say his bit while the padre remained silent and a few steps behind him. The notifying officer would then leave, hopefully never to be seen again by the family, and the padre would be left with the wreckage. As soon as the notifying officer was clear, Tom would join the padre to do what he could.

"I will do, padre," Tom replied. He nodded at the station commander and turned to leave the office. It was going to be a long day and a painful one. But nowhere near as painful as it was going to be for the young woman whose life they were about to ruin.

33

"Sirs, ma'ams, ladies and gents," a male voice boomed through the public address system in the terminal building. Adams was in Cyprus where his plane had landed about an hour ago, and when he heard the announcement, he opened his eyes to see who was speaking. "I've got some good news and some bad news."

The voice belonged to a stout flight sergeant dressed in a flying suit who had been the chief purser on their flight here from Brize Norton. Adams stretched and sat forward. The hard plastic chair he'd been trying to snooze on was about as uncomfortable as his seat on the plane had been.

"The bad news is that there's a delay to the takeoff for Kandahar." As the flight sergeant said this, a collective groan went up from the soldiers in the terminal. There were almost three hundred of them crammed into the building. When the terminal at Akrotiri air base had been designed, the Royal Air Force didn't have any passenger planes that could carry that many passengers. Beside him,

Adams heard several squaddies swearing about the RAF. "The good news is that we've opened up the exterior seating area so you can catch some rays while you're waiting. Lunch will be made available later on."

"For fuck's sake," the soldier next to Adams muttered to no-one in particular. "That's the good news? We can go outside when it's redders to wait for a butty box?"

"Yeah," another squaddie replied. "A dead dog roll and some warm Rola Cola. Can't bloody wait."

Adams got to his feet, grinning at the soldiers' complaints. It was their prerogative, he guessed, and he'd never met anyone from the Army who couldn't whinge like a professional. He walked over to where the flight sergeant was trying to escape through a door with a combination lock on it before anyone asked him any questions.

"Excuse me, Flight?" Adams said. The flight sergeant turned around with a frown and looked as if he was about to say something when he saw Adams's rank slides.

"Hey, sir," the flight sergeant said. "Everything okay?"

"Sure," Adams replied. "I was just wondering how long you think the delay will be?"

"Bear with me a moment, sir. Let me just get this door open and we can go through." He glanced at the gathered soldiers in the terminal building, several of whom were staring at him with barely disguised hostility. "Bloody thing. This always sticks."

"C, X, and then 5,4,3,2,1," Adams said with a grin. The flight sergeant entered the combination on the lock and the door swung open. With an embarrassed smile, he stepped through the door, followed by Adams. "Don't want that lot out there overhearing," the flight sergeant said when the door had swung shut behind them, "but we're looking at about five hours, maybe more. There's a medical team on a Herc that needs to catch us up."

"From Brize?"

"Yep. A critical care team. There's a few lads been hurt. RAF regiment is what I heard."

"Oh, right. Okay." Adams thought for a moment. "Any chance I could nip out onto the base? I'll be back in plenty of time for the flight."

"Not really supposed to let you do that, sir," the flight sergeant replied, looking at his watch and then at the Red Cross on Adams's arm. "Sorry."

"I was just going to nip to the officers' mess, and probably the NAAFI. Maybe I could pick you something up there?"

"Such as what, sir?" the flight sergeant said as a slow smile crept onto his face.

"Something cold and wet, perhaps? For you and your crew when you get stood down?"

"Takeoff is estimated as being at sixteen sixty four, sir." Adams grinned. A slab of Kronenburg 1664 it was, then. "So you need to be back for seventeen hundred."

"Roger dodge, flight," Adams replied.

The heat outside the terminal building was stifling, but Adams knew it was only a precursor for the heat at Kandahar. When they eventually got there. He walked down Vulcan Road to the junction with Phantom Way and followed the dog leg round until he was on Church Rise Way. The sun was reflecting from the large white workshop buildings he walked past, and he wished he'd not left his sunglasses on the plane. On his right-hand side was the Station Headquarters, a two storey red-brick building with an RAF ensign fluttering in the breeze outside it. Beyond the station headquarters he could see the medical centre, and for a moment he thought about nipping in to say hello to a few people he knew working there.

His stomach had other ideas, however, and the idea of a nice lunch in the mess was more appealing. When he reached the end of the road, he turned right and walked along Jacaranda Drive to the mess. He could eat first, and maybe nip into the medical centre later.

A COUPLE OF HOURS LATER, Adams was sitting back outside the terminal building in the shade of a large eucalyptus tree. He'd had a much nicer lunch than the soldiers back at the terminal would have had and had bumped into a friend who worked in the RAF's equivalent of Human Resources in the Station Headquarters. The conversation had been muted. Adams knew that his friend would know about the casualties—the same signal that informed units back in the United Kingdom came through his desk—but other than confirming there was a medical team on its way, he'd not said a word about what had happened.

Adams toyed with the idea of phoning Lizzie to see if she'd found out anything. She was working with the RAF regiment so would probably know something. But if she didn't, he didn't want to have to be the one to tell her.

He glanced at his watch. It was almost four o'clock, so he got to his feet and walked over to the wire that separated the live airfield from the rest of the base. About thirty minutes ago, a C130J Hercules had landed, the distinctive noise of its engines a familiar sound to anyone who had served at Lyneham or Brize Norton. Adams pressed his face against the wire and watched tiny figures in the distance unloading large green containers from the ramp at the back of the plane that was known fondly as a 'Fat Albert'. The critical care teams carried a lot of equipment so they could run an intensive care unit in the air. He didn't envy them one bit. At least his speciality, emergency medicine, had some excitement. Intensive care nursing, by contrast, was ninety-nine percent boredom and one percent pure panic.

Adams returned to the tree, picked up the slab of beer that he'd bought in the NAAFI, and tucked it under his arm.

34

Lizzie sat down in one of the chairs in the classroom and turned to the chief instructor.

"What going on, Flight?" she asked him.

"No idea, mate," Flight Sergeant Hughes replied. "All I know is that the SWO wanted us all in here."

"Shit, that doesn't sound good," Lizzie replied. Around them, the rest of the regiment squadron were filing into the room and taking up the seats usually used by students.

"No, it doesn't," Hughes said. "Here's Su Pollard, best hush up."

"Who's Su Pollard?"

"She's an actress, and that's what we call him."

"Why?" Lizzie asked as she watched Warrant Officer Fowler walk to the front of the room.

"She played a character called Peggy in *Hi-de-Hi*. Peggy. Peg leg."

"You do know he'll kill you if he hears you call him that?" Lizzie replied.

"You do know I'll kill you if he finds out?" Hughes

whispered with a grin.

"What's *Hi-de-Hi,* anyway?" she asked, and Hughes's grin slipped a notch.

"Before your time, Lizzie," he replied. "Now, shh."

"Gentlemen," Warrant Officer Fowler's voice boomed from the front of the room. When he noticed Lizzie, he nodded at her. "And Sergeant Jarman, of course." He took a breath, and Lizzie looked at him carefully. He looked exhausted. It was more than that, but Lizzie wasn't quite sure how to read the look on his face. "I've got some bad news, I'm afraid. Earlier this morning, just outside Kandahar, a regiment patrol took a direct hit from an IED."

The room remained absolutely silent as the Station Warrant Officer went on to tell them that three of the patrol had died. Two immediately, and one in the field hospital from a head injury. When he read out the names of the airmen who had died, there were a couple of audible gasps in the room as the names were recognised as belonging to friends.

"Did anyone know Corporal Russell?" the SWO asked. When there was no reply other than a few heads shaking, he continued. "His wife's on the patch, so be careful what you say or do if you live on it. There were also some personnel injured, including Sergeant David Miller. Known as Windy." Warrant Officer Fowler was looking directly at Lizzie as he said Windy's name, and she felt her heart run cold. "I don't have any more information, but there's a medical team on their way from Brize as we speak to bring them home."

Lizzie could feel a lump in her throat. If the medical team had already left, then the casualties must be really serious. Otherwise, they would be brought back on a routine flight.

"Do you know how badly hurt Windy is, Tom?" Lizzie asked. "Sorry, Mr Fowler?"

"He's listed as Very Seriously Ill, Lizzie, but I don't have any more than that."

Lizzie felt a hand on her shoulder as the warrant officer said this. Everyone in the room knew that this was the highest possible category in terms of being sick or injured.

"Are you okay?" she heard Hughes whisper in her ear. Lizzie nodded, too numb to speak. As Warrant Officer Fowler spoke to the room about pulling together in a time like this, her mind wandered as she tried to remember the last time she'd seen Windy. Lizzie wasn't sure when it was, but she remembered being quite drunk at the time. Adams had been there as well. When she turned her attention back to the room, the warrant officer was talking about battle casualty replacements.

"So we'll be sending replacements from here for the regiment lads. Listen in, and if your name's called, just raise your hand so I know you're here." He read out four names, and the room remained silent as five hands were raised in the air. "They're the nominations from Air Command, so you'd best get cracking, lads." Several of the regiment gunners whose names had just been read out started shuffling.

"What about Windy, Mr Fowler?" Lizzie asked, raising her own hand. The SWO looked down at his notes.

"Sergeant Ferris will be replacing Windy," he said. There were several groans from across the room. Sergeant Ferris wasn't the most popular man on the station by a long stretch of the imagination.

"But his wife's pregnant," Lizzie replied.

"It wasn't me," a male voice said behind Lizzie.

Warrant Officer Hughes put his hand up to stop the muffled laughter in the room.

"Well, he's the nomination from Air Command."

The next words out of Lizzie's mouth surprised even her. "I'll go," she said, her voice coming out much more confidently than she felt. "I'll go instead."

"Lizzie, you're not long back," Fowler replied.

"That doesn't matter. I want to go. Can you ask the group captain to speak to Air Command, please?"

"Mr Fowler?" Lizzie turned to see one of the regiment gunners, Corporal Perkins, was talking. "Not being funny like, but if I get hurt over there, I'd much rather have Sergeant Jarman looking after me than that fat Scottish twat."

"Me too," another voice said. "Ferris is a complete bell-end." There was another voice in the background saying something that Lizzie didn't catch other than it rhymed with anchor.

"Enough, gentlemen," Fowler said, fixing them with a hard stare. "Now's not the time for your opinions of Sergeant Ferris." He turned to Lizzie before continuing. "I'll speak to Group Captain Leeson and see what he says."

"No need, Mr Fowler." Lizzie turned to see the station commander standing in a doorway at the back of the room. "I think the lads have made it clear who they'd prefer. Are you sure, Sergeant Jarman?"

Lizzie licked her lips before replying. She looked around the room and saw every set of eyes on her. Even if she had wanted to back down, which she didn't, there was no way she could let her colleagues down.

"One hundred percent, sir," Lizzie said, trying to put as much confidence into her voice as she could.

35

"You're a bloody idiot, Delaney." Delaney turned at the mention of his name to see Rubenstein standing with his arms folded across his chest, glaring at him.

"Why?" he asked his boss. "What have I done now?"

"What, apart from slicing your hand open, you mean?" Delaney sighed. To say Rubenstein was unimpressed with the fact that Delaney had taken most of the previous day off while he was waiting for his hand to be stitched was an understatement. "Your figures are all wrong. Are you off your bloody meds or something?"

Rubenstein nodded at the large map on the table, held in place by a can of soda in each corner. They were from Rubenstein's personal stash of drinks that he kept in the fridge. In the short time that Delaney had been in Kandahar, he'd not been offered a single one.

"What do you mean, wrong?" Delaney replied, getting to his feet and crossing to the map. He looked down at it and examined the pencilled lines that they'd spent a couple of hours plotting that morning. Rubenstein jabbed a fat finger at one of the lines and ran his finger back to the start of it. According to the map, the line started in the foothills of the mountains that overlooked the base.

"Here's the firing point of the rockets," he said, running his finger along the line, "leading to the point of impact." Rubenstein prodded at a small circle that Delaney had drawn on the map. "You're suggesting that we deploy Steel Sky here."

"Yes, and that will cover most of the area that it's supposed to cover." Delaney ran his eyes over the various lines and symbols on the map, but he was sure he was right. "Where do you think we should put it?" By way of a reply, Rubenstein pointed at a large dark circle on the aerial photograph.

"Ideally, slap bang in the middle of that," he said, glancing at one of the cans of soda that was holding the map flat. Delaney stifled a laugh, realising that his boss must have run out of cold ones in his fridge.

"Good luck with that one," Delaney said. "That's the waste treatment plant."

"The poo pond," Rubenstein replied with a grimace.

"Yep, and I don't want to go anywhere near it."

Delaney looked again at the map. Much to his chagrin, he could see that his boss had a point. Deploying Steel Sky in the vicinity of the poo pond would make sense, although it still left a lot of the crucial infrastructure on the base vulnerable. When he realised that deploying Steel Sky where Rubenstein was suggesting would bring the field hospital into its protective shield, he acquiesced.

"I think you're right, boss," Delaney said quietly as an image of Isobel flashed across his mind's eye. "That might work better. There's a space next to the treatment plant where it could go." He pointed at the map. "Just here."

Delaney watched as Rubenstein stood and folded his arms across his ample chest. A well-placed punch to the face would wipe off the smug grin he was wearing, but would also split Delaney's stitches and probably result in him being sacked. Delaney suppressed the urge. Rubenstein's time would come, of that there was no doubt.

"The kit will be here later tonight," Rubenstein said, "so we can set it up tomorrow. The base commander wants a brief before it's fully operational. You're giving it."

"Why do I have to do it?" Delaney asked, irritated. "You're supposed to be the chief engineer."

"That's the key word," Rubenstein replied, finally giving in to temptation and picking up one of the cans of soda. Delaney watched as the map started to curl up at the corner. "Chief. Therefore, I have lackeys to do stuff for me, like brief people."

"I'm sure the base commander would rather hear from the chief, though, not one of his lackeys," Delaney replied as Rubenstein took a long pull from the can. There was a pause in the conversation as Rubenstein smoothed the map back down and replaced the half-empty can onto the corner. Then he belched loudly and rubbed his sternum.

"Well, tough titties, Delaney. Consider it a career opportunity."

"Gee, thanks, boss," Delaney replied, not even trying to hide the sarcasm in his voice. He got to his feet and returned to his computer in the corner of the room. The screen was angled so that Rubenstein couldn't see what was on it, which was just as well as Delaney had found Isobel's Facebook page. He had been in the process of downloading all the photographs she had posted there to a private folder when Rubenstein had interrupted him.

There was one photograph of Isobel standing in front

of a lake wearing a bikini. Her hair was tied back, and she had a broad smile on her face, obviously not fazed by the fact that she was almost naked. From the shit-eating grin on the face of the man with his arm around her, neither was her companion. Delaney frowned as he looked at the photograph. It was going to take him ages to Photoshop the bloke out and replace him. But while he was doing that, he could also remove the tiny green bikini, pixel by pixel.

"So, re-do those bloody figures," Rubenstein called over to Delaney. "I want to see the presentation for the base commander before you finish today."

"Yes, chief," Delaney muttered under his breath as he fired up Photoshop. When it had loaded, he selected the spot healing brush and started work on the strap of Isobel's bikini. With any luck, Rubenstein would fall asleep after lunch like he normally did and leave him to it.

36

Adams opened his eyes as the public address system on the plane crackled into life.

"Gentlemen, wakey wakey, rise and shine." It was the pilot sounding ridiculously chirpy. "We're about to start our descent into Kandahar, so if you could put your body armour and helmets on before I dim the lights, that would be appreciated."

Around him, soldiers stirred into life, most of them grumbling as they did so. Adams undid his seatbelt and stood up to get his body armour and helmet from the overhead locker as around him almost three hundred other people did the same thing. It took them a few moments, and Adams struggled to get his seatbelt over the body armour, but he managed it eventually and slid gratefully back into his seat.

"Window blind down, please, sir," a steward said as he walked down the aisle. A few minutes later, Adams felt his ears pop as the plane started its rapid descent, and the lights were extinguished.

It was a surreal experience. Adams was sitting on a

plane that was almost in pitch darkness, wearing heavy body armour and a Kevlar helmet, while it was descending at a rate that would have terrified most people. Adams knew why—although the insurgents on the ground below them hadn't yet had a pop at a large plane coming into Kandahar, they would at some point. Adams just hoped it wasn't tonight.

Before he'd decided to try to sleep, Adams had wandered down to the rear of the large Voyager aircraft to speak to the medical team that had boarded at Cyprus. The news he'd got from them was sobering, to say the least. Three dead, one of them who had died on the operating table with an unexpected intracranial bleed. One triple amputee, one with a smashed femur, and one with a head injury. He had chewed the fat with the medics for a few minutes, but they weren't really in the mood for small talk.

Beneath the aircraft, there was a noisy bang which made several of the soldiers around Adams jump and then look around to see if anyone had noticed. Adams knew that they were at about two thousand feet and that the landing gear had just dropped. It wasn't as if he could look out of the window to see how close to the ground they were. A moment later, the plane touched down, and the brakes screeched into life.

Unlike on a normal passenger plane, there was no-one hurrying to get bags out of the lockers and being told off by the crew. None of the passengers seemed to be in any particular hurry at all. When the pilot's voice said *Welcome to Kandahar,* even he didn't sound as chirpy as he had done a few moments before. It took a few moments, but eventually the plane stopped and the doors were opened with a pneumatic hiss.

Adams waited until the plane was almost empty before he got to his feet. He retrieved his carry-on bag from the overhead locker. It didn't have much in it. His laptop, toiletries, and some spare underwear in case his main bag ended up on the Falkland Islands. He walked to the front of the plane, thanked the flight sergeant, and walked down the portable stairs into the fierce heat of the Afghan night.

"Adams?" a female voice said as he reached the bottom of the stairs. "You're supposed to bring yourself to attention when a senior officer addresses you."

Adams looked at Squadron Leader Christine Beckett, the woman he was replacing, who was silhouetted against the bright lights from the terminal building.

"You can piss off, Christine," Adams replied with a good-natured grin. "I'm your new best friend, aren't I?"

"Don't you mean you can piss off, ma'am?" she replied. Adams stepped forward, and she saw the rank slide on the front of his uniform. "Oh my God," she laughed. "When did that happen?"

"About eight hours ago."

Christine laughed and put her arms out for a hug. She was a couple of years older and a couple of inches shorter than Adams, and was wearing a pair of oversized combats with an embroidered name badge. Her blonde hair was cut into a short bob. Probably not a bad idea, Adams reasoned, given how hot it was outside.

"Bloody hell, they must be desperate." She ran her eyes up and down him. "You're looking well, Adams."

"You look pretty swamped by those combats. Have you lost weight?"

"They're awful, aren't they?" she replied, smoothing her hands down her sides. "It feels like I'm wearing a twelve by twelve tent. But you're right. I've been on the Kandahar weight loss plan. I can't say I recommend it. You're looking well. Any gossip?"

"I just couldn't stop thinking about you, Christine," Adams said with a broad grin. "So I got on a trooper flight to come and see you."

"You old charmer," she replied, "but you do know I wouldn't sleep with you if you were the last man in NATO, don't you?"

"No way!" Adams laughed. "I've come all this way for nothing?" It had been a standing joke between them for years. "How is the wife?" he asked Christine.

"Julie's good, we're good. She can't wait for me to go home. Let's get your bag and your weapons. Are you dropping your rifle off at the armoury?"

"Yep, if I can. Carrying a pistol around all day will be bad enough, let alone a rifle."

"You get used to it," Christine replied, touching her hand to the pistol on her belt. "Just don't drop it in the toilet like I did."

"You didn't?"

"Afraid so," Christine said with a laugh. "Before I'd used it, fortunately. And I dropped it on my big toe once, as well. We'll square the rifle away and I'll take you to your accommodation. We can grab a coffee on the way, if you want?"

"Sounds good to me. You have got a car, haven't you? It's bloody hot."

"Of course I've got a bloody car, Adams."

A FEW MOMENTS LATER, Adams and Christine were sitting on the boardwalk outside an all-night coffee stand. To

Adams's relief, it was much cooler where they were courtesy of a gentle breeze, but the stench it was carrying made it much less appealing than it could have been.

"What in hell is that smell?" he asked her, wrinkling his nose.

"That's the poo pond," she replied. "It's a large lake that used to be on the edge of the base. Now it's almost in the middle."

"What's in it?"

"It's called the poo pond, Adams. What do you think's in it?"

"Oh," he said. "Nice."

"I'll take you to see it tomorrow if you want? You can taste the rainbow up close and personal."

"I can't wait."

The poo pond was a lake of sewage that sat on a grim intersection between All-American Boulevard and Louisiana Road. It was an enormous liquid pit that held the contents of over eighteen hundred portable toilets dotted around the base. There was an urban legend, that Christine went on to tell Adams about, about a soldier who had swum across it for a dare. According to Christine, the nationality of the swimmer changed according to the nationality of whoever was telling the tale.

"Yeah, well," Adams said with a grimace, "never let the truth get in the way of a good story."

They spent a while catching up with each other. Adams hadn't seen Christine for at least a couple of years since her wedding. That had been a riotous evening, or at least what he could remember of it had been. Christine told him about how she and Julie were looking into having a child. "No," she had said with her hand in the air, "we do not need a sperm donor. Especially one from Norfolk."

In turn, Adams told Christine about how he'd managed to persuade the manning desk to get him acting rank for the tour. He exaggerated slightly as he told the story, making it sound as if the wing commander only wanted him for the job and no-one else. Christine, as he'd expected, didn't believe a word of it.

"You know why your flight was delayed, don't you?" Christine asked, taking a sip of her coffee.

"Yeah, I spoke to the medics on the plane," Adams replied. "Sounds pretty bad."

"Do you know David Miller?" Christine asked Adams. "He's a paramedic?"

"Windy? Yeah, I know Windy. I got really pissed at his promotion a while ago. He's a great lad."

"He's the triple amputee."

Adams paused with his coffee cup half-way to his mouth.

"Oh my God!" He replied, putting his coffee down. "Poor bloody bloke. That's desperate."

"I know," Christine replied, looking into the darkness beyond the fluorescent lights above their heads. "Isn't it? I can't wait to go home."

37

"I'm just not sure that she's ready, Paddy," Warrant Officer Fowler said. "That's all I'm saying." He was sitting in the station commander's office. Group Captain Leeson turned from his position at the window to face him.

"Tom, she just volunteered in front of the entire squadron," Leeson said. "She certainly sounded as if she was ready to me. You know the manning desk will bite my hand off if I give them a volunteer."

"With all due respect, sir," Fowler replied, using the universal code for *I think you're talking bollocks, and I'm about to tell you why*, "I do know her a bit better than you do."

Leeson crossed the room and sat down in the armchair opposite Fowler's.

"That goes without saying, Tom," he said, "and if you tell me that she shouldn't go, then she won't go. But after she's piped up in front of everyone, if we don't send her then we need to manage what we say to the others." He paused for a moment, and Fowler looked at him. The group captain looked exhausted, as was he. "Why don't you think she's ready? I've read her file. She's medically fit for deployment and she appears to want to go."

"I just think it might be too soon after what happened to her last time, that's all."

"She was under the care of the shrinks, wasn't she?"

"She saw them, yes," Fowler replied, "but I wouldn't say she was under their care. It was more of a precautionary measure to make sure that she was okay, if I understand it correctly."

"But if they had felt that she wasn't fit, then they would have downgraded her on mental health grounds, wouldn't they?"

"Yes, Paddy. They would." Fowler sighed. He knew that the group captain was talking sense, but at the same time that didn't mean he had to like it.

"Let me ask you a question, Tom, if I may."

"You are the station commander," Fowler replied with a faint smile.

"Would it be any different if she were male?"

Fowler paused for a moment before replying. It was a good question, and one which he had been anticipating. The problem, or at least as far as Fowler was concerned, was that it did make a difference. At least to him.

"If I'm honest, Paddy, I think it would."

"There you go then. We can't not send her just because she's female. What time is it?"

Fowler looked at his watch.

"Just gone six. Are you thinking about phoning Air Command to let them know?"

"I've already spoken to them," Leeson replied. "Warmed them up to the idea."

"So when you said if I said she shouldn't go, you

wouldn't send her, you were actually talking out of your arse?"

"Not at all, Tom," the station commander said as Fowler smiled at him. "I knew you'd come round, eventually."

Leeson got to his feet and crossed to a bureau next to the wall of his office. When he returned, he had a bottle of scotch and a couple of tumblers in his hands.

"It's been a long day, Tom," Leeson said as he sat down. "I think a drink wouldn't be a bad idea."

"Took you long enough, Paddy," Fowler laughed. "I've been gasping sitting here."

The station commander poured them both a generous amount of whiskey and they clinked their glasses together in a silent toast. Fowler sipped his drink, enjoying the warmth of the single malt. One thing the station commander couldn't bear was cheap whiskey, which had made buying his Christmas present a lot easier for Fowler.

"She would be the first woman to serve on the front line with the regiment if we do send her," Leeson said after a few moments of silence.

"That thought had occurred to me," Fowler replied. "The papers will love it. A young, pretty female medic putting her life in danger to help others."

"There could be some good press to be had out of it, I guess."

"I would imagine the public relations people in Main Building have got a hard on for her already," Fowler said with a grim smile.

"Probably not the best turn of phrase to use, Tom," Leeson replied. "Makes you look like a bit of a dinosaur. I might even send you on one of those equality courses Air Command keeps on trying to send me on."

"Don't you dare, Paddy," Fowler said. "I'm far too long in the tooth for all that nonsense."

"Are you likely to see the young lady in the mess later?"

"I expect so."

"Perhaps you could let her know our decision?"

"Oh, it's our decision now, is it?" When Fowler turned to look at Leeson, they were both smiling.

"Just tell her to bloody well stay safe over there," the station commander said as his smile started to fade.

38

Even though it was less than five inches long and weighed one and half pounds, the round device was arguably the most important part of the rocket because if it failed, the rocket itself failed. Its correct name was the Jiàn-1 point detonating fuze and within its upper body there were centrifugal weights, a firing pin, and a locking bushel. Below these components, in the lower body, was a delay screw designed to pause the detonation of the explosives within the fuze by 0.1 seconds.

When the outer skin of the fuze struck its target, the firing pin was forced into the firing cap, resulting in a flame. This flame ignited the detonator which, in turn, ignited the booster charge. This ignited the primary charge of the rocket's warhead. This entire sequence took place between the time it took the rocket to pass through the thin ceiling of the dining facility and impact the floor, giving the soldiers eating their breakfast below no time to react before the explosive wave ripped through the building at well over one thousand kilometres per hour.

The DFAC—short for Dining Facility and pronounced *Dee-Fack*—was one of five similar facilities on Kandahar air base. They were loosely named after the region that the food they served was from. The one that the rocket had just landed square in the middle of was called the Luxemburg DFAC, although as it was breakfast time there wasn't anything particularly European about the food. As it was the smallest DFAC on Kandahar, it only had boxed cereal, long life milk, and varying types of fruit to offer. Any residents of Kandahar who wanted a cooked breakfast would have to make their way to the Cambridge DFAC for a full English breakfast, or the Niagara DFAC for an American one. When the rocket punched through the roof, there were four American soldiers eating in the facility and one Indian chef, although all he had to do was supervise the soldiers to make sure they only had one box of cereal and one piece of fruit each.

Three of the soldiers and the chef were killed instantly, their bodies shredded by the detonation of the TNT inside the warhead. The fourth soldier died about twenty seconds later. He had been shielded to an extent by one of his colleagues' bodies, but as his friend's body was torn apart, parts of him became lethal shrapnel. The surviving soldier, a twenty-two year old lad from Missouri whose girlfriend was at that very moment writing him a letter to tell him how much she loved him, only remained alive long enough to realise that he was dying and would never see her again.

Adams heard the *crump* of the rocket exploding from his bed, followed a few seconds later by the mournful wailing of the sirens. As he had been trained to do, he put on his body armour and helmet and lay flat on the ground of his accommodation. He was technically supposed to roll under the bed, but couldn't see the point. Adams mumbled to himself under his breath. He hadn't even been in theatre for twenty-four hours and already there was incoming fire.

The previous evening, Christine had told him about the increase in indirect fire over the last few weeks. The intelligence lot thought there was a new rocket expert who the insurgents had drafted in from somewhere else to increase their activity. For the first few months of her tour, there had been nothing but drills, but then, two weeks ago, they had started for real. It was the complete randomness of them that terrified her, she had confessed to him. The alarm system always seemed to go off after the first rocket had hit the ground, just as it had done that morning, but by the time people had been able to react to the alarm, the projectiles had already landed.

Adams lay on the floor, starting to feel foolish even though he had his own room. It was a privilege of rank, apparently. If you were a squadron leader or above, you had your own space. Any lower than that and you were in shared accommodation, with the number of occupants sharing the same space being inversely relational to their seniority.

The room had a single bed, a small chest of drawers, and a large grey metal cupboard. Christine had bought a television that she was going to sell on to Adams when she left after her handover, and Adams had already decided that he was going to invest in a new PlayStation to make the tour go quicker.

When the all-clear sounded a few moments later, Adams took off his helmet and body armour and made his way to the communal area between the accommodation blocks. The blocks themselves were rows of pre-fabricated buildings separated by a strip of gravelled land with makeshift furniture constructed by amateur carpenters. When Christine had shown him to his accommodation the previous evening, there had been a few of the occupants sitting outside, smoking and talking. Adams had been too tired to talk to them and introduce himself.

Adams stepped out into the communal area to see a group of people already standing around one of the tables. As he approached, he could see that it wasn't a proper table, but a huge drum from a cable roll that had been cut in half. He walked closer to the group, all of whom were dressed or half dressed in combat fatigues, and was grateful to see Christine standing with them.

"Morning, mate," Adams said to her as he approached. Her face lit up when she saw him.

"Hey, it's my new best friend!" she replied brightly, seemingly ignoring the fact that the base had just been rocketed. "Let me introduce you to this motley bunch."

She had just started the introductions when the rocket alarm started warbling again. The group dispersed in a matter of seconds, everyone running back to wherever their protective equipment was.

As he wriggled back into his body armour, Adams knew that this was going to be a long four months.

39

Lizzie could feel a warm trickle of perspiration running down her back, and she wriggled on the stool she was sitting on to try to get rid of it. In front of her, the station photographer was fiddling with his camera.

"Nearly there," he muttered. The man had to be in his sixties and was in no hurry. By contrast, Lizzie was desperate to get out of her Number One dress uniform. The thick wool was heavy enough at the best of times, and the lights of his studio weren't helping. Neither was Corporal Perkins, one of the regiment gunners who had come with her to get his official photograph done as well. Known as 'Travis', he had been the first to speak up for her when the Station Warrant Officer had told them about the casualties.

"Would you stop pulling faces at me, Travis," Lizzie said, trying not to laugh. "It'll be your turn in a minute, mate. See how you like it then."

"Right then, we're good to go," the photographer said, cutting off any response from Travis, witty or otherwise.

"Can you slide your backside round a bit, love, so that you're a bit more side on to the camera?" Lizzie did as instructed. "Perfect, now look at the camera. That's it."

Lizzie flinched as the umbrella soft box lights flashed either side of the photographer. He leaned in to the camera and examined the small screen on the back.

"Okay, one more. Try to keep your eyes open for this one if you can." Lizzie ignored Travis's stifled laugh and stared at the camera as the lights flashed again. "Perfect," he said when he examined the second photograph. "Right then, Perkins, is it?"

A FEW MOMENTS LATER, Lizzie and Travis left the photographer's studio.

"Well," Travis said, "that's the coffin shots done."

"You're so morbid, Travis," Lizzie said with a laugh as she slapped his arm.

"What?" he replied. "It's true. If you come home as freight, then they've got a half decent picture for the top of your coffin as opposed to one of you in Magaluf with your tits out."

"Please tell me you've not seen that picture?" Lizzie asked with a grin on her face.

"No, but I'd like to," Travis replied, also grinning.

"Well, sorry to disappoint you but I've never been to Magaluf, and there are no pictures in existence of me with my tits out."

"There will be by this evening."

"How d'you mean?" Lizzie asked. Travis nodded back in the direction of the photographer's studio.

"When matey boy back in there fires up Photoshop, he'll have you doing all sorts of nonsense."

"Maybe he bats for the other side? Even if he does, he'll have to be pretty good at Photoshop to make you look presentable," Lizzie countered. "What do you still need to get done then?"

Travis fished a crumpled piece of paper out of his pocket. Lizzie had a similar one in hers, but they were both the same, so she leaned over his shoulder as he read down it.

"Let me know if you get stuck on any of the long words, Travis."

"Very funny, Lizzie. Just stores, I think."

"Me too. I need some more t-shirts."

"You have got them in stock," Lizzie said to the store man a few moments later. "Look, there on the shelf." She pointed at a box full of t-shirts behind the miserable civilian who could have been the photographer's brother.

"Yes, but you can't have those ones. Someone might need them, so we have to keep some back for spares."

"But I need them. I'm deploying in a couple of days."

"Sorry, can't be done."

"What's the point of having them then, if you can't actually give them out?" Travis joined in the conversation. The store man just crossed his arms and glared at him. "This is pointless," Travis said. "Come on, Lizzie, let's go."

They walked out of the stores and into the sunshine.

"Do you want to grab a coffee in the NAAFI?" Travis asked her.

"Probably not, mate. I'm going to nip into Norwich this afternoon and go to Primark. I've got a better chance of coming out of there with some t-shirts," Lizzie replied. "Do you want to come?"

"Nah, I've got to go and see the old girl and listen to her sobbing for half an hour when she finds out I'm going away. But at least I'll get a decent meal once she's finished blubbing."

LIZZIE WALKED BACK TO THE SERGEANTS' mess, mentally running through her final preparations as she did so. She could have ordered some t-shirts on the internet and had them delivered instead of driving all the way to Norwich. It was almost an hour each way, but she didn't want to go just for the shopping. It would be the last time for a while where she could just be normal. Not wearing a uniform with a rifle slung over her shoulder and a Kevlar helmet ruining her hair.

In the centre of Norwich was a pasty shop with a seating area upstairs that looked out over the market. It was the perfect place to people watch without being disturbed. Lizzie was fairly sure that the pasties they sold were nothing like the traditional Cornish ones she used to have when she went there on holiday as a child—great big hulking lumps of pastry filled with steaming meat and vegetables—but they were nice enough.

"It's the simple pleasures," Lizzie muttered to herself as she considered what type of pasty she would have once she got to Norwich. She would have gone to see her own mother, but she was away on holiday and would have to find out via e-mail.

When she got to her room, Lizzie looked at the large black bag with all her clothes in. By the time she had included her combats and other military equipment that she had to take with her, there wasn't much room for personal clothing. Not that she would have much of a chance to wear it, anyway. Lizzie fired up her laptop and opened her e-mail. It took her a few moments, but she composed an e-mail to her mother to let her know that she was deploying at short notice. She didn't say why, though, just that she didn't have a choice. If her mother knew that she had effectively volunteered to go, she would go ballistic on Lizzie.

After sending the e-mail to her mother, she opened up another blank e-mail and chewed the inside of her lip as she thought for a few moments. Lizzie wanted to let Adams know she was coming out, but as with the e-mail to her mother, wasn't quite sure how to phrase it. Instead, she closed the laptop down and got to her feet.

When she got out there, she could see him and tell him in person.

40

Delaney looked at the single-storey building in front of him. It was half hidden behind concrete blast barriers topped with barbed wire. Any gaps in the barriers were filled with secure fencing, similarly topped. Standing in front of the main entrance to the building was a surly looking American soldier, his M4 carbine clutched tightly to his chest as if Delaney was about to make a grab for it.

"Identification?" the solider barked at Delaney. He held out his contractor ID card that he wore on a lanyard around his neck for the soldier to examine.

"Purpose of visit?"

"I'm here to brief the base commander," Delaney replied. If he was impressed, the soldier didn't show it. He handed Delaney back his ID card and regarded him for a few seconds, enjoying his brief moment of power before nodding his head and standing to one side.

Delaney looked at the entrance to the building, noticing the pockmarks in the outer brick and stucco walls. There was a tall archway with a door set into it. The original door had been replaced with a plywood one, and above the doorway was a rectangular sign with the Afghanistan flag and the words *Welcome to Kandahar* in white letters.

The building was known as the TLS, which stood for *Taliban Last Stand*. Delaney had looked it up on the internet, and apparently this was where the last vestiges of the Taliban had attempted to resist the US Marine Corps back in 2001. The battle had ended when the Americans had dropped a thousand pound bomb known as a JDAM through the roof of the building.

He stepped inside the plywood doorway, relieved to be out of the sun. Although there wasn't any air conditioning that he could see or hear, the interior was much cooler. Just inside the doorway was a large hallway, its walls blackened by a fire in the past, with several more clusters of pock marks visible. Delaney smiled, imagining what it must have been like for the Taliban trying to defeat the Marine Corps. It must have been pretty cool, he thought, but perhaps not for the Taliban.

A woman dressed in combats approached him.

"Can I help you?" she asked, glancing at his ID card.

"I'm here to brief the base commander," Delaney replied.

"Air Commodore Maugham?"

"No, my name's Mark Delaney." The woman gave him an odd look.

"The base commander's called Air Commodore Maugham," she said. Realising his mistake, Delaney grinned awkwardly, but the woman didn't smile back. "The briefing room's through there. Make sure you're there at exactly five to. He's a stickler for timing. Have you got a brief?"

"Yes, I e-mailed it to one of his staff yesterday."

"Just make sure you stick to your time for it. He's been known to throw people out who go on for too long."

"Right, cheers," Delaney replied uncertainly.

AT EXACTLY FIVE minutes before nine, Delaney was sitting in what passed for the briefing room. It was a fairly large room with high ceilings and the now familiar pock marks in the walls. In the centre of it was a large oval table, already prepared with papers, pens, and bottled water for the occupants. At the far end of the table was a projector, its lens pointing at a white sheet that was tacked to the wall.

Delaney had chosen to sit on one of the chairs that were lined up along the walls, figuring that the oval table would have some sort of seating plan. As the door opened and men and women in combats filed in, Delaney realised he was right and suddenly wondered if he was in someone's seat.

The woman from earlier came in, followed by a male colleague. They both had Red Cross armbands on.

"Am I okay to sit here?" Delaney asked the woman.

"Yeah, these are the cheap seats. The boss will be in soon, just stand up when he walks in," she replied.

The other attendees of the brief milled around in loose groups and chatted. Over the next few moments, they gradually took their places. There were perhaps fifteen of them altogether, not counting himself and the two medics in the cheap seats. One of the younger soldiers walked to the front of the room and started fiddling with a laptop. A few seconds later, the projector whirred into life and a military crest appeared on the sheet.

On the stroke of nine o'clock, the door opened and a tall man walked in. On the front of his uniform was a thick bright blue rank slide. As he walked in, the few people who had been sitting got to their feet sharply.

"Sit down, sit down," the base commander said.

Delaney took a closer look at the air commodore. He was over six feet tall, but thin with it, as if he was a keen runner. In one hand was a large mug, and he used the other hand to smooth his hair down, although he didn't have a massive amount of it and what little he had was white.

Around the room, the attendees took their seats and, once settled, looked expectantly at the air commodore. He ran his eyes around the room and settled on Delaney.

"Who are you?" the air commodore asked, his voice not particularly welcoming but not that unfriendly either.

"Mark Delaney, Mr, er, Maugham," Delaney replied.

"I've not been called Mister for quite a while," Maugham replied, his expression softening. "Are you briefing on the new defence system?"

Next to Delaney, the woman with the red armband covered her mouth with her hand and whispered from under it.

"Call him sir, for God's sake."

"Yes," Delaney said. "I am, Sir Maugham. I work for Aeolus." There was laughter around the room, and Delaney wondered what he'd said wrong. Had the woman just set him up? She was a bitch if she was. Delaney shot her a dark look, but both she and her companion were laughing too much to notice.

"Good," Maugham said. "Now, unless your security

clearance is higher than your lanyard suggests, you'd better go first. You're not cleared for the rest of it. Mark, wasn't it?"

"Yes."

"We're all ears, young man."

41

Adams watched with amusement as the young man got to his feet and made his way hesitantly to the front of the room. At least the poor bloke had given them all a cheap laugh by calling the air commodore *Sir Maugham*. As Delaney had walked past Christine, she had leaned forward and whispered something in his ear. He had nodded in response and took up his position next to the screen at the front of the room. A soldier said something to him before handing Delaney a small remote control.

"He looks so nervous," Christine whispered.

"He does, doesn't he?" Adams replied. Even from the back of the room, Adams could see Delaney's hands shaking.

"Sir, ladies, gentlemen," Delaney said. "I understand it's just *sir*, with no need for anything else."

Air Commodore Maugham leaned back in his chair and laughed. This was followed by dutiful laughter from the rest of the room. Delaney clicked the remote control and a blocky picture appeared on the sheet that was pinned to the wall at the front of the room. It was a vehicle, obviously military from the paint job, but it wasn't one that Adams recognised.

"This is a COBRA unit," Delaney explained, "or counter battery radar to give it the proper name. It's a collaboration between Germany and France, which makes reading the technical manuals a challenge." Delaney paused, obviously waiting for a laugh or two, but the occupants of the room remained silent.

"Tough crowd," Adams whispered to Christine, who nodded in response.

"The main problem with the COBRA is that it can only detect incoming fire when the projectiles are three thousand metres above sea level." Delaney paused and looked at the air commodore. "Is metres okay, sir, or would you prefer feet and inches?" Maugham didn't reply, but Adams saw him frowning for a few seconds before he started grinning.

"Nine thousand, eight hundred, and forty feet," the air commodore replied. Delaney returned his smile and Adams saw his brow furrow for a couple of seconds.

"Close, sir. Nine thousand, eight hundred and forty-two and a half, to be precise."

Beside him, Adams heard Christine wince.

"He's not going to like that," she whispered, but she was wrong. Maugham guffawed with laughter.

"I like you, Mr Delaney," he said. "Please, carry on."

As Delaney started talking about active solid-state phased array antenna and state-of-the-art digital processing, Adams could feel his eyelids getting heavy. Christine nudged him in the ribs.

"Try to stay awake, Adams," she whispered. "It

wouldn't be the best introduction to your new boss to snore in morning prayers."

Adams sat himself more upright on his chair and leaned forward, trying to concentrate on what Delaney was saying. He had advanced his presentation by a couple of slides and there was a different picture on the sheet. It showed a dark green metal box with an antenna on top of it. Whatever it was, not much effort had been put into making it look pretty.

"This is the first generation of Steel Sky," Delaney said, pointing at the sheet. Next to the green box was a thick metal pole supported by a tripod with a strange looking circular device on the top that reminded Adams of a honeycomb. The next image Delaney showed had a man standing next to the antenna, which was almost twice his height. "Unlike the COBRA system, which has a limited arc of detection, Steel Sky provides three hundred and sixty degree coverage." The next slide showed the addition of four heavy machine guns mounted on motorised units that were connected to the metal box with thick cables. "Is it possible to dim the lights for the video?" Delaney asked the soldier sitting next to the projector.

As the soldier crossed the room to the light switch by the door, Delaney continued his sales pitch. He looked to Adams to be much less nervous now that he was on familiar ground.

"This video shows three incoming missiles, all fired from a different direction within a few seconds of each other. It's not a very long clip, and I would suggest that you focus your attention on the horizon just behind this tree." He pointed at the screen as the lights dimmed.

Adams squinted at the tree as Delaney started the video. A few seconds in, a smoke trail appeared behind the tree. Two of the machine guns—moving so quickly that they blurred in the video—snapped round and after a pause of a few seconds, started spitting rounds. A couple of seconds after that, there was a puff of smoke in the distance as the missile was obliterated. Adams saw the other two machine guns also firing, but the projectiles they were firing at weren't visible on the video clip.

"That was a Chinese 107mm rocket fired from approximately six kilometres away. The radar locates the firing point, calculates the trajectory of the missile and determines that the landing point would be within the area that we had told the system to protect."

"How long does it take the system to do that?" Air Commodore Maugham asked.

"Under a second," Delaney replied. "It would be quicker, but it needs at least five deciseconds to calculate the trajectory properly. Then, when the missile is within range of the machine guns, they put enough rounds in the missile's path to destroy it."

"Can we see that video again?" another soldier asked from the front of the room.

"Sure," Delaney replied. As Adams watched the video replay, Christine leaned in to whisper in his ear.

"I challenge you to use the word *decisecond* in a normal conversation at some point today."

"If I knew what it meant," Adams replied with a grin, "I would happily accept that challenge."

He watched as Delaney finished his presentation and took a couple of questions from the people in the room. The air commodore introduced a major at the front of the room to Delaney, suggesting that the two of them get together to talk about the details of where and when Steel Sky could deploy. Delaney spoke briefly to the major and retrieved his memory stick from the laptop before leaving the room.

"Well, that was interesting," Maugham said to no-one in particular. "Let's hope it bloody well works. Right then, who's up next? It's the weather man, isn't it?"

"Do you mean the meteorologist, sir?" the soldier next to the laptop said with a smile. A chart appeared on the sheet with a complicated looking set of graphs and figures, and a man in civilian clothes near the back of the room got to his feet.

"No, I want someone to tell me about the weather," Maugham replied, "and not just that it's going to be hot and sunny. Come on, Michael Fish. Do your thing."

42

"Il est stupide," Adèle muttered under her breath as she looked at the American soldier lying on the trolley in front of her. *He is stupid.* They had stripped the soldier down to his underwear and Isobel was sponging him down with a cold flannel. Behind her, several fans whirred to blow air over the solider. "Quelle est sa température maintenant?" *What's his temperature now?*

Isobel glanced at a small device resting between her patient's legs. When he was more conscious than he was at the moment, he would find out that the wire leading from it belonged to a temperature probe in his rectum.

"Trente neuf cinq," Isobel replied. *Thirty-nine five.*

"Okay," Adèle said. "It's coming down. I'm going to speak to his sergeant."

She left Isobel to continue sponging the soldier down and walked to the front of the hospital where there was a small waiting area for the emergency department. Sitting on one of the seats looking nervous was a thick-set man in US fatigues. As Adèle approached, he got to his feet.

"Ma'am?" he said. "How's he doing?"

"He'll be okay," Adèle replied. "But no thanks to you."

"Sorry, ma'am, but how is it my fault? I didn't tell him to go out running in the heat."

"You are his sergeant, yes?"

"Yes, ma'am."

"Then you should have stopped him." Adèle looked at the sergeant and saw the look of resignation on his face.

"Yes, ma'am."

"That's the third one this week from your unit. I'm going to have to raise it with your chain of command. At some point, one of them will die."

She turned, not waiting for the sergeant to reply, and walked out of the waiting room into the main corridor of the hospital. Walking toward her were two people in British uniforms, both with red crosses on their arms.

"Christine," Adèle said. "How lovely to see you." She looked at her companion, realising from his pale skin that he had only just arrived in theatre. "And who is this?"

"Ma'am, this is my new best friend, Paul Adams. He's my replacement."

"Pleased to meet you, Paul. You are the new medical advisor for the commandant?"

"I am, yes. I mean *oui*." He put out a hand for Adèle to shake and grinned at her.

"Vous parlez français?" Adèle said. *Do you speak French?*

"Um, if you just asked me if I speak French, I'm afraid I don't." He had a disarming smile, and Adèle warmed to him straight away. "I go by Adams, by the way. The only people who call me by my first name are my mum and, er..." His voice tailed away.

"Adams it is, then. Would you like me to show you around the hospital? There's not much to it, I'm afraid."

"Sure, that would be great," Adams replied. "Thank you."

"Adams, I'll come back for you in half an hour," Christine said.

FOR THE NEXT TWENTY MINUTES, Adèle walked around the hospital with Adams. She showed him the ward area with its ten beds, the operating theatre which was empty, and the various other departments that made up her facility. When they reached the emergency room, she saw his eyes light up.

"This is more like it," he said as they walked into the room. She saw him cast a practised eye over the patient who Isobel was still sponging down before picking up the chart that was hanging on the end of the trolley. He looked at the lines on the chart for a few seconds. "Temperature's coming down nicely," he said.

"Isobel, can I introduce Adams. He's the new medical advisor."

"Hi, Adams," Isobel replied, continuing with the sponge. "Welcome."

"Thank you," Adams replied, glancing up at the monitor on the wall. Adèle realised he'd barely even looked at Isobel. "Let me guess, he went out for a run?"

"He did," Adèle said. "In full combats with a thirty kilogram pack on his back. If I give you his unit details, could you speak to the base commandant? There's been three of them this week from the same section."

"Sure," Adams replied. "Or I could speak to the unit

first, if you'd prefer? Before wading in with an air commodore?"

"I don't mind," Adèle said. "As long as it gets flagged up by someone."

"Leave it with me."

Adèle thanked him and was just about to offer him a drink when a large explosion sounded somewhere nearby. The canvas walls of the hospital shook, and dust started falling from the light fittings. She instinctively crouched down, as did Adams. Next to the trolley, Isobel shouted.

"Attention, une roquette!" *Look out, a rocket!* When Adèle looked up at her, Isobel had thrown her body across the patient. Next to the trolley, an intravenous fluid bag was swinging from side to side.

"Going for my kit," Adams said before getting to his feet and running from the room. Adèle stood up as well and dashed over to the corner of the room where her body armour and helmet were neatly stacked in the corner.

"Isobel!" Adèle shouted as she picked up her kit. "Get your protective equipment!"

Outside the hospital, the public address system started wailing. It was followed a few seconds later by the internal speakers. The mournful wail was so loud inside the tent that it made Adèle's ears ache.

Adèle struggled into her body armour and put her helmet on. She was trying to buckle up the strap under her chin when Isobel lay down next to her. She had already fastened up her own helmet and reached out to help Adèle with hers.

"Isn't it supposed to be an early warning system?" Isobel shouted over the din.

"Yes," Adèle replied, grateful for the younger woman's help with the buckle.

"So why does it go off after the rockets have started landing?"

43

Lizzie was standing in an office on the top floor of the terminal building at RAF Brize Norton, looking out over the pan. A hundred feet in front of her was a squat Hercules plane with its ramp down. Behind the Herc were three hearses, all parked with their open rear doors facing the plane. At the base of the ramp, standing smartly to attention, was a warrant officer.

She knew that below her in the VIP suite of the terminal were the families of the airmen who were about to be brought down the ramp. A gentle breeze blew through the open window of the office, but outside it was silent. The whole base was locked down. There were no cars on the roads and very few people would be walking about.

"It's sobering, isn't it?" Lizzie turned to look at Travis, who she had managed to bring into the business area of the terminal with her.

"You could say that," she replied quietly.

They stood in silence as six men dressed in their Number One RAF uniforms marched up to the back of the plane. They were dismissed by the warrant officer, his barked command audible to Lizzie and Travis, and the six of them broke ranks to walk up the ramp of the Herc. A few moments later, they reappeared.

The coffin had been tightly wrapped in a union flag, it's red, white and blue colours bright in the sunshine. The pall bearers moved slowly, their feet in perfect unison as they carried the coffin on their shoulders down the ramp. Lizzie knew that the man at the back on the left would be whispering commands to keep them in time. Even from this distance, she could see the grim determination on their faces.

Lizzie and Travis watched the first coffin being loaded into the back of the first hearse. As the pallbearers walked back to the plane, the black car moved away and the next one moved into position.

"I can't watch," Lizzie said, turning away from the window. She had a lump in her throat but didn't want to cry in front of Travis.

"Are you okay?" he asked her, but she waved his enquiry away with her hand. She didn't trust herself to speak. "It's bloody grim," he continued. "At least they're not going back through Wootton Bassett any more. What a bloody circus that turned out to be."

Travis was referring to a small town near RAF Lyneham that had started paying their respects to the flag-draped coffins being driven through it while the main runway at Brize Norton was closed for repairs. What had started out as a genuine gesture had soon caught the attention of the press. As the press started attending, so had more people and before long, people were lining the streets.

"That's what Adams said," Lizzie said, "the last time

we were away. He told me he'd told his family that if he came back in a box, under no circumstances was he to be taken anywhere near the place."

"That your other half, is it?" Travis asked. Lizzie felt a smile creeping onto her face as she considered the question.

"Yeah, he is," she replied.

"You been together long?" *One night*, Lizzie thought, but she wasn't about to tell Travis that.

"We've known each other for ages, but not long got together."

"He's a medic, I take it?"

"Yep. He's an emergency department nurse by trade, but he's out in Kandahar as the medical advisor to the base commander."

"What, he's an officer?"

"What's wrong with that?"

"Nothing wrong with it, Lizzie. I just didn't take you for the type to be shagging an officer." Lizzie felt herself blushing at Travis's words. "Did he go to posh school, then?"

Lizzie paused before replying.

"I've got no idea, to be honest. I've never asked him."

"I used to go to posh school," Travis said. He looked offended when Lizzie started laughing.

"You so did not go to posh school, Travis," she said, slapping him on the arm. "You lying git."

"I did too," Travis countered. "Every Friday afternoon me and my mates used to go to posh school to beat up the posh kids."

Lizzie laughed, grateful to Travis for changing the subject away from both what was happening outside the window and Adams. His next words brought her laughter to an abrupt halt, though.

"Would you carry me, mate?" he asked, nodding at the window. "If I come back in one of them, would you carry me?"

"They might have to find five other short people," she replied, trying to lighten the moment, "or I wouldn't be able to reach and that would just look silly."

"I mean it, Lizzie," Travis said. "Promise?"

"Travis," Lizzie said, crossing over to where he was standing. "You are not coming back in one of them. For a start, if anything did happen to you, you've got the best medic in the RAF to look after you."

"Sergeant Ferris is still at Honington, though?" Travis said with the ghost of a smile.

"You're a fool, Travis," Lizzie replied, "but we're all coming back together in a few months' time. Then we're all going to go to Swindon and get hammered."

"Now you're talking," Travis said, and Lizzie could see that he was forcing himself to smile.

They looked out of the window just as the third and final coffin was being loaded into the hearse. As it moved away and the pall bearers started marching back to the terminal, Travis turned to her.

"We'll be okay, won't we?" he asked Lizzie. Even though she knew it was a lie, she said what she knew he wanted to hear.

"Of course we will," she replied. "We'll be fine. You'll see."

44

Adams sprinted down the central spine of the hospital corridor as his pistol smacked painfully on his thigh, passing several medical personnel who were already wearing their body armour and helmets. He should have kept his stuff with him, but he'd been carrying it round all morning and was sick of it. That wasn't a mistake he was going to make again.

When he reached the area where he'd stored his equipment, Adams was blowing hard even though he'd run less than a hundred metres. He shrugged himself into his body armour, jammed the helmet on his head, and was about to lie down on the floor when the doors to the hospital burst open. It was Christine and an American soldier. Between them was a female soldier, blood pouring from a wound in her head.

Adams remained on his feet and ran across to the door to help Christine and the soldier. When he looked at Christine, he could see that her face was covered in dust and she had an abrasion above her right eye.

"Are you okay, Christine?" Adams said, glancing at her

quickly before turning his attention to the woman they were half dragging and half carrying into the hospital.

"I'm fine," she gasped. "Got blown off my bloody feet though."

"Here," Adams replied, "let me take her."

Adams took the female soldier's arm from Christine and wrapped it over his shoulder. He looked at the other soldier.

"We'll take her to the emergency room," Adams said. "End of the corridor." As the two men carried the injured woman down the corridor, several medical personnel rushed past them, but none stopped to help.

"Are there more casualties, Christine?" Adams asked. Christine, who looked as if she was about to faint, just nodded her head.

"There was a group of three or four of them sitting outside their accommodation." Adams saw her examining the palms of her hands. He glanced at them, seeing that both hands were badly scraped up and covered in dirt. "The rocket hit about thirty yards away. I'd not long walked past them."

"Are you sure you're okay?" Adams asked.

"I'm fine. Let me get the doors for you."

Christine opened the doors to the emergency room and Adams and the soldier dragged the woman through them. Adams had noticed that as they had been moving down the corridor, she had made less and less of an effort to help them move her. When they got into the room, two figures who had been lying on the floor got to their feet.

"On here," Adèle said in a no-nonsense voice as she pointed at the closest trolley. Adams and the soldier manhandled the woman onto the trolley and pulled her up so she was fully on it. "Isobel, could you go and see where Colonel Gagnon is, please?" She turned her attention to the soldier who had helped Adams with the patient. "Sergeant? Take Christine here to the front desk and get her booked in."

"Adèle, seriously," Christine said. "I'm fine."

"Do as you're told, Christine. My hospital, my rules." Adèle was smiling as she said this, but at the same time, it was obvious that arguing with her wasn't an option. With a reluctant look at Adams, Christine did as instructed and followed the sergeant out of the room.

"Adèle?" A male voice called out from the direction of the door. She looked up, irritated, and barked something in French to the major who had just walked in. Adams didn't understand what they were talking about, but from the tone of his voice when the new arrival replied, he wasn't taking no for an answer.

"Adams," Adèle said, "I'm needed in the ops room. Isobel should be back soon with the doctor. Can I leave you here?"

Adams glanced around the room, noting where the equipment he might need was.

"Sure," he replied. "I've got this. Could you grab me a field bandage, though?" That was his most pressing need, and he didn't want to be wasting time looking for a piece of kit that could be anywhere. Adèle crossed to a cupboard and pulled out a rectangular green packet, throwing to Adams.

"I'll be as quick as I can," she said before turning to leave the room.

Adams tore open the bandage as he looked at the woman lying on the trolley in front of him. She was in her mid-twenties with blonde, almost white, hair that was covered in congealed blood. Above a pocket on her uniform was a name badge that read *Browning*, and her rank slides were comprised of three chevrons like a sergeant's rank slides in the British military but upside down.

"Specialist Browning?" Adams called out, hoping that he'd got the rank right. "Can you hear me?" The woman's eyes flickered, but she didn't open them. "You've got a cut on your head that I'm just going to put a bandage on." Her eyes flickered again.

As he placed the field dressing over the laceration and wound the bandage around Browning's head, Adams ran his eyes up and down her body. She wasn't haemorrhaging from anywhere that he could see, and they hadn't left a trail of claret down the hospital corridor, so he was happy that apart from the gash on her head, she didn't have any other obvious points of bleeding. She would need to be fully undressed to be examined properly, but Adams was able to rule out a catastrophic haemorrhage pretty much straight away. He wasn't about to be distracted by the cut to her scalp. They generally looked worse than they actually were.

"What's your first name, Specialist Browning?" Adams said, louder than he would have done had he been talking to her normally. If she had been that close to the explosion, then her eardrums could have been ruptured by the pressure wave. Adams knew that if that was the case, then Browning could also have lung tissue damage, or even rupturing of the alveoli and pulmonary veins. If so, and she had an air embolism from the damage, there wasn't going to be anything he could do about it. "Specialist Browning?" Adams said again, even louder this time, as he reached behind her head to grab an oxygen mask. He could see her lips moving as she struggled to speak while he turned the dial on the oxygen cylinder.

"Sally," the woman said, although he struggled to hear her.

"Hey Sally, my name's Adams. I'm just going to put an oxygen mask on you if that's okay?" Adams didn't wait for a reply, but once the rebreather bag was full of oxygen, he placed it on Browning's face.

Outside the hospital, the Giant Voice burst back into life. At least this time it was sounding the all clear.

45

Delaney thanked Darpak for letting him use his computers again and walked back out into the sunshine. He had been in the middle of reading an e-mail from back home when he had heard a distant explosion, followed a few seconds later by the alarm sounding. Despite the adrenaline that had started coursing through his veins, the second he heard the muffled thump and the alarms, Delaney had still had the presence of mind to close down his browser before taking cover under the table. Once he had managed to get his body armour and helmet on, Delaney had looked across at Darpak who didn't even seem to have noticed the warbling noise outside.

"Are you going to take cover?" Delaney had asked Darpak over the noise of the alarm. Darpak had just shrugged his shoulders and returned to his newspaper.

As he walked toward the boardwalk, Delaney wondered where the rockets had hit this time. With any luck, he told himself, he would get back to the Portakabin he and Rubenstein called an office to see it as a smouldering wreck with the rescue crews picking up pieces of the fat bastard. That would solve one issue. At some point, Rubenstein was going to have to go. The e-mail Delaney had just read made that very clear.

Delaney stopped off at the coffee shop on the boardwalk and grabbed a couple of coffees. Much as he hated the man, bringing him a drink might keep him off his back for a while. He watched a heated game of hockey being played by some Canadian soldiers while he waited for his drinks to be prepared. In the centre of the boardwalk was an oval concrete hockey rink that always seemed to have groups playing on it. As he watched, a couple of the players squared up to each other, but they were soon separated by the other players. It was a shame, Delaney thought, that they hadn't all just piled in like he'd seen on the telly.

By the time Delaney got back to the office, he was sweating hard in the heat. It was just after ten in the morning and promising to be another scorching hot day. Just like every other day in this Godforsaken place.

"I got you a coffee," Delaney called out as he walked into the Portakabin, grateful for the relief that the air conditioning brought. "Rubenstein?"

"I'm out the back," his boss replied through the thin door that separated the main office from the small storeroom. Delaney didn't want to know what his boss had been doing in there, especially as his face was flushed when he walked back into the office. "How did the brief go?"

"Very good," Delaney replied, placing the cups of coffee on the table, "and the fact that there was another rocket attack just after I gave it was priceless. Couldn't have timed it better, could they?" He sat down and picked up his medication, careful to count out the pills so that Rubenstein could see.

A rare smile appeared on Rubenstein's face.

"True, true. The kit should be here tonight so we can get it set up over the next few days," he said to Delaney. "First piece we need operational is the radar. Once that's calibrated, we need another couple of rockets to come in so we can test the system. Then we should be good to go live with the weaponised version."

"Won't take long for them to come, will it?" Delaney replied, putting the pills in his mouth and washing them down with a bottle of water. It was a rare attempt at a conversation with the man and, once his pills were gone, Delaney sat down at his computer and fired up his browser.

"Not at the rate they've been coming in the last few days. Have you seen the new bunkers being put up everywhere?"

"Yeah, I saw one on the way here." Delaney didn't admit that although he'd seen some engineers building something, he'd not recognised it as a bunker. That would just give Rubenstein one more excuse to put him down, even though Delaney knew he was far smarter than the smug bastard.

Delaney looked at his screen and spent the next few moments idling around on Google to see if there was a relatively easy way to encourage a heart attack in someone. Looking at Rubenstein, he wouldn't need much of a nudge in that direction. While he scrolled through an article on morbid obesity and the effects it had on the cardiac system, Delaney fought the urge to itch his stitches. He had another four days until he could get them taken out, and he didn't want to wait that long before seeing Isobel again.

"Why don't you take the rest of the day off, Delaney?" Rubenstein called over. Shocked, Delaney stopped scrolling and looked up.

"Sorry, what?" he asked, not sure he'd heard him correctly.

"Take the rest of the day off," Rubenstein repeated himself. "You might as well seeing as we're going to be working most of the night installing the radar."

"We're doing it tonight?" Delaney replied, instantly annoyed. Why hadn't Rubenstein just told him not to come in to work in the morning?

"Sooner the better, Delaney," Rubenstein replied with a smug grin on his face. "The rockets are mostly in the mornings, so if we install it tonight we might catch some tomorrow."

Delaney frowned. Rubenstein was right, but that didn't make him any less irritating. Closing the computer down after clearing his browsing history, Delaney got to his feet. He could go for some lunch in one of the DFACs and then just chill for the afternoon.

"Well, I don't need telling twice," Delaney muttered as he pushed past Rubenstein and walked to the door. As he left, he thought that maybe having to do some manual labour would give Rubenstein a heart attack? That would be fitting and would save Delaney some time.

The e-mail he'd been reading earlier hadn't said when Rubenstein needed to be taken out of action, just that it needed to be done soon.

46

Adèle pushed her fork into the sloppy mess on her plate. It was, according to the menu, mashed potato, but it was unlike any mashed potato she'd ever seen in her life. Across the table from her, Isobel was doing the same thing, but she was prodding at something that was supposed to be chicken.

"Mon dieu," Adèle said. "C'est incroyable." *My God, it's incredible.*

"Que c'est ce que?" Isobel asked. *What is it?*

"Pomme de terre, apparemment." *Potato, apparently.*

The two women exchanged wan smiles, and both laughed.

"I suppose," Adèle said, "that as a weight loss plan this is pretty effective. That and the heat."

"You're right," Isobel replied. "I've lost a couple of kilograms already." Adèle looked at Isobel's slim shoulders and raised her eyebrows.

"You're not exactly obese, Isobel. I can afford to lose a few pounds. You can't, not really."

"Sorry mom," Isobel replied with a smile. A few

seconds later, when Adèle looked again at Isobel, she saw a tear running down the younger woman's cheek.

"Hey," Adèle said, putting her fork down and reaching out for Isobel's hand. "What is it?"

"I miss them, Adèle," Isobel replied with a sob. "My family. I miss them so much." Adèle wanted to get to her feet and give Isobel a big hug, tell her that everything would be okay, but she didn't want to draw attention to her upset.

"You'll see them soon enough," Adèle said, "and then you'll be wondering what you ever missed about them." Isobel smiled through her tears. "Have you got brothers and sisters?"

"One brother. He's a couple of years younger than me, but twice my size. He wanted to be a professional hockey player when he was younger, but never made it."

"Did he get injured?"

"No, he just wasn't as good as he thought he was," Isobel replied. Adèle laughed, thinking about her own son, William. She had spent years ferrying him from hockey match to hockey match, but other than a few school medals, he had nothing to show for it.

"So your brother's, what? Early twenties?"

"Twenty last year. The same age as many of our patients."

The two women sat in silence for a few moments, Adèle still clutching Isobel's hand. Every time a young patient was brought to them, Adèle couldn't help but think of William. It was no doubt the same for Isobel, who would be thinking about her brother.

"It's hard, isn't it?" Adèle said. "When they're so young? But it's what we do, Isobel. Never lose sight of that. If they don't make it, it's not because we haven't tried."

Isobel reached out for a serviette on the table and used it to pat her face dry. She nodded as she replied.

"I know, I know," Isobel said, "but it's still hard."

"That's because you care, Isobel. When you stop caring, it's probably time to find something else to do."

"Bonjour," a male voice said behind Adèle. She turned to see who it was, knowing before she did that it wasn't a native speaker. When she saw Adams standing behind her with a tray in his hands, she smiled. "Do you mind if I join you?"

Adèle looked at Isobel to see what her response was likely to be, but the younger woman spoke before she did.

"Of course," Isobel said, switching to English. She gave Adèle a brief smile of her own, and Adèle thought that perhaps she was happy to have to change the subject. One thing Adèle did know, though, was that she was going to have to keep an eye on the young woman. She was more fragile than she'd realised.

Adams sat down next to Adèle and put his tray on the table.

"What did you decide to have?" Adèle asked him as he regarded his plate with suspicion.

"Macaroni cheese," he said as he picked up a fork. "I think." He took a mouthful of the yellow gloop and chewed it thoughtfully for a few seconds before swallowing it with a grimace. "How's Specialist Browning?"

"She's going to have a hell of a headache," Isobel replied with a warm smile in Adams's direction. "The cut on her head was quite deep, but it came together well. It's above her hairline as well, so she won't have a visible scar."

"Thank you for helping earlier, Adams," Adèle said. "It was a bit busy for a while."

"Not a problem," he replied, taking another mouthful of food.

"Your, er," Adèle said before pausing to search for the right word in English. She switched to French and spoke to Isobel. "Comment dit on prédécesseur en Anglais?" *How do you say predecessor in English?* Isobel just shrugged her shoulders in reply. "The woman before you? She never really came to the hospital that much."

"My predecessor?" Adams replied. "Christine's not clinical. She's a Medical Support Officer. Kind of like a healthcare manager or administrator."

"Ah, we have them too," Adèle said with a wry grin. "Some are good, some not so good."

"It's no different in the British Forces."

The three of them laughed at the similarity. Adams pushed his plate away, having barely eaten half of his lunch.

"Have you been to Afghanistan before, Adams?" Isobel asked, picking up her own fork and sampling some macaroni cheese. From the look on her face, Adèle realised it was as bad as it looked.

"Yes, last year I was in Helmand working on the back of Chinooks."

"As a medic?" Isobel replied.

"Yes," Adams said. Adèle saw a brief frown cross his face, but as soon as it appeared, it had gone. "It was a tough tour. So, have you had many casualties from the incoming fire?"

"Too many," Adèle said, noting the change in subject. "Eight dead since the start of the week, and three wounded this morning."

"Bloody hell," Adams replied, his mouth open. "I didn't realise it was that many."

"It's the, how do you say, random nature of them that hurts so much," Isobel added. Adams nodded, and Adèle could see that what she had just told him had shocked him.

"I went to a brief this morning," Adams said, "with the base commander. There's a new system coming online at some point that's supposed to shoot them down before they land."

"Wasn't that your patient the other day, Isobel? What was his name?" Adèle asked.

"Mark Delaney," she replied. "He cut his hand on some metal."

"That's the chap," Adams said. "He was briefing this morning. Steel Sky or something. That's what he's out here to install."

"Well, I hope it works," Adèle said. "I just hope it works."

47

Despite promising herself that she was going to be fine, Lizzie tried as hard as she could to hide her nervousness as her plane took off from RAF Brize Norton. She'd flown probably a hundred times in passenger planes since joining the RAF, but for some reason the take off and the landing always made her nervous. Probably because she knew that if there was going to be a serious problem with the aircraft, it would almost certainly be while it was taking off or landing.

"You alright there, pet?" Travis said from his seat beside her. "Bit jumpy, are you?"

"Bugger off, Travis," Lizzie replied. "I was just about to nod off. Bloody take off woke me right up."

"Sure it did, Lizzie," Travis said with a lop-sided smile. Lizzie looked at him, wanting to be annoyed with the man but not able to. Travis was the sort of person who you could never be irritated with for more than ten seconds. It was a standing joke on the squadron that he was so laid back that he was almost horizontal.

Lizzie had seen a different side to him, though. Not long after she'd joined the squadron, most of the squadron had been on a night out in Kings Lynn, a town not far from the base at Honington. As the only female, Lizzie hadn't been that bothered about going, but they had all insisted. Towards the end of the evening, Lizzie had been approached by a young Portuguese man who barely spoke any English but was determined to talk to her. When her would-be suitor had touched her for the third time, despite Lizzie telling him in no uncertain terms not to put his hands anywhere near her, he had found himself pinned up against the wall by Travis.

"Leave. Her. Alone." There was no way that Travis's intentions could be misunderstood, language barrier or no language barrier. It was the look in her colleague's eyes that had surprised Lizzie. Travis's easy going expression had been replaced in a split second by a hardened expression that left no doubt he was quite happy with violence.

"Well, you're now officially fit, Lizzie," Travis said. "We're in theatre, therefore the bar for attractiveness is on the floor."

"What?" Lizzie asked. "I wasn't fit before we left Brize?"

"Maybe a bit, but now it's official. Every man on this plane would shag you."

"Travis?" Lizzie said.

"What?" he replied with his trademark easy grin.

"Shut up."

"Yes, sarge. Sorry, sarge." He settled back into his seat and closed his eyes, although he still had a grin on his face. Lizzie thought about doing the same thing, but knew that she was too hyped up to sleep just yet. Instead, she pulled her Kindle from her pocket and started reading the latest Peter James novel.

A COUPLE OF HOURS LATER, Lizzie decided to stretch her legs and wandered to the back of the plane, climbing over Travis's legs. There was normally a stretcher fit installed where the rear three or four rows of seats should have been, ready to bring casualties back on the return flight. Lizzie wanted to see if there were any medics outbound who she knew but, to her surprise, where the stretchers should have been was a tower of green rectangular storage containers known as lacons.

"What's in these?" Lizzie asked a passing steward.

"Not sure, sarge," the steward replied. "Some sort of fancy electronic stuff."

"It can't go in the hold?"

"Obviously not."

Lizzie studied the lacons for a few moments, wondering what was in them. She had once flown into Helmand in a Herc as the only passenger with a bunch of freight in similar containers. She had later found out that they contained several tonnes of high explosives. Had she known that in advance, there was no way she would have boarded the plane. But surely cargos like that one weren't allowed on passenger planes?

When she returned to her seat after using the bathroom and persuading the steward to make her a cup of tea, Travis was still fast asleep. She put one leg over his and was about to climb over him when his eyes opened. Lizzie was standing astride him with one leg on either side of his thighs.

"That's not a bad way to wake up," he said, smirking.

"Go back to sleep, you pervert," Lizzie replied, grinning at him.

"Have you got a jack brew there?" Travis eyed the cup in her hand.

"Oh, for God's sake." Lizzie put her tea down on her table and went back to speak to the steward to sweet talk him into another cup.

"Problem is, sarge," the steward said when she asked him, "is that if that lot see you with a cuppa then I'll have a queue all the way to the cockpit." Lizzie ignored the obvious retort, which was that he didn't have a great deal else to do, and tried to turn on the charm.

"Just this once?" she asked, smiling sweetly and hating herself for it. The young steward looked at her for a moment before relenting.

"Just this once."

When Lizzie got back to her seat, she made Travis stand up so she could get to her seat without having to step over him again.

"There's your tea," she said, handing him the polystyrene cup.

"Has it got sugar in it?"

"No, Travis," Lizzie said with a sigh. "It hasn't got sugar in it. You'll have to go and ask the steward."

"One job," Travis muttered under his breath as he walked down the aisle. Lizzie giggled to herself as she settled back down with her book. A few moments later, Travis returned with a dark look on his face.

"What's the matter?" Lizzie asked him, looking up from her Kindle.

"He didn't have any."

"Yes, he did. I saw some in a jar next to the boiler. What did he say?" Travis's look darkened and Lizzie started laughing. It only took a few seconds before his face lightened and he joined in.

"He told me to piss off back to my seat because he wasn't running a sodding coffee shop."

48

Delaney thanked the man behind the counter and took his tray to a table with no-one else sitting on it. He sat down and shifted himself along the bench so he could get a good look at Isobel. She was sitting at a table with the nurse who had stitched his hand up earlier in the week—Adèle, he thought her name was—and a British soldier who Delaney remembered from his presentation that morning.

Isobel was wearing her combats but had taken her jacket off while she was eating. Under the jacket she was wearing a brown t-shirt that left little to the imagination. At least, it left little to Delaney's imagination. He squinted at her, trying to conjure up an image of her in his mind where she wasn't wearing the t-shirt. It wasn't difficult. Delaney had always had an active imagination.

He spooned the tasteless food into his mouth and watched her as she chatted with the other two. At one point, the Brit said something that made her laugh out loud, and the way she tilted her head back to show Delaney her throat was irresistible. Delaney had a thing for women's necks. No matter how much make-up they wore—which in Isobel's case was none—or how much work they had done to their faces, women couldn't do anything about the skin on their throats. And Isobel's was particularly smooth and unlined. He imagined running his fingertips over it, starting just below her ears and down to the top of her shoulders while she looked at him with her mouth open just a few millimetres. Delaney shoved another spoonful of food into his mouth and shifted on the bench to relieve his discomfort.

A few moments later, Delaney had almost finished his meal when the Brit and the older woman got to their feet. Adèle reached out for Isobel's tray and took it from her before walking with the Brit to the bins in the corner of the DFAC.

Delaney got to his feet, moving quickly. This was his chance.

"Excuse me," he said to Isobel as he approached her table. She had turned around to get her combat jacket, and he made sure that he wasn't staring at her chest when she turned back around. "Isobel?"

"Oh, hello," she replied with a broad smile. "How is the hand?" Delaney looked down at the plaster he had used to cover up the sutures with before realising it was filthy.

"It's fine," he replied, talking quickly. In the corner of his eye, he could see that Isobel's companions were talking to someone else near the bins. Perhaps he had a bit more time that he thought? "I just wanted to say thank you for looking after me the other day."

"That's no problem," she replied. "If only everyone's injuries were like yours, our job would be a lot easier."

"Sure, I can imagine."

Isobel put one arm into her combat jacket and arched her back to slip the other arm in. Delaney kept his eyes resolutely on hers as she did so, much to his chagrin.

"I'm just about to go back to work, I'm afraid," she said as she buttoned up her tunic, "otherwise I would love to stop and chat with you for a while. My English is not so good, and I need all the practice I can get."

"Your English is a lot better than my French," Delaney replied with a grin.

"That's very kind of you to say so."

"Um, listen, Isobel. I was wondering." Delaney paused, suddenly unsure what to say, and she looked at him curiously. He should have practised this in the mirror, but he'd not been expecting to see her in the DFAC, much less be talking to her on his own.

"What were you wondering?" she asked, her eyebrows going up a touch.

"Maybe I could buy you a drink to say thank you?" Delaney replied, his mouth suddenly dry. "A coffee, I mean."

"Oh," Isobel replied. Her smile slipped as if that wasn't what she had been expecting him to say, and Delaney felt his stomach lurch. He'd blown it, idiot that he was. "That sounds like a great idea. Perhaps you could help me with my English?"

"Sure," Delaney replied, aiming for nonchalance. Had she really just said yes? He was just about to ask Isobel when she would like to go for a coffee when Adèle approached the table.

"Come on, Isobel, we'll be late," she said before glancing at Delaney. "Hello young man. How's the hand?" What was it with nurses, Delaney thought, and their obsession with reminding people of their own stupidity? "Let me see."

Adèle grabbed Delaney's hand before he could do anything else and looked at the dirty plaster. She mumbled something in French and tutted.

"Oh dear," Adèle said, frowning at him. "When did you last change that?"

"Um, yesterday, I think. Maybe the day before?"

"You need to come to the hospital and let us redress that for you. I'm sure Isobel won't mind."

Isobel smiled shyly at Delaney before replying.

"Not at all," she said. "Why don't you stop by this evening at about six thirty? I'll change your dressing and we can go for a coffee when I've finished my shift."

"Okay, excellent," Delaney replied, his heart thudding in his chest at the thought. Adèle said something in French to Isobel, and whatever she said made the younger nurse's cheeks flush instantly. She shook her head and replied, also in French, before looking back at him.

"I'll see you then," she said. As the two nurses turned to walk away, Delaney had to resist the temptation to punch his fist in the air. He had just asked a beautiful Canadian woman out for a drink. Not only that, but she had said yes. But the icing on the cake, as far as Delaney was concerned, was the look she had given him just before she'd walked away.

Delaney had seen that look before in other women's eyes. It was the look they gave him just after he'd paid them, and they both knew what was going to happen next.

He loved that look.

49

Adams glanced at his watch. It was a couple of minutes before two in the afternoon, and he was standing with Christine outside the base commander's office. After her close shave that morning, she had spent a couple of hours packing her stuff before meeting him after lunch. Although she'd not said anything directly to him, Adams could see that she was rattled.

"I bet you can't wait to get home," he said, conversationally. Christine looked down at the palms of her hands before replying.

"You could say that," she replied. "Can you imagine getting slotted the day before you leave?"

Adams didn't reply. He knew she didn't mean anything by the comment, but he had four months to go and would be running that risk every day if the momentum of the rockets continued.

"I'm sure that's happened to some people," he said. Adams was about to continue when the door was thrown open from the inside. He glanced again at his watch. It was two o'clock on the nose.

"Come in, chaps," Air Commodore Maugham's voice boomed from inside the room. He had opened the door and hurried back across his office so he was standing behind his desk when they entered. Adams suppressed a smile as he followed Christine into the room. The man was an air commodore whereas they were both squadron leaders, but the big man obviously felt the power play was important. Adams had asked Christine if he should wear a beret and salute when he went in, but she had said the boss wasn't that bothered about that sort of thing. Adams wasn't so sure, but it was too late now.

"So, you're my new medical advisor?" Maugham said, stepping back from behind his desk and extending a hand to Adams.

"I am, sir, yes," Adams said. He shook Maugham's hand, noting the other man's firm grip and intense look as they shook. Adams warmed to the man instantly. There was nothing, in Adams's opinion, like a man with a genuine handshake.

"Welcome aboard, Squadron Leader Adams," Maugham replied, finally letting go of Adams's hand and nodding his head. Adams couldn't help but smile then. It was the first time anyone had actually addressed him with his new, albeit temporary, rank.

"Thank you, sir."

"Now then, young lady?" Maugham turned his attention to Christine. "I hear you had a narrow escape this morning?"

"I did, sir," Christine replied.

"Were you hurt?"

"Not really, no." She extended her palms out for him to look at. "Just a few scratches."

"My word," Maugham replied, taking her hands in his. "If you were an American, you'd get a Purple Heart for those." He looked at the obligatory framed photograph of the Queen that was hanging above his desk. "But I'm afraid Her Majesty is a bit stricter about dishing out tin."

Adams tuned out the conversation between the air commodore and Christine and took in the office. It was, like most of the other rooms in the building, pockmarked with bullet holes and blackened from fire damage, but at least it was intact and an entire room. His own much smaller office, by contrast, was a partitioned area within a much larger room. It was private in a sense in that he couldn't be seen once he was inside, but there was no soundproofing from the plywood walls.

The air commodore's large table was about five times the size of the desk Adams had just inherited from Christine, which had room for a computer and not much else. The one luxury item in Adam's office was a tiny sofa that had been acquired by a previous occupant. Unsurprisingly given his rank, the air commodore also had sofas, but they were proper ones, and Adams took a seat in one of them as instructed by Maugham when he had finished talking to Christine.

"Christine," Maugham said, "you're booked in for your departure interview with me at fifteen hundred, so I'll see you then."

"Yes, sir," Christine replied. Before she turned to leave, she winked at Adams. Maugham waited until she had closed the door and sat down in the sofa opposite him.

"So, Adams. That's your moniker, is it?"

"It is, sir, yes. First name's Paul, but I go by Adams."

"Public school, was it?" Maugham replied, referring to the common practice of only referring to people by their last names in British private schools.

"No, sir," Adams replied. "I'm afraid not. I went to a grotty comprehensive on the outskirts of Norwich."

"Well, you've done okay for yourself," Maugham replied with a warm smile. "You've made it to squadron leader and you're still quite young. Plenty of space for you ahead, I would imagine?"

"Time will tell, sir," Adams replied.

Over the next twenty minutes or so, Adams realised that either the air commodore had plenty of time on his hands, or he was genuinely interested in the people who worked for him. He wanted to know everything about Adams, it seemed. Where he grew up, what his hobbies and interests were, did he have a significant other? At that question, Adam's had paused for a few seconds before saying that yes, he did have a significant other. Maugham narrowed his eyes at Adams's response, but didn't press.

Unlike any other senior officer that Adams had ever spoken to, at least over the rank of group captain, Maugham didn't once mention himself as they spoke. It was, as far as Adams was concerned, just one more reason to like the man. He had heard that the air commodore could be brusque at times, and didn't suffer fools gladly, but Adams didn't mind that.

Maugham was just in the middle of asking Adams a question about his previous operational experience when there was a low rumble in the distance. It sounded to Adams like thunder but when the Giant Voice burst into life as the rumbling was starting to die away, he realised it wasn't.

"Oh, for goodness' sake," Maugham barked as he

jumped out of the sofa to get his protective equipment. Adams's own body armour and helmet were by the side of the sofa, so he reached down for them.

Adams was just getting to his knees so he could lie down in the prone position when he heard the air commodore calling out to him.

"Adams, over here, old chap!" Maugham shouted over the noise of the alarm. Adams looked up to see his boss crouched on the floor underneath his table. He was doing up his chin strap with one hand and beckoning to Adams with the other. Adams shuffled across to join him. It was cramped, but there was room enough for them both.

"I have to say, Adams," Maugham shouted in Adams's ear, "I know you youngsters might think this is all rather sporty, but I'm beginning to get really pissed off with all this."

50

"Merde, c'était quoi ça?" Adèle jumped when she heard what sounded like a rumble of thunder. Next to her, Isobel started as well and grabbed onto Adèle's arm. *Shit, what was that?* The two women were walking back to the hospital from the DFAC on the gravelled road chatting about the new medical advisor when the sound interrupted their conversation.

"No idea," Isobel replied, looking in the direction that the low rumbling was coming from. It wasn't the same noise as the explosions from the rockets over the last few days. This was different. It was lower and went on for a few seconds instead of the loud but temporary sound that a rocket exploding made.

A couple of hundred yards away, in the direction of the pan where the aircraft were located, was a slowly rising black plume of smoke.

"Has a plane crashed or something?" Isobel asked Adèle. She was about to reply when the Giant Voice sounded.

"Quick!" Adèle shouted, pushing Isobel toward the drainage ditch at the side of the road. "Into cover!"

The two women knelt down in the ditch and put their protective equipment on before lying down with their heads next to each other so they could speak over the sound of the alarm.

"It didn't sound like a rocket," Isobel said, "did it?" Adèle shook her head.

"Not like the other ones, anyway. Maybe the insurgents are using something else?"

"Should we stay here, or should we go to the hospital?"

Adèle thought for a few seconds. Her gut instinct was to get to the hospital. If there were any casualties from whatever had caused the large smoke plume, they should be there. But her rational side won the internal debate. They were safest where they were. Lying down, especially in a ditch, would mean that only a direct hit from above could hurt them.

"We stay here," Adèle said, looking at Isobel. From the look in her eyes, the young woman was terrified. She probably wanted to be in the hospital because it was familiar to her and therefore felt safer. "Isobel, listen to me. Lying in this ditch is probably the safest place on the whole camp at the moment." Isobel nodded, but her expression didn't change. Knowing there was nothing she could say to make her feel any better, Adèle just reached out her hand and took Isobel's in hers.

When the Giant Voice faded away a few seconds later, it was replaced by the distant wail of sirens. Adèle couldn't tell if they were fire engines or ambulances, but decided that it was almost certainly both. Perhaps they should go to the hospital after all? When the rockets had landed previously, they had only been in small groups that all landed within a few seconds of each other. But the rumbling hadn't sounded like a rocket.

"Stay there," Adèle said to Isobel. "I'm going to have a look over the top of this ditch, see if I can find out what's going on."

"Be careful!" Isobel replied, her eyes wide.

When she tried to let go of Isobel's hand, Adèle realised she was gripping it even harder.

"Let me go, Isobel," Adèle said as gently as she could as she prised the younger woman's fingers apart.

Keeping low, Adèle shuffled up the side of the ditch until her head was just peering over the top. She could see what was now an angry column of thick black smoke rising into the air, but couldn't see anything else. Everyone apart from the emergency responders was under cover, or at least they were supposed to be.

"All I can see is a big pillar of smoke," Adèle said when she slid back down to join Isobel.

"I wonder what's happened?"

"We'll find out soon enough," Adèle replied. "So, you're going for a coffee with that British contractor, are you? Mark, isn't that his name?"

"You're just changing the subject."

"So?"

Isobel smiled faintly.

"He's called Mark, yes. I thought it might be good to practise my English with a native speaker."

"It's a good idea, Isobel," Adèle said. "I could probably do with something like that."

"Well, come with me then?"

"I can't see him wanting me there, Isobel."

"What do you mean? It's not a date, Adèle. I'm just meeting him for a coffee. Besides, I have a man at home."

"Does this Mark know that?" Adèle asked, pretty sure he didn't. She looked at Isobel, remembering how young she was. She'd not thought her to be naïve as well, but perhaps she was?

"No, I mean, he just asked me if he could buy me a coffee to say thank you for helping him when he hurt his hand."

"But I was the one who stitched up his hand," Adèle replied with a wry smile. "But he's not asked me out for a coffee, has he?"

"Oh," Isobel replied, her face falling. "I see what you mean. I never realised."

Any further conversation was stopped by the wail of the all clear from the Giant Voice. The two women got to their feet and took their helmets off before climbing out of the ditch. Adèle's knees were trembling as they set off toward the hospital. She was getting too old for clambering around like this, she thought as she tried to keep up with Isobel. The younger woman seemed determined to get there as soon as possible.

"Isobel, slow down a bit," Adèle called out eventually. She was perspiring in the heat and could feel how red her face had become from the exertion. "Don't forget I'm twice your age."

"Sorry, Adèle," Isobel replied over her shoulder. "I'd forgotten how old you were."

"Isobel, come here for a second," Adèle replied. Isobel stopped walking to let her catch up. When she reached the younger woman, Adèle reached out and playfully slapped her round the back of the head.

"What was that for?" Isobel said, smiling but with a mock look of indignation on her face.

"Being cheeky."

51

"Travis," Lizzie said, pushing her sunglasses back onto her face. "Stop whinging and try to enjoy the sunshine." She was lying on a bench in a fenced-in area within the arrivals terminal at RAF Akrotiri. The other passengers from the plane were milling around, and some of them had even organised an impromptu game of football.

"I just don't see the point of us all being caged in here. It's like an exercise yard in a prison," Travis replied. Lizzie closed her eyes and enjoyed the heat on her face.

"Have you ever been to prison?" she asked him.

"Nope, not planning on it, either."

"Well, how do you know what it's like then?"

"Seen it on telly, haven't I?"

Lizzie sat up, propping herself up on one elbow and looking at Travis over the top of her sunglasses.

"I'd bet you'd be popular in prison," she said with a grin.

"What do you mean?"

"Pretty boy like you. You'd be someone's bitch in no time, you would."

"Piss off," Travis replied with a snort. "No chance of that happening."

"I reckon you'd take it to make it." Lizzie started giggling at Travis's expression. She could tell that he wanted to be annoyed, but at the same time was trying not to laugh.

"Where the hell did you get that expression from?" he asked, working hard to suppress a grin.

"You would, wouldn't you? Go gay for the stay?" Lizzie's giggles turned into all out laughter, and a couple of nearby passengers looked over to see what she was laughing at. Travis got to his feet and flashed them a look until they turned away to mind their own business.

"You're just obsessed with me, Lizzie," he said, flashing her a cheeky smile. "I get that, I seriously do, even though we're both spoken for. Now I'm going to go and play football with that lot over there." He raised his arms and flexed his biceps as he pointed at the football match before swaggering away.

Lizzie's giggles continued for a few moments as she watched him. She'd never met his girlfriend, but the other lads on the squadron had told her he was so far under her thumb, they were considering changing his nickname to 'drawing pin'.

She lay back on the bench and closed her eyes again. They had at least two hours in the compound while their plane was being refuelled. Another reason for the brief layover was so it would be dark by the time they landed in Kandahar. It was, apparently, safer to land in the dark for the large, slow-moving aircraft.

Her thoughts turned to Adams as she lay there, triggered by Travis's words. The last time she had been in Cyprus was for Staff Sergeant Partridge's court martial. She and Adams had come close to having something between them then, but she hadn't been in the right place in her head at the time. The time before that—when they were both delayed returning to Helmand Province—was when he had first made a clumsy pass at her in a Cypriot hotel. A pass that she'd rejected.

There was a part of her that was sad that they hadn't got together in the hotel that first time. If they had, they would have been together for six months by now. But Lizzie didn't think it would have been the same back then. If they had gone to bed together, it would have been just sex. And what they had experienced a few short days ago was nowhere near just sex. Perhaps she was overthinking, but that wasn't how it had felt. It had been far more than that.

Lizzie's experiences with men hadn't been brilliant. There had been the obligatory first time with a lad called Ryan when she was not long out of school and drunk so much that she could barely remember anything. Then a brief but unsatisfying relationship with a lad who thought he was going to be the next big thing at Norwich City Football Club's academy. When the club had dropped him, he had dropped her. And that was it. Adams had been Lizzie's third notch on her bedpost.

She thought back to the night in his hotel room. How nervous she had been, not wanting to disappoint Adams but at the same time not really knowing how not to disappoint him. He had been so tender in the way he had treated her that she hadn't known what to do. In the end, she hadn't needed to. Adams had a plan, and it was one which he had executed very well.

Lizzie opened her eyes and stared into the blue sky above her. She couldn't wait to see him again. Couldn't wait to be with him again, although whether that would be possible in Kandahar was debatable, perhaps unlikely. She let her eyes close and thought back to that evening, when she was lying on the bed in his hotel room and Adams had his hand on her hip with his thumb hooked into the elastic of her panties. Then, while he slid them off her, he'd whispered in her ear that he was going to do something for her, and once he'd started, he wasn't going to stop. And he hadn't.

"Did you see that?" Lizzie jumped at the noise. She opened her eyes to see Travis standing in front of her, his face red and flushed with excitement. "Did you see that goal? It was like, boom, back of the net!"

"Travis," she said, swinging her feet round and sitting up on the bench, "I'm trying to have a sexual fantasy here. Would you bugger off and leave me alone?"

"Oh," he replied, looking down at his feet. "Sorry. I'll, er, I'll leave you to it, will I?" Lizzie giggled, grateful for the distraction from her memories of Adams's insistence on her pleasure. Travis shrugged his shoulders and turned to walk away.

"Hey, Travis," she called after him. "Score another one, I'll be watching this time."

52

Adams had just put his body armour and helmet down on the floor when there was a brisk knock on the air commodore's office door.

"Come in," Maugham barked. The door opened and a young man's head appeared around it.

"Hello, sir," the new arrival said. "Thought you'd want a sitrep."

"Yes, please," Maugham replied, and Adams noted the irritation in his voice. "Seeing as how I'm the base commander."

"There's a fire down at the bulk fuel installation, sir."

"Bloody hell," Maugham said. "Come on, Adams. Might as well get your hands dirty in the ops room. This is Simpkins. He's supposed to be an ops officer, but he's still learning." Adams saw Simpkins's mouth open to respond, but he closed it again, saying nothing. Probably not a bad idea, Adams thought as he looked at the young officer's rank slides. He was only a lieutenant which was as about as far down the pecking order as it was possible to get.

Adams followed Maugham as he strode out of his

office and down the main corridor within the TLS building.

"What do we know so far, Simpkins?" Maugham asked the ops officer.

"Not a great deal, sir," Simpkins replied, "other than we don't think it was enemy action. The explosion set off the seismic sensors. That's why the alarm sounded."

"So it wasn't a rocket attack?"

"No, sir," Simpkins said, "we don't believe so."

"Are there any casualties?" Adams asked. Simpkins looked at him and obviously hadn't got a clue. "Sorry, I should have introduced myself," Adams continued to save the poor lad some face. "I'm Adams, the new medical adviser."

"Pleased to meet you, sir," Simpkins replied as the two men shared a swift handshake as they walked. "Regarding casualties, I'm—"

"Don't worry, mate," Adams said, cutting him off. "We'll find out soon enough, I'm sure."

Adams followed the air commodore through another door and into the main operations room for the air base. It was a hive of activity, with uniformed personnel darting around. Detailed maps covered the walls. Adams could see that most of them were of the airfield itself, but there were also several regional and country wide maps. On one wall was a series of clocks with labels underneath them. The one on the left was local time, and the next few clocks detailed the current times in Cyprus, London, and Washington.

"Where's Major Persimmon?" Maugham shouted to no-one in particular. Adams looked around the room to see an Army officer rushing toward them.

"I'm here, sir," Persimmon said as he stood to attention in front of the air commodore. The major then spun on his heel. "Right, listen in, everyone." A hush spread across the room as the occupants stopped what they were doing. Persimmon walked to a large crash map of the airfield on the wall and started his brief. "At fourteen twenty two, there was an explosion in the BFI situated here." He stabbed at the map with his finger. "Cause is unknown, but likely to be a fuel air ignition as opposed to enemy action. The COBRA didn't pick up anything incoming, and the tank that exploded was being re-filled at the time. First responders are at the scene and report that the fire is isolated and under control. There are..." Persimmon paused and checked his notes, "three confirmed casualties, one serious. The flight line is closed, and all personnel within a three hundred metre radius have been evacuated and accounted for." Persimmon took a deep breath, pleased with his performance. "Any questions, sir?"

"Have we got visuals?" Maugham asked. Persimmon nodded to another officer who turned to his computer screen. A few seconds later, a projector whirred into life and a video of the fire appeared on a blank wall. Maugham took a couple of steps toward it and regarded the scene. "What's up in the air at the moment?" An RAF officer in the corner stepped forward.

"We've got a couple of Dutch F16s out on close air support and two of our GR4s doing a recce up country," the flight lieutenant said. "Rotary wing wise, there're a couple of Apaches up at Kajaki Dam, but they should be able to get back in without any problems. We've got four civvy transports circling, waiting for instruction. There's also a trooper on the ground in Cyprus, which is due here this evening, but I've warned them off that we might delay them."

"Okay," Maugham replied. "Thanks. So it's pretty quiet up there. The smoke's not occluding the runway, so the line can be reopened, but the minute the wind looks like it's about to change, close it again straight away."

"Sir?" It was the flight lieutenant.

"What?" Maugham replied.

"I would suggest keeping it closed for another hour or so. By then the smoke should have dissipated if what the fire crews are telling us is correct. If something's on finals and the wind changes, that would be a tricky landing to say the least." Maugham crossed his arms and considered the young officer's words for a few seconds.

"Yep, happy with that. Persimmon, give me another sit rep in thirty minutes. I want a full one through nine this time."

Adams started going through the numbers in his head. A one through nine was a way of briefing that covered all the main areas within the military. One was for personnel, two was for intelligence, but he could never remember what three and beyond were, which was why he had them written in the front page of his notebook.

"Adams, advise me, please." Adams looked up to see the air commodore looking at him with his eyebrows raised. There was nothing like being put on the spot.

"Um, okay, sir. I'll go to the hospital to get some more information on the casualties." He squinted at the screen. "The smoke plume is going over the top of some accommodation blocks from the looks of it, but they should have all been evacuated, anyway. I'd like to check that the area they've been evacuated to is upwind. If the berm hasn't been breached, then there shouldn't be any environmental contamination to worry about." Maugham looked at Adams and nodded sharply.

"Good. Persimmon?" The air commodore looked away and Adams realised that he'd been dismissed. Hopefully, he'd passed his first test. "Persimmon? Where's my coffee?" He turned back to Adams and lowered his voice. "Bloody Army," he whispered with a smirk.

53

Delaney was standing outside the hospital, waiting to see if Isobel was still going to be able to meet him for a coffee. There had been a fire earlier down near the runway, and Darpak had told him that there'd been some casualties. Hopefully she would still be able to get away on time.

When he had checked his e-mails earlier, there had been another one from back home. It wanted to know what he was planning to do about Rubenstein, and he could sense the urgency in the text. *I don't know,* he had replied, *but I'll think of something*. The problem was he didn't really have a plan as yet. He had spent most of the afternoon on the internet, researching possible ways to achieve his goal, but there was nothing straightforward that he could come up with.

Perhaps, Delaney thought as he shifted his feet in the sandy ground, he could get in with Isobel and somehow get access to the hospital pharmacy? There had to be something in there that he could use, surely? Maybe he could even get Isobel to help him? Delaney smiled as he thought of them both as partners in crime. He liked that idea a lot.

She could be his very own femme fatale. Isobel could seduce Rubenstein—that wouldn't be difficult at all—and take him to an isolated location on the airfield somewhere with the promise of sex. But Delaney would be there, waiting for him, with a gun. Then they could bury his fat, stinking corpse in the sand before going back to the office to *do it*.

The thought of *doing it* with Isobel made him think for a few minutes. When they did get together, where could they go that was private? She would be noticed in the accommodation block, that much was for certain. The office perhaps? At least that would be private enough, and they could always use the storeroom in the back. He might have to make it a bit more comfortable for them, though.

"Hey, Mark," Isobel's voice interrupted his daydream and his hands shot to his crotch to make sure there was nothing obvious that she could see. Not that he would mind. She would be seeing him in all his glory at some point soon anyway, but he wanted to save the moment. "How are you?"

"I'm good, Isobel," Delaney replied. "Did you have a good shift?" She was supposed to be changing the bandage on his hand, but when he'd got to the hospital earlier, he'd been turned away when he explained what he was there for.

"It was busy," Isobel said with a sigh. "You heard about the fire?" He nodded his head and looked at her. She looked tired, but was still beautiful. Delaney preferred her in scrubs, though. She had changed back into her combat uniform, which wasn't exactly designed to show off her figure.

"I did, yes," Delaney said. "Were many people hurt?"

"There were three contractors hurt. One of them might not make out."

"Make it."

"Excuse me?"

"One of them might not make it. Not make out." Delaney grinned. "That means something else."

"You see!" Isobel said with a laugh. "You're already helping me with my English."

"Where would you like to go?" Delaney asked, watching her closely. He liked it when she laughed.

"We'll go to the boardwalk for a coffee?"

"Okay," Delaney said.

The two of them set off toward the boardwalk. It wasn't far, and Delaney loved the fact that she was with him. He wanted her to loop her arm through the crook of his elbow as they walked like he'd seen couples doing back at home and thought for a moment about suggesting it.

"So, where are you from in Canada?" Delaney asked.

"Quebec," Isobel replied. "Do you know it?"

"No, I've never been."

"I live in a place called Saint-Hyacinthe. It's to the east of Montreal."

"What's it like there?"

"It's pretty quiet," Isobel said, "but Montreal is less than an hour away, which is good."

A few moments later, they were sitting at a picnic bench outside the Starbucks coffee. The boardwalk was quite busy, and they had been lucky to get a bench at all.

Delaney had bought the coffees and offered Isobel some donuts.

"I'm fine, thank you," she had said. "I need to watch my figure."

"No, you don't," Delaney had replied. "Your figure's perfect." When he had said this, Isobel had given him a strange look but not said anything. He knew exactly what she was thinking, though. Which was fine, because he was thinking exactly the same thing. She was looking forward to *doing it* as much as he was.

"Do you have any books in English?" Isobel asked him.

"Er, yes. I've got a few. Why?"

"Maybe I could read one and then we could talk about it? Adèle told me that's a good way to learn."

"Sure, what sort of books do you like reading?"

"Anything, really. What do you have?"

They chatted for a few moments about the few books in Delaney's small collection before he saw over her shoulder that Rubenstein was in the coffee shop. Delaney moved on the bench slightly so he wouldn't be able to see him, but it was too late. When Rubenstein had got his coffee, he walked directly over to them.

"Delaney," Rubenstein said, leering at Isobel. "Who's this?"

"This is Isobel, Rubenstein," he replied, shooting his boss a dark look. "We're just in a private meeting here."

"Isobel, what a pleasure it is to meet you." He held out a hand for her to shake and she awkwardly half got to her feet. "I'm his boss. What are you doing here with this loser?"

"Sorry, loser?" she replied with a frown. "What does this mean?"

"Waste of space." Rubenstein spoke slowly and stared at Delaney as he said this. "Do you understand that?"

"That's not very polite, Mr Rubenstein," Isobel said with a frown. "Now if you don't mind, we are in a private meeting just as Mark said."

"Whatever," Rubenstein replied with a dismissive wave at Delaney. "Just don't believe a word he tells you."

As he watched Rubenstein wobble away from their bench, Delaney was on the verge of tears. His boss had embarrassed him in front of Isobel and completely ruined everything. She would never want to be with him now.

"Hey," Isobel said, putting her hand over his. "Don't be upset. He's a nasty fat man." She frowned at Delaney. "I don't know how you work for him."

Delaney looked around him and lowered his voice.

"Isobel," he said in a loud whisper, "will you help me kill him?"

Isobel let go of his hand and tilted her head back to laugh. It was Delaney's turn to frown. He didn't understand what she was laughing about.

54

Adèle walked over to the table outside the accommodation block where she could see Isobel sitting. It was almost ten o'clock in the evening, and Isobel was sitting reading a book. She was wearing pyjamas and a pair of flip-flops.

"Comment s'est passée ta soirée?" Adèle asked. *How was your evening?* Isobel jumped slightly at the sound of Adèle's voice.

"It was fine," she replied, folding the corner of the page in her book down to mark the place before placing it on the table. "Delaney and I just had a coffee and chatted for a while. I met his boss, too. Horrible man."

"Are you going to meet up with him again?"

"Definitely," Isobel said. "He said he'd be more than happy to help me with my English. He's lent me a book to read. We're going to discuss it." She nodded at the book she had just put down, and Adèle picked it up to see what she was reading. It was a translation of a book by Vladimir Nabokov. *Lolita*.

"Have you read this before?" Adèle asked as she put the book back down.

"No," Isobel replied. "I'm only a few pages in, and it's a bit weird, to be honest."

Adèle sat down opposite Isobel. In her pyjamas, she looked so young that it broke Adèle's heart. Especially as Adèle knew exactly what the book was about. She had thought, when she had met him, that this Mark Delaney character was a bit strange, and his choice in literature had just confirmed that for Adèle.

"Tell me about this man of yours back home?" Adèle asked, trying to keep her voice light and conversational. "Have you been together for long?"

"Oh, yes," Isobel said, a broad smile appearing on her face. "He first asked me out on a date fifteen years ago." Adèle did the maths in her head. That didn't make sense.

"When you were about eight years old?" In reply, Isobel laughed.

"I had just turned nine, and it was his birthday party," she replied. "He didn't like the present I got him, so I asked him what he would like instead for his birthday. He said that he would like to go on a date with me."

"And did you?"

"Kind of," Isobel said. "Our mothers took us to the ice skating rink a few weeks later. We didn't get together properly for a few years after that, but Édouard and I have been sweethearts since childhood."

Adèle smiled. It was a very sweet story, and for some reason it suited Isobel's character perfectly. It also explained some of her apparent naivety around Delaney.

"So you've never been with anyone else?"

Despite the dim light, Adèle saw the colour rising to

Isobel's cheeks at the question. She glanced around her before replying.

"I've never been with anyone, Adèle," Isobel whispered. "We've decided to wait until we're married."

"Oh, my word. Really?"

"What's wrong with waiting?" Isobel looked upset and Adèle realised that she had misinterpreted what she had just said. She reached across the bench and put her hand over Isobel's.

"Nothing at all, Isobel," Adèle said, smiling gently. "It's just that so few people do these days. We waited, and it was well worth it."

"It's difficult, though. But Édouard is determined not to give in to temptation, no matter how hard it is."

"Do you go to church?"

"He does," Isobel said with a sigh. "I'm not so keen, but I go anyway."

"He sounds like a lovely young man," Adèle replied, letting go of Isobel's hand. "I'm sure you'll have an amazing life together."

The two women sat in companionable silence for a few moments. Adèle was thinking about how best to broach the subject of Mark with her, and the fact that his intentions were nowhere near as honourable as Isobel's boyfriend's appeared to be.

"Can I offer you some advice, Isobel?" Adèle asked eventually. She was just going to have to get on with it.

"What sort of advice?"

"Just, well..." Adèle paused, wondering how to put it. "Some advice from one woman to another." Isobel started giggling despite Adèle's earnest expression.

"You sound like my mum."

"It's the sort of advice your mum would offer if she was here, Isobel."

"Is it about Mark?" Isobel replied, nodding at the book on the table and jiggling her leg up and down.

"It is," Adèle said. "I saw him looking at you in the DFAC earlier. I don't think he realised I was watching him, but I was."

"Looking at me how?"

"Probably the same way Édouard looks at you when he's struggling with temptation."

"Oh," Isobel replied. The smile she'd had on her face disappeared. "I know that look."

"I'm just saying, be careful. That's all. There's just something about him that's a bit strange."

"Okay, thanks. Maybe I should tell him about Édouard?"

"I think that's probably a good idea, Isobel." They sat for a few more moments and Adèle was about to leave Isobel to her book and go to bed when the younger woman spoke.

"I miss him so much," Isobel said. "Édouard, I mean," she added, even though it was obvious to Adèle who she was talking about. "I do wish I had his faith, sometimes." Isobel shrugged her shoulders. "But I don't. I mean, I believe there's a God, but I don't understand why if there is, and if He loves us so much, He lets such bad things happen."

Adèle unconsciously touched the crucifix around her neck.

"Neither do I, Isobel," she replied. "Neither do I."

55

Delaney winced as he felt something pop in his lower back. The green container he was trying to unload from the back of the Land Rover weighed a ton, and Rubenstein didn't seem in the slightest bit interested in helping him.

"Can I have a hand please, Rubenstein?" Delaney called out. Rubenstein looked up from the concrete plinth he was standing on with a derogatory look on his face.

"Give me a second," he replied, turning his attention back to the metal cradle he was trying to secure to the plinth.

It was half-past one in the morning, and for once, there was a slight chill in the air. Delaney pulled his t-shirt up over his nose, fully aware that the smell from the poo pond a few feet away from where they were working was particulate. A faint shaft of moonlight illuminated the black surface of the disgusting lake in front of him, and the rubber liner surrounding it made it difficult to tell where the liner ended and the pond itself began. Of all the places to site Steel Sky, they had to choose this one.

Not only that, but Rubenstein was insisting that they put it together in almost pitch blackness.

Rubenstein stepped down from the plinth, one of four that had been laid out in a square by a group of irritated US engineers over the previous few days. There was a further, larger plinth in the centre which would house the main radar array and ultimately connect to the large calibre machine guns on the other four. Fifty yards or so away from the poo pond was the last plinth. This one was much larger and was designed to house a counter battery unit. When Delaney had checked the measurements of the plinths, to the engineer's credit, they were sited to within millimetres of their original specification.

Delaney watched as his boss meandered over to the back of the Land Rover, seemingly unperturbed by the smell.

"You're bloody useless, you are," he said as he grabbed the other end of the container. "You might be good with numbers, but you're no use with anything else." Delaney ignored him as they both lifted the container off and placed it on the ground, grunting as they did so. "So what happened with that bird earlier, then?" Rubenstein asked. "That one you were sniffing around at the coffee shop?"

"I wasn't sniffing around her. She's my friend," Delaney replied as he reached back into the Land Rover to pull out two long poles.

"Sure she is," Rubenstein said with a smirk. "I bet she's filthy in the sack, though. For those who manage to get her into it, which won't be you."

"Don't talk about her like that, Rubenstein," Delaney replied, not bothering to hide his anger.

"Or what?" Rubenstein was looking at him with an incredulous expression. Delaney put the poles on the ground and stared back at him. "What are you going to do about it, little boy?"

The two men stared at each other for a few seconds before Delaney looked down at the poles on the ground. This wasn't an argument he was ever going to win. He knelt down and started arranging them so he could screw them together.

"Yeah, that's right," Rubenstein said with a sneer. "You erect your little antenna." He turned his back on Delaney and walked away, slipping on the black surface as he did so.

Delaney screwed the two ends of the antenna together before fastening them with their retaining screws. The honeycomb sensor was in the box they had just placed on the ground. Delaney watched Rubenstein as he spooled a cable between the main plinth in the middle and the one with the metal cradle. It was the main control cable, which would mean the honeycomb sensor could transfer the information required for the machine gun to shoot down the incoming rockets before they delivered their deadly cargoes.

The honeycomb sensor was probably the most sensitive part of the entire assembly, and Delaney took his time taking it out of its protective container. He placed it gently on the ground next to the antenna and sat back on his haunches to watch Rubenstein. It wasn't right, what he'd said about Isobel. That wasn't right at all.

"Do some sodding work, Delaney!" Rubenstein shouted to him. "Come over here and help me, would you?"

"Now who's bloody useless," Delaney muttered as he made his way carefully over the slippery liner to where Rubenstein was crouched over the plinth. As he approached, Delaney wrinkled his nose at the smell. The closer he got to the edge of the pond, the worse it got.

Rubenstein was trying to thread the spool of cable up through the centre of the metal cradle. Saying nothing, Delaney took the cable from him. It had been wound round on itself, which was why Rubenstein hadn't been able to thread it through. It took Delaney a couple of attempts, but eventually he managed to pull the cable through so it stretched between the central unit and the plinth a few inches above the ground. As Rubenstein tightened the retaining bolts, Delaney could feel his anger building as he thought about what his boss had said about Isobel.

When the cable was fully secured, both men got to their feet. Delaney pulled himself up to his full height and took a deep breath.

"I want you to apologise," he said through gritted teeth. Rubenstein just laughed in response.

"For what?"

"For what you said about Isobel."

"No chance. Get out of my face, would you?"

What happened next took them both by surprise, especially Rubenstein. Delaney raised both hands, planted them firmly on Rubenstein's chest, and shoved him as hard as he could. Rubenstein's heels caught on the taut cable behind him, and he lost his footing. When he landed, he was only a few feet away from the edge of the poo pond.

"You fucking idiot," Rubenstein snarled, trying and failing to get up. The slope of the liner was steeper near the edge, and he couldn't get any purchase on the slippery rubber. He swore as he slipped, this time ending up even closer to the edge. "Delaney, help me up, for fuck's sake."

"Not until you apologise," Delaney said, staring at his boss in disgust. He was too fat to even stand up. Rubenstein tried again to stand, but couldn't.

"Alright, alright. I'm sorry. Now help me up."

As Delaney turned and walked back to where he had put the antenna on the ground, he was still seething. Pushing Rubenstein over hadn't solved anything. The minute the fat bastard was back on his feet, he would be on Delaney's back again immediately. Not only that, but given his weight, Delaney wasn't even sure if he would be able to pull Rubenstein to his feet when the man probably weighed twice what he did.

Delaney picked up the antenna and walked back to where Rubenstein was still floundering. He extended the long pole towards the pond.

"Grab the end," Delaney said, making sure that his feet were on solid ground. "I'll pull you back up." Rubenstein grabbed the end of the antenna with both hands and yanked on it, almost pulling Delaney off his feet. "Hang on," Delaney said urgently. He readjusted his feet so that he had as much purchase as possible. Then he took a deep breath and put all his weight behind the antenna, pushing the end of it against Rubenstein's chest and sliding him towards the edge of the pond.

When Rubenstein realised what Delaney was doing, he screamed, his eyes bulging with the effort, but all this did was increase Delaney's resolve. A few seconds later, when Rubenstein disappeared into the inky black sludge, the only sound was a couple of large bubbles breaking on the surface of the lagoon.

56

Despite the lateness of the hour, the wave of heat that hit Lizzie the minute she stepped out of the plane was stifling. She sniffed before wishing she hadn't. The air stunk of aviation fuel, but there was something much more venal underneath the acrid smell of the fuel. Lizzie didn't know what it was, other than it was nasty.

"My God," Travis said over her shoulder. "Whatever that is, it stinks."

The two of them made their way down the steps and onto the asphalt of the airfield. There were several young soldiers standing in a line holding cyalumes in their hands. The small plastic tubes were filled with an illuminescent chemical that formed a line from the plane to a dark building a few hundred yards away.

"Now what?" Lizzie muttered to Travis, knowing what the answer to her question would be as they followed the cyalumes toward the building.

"Now we arse about for a couple of hours while they get all the paperwork squared away and then try to find our bags in the dark. I thought you'd been away before, Lizzie?"

"I have," she replied with a grin, "I was just wondering if maybe something had changed since last time."

"No such luck," Travis said. "We just have to hurry up and wait. I hope they don't take too long about it, though. They want us out and about on patrol as soon as possible."

"What, you think we might be going straight out tomorrow?"

"Reckon so," he replied. "Visible deterrent and all that jazz."

Lizzie thought about Travis's words as they walked into the building. It was a large warehouse, dimly lit with fluorescent strip lighting, with a series of desks about halfway down it. Passengers from the plane were forming orderly queues in front of the desks, so Lizzie and Travis joined the end of one of them.

To Lizzie's surprise, the lines to be processed into theatre moved fairly quickly. She and Travis watched as behind the desks, in the rear half of the warehouse, their bags were unloaded and placed in neat lines by a couple of Indian contractors. When she got to the front of the queue, Lizzie looked at the young soldier sitting behind the desk.

"Service number?" he said without even looking at her. Lizzie reeled off her service number, and he tapped it into the laptop in front of him. "ID card?" Lizzie handed him her service identity card, and he gave it a cursory glance before handing it straight back to her. He tapped a few more keys on the keyboard and then looked up at her. "All done."

"Blimey, that was quick," Lizzie said, flashing the

young soldier a quick smile. "Last time I was here it took bloody ages to get processed into theatre."

"Yeah, we've tried to get it as quick as we can." The soldier looked as if he welcomed the conversation, but Lizzie was conscious of the queue of soldiers behind her.

"Nice one, thanks."

Once Travis had been processed in the same manner, the two of them walked to the back of the warehouse and regarded the lines of identical black bags.

"Let me guess," Lizzie said as they walked down the line, "yours is a black one?"

"Very funny," Travis replied. A few yards further down the line, Lizzie saw the yellow and green ribbon that she'd attached to her bag to differentiate from all the other ones.

"You did mark yours, didn't you Travis?" she asked him, but he just glared at her in reply. "I'll be over here, then," Lizzie said, hiding a smile and nodding to the exit to the warehouse. There was a bunch of people in uniform milling about and waiting for the new arrivals.

Lizzie slung her bag onto her back and walked over to the group, looking around for someone with the familiar *RAF regiment* fabric badges on his shoulders. They were known as mudguards, but Lizzie had yet to find out anyone who knew why they were called that. It appeared they just were. Finally, she saw a flight sergeant wearing them.

"Hey, Flight," Lizzie said as she approached him. He turned to look at her, but she didn't recognise him. The flight sergeant was in his late thirties by her estimation and was as thin as a rake. She was tempted to make a joke about the food, but was deterred by the sour look on his face. "I'm Sergeant Lizzie Jarman. Windy's replacement?"

"Have you got a regiment corporal with you?"

"I have, yes," she replied. "Corporal Perkins is over there, looking for his bag."

"Did he mark it?"

"I'm sure he did, yes," Lizzie said. Travis could owe her one for not dropping him in it.

"My arse he did," the flight sergeant replied. "I've known him since he went through phase two training. He couldn't find his own cock if it wasn't attached to him." Lizzie hid a smile at the comment. "I'm Ricky, anyway. Come on, I'll take you to your accommodation and come back for that muppet."

The two of them walked to a green Land Rover parked outside the warehouse. He didn't offer to carry her bag for her, which Lizzie was pleased about. She didn't want to be treated any differently to any of the lads, and it was a good start.

"How's it been?" Lizzie said once Ricky had started the vehicle and pulled away.

"It's been shit," Ricky replied, not taking his eyes off the road. "Proper shit." That was the extent of their conversation. Lizzie knew she could have made more of an effort, but she was tired and Ricky didn't seem in the mood for small talk, so she just looked out of the window at what she could see of the base outside.

A few moments later, Ricky dropped her off outside the accommodation block. It was a two-storey building that glowed orange in the reflection of the few streetlights. Each window had an air conditioning unit underneath it, even the ones on the upper floor.

"There should be some paperwork inside the door for you with your room number," he explained as she got out of the Land Rover. "They're four man rooms. The juniors have got a dormitory, so you've lucked out there. I'll pick you up at oh six hundred from here."

Lizzie groaned. That was just over five hours away. By the time she'd located her bed and sorted her stuff out as best she could, she would only get about four hours sleep.

"Okay, thanks Ricky," she said, picking up her bag. Lizzie turned to say something else to him through the window of the Land Rover, but before she could speak, he had already started pulling away.

"No problem, Lizzie," she muttered as she made her way to the entrance of the accommodation block. "Nice meeting you and all that."

57

Adams left Air Commodore Maugham's office, closing the door softly behind him. If it weren't for the fact that the base had no alcohol on it, and that the air commodore was a strict tee-totaller, he would have sworn that the man was hung over from the night before. He looked as if he'd aged five years since Adams had last seen him and had large bags under his bloodshot eyes.

"Is everything okay, sir?" Adams had asked him when the base commander had finished telling him about the environmental health report following the fire.

"I'm fine," Maugham had replied. "Just not sleeping very well, that's all."

Adams had been wrong about the contamination. The fuel leak had breached the bund that was designed to stop the spread of fuel in just such a situation, and the ground around it was contaminated. Adams's first job that morning, among many others that the air commodore had dished out to him, was to try to find out what that actually meant.

Adams walked out into the corridor in the TLS building and was making his way to his small office when the American soldier who was guarding the entrance caught his attention and beckoned him over.

"Excuse me, sir," the soldier said. "There's a Brit outside wants to talk to someone."

"Who does he want to talk to?" Adams asked him.

"He's not sure."

Great, Adams thought. Now he was doing customer service instead of making a start on the list of tasks that the air commodore had given him.

Adams walked out of the front door of the TLS to see the contractor who had given the presentation on the base defence system standing outside.

"Hey, you okay?" Adams said before offering him a hand. "We've not properly met. I'm Adams, the medical advisor." As they shook hands, Adams looked at the contractor. "Mr Delaney, isn't that right?"

"Yeah, that's me." Adams let go of his hand, resisting the urge to wipe it down his trousers. Delaney was hyped about something. "Can I talk to you for a moment?"

"Come on in," Adams said, glancing at the American soldier. "Get yourself out of the heat." Even though it wasn't yet nine in the morning, it was already stifling. "Did you need to speak to me or just anyone?"

"I'm not sure who to speak to, to be honest."

"Come through to my office. We can talk there." Adams led the way to his office and pointed at the sofa when they entered it. "Have a seat. Do you want a cold drink?"

"Er, sure. I'll have a bottle of water if you have one?"

"I've got Coke, Tango, or some weird American drink that's full of sugar if you'd prefer?" Adams watched as

Delaney sat down. He kept clenching and unclenching his fists as if he was about to be attacked, and Adams regretted offering him the sugar-filled drink. He didn't look like he needed any.

"Coke would be great, thanks." Adams reached into the small fridge under his desk that he'd inherited from Christine. As he did so, he realised that his predecessor would be halfway back to the United Kingdom by now. The transport plane that had come in last night had left a few hours after arriving, full of grateful passengers. "Nice one, cheers," Delaney said as Adams passed him the can.

"So, how can I help?" Adams asked when Delaney had taken a long drink.

"Um, it's my boss. I'm not sure where he is."

Adams frowned. That wasn't what he'd been expecting the contractor to say.

"When did you last see him?"

"Last night, down by the poo pond. We were installing Steel Sky, and he'd left one of the toolkits back in the office, so he sent me back to get it because he's a lazy bastard." Delaney took another drink from the can as Adams grinned at his description of his boss. "When I got back, he wasn't there. He's not in his accommodation either."

"So, you think he's missing?"

"Something like that, yeah." Delaney wiped his hand across his mouth, and Adams noticed a slight tremor in his fingertips.

"Okay, well, there's a police section on base. Maybe you need to speak to them?"

"Yep, okay. Do you know where they are?"

"Down near the Cambridge DFAC, I think," Adams said. Christine had pointed out the police section during the brief windscreen tour she'd given him earlier that morning. She'd also shown him the poo pond, but they hadn't hung around there. "Listen, I can give you lift there if you want? I'm going that way."

"Would that be okay? Only I'm a bit worried about him. I don't think he's in the best of health, and I'm concerned that he's had some sort of accident."

Adams smiled at the comment. A lot of the contractors weren't in the best of health. Probably the busiest medical facility he'd visited with Christine as part of their handover had been the one for civilian employees.

"Of course it is," he said to Delaney. "Beats walking in this heat."

As Adams and Delaney walked to where Adams's car —a battered white 4x4 with the radio callsign *Medic 1*—he tried in vain to have a proper conversation with Delaney. Apart from the fact he was from Hastings on the south coast and didn't follow football, Adams wasn't able to get much out of the man.

Adams dropped Delaney off at the police section and made his way to the pan. He was due to meet with some environmental health technicians at the site of the fire to watch them do whatever it was that environmental health technicians did. As he drove, he drummed his fingers on the steering wheel and thought back to the presentation that Delaney had given. At least there hadn't been a rocket attack that morning. But, he realised as he looked at his watch, there was plenty of time.

58

Lizzie yawned so hard that she felt something click in her jaw. She was exhausted, having only slept for a couple of hours. In the passenger seat next to her, Travis yawned a few seconds later.

"Bloody hell, Lizzie," Travis said. "You've set me off now, so you have. I got even less sleep than you did."

"Well, if you'd marked your bag with something, you would have found it sooner and not spent half the night trying to find it."

"Yeah, thanks for reminding me. Again."

"It's not a competition, Travis."

"Ooh," he said in a snide voice. "Someone's tired."

"Bugger off, Travis," Lizzie replied. "I'm not in the mood."

The Ridgeback vehicle they were sitting in was the third in a convoy of three armoured cars. Ahead of them, chugging out clouds of black exhaust, were the other two, both bigger brothers of Lizzie's Ridgeback. They were all part of the same vehicle family produced in the United

States, but seriously up-armoured from the original versions.

Their Ridgeback was a strange-looking vehicle, of that there was no doubt. It was squat, heavy, and cumbersome despite the three hundred and thirty horsepower Caterpillar C-7 diesel engine. The exterior, not just of Lizzie's vehicles but also the other two larger Mastiffs in the convoy, were painted a sand colour and fitted with add-on side armour that was supposed to protect them against projectiles, shell splinters, and rocket-propelled grenades.

Lizzie shuffled awkwardly on the armoured seat and tried to shift the harness that was holding her to it.

"Open the door for a bit, Travis," she said. "It's stifling in here."

"Very funny, Lizzie," Travis replied. They both knew that the doors at the front of the Ridgeback were welded shut.

The two Mastiffs in the convoy, broadly similar to Lizzie's Ridgeback but bigger and with more of everything —wheels, weapons, and people—were revving their engines hard. Both of them were fully manned, but Lizzie's Ridgeback only had her and Travis in it. The back of their vehicle was fitted out as an ambulance, which seemed to make it less attractive to the other gunners. That didn't bother Lizzie. She knew that as soon as they got outside the wire, Travis would move to man the 12.7mm heavy machine gun in the rear of the Ridgeback.

"At least all you've got to do is follow that lot," Travis said with a smirk. "Not like you're going to get lost or nothing like that."

Lizzie ignored Travis's jibe, knowing full well that he was much worse at reading a map than she was.

"Yeah, you're bang on there. If you were navigating, then it would be a different story," she countered.

"Ha bloody ha," Travis replied. "Looks like we're off."

The lead Mastiff, captained by the flight sergeant who had collected them the previous evening, juddered into motion accompanied by a thick billow of smoke. Lizzie put the Ridgeback into gear and inched forward, ready to follow.

"They're hardly discrete, these things, are they?" she muttered, more to herself than to Travis.

"They're not supposed to be," Travis replied, raising his voice as the noise of the engine increased. "That's the whole point of a visible deterrent, mate."

Lizzie ignored him as she adjusted her goggles. With the heavy body armour she was wearing, Kevlar helmet, and tactical vest full of medical equipment, she was already sweating, and it wasn't as if it was going to get any cooler.

According to the brief they'd had back in the accommodation, this morning's patrol was intended to reassure the locals and also do some reconnaissance. There was another patrol that had left before dawn, and they were going to rendezvous in the foothills of the mountains beyond the base. The only problem with trying to reassure the locals, as the flight sergeant had told them all bitterly, was that the locals didn't seem to appreciate that. Up until the improvised explosive device that had taken out Windy's patrol, the most serious injuries the Brits had had in the area were from children throwing rocks at them as they drove past.

Lizzie looked at the high T-walls on either side of the road. They were apparently a fairly new addition, designed to protect against vehicle borne explosive devices, and were at least twenty foot high and solid concrete. In front of her, concrete barriers placed for the same reason turned the road into a chicane that she had to negotiate carefully.

"Loads of room this side, mate," Travis said as he looked down at the side of the Ridgeback.

"Cheers," Lizzie replied gratefully. Putting a deep scratch down the side of the vehicle wouldn't be the best start to the day.

The schedule they had for the day meant that, all being well, they should be back in the base just after lunch. Lizzie's plan was to shower, grab a couple of hours' sleep, and find out where Adams was hiding himself away. She'd found out from one of the other women in the accommodation block who'd known his predecessor that the medical advisor worked out of a building called the Taliban Last Stand.

A few moments later, having successfully negotiated the concrete chicane, the convoy was on the road. Lizzie eased up on the accelerator until her vehicle was the correct distance from the one in front—as close to fifty meters as she could get it—and tried to relax. Beside her, Travis started manoeuvring himself so that he could get into the rear of the Ridgeback and up onto the top to man the machine gun. As he did so, he put his hand on Lizzie's shoulder. At first, she thought he was using her as leverage so he could get in the back, but when he squeezed his hand, she realised he was reassuring her.

"We'll be fine, Lizzie," he said over the noise of the engine. "If anyone tries to tailgate you, they'll be looking down the wrong end of an HMG."

Once Travis was in the back of the Ridgeback on the

machine gun, Lizzie tried to relax. She picked up a bottle of water from the well between the seats and took a drink. It had been cold when they'd done the pre-inspections of the vehicles earlier, but was now lukewarm. She took another small sip and replaced the bottle. It was a fine balancing act, she thought as she watched the vehicle in front of her. She needed to drink enough water to stay hydrated, especially as she wasn't acclimatised to the heat, but at the same time she didn't want to drink so much that she needed to pee.

It was alright for the blokes, Lizzie thought. They could just go anywhere they wanted. But for Lizzie, that wasn't the case. It wasn't something that had occurred to many people, particularly because there weren't that many women in positions such as the one Lizzie was in now. Although she was there as a medic and her sole job was to look after any of the patrol who were wounded, she was still further forward on the front line than almost any other woman in the military.

Around thirty minutes later, after the desolate area surrounding Kandahar air base had given way to orchards and forests, the brake lights of the vehicle in front of her flared into life. Lizzie brought the Ridgeback to a halt and waited. A few seconds after she had stopped, the flight sergeant's voice came over the radio.

"Village ahead," he said, his voice crackling over the airwaves. "Lower Barbur. Keep them peeled. The natives aren't known to be hostile, but the Americans think there's a bomb factory somewhere in the village so if you get eyes on anything unusual, call it in. Okay, bunch up."

The Mastiff in front of Lizzie moved forward to within about twenty metres of the flight sergeant's lead vehicle, and Lizzie put her own Ridgeback back into gear. Her mouth was suddenly dry and she could feel her heart hammering in her chest at the thought of driving through the village. This was going to be the closest she'd ever come to the local population, and any one of them could be the enemy. It wasn't as if they were wearing uniforms.

59

"Help you?" the bored-looking American military policeman said without looking up from his magazine as Delaney walked into the police section. The building he was in was one of a collection of three pre-fabricated cabins next to each other together with a large tarpaulin covering them, and although a sign outside promised a reception, so far it wasn't meeting up to expectations.

"Hi, I er, I need to report a missing person," Delaney said. Even then, it took the policeman several seconds to tear himself away from his magazine. When he eventually placed it down on the desk he was sitting behind, Delaney saw it was a copy of *Guns 'n Ammo*. There was nothing, Delaney thought, like a stereotype. He looked at the policeman who was wearing a t-shirt several sizes too small to emphasise his upper body along with an obligatory crew cut hairstyle.

"Is that right?" the policeman replied after regarding Delaney for a few seconds with a disinterested expression.

Delaney wouldn't have been that surprised if he'd spat some tobacco into a pot.

"Yes. My boss, Mr Rubenstein, has disappeared." Delaney tried to inject some authority into his voice. He was, after all, doing the right thing by reporting Rubenstein missing.

"Sure, let me take some notes. Have yourself a seat."

Delaney sat on the offered plastic chair in front of the desk and waited as the policeman grabbed a notepad. The first few questions were relatively simple and were about Rubenstein's appearance, where Delaney had last seen him, that sort of thing. Delaney answered them as honestly as he could, grateful that the chemical fog the tablets caused seemed to be lifting even though he'd only missed one day's worth of medication. A few moments later, the policeman seemed to have all the information that he needed.

"Okay, I guess we'll go and have a look at the location he was last seen. You're coming with us, right?"

"Yes, of course," Delaney replied.

LESS THAN TEN MINUTES LATER, Delaney was sitting in the back of a police car with the policeman and one of his colleagues. It was the first time he'd ever been in a proper police car, and he tried to hide his excitement. It looked just like the ones he'd seen on the television, even down to the metal grille that separated the rear compartment from the officers in the front. Delaney's imagination started running through various scenarios where he might be in the back of a police car for real, not just because he was being given a lift somewhere. The scenarios got more and more outlandish as they drove, and he was buzzing with excitement by the time they arrived at the poo pond. The moment the policeman opened the back door and the all too familiar smell swept into the back of the car, any excitement he had been feeling disappeared in an instant.

"Man, that stinks," the policeman holding the door open said as he tried to put his elbow over his face. On the other side of the car, the second policeman was doing exactly the same thing.

Delaney got out of the car and started explaining to the two policemen what the plinths were for. The previous evening, while Rubenstein was hopefully sinking to the bottom of the lake, Delaney had got the radar assembly up and, as far as he could tell, running. The only thing he'd not tested was the feed from the assembly back to the office. If that worked, then he wouldn't have to come here that often.

"So he was putting this thing together when he disappeared?" the larger of the two policemen asked.

"Yes," Delaney replied, pointing at the plinth nearest the edge of the lake. "He was just there when I went back to the office. When I came back, he was gone."

The policeman wandered over to the plinth and started looking at the surrounding ground. After a couple of seconds, he beckoned to his colleague and the two of them started a hushed conversation. Delaney looked back at the police car, wondering what the sirens would sound like. Would they be like the ones on the television, maybe? Maybe if he asked the policeman, he could have a go at turning them on?

"Sir?" Delaney jumped slightly at the sound of the policeman's voice. "We're going to have cordon this area off, I'm afraid."

"Why?"

"There are some skid marks leading from that concrete square down to the edge of the pond. You said your boss wasn't particularly fit earlier?"

"I said he was about twice the size he should be," Delaney replied, looking at the area on the ground near the plinth. He closed his eyes for a brief second, remembering the previous evening and the sound that Rubenstein had made as Delaney pushed him into the lake. He had to concentrate so he didn't smile. "Do you think he's fallen in?"

"Possibly," the policeman said. "The ground slopes down toward the pond and the liner looks pretty slippery."

"It was last night," Delaney replied, suddenly realising that he could perhaps influence what the two policemen were thinking. "There was like a dew on the ground. Does that make sense?"

"Sure does," the policeman said with a knowing look at his colleague. Delaney had to concentrate even harder on keeping a straight face. This was turning out to be too easy. "So can I ask you to return to your office? We'll take it from here."

"You will let me know if you find anything?"

"Absolutely, sir. We'll be in touch directly."

Delaney thanked the policemen and turned to walk away. When he was about fifty yards away from the pond, he finally allowed the smile he had been suppressing to appear. He wanted to punch the air and whoop with delight. Not only had he managed to get rid of the fat bastard as he had been told to do, but he'd made it look like an accident.

It was time, Delaney thought, to go and see Darpak

and check in with home. They would be delighted, Delaney was sure.

Mission accomplished.

60

Adèle sat down in one of the battered armchairs in the makeshift crew room of the hospital. For once, the hospital was empty of patients. There was no restocking to do, and each of the clinical areas was as clean as it could be. She had just sent Major Laurent to the coffee shop to get some take outs, knowing full well that he would come back with some donuts. Adèle had stood down around half of the nursing staff due to be working that morning.

"Just make sure you're at the accommodation block or in the gym," she had told them. "If we get busy, then I'll send a runner to both those locations. I'm trusting you not to take advantage of my good mood." She had asked them all to be back after lunch for some teaching sessions. One of the reasons for standing them down was to give Adèle and Laurent some time to prepare the lessons.

Adèle looked at her watch. It was just after ten. When Laurent got back, that gave them a couple of hours to prepare the scenarios for the training. Then they could have a leisurely lunch before meeting the staff again.

Assuming nothing happened in the meantime, of course. She was just about to nip to the bathroom when the phone in the corner of the crew room rang.

"Bonjour?" Adèle said as she answered the call. *Hello?*

"Hi, er, is that the hospital?" a male voice replied in English with an American accent. Adèle was no expert, but it sounded like a southern drawl to her.

"Yes, this is Lieutenant Colonel Gautier. How can I help?" she said, switching to English.

"This is Robert Bertram from Mortuary Affairs. We have a bit of a developing situation that I might need your help with."

"Sure, how can I help?"

"We're down at the poo pond currently. A contractor's gone missing, and he was last seen in the vicinity."

"What, you think he might be in there?" Adèle asked with a gasp, even though she knew the answer to the question before she'd asked it. Mortuary Affairs wouldn't be involved unless that was the case.

"That's one option that the police are exploring." The way Bertram pronounced the word police, extending it out over two very distinct syllables, confirmed him as being from the south. "But if he is, then we have a problem."

Adèle grimaced as two concurrent thoughts ran through her head. The first was what it would be like to drown in that disgusting lake of human sludge. The second was how a body could be recovered from it, and what state it would be in when it was.

"How can we help?" Adèle asked. They weren't really set up for dealing with cadavers. That was the whole point of the Mortuary Affairs team.

"You have a decontamination rig, right? For, like chemical weapons and stuff?"

"We do, yes," she replied, thinking back to an exercise she'd been involved in back in Canada where they'd practiced a nerve agent scenario. "It's all packed away, though. We've got one, but never used it."

"It's just if this guy is in there, well, he's going to need decontaminating. We're not configured for, uh, that level of contamination if you get me?"

"Yes, I understand," Adèle replied. "My Lord, I hope he's not in there."

"He's probably sleeping off a potato moonshine hangover somewhere in the contractor's accommodation," Bertram said with a chuckle. "But if he is in the pond, then we're going to have to wash him off. And I wouldn't want to be doing that without the right kit."

Adèle told Bertram to keep her in the loop on what was going on and put the phone down. Just as she did so, the door to the crew room opened and Laurent walked in with a cup of coffee in each hand. Under his arm was a half crushed box of donuts.

"Qui était-ce?" he said as he put the coffees down on a table and tried to un-crush the box. *Who was that?*

"It was Mortuary Affairs."

"What did they want?" Laurent's scowl wasn't unexpected. Adèle knew that he and the department that had just called didn't get along that well. She also knew that the main touch point between their hospital and the Mortuary Affairs department was when the hospital had failed in its primary duty, which was to not let people die. Laurent always seemed to take it personally when one of their patients passed away and often took out his frustration on the Mortuary Affairs team.

"They're looking for a body in the poo pond," Adèle replied. "If they find it, they want our help to decontaminate it."

"The poo pond?" Laurent replied with a frown. "What, has someone actually tried to swim it, do you think?"

"I don't know. All he said was that a contractor had gone missing, and that was the location he was working in when he did."

"Merde," Laurent said. *Shit.*

"Literally," Adèle replied, lifting the lid from one of the coffees. "Is this one mine?"

"They're both the same."

"You've given up sugar?"

Laurent reached into his pocket and pulled out a handful of sachets of demerara sugar.

"Nope," he said with a grin. "Not a chance."

Adèle watched Laurent as he ripped open the sachets and poured them into his coffee. He was a big guy. Not fat, but muscular, and he probably spent more time in the gym than doing anything else. He wasn't just gym fit though. She had watched him on the hockey rink several times, and he had a natural athleticism to go with his size.

"What are you thinking about?" he said as he stirred the coffee with a spoon.

"We could do a training session on the decontamination equipment," she replied. "It would be a good drill and then if they do find a body in the poo pond, it's all there to use."

"Nice," Laurent said. "I like your thinking. Although if they find this man, the Mortuary Affairs lot can do the decontaminating."

"I had a feeling you might say that." Adèle took a sip

from her coffee and smiled. "After all, once they're dead, they're not ours. Right?"

"Damn straight," Laurent replied with a wry smile.

61

Lizzie made sure that the Ridgeback stayed the right distance behind the Mastiff in front as they approached the village. The first sign of life was a shepherd with a collection of scrawny goats. He stood by the side of the road and stared at the convoy as it went past. The shepherd was dressed in a simple long white robe that reached to his feet and a complicated-looking piece of headgear that looked to Lizzie like it was made of a roll of material. His face was impassive, and he just looked at the convoy through dark eyes as his goats wandered amongst the vehicles.

The first building she drove past was a low-slung, single storey affair made of brown mud and a tin roof. Perhaps, Lizzie thought, it was the shepherd's hut, and he lived in it with his goats. The closer they got to the village proper, the more buildings appeared, all constructed similarly. Children were running between the vehicles, paying them no mind, which to Lizzie was a good sign. It was normal, or at least it was for the Afghan villagers. She cast her mind back to the briefing that morning where the flight sergeant had reminded them that signs of life were a good thing. The Afghans weren't stupid—far from it—and a lack of activity in an area was a sign that something wasn't right. If there was an IED or planned attack, the locals wouldn't want to be caught up in it.

Standing in the doorway of one of the simple buildings was a woman, dressed in a full length light-blue burqa. Lizzie had no idea how old the woman was—she could have been Lizzie's age or she could have been in her eighties, unlikely though in Afghanistan—as the mesh covering hid even her eyes. Behind the woman, half-hiding in the folds of the traditional dress, was a small child. He was perhaps five or six and was staring at Lizzie with wide eyes. Lizzie smiled and waved at the boy. But the only effect this had was to cause him to hide behind the woman.

"You okay there, Lizzie?" Travis called from behind her. She craned her neck over her shoulder to look at him. He had canted the heavy machine gun so that it was pointing directly at the ground behind their Ridgeback, presumably to be less aggressive looking.

"Just trying to make friends with the locals," Lizzie replied.

"What, these rag-heads?" Travis said with a sneer. "They'll kill you as soon as look at you, you know that."

Lizzie looked around the village, determined not to feel sorry for the locals just because their lives were different to hers. What Travis had said was wrong, in her opinion.

"They're just living their lives, Travis," she shouted back to him. "They didn't choose to live here, did they?"

"Don't go getting soft on me, Lizzie," Travis replied. "Every man, woman, and child in this shit hole would come and watch you or me getting our heads chopped off if they could."

Lizzie pressed her lips together in a thin line. She loved Travis like a brother, but hadn't heard him talk like this before. What she wanted to say could wait until they were back in the relative safety of Kandahar. His words made her think back to some training she'd done back in the United Kingdom. Conduct after capture.

It had been one of the harshest lessons she'd ever had to sit through and detailed what they could expect if the enemy—whoever that was—took them prisoner. It had been particularly hard on her as a woman, as the threats she might face could be different to those of her male colleagues. Rape was the obvious one, and the advice offered had been to make every effort to be unattractive to a potential rapist. That advice had included soiling herself, and if it weren't for the fact that the lesson had been delivered by a woman who'd been held hostage by Somali pirates for several months, Lizzie would have been utterly disgusted.

She shook her head to dispel the unwelcome thoughts that Travis's words had caused and concentrated on keeping the Ridgeback the right distance from the one in front. They drove past an open square which Lizzie imagined was the centre of the village. There were several dilapidated market stalls, all empty and seemingly abandoned. Then there were more clusters of buildings.

As they drove through the village, time almost seemed to stop. The locals ceased whatever they were doing as the vehicles approached, and Lizzie felt the eyes of the villagers on her and the others as they drove past them. When she realised they were approaching the end of the village, she could feel the relief in her chest.

The final building before the road gave way again to open countryside was almost a mirror image of the first. It was a single story shack with a tin roof and holes for windows. In the doorway was a man, maybe in his forties, with a thick beard several inches long. He had the same complicated headgear as the goat shepherd, and Lizzie made a mental note to find out what their significance was when she got back to Kandahar. As Lizzie drove past him, she glanced at the man and realised he was smiling at her.

Lizzie smiled back and raised her hand from the steering wheel of the Ridgeback to wave at him through the small reinforced glass window. Finally, she thought. A friendly face. In response, the man in the doorway raised his own hand. His smile disappearing, he put his hand out flat and drew it across his neck as if miming a knife.

"See, Lizzie," Travis shouted down from the rear of the Jackal a few seconds later. "Told you so."

62

Adams replaced the handset and took a deep breath. That wasn't a call he'd been expecting at all. Muttering to himself under his breath, he thought for a few moments. Technically, the issue that the caller had just reported to him wasn't Adams's problem. But it also wasn't one that he could ignore. Noting the time of the call and the name of the caller on a scrap of paper, he made his way down to the ops room. They should be the first to know about the developing situation, then he would need to tell the air commodore.

He knocked on the flimsy plywood door of the ops room and was greeted a few seconds later by Lieutenant Simpkins.

"Hey, sir," Simpkins said with a smile. "What can we do for you?"

"I need to let you know about an issue," Adams replied. Simpkins's smile faltered slightly.

"What sort of an issue?"

"I had a phone call a few moments ago from the police section. They're down at the poo pond."

"Lucky them," Simpkins said. "What's going on down there?"

"They think there's someone in there."

"What, another swimmer?"

"No." Adams's next words wiped what was left of the smile straight off Simpkins's face. "A body."

"Seriously? Someone's drowned in there?"

"Possibly," Adams said. "There's a contractor who's disappeared. He was last seen by the poo pond, and apparently there's some evidence to suggest he might have fallen in."

"Jesus, can you imagine that?"

"I'd rather not." Adams handed the lieutenant the piece of paper in his hand. "That's the time of the call and the name of the American copper who called it in." Simpkins looked at him blankly. "For your ops room log?"

"Oh, yeah," Simpkins said. "Cheers, sir. Appreciate that."

"I'll let the boss man know and then head down to find out what's going on."

Adams left Simpkins to it and made his way down the corridor to the air commodore's office. When he reached the door, he reached up and rapped on it.

"Two seconds," the base commander's voice came through. Adams waited and then heard Air Commodore Maugham call out. "Come in."

The air commodore was standing behind his desk, both fists pressed to the surface just as he had been standing when Adams had come for his arrival interview. Adams glanced around the room and saw a large cup of coffee with small wisps of steam coming from it on a small table, and a copy of *The Times* newspaper that was several days old on the armchair next to the table.

Maybe when he had knocked, Maugham had been reading the paper in his chair but got to his feet so he was standing behind the desk when Adams entered? Adams didn't really care either way, but it was an amusing affectation if that was what the senior officer had done.

"Squadron Leader Adams, my favourite medical adviser," Maugham said with a toothy smile.

"I'm your only medical adviser, sir," Adams replied, returning the smile.

"Precisely, you are therefore my favourite. What can I do for you this fine, er…" Maugham's voice tailed away, and he frowned before continuing. "Friday?"

"Saturday, sir," Adams corrected him. "But I only know that because the football's on later."

"Who do you follow?" Maugham asked. Adams's ears pricked up at the phrase. It was the way a fellow football fan would ask another which was his team.

"Norwich City, sir. Man and boy. You?"

"Huddersfield Town, for my sins."

"I went to Leeds Road once to watch Norwich against the Terriers, many years ago, with my dad," Adams said with a grin. "It wasn't the most memorable day out."

"What was the result?"

"City won, I'm afraid." Maugham laughed at Adams's reply. "Knocked your lot out of the FA cup."

"That must have been a while ago if it was at Leeds Road?" The stadium had been knocked down years ago, and wasn't missed by many football fans, home or away.

"Late-eighties, maybe?"

"Hang on," Maugham said, clicking his fingers. "That was 1987. I remember going to that match." The air commodore laughed. "What a small world!"

"I had you down as an odd-ball man, to be honest," Adams said.

"No chance. Rugby's just the bastard child of the beautiful game, in my opinion. No real skill to it, no real passion in the stands. Not for me. Cricket's my game for playing."

"Batter or bowler?" Adams asked, nodding in agreement with Maugham's sentiments about rugby.

"Batter." Maugham extended his arms out. "Long arms, see. Do you play?"

"Not really," Adams replied. "Plenty of enthusiasm, not much talent was how my physical education teacher described me."

"Well, he could have been talking about me," Maugham said. "Anyway, you didn't come here to talk about football or cricket, did you Adams? We've done the polite conversation, so have a seat." He pointed toward a white plastic chair near the armchair with the newspaper on it. "What's occurring?"

"Er, bit of a situation developing down at the poo pond, sir," Adams said as he sat in the chair, putting his weight on it carefully to make sure it didn't collapse under him.

"Really?" Maugham replied as he sat down in his far more comfortable armchair. "What sort of situation?"

"The police are down there, sir. They think there might be a body in the pond."

"In all that ghastly sludge? My word, how awful." Maugham grimaced. "Do they know who it might be?"

"Do you remember that presentation on the new rocket defence system given by that young lad?"

"It's not him, is it?"

"No, his boss, a chap called Rubenstein. I spoke to him earlier. The lad who gave the presentation, that is."

"Right. Is this Ruebenstein British?"

"I don't know, sir, to be honest." Adams paused. It wasn't something that would have occurred to him. "Does it make a difference?"

"Only if they find his body," Maugham replied, picking up his mug of coffee. "Different countries have different rules for handling things like that. I just hope that if it is that young lad's boss, it doesn't delay the new rocket protection system." Maugham took a deep gulp of his coffee and sighed in contentment. "I think this morning's the first all week we've not had incoming fire."

"Well, I'm going to head down there and see if I can find out what's what. Do you want me to let you know the score once I know?"

"Seeing as I'm the base commander," Maugham replied with a smirk, "that would be nice. Thank you."

63

Delaney drummed his fingers on the formica desktop as he stared at the computer screen. A few feet behind him, sitting behind his desk, was Darpak. Delaney was the only customer in the Internet cafe, and he started to wonder how much trade Darpak actually got. Delaney didn't think he'd ever seen another customer in the place when he'd been in there.

"Do you have, like, busy periods, Darpak?" Delaney asked the proprietor. "Only every time I come in here it seems to be just me."

"Sure, sure," Darpak replied, stirring into life and putting down his newspaper. "Evenings it gets busy, when most people finish work. Not everyone is a boss man like you are."

Delaney smiled at Darpak's words. With Rubenstein out of the way, Delaney was indeed the boss man. Whether the company would send someone else out to replace Rubenstein or not, Delaney didn't know. But as far as he knew, Rubenstein was still missing. Not dead. Maybe his body would never be found? A soft ding from the computer in front of him caught Delaney's attention, and he broke off from the conversation with Darpak to read the e-mail that had just arrived in his account.

What do you mean, 'mission accomplished'?

He paused for a moment before composing a reply. The response had arrived moments after his original e-mail, which meant that the man on the other end of the e-mail exchange was on-line at the same time as Delaney.

You told me to get rid of Rubenstein, and I have. Before he pressed send, Delaney thought for a moment about providing some more information, but decided not to. The response this time was even quicker.

What do you mean, get rid? You were told to get him out of the picture?

Delaney grinned as he composed his reply. That was exactly what he had done.

He's out of the picture, as requested.

As Delaney waited for a reply, his thoughts turned to Isobel. He didn't need much in the way of motivation. The clearer his head became, the less foggy it was from the medication that Rubenstein had been forcing down his throat, the more he could see what he knew to be the truth. With the fat bastard out of the way, he and Isobel could have the office to themselves. Their own private space where they could *do it* all day and all night. He knew that was what she wanted. He'd seen it in her eyes. Her lust for him. The meds had dulled his perception of the way that she looked at him, but now that the fog was lifting, what Isobel was desperate for was becoming clearer. Much clearer.

The computer in front of him pinged again, and Delaney looked at it with annoyance.

What have you done, Mark?

"Oh, for God's sake," he muttered. Did he really have to spell it out?

He's dead. The system is live. I just need some data sets from another set of incoming rockets to calibrate it and then I can assemble the defence suite, just like you told me to. When he pressed the send button, he did it so hard that the fingernail on his index finger broke. Swearing, he put his finger in his mouth and tasted blood. The reply to his email was almost instantaneous.

WTF, Mark? I didn't tell you to kill him?

Delaney frowned at the response. That was exactly what he had been told to do. Get Rubenstein out of the picture. Those were his instructions. How else was he supposed to do that without killing the bastard? Delaney didn't want to be having this conversation. He wanted to be somewhere else, with someone else. Maybe he should dial things down a bit?

I didn't kill him. He had a heart attack. Delaney thought back to his research of how to trigger a cardiac event. *We were installing Steel Sky in the centre of the base and he just clutched his chest and fell over. I did what I could, but the nurse at the hospital said that even though I did everything right, he was too fat to live.* Delaney winced as he pressed send, his index finger leaving a smudge of blood on the mouse.

Maybe he shouldn't have included so much information, particularly when Rubenstein's body hadn't even been found yet. What if the man he had just e-mailed contacted the hospital? Delaney could be in serious trouble if he did that. He would have to get Isobel to cover for him.

He waited for a few moments longer to see if there would be a response from home, but there was nothing. Delaney swore to himself and closed the computer down after carefully wiping his history and also the mouse. He wasn't bothered about leaving DNA or anything like that. He just didn't want to leave a bloodstained mouse there for other people to use. After all, he wouldn't want to use one.

"Right then," Delaney said to Darpak as he got to his feet. "Back to the office."

AFTER HE'D SAID goodbye to Darpak, Delaney walked out onto the boardwalk. It was quiet, which wasn't surprising given the time of day or the heat. Even the hockey rink was empty. He contemplated getting some donuts and maybe taking them to the hospital for the staff there, but decided against it when he realised it was almost lunchtime.

Delaney walked to the end of the wooden covered walkway to a small sandwich shop that was manned by a perpetually smiling Bangladeshi contractor. He ordered a cold meat and salad baguette, or at least something that passed for a baguette, and a can of soda before returning to his office. As he walked along the gravel road, he wondered what was happening down at the poo pond. Had Rubenstein been found? Or was he right at the bottom of the lake where he belonged? Delaney smiled when he realised that he didn't care either way. Missing worked more in Delaney's favour, but even if Rubenstein was discovered, he was still in charge. That meant he could do what he wanted without anyone interfering.

By the time he got to the Portakabin, neither the baguette nor the soda were cold any more. He put them into the small fridge before looking at the cans of soda already in there. Delaney reached in and took out a cold can of Coke.

"Sorry, what was that, Rubenstein?" he called out over his shoulder. "Why, thank you. I'd love a can of drink. Very kind of you." Careful not to use his index finger, Delaney popped the ring-pull on the can and took a long drink. "Very kind of you indeed."

64

Lizzie put her hand over her eyes to shield them from the bright sunshine. She was sitting in the shade next to the Ridgeback munching on a warm sausage roll and looking up at the flight sergeant, Ricky, who was in the middle of telling a long-winded joke. Next to her, also sitting in the shade, was Travis. He was already chuckling at the story that the flight sergeant was telling.

After they had driven through the village, the vehicles in Lizzie's convoy had met with the other patrol. They were currently on a high ridge, the village a few hundred feet below them. All six armoured vehicles were now arranged in a loose circle with a few of their occupants milling about in the centre while the others were also sitting in the shade of their vehicles. Only Lizzie, Travis, and the flight sergeant were facing outwards.

Lizzie jumped when she was sprayed with warm liquid. She looked up at the flight sergeant and was about to remonstrate with him for spraying her with his water bottle when she realised two things. One was that he was falling toward her and Travis. The second was that he was missing a large section of his forehead.

"Travis!" Lizzie screamed as she scrambled to get out of the flight sergeant's way so she could help him to the floor. The sausage roll, now covered in blood and tissue, fell from her hands as a loud crack echoed through the air.

"Sniper! Sniper!" Travis shouted at the top of his voice. He managed to break the flight sergeant's fall and started pulling at one of his arms. "Lizzie, get into cover. Other side of the car. Go!" Lizzie ignored him and grabbed the flight sergeant's other arm. Between them, she and Travis dragged Ricky behind the Ridgeback and into cover.

Her heart thudding in her chest, Lizzie reached into the front of the Ridgeback for her medical bag as the other regiment gunners ran to man their vehicles.

"Stay! In! Cover!" It was Travis, shouting at them not to make themselves targets. Lizzie tried to ignore what was going on around her and looked down at the flight sergeant. He had a large section missing from his forehead. It was so big that Lizzie probably could have put her entire fist in it, and she knew that on the other side of Ricky's head there would be a small entrance wound.

"Fuck," Travis whispered as he knelt down next to Lizzie and looked at Ricky's ruined head. "What can I do?"

Lizzie's hands were shaking as she struggled to rip open the field dressing she had pulled from her medical kit. The flight sergeant was staring over her shoulder, and he was taking deep, intermittent breaths. There was nothing that any of them could do. He was dying in front of them. Lizzie recognised the agonal breathing for what it was. Ricky's last breaths.

"Hold his hand, Travis," Lizzie said as she unwrapped

the bandage. Travis looked at her and their eyes met for a second. She shook her head ever so slightly, just in case Ricky could see them. She was fairly sure he couldn't. "Talk to him. You know him better than me."

Travis leaned forward and took Ricky's hand in his. He put his mouth close to his ear, and Lizzie heard him trying to reassure the man.

"Mate, I tell you what," Travis said, his voice on the verge of breaking, "you're going to have a right old headache in the morning from that one. Like when we went out that night in Swindon? You were mullered by the time we left the base. Remember?"

Lizzie tried to tune Travis out as she gently placed the dressing over the wound in Ricky's forehead. She lifted his head a fraction and wound the bandage around it. As she placed his head back on the sand, Ricky gasped. She looked at him, knowing that he had gone and there was nothing she could do about it.

"Has he died?" Travis asked her, his voice finally breaking into a sob. He tightened his grip on the flight sergeant's hand. "Ricky? Can you hear me, mate?"

Above their heads was a metallic clang, followed a few seconds later by another sharp crack that boomed around the vehicles. Both Lizzie and Travis ignored it, but the noise generated some shouting from the other gunners. Someone was shouting about getting to cover, and Lizzie heard several engines starting up.

"He's gone, Travis," Lizzie said over the noise of the Mastiffs.

"Can't you do something?" he asked her desperately. "You're the medic, Lizzie. Can't you do something?"

"Not this time, Travis," she replied, her eyes filling up with tears. Irritated, she wiped them away with the back of her hand. "Come on, we need to put him in the back of the Ridgeback. Looks like we're leaving."

"Wait," Travis said, putting his hand on her arm. "Wait here."

Travis got to his feet and, staying crouched down, ran to the Mastiff next to their Ridgeback. A moment later, the vehicle swung around and parked toward the end of their own vehicle. The driver hopped out and ran over to them.

"There, we've got some cover." The new arrival glanced at Ricky's body and swallowed hard. "Fuck."

"Come on, mate," Travis said. "Let's get him in the wagon and get the hell out of here. We're too exposed."

Lizzie pinched the bridge of her nose with her fingers as the two men started to lift Ricky. This wasn't how her first day was supposed to go. She knew she hadn't failed as a medic. Even if Ricky had been standing in the middle of a fully equipped and staffed emergency department when he'd been shot, he still would have died. But the gunners weren't going to know that, were they? She would be forever remembered as the medic who'd lost someone on her first ever patrol.

"Come on, Lizzie," she muttered to herself as she threw her medical bag back into the Ridgeback and climbed into the driver's seat, fighting tears as she did so. "Focus, for God's sake."

65

Adams looked at the white van parked up next to the poo pond. It was an American van, about the same size as a Transit, with the words *Mortuary Affairs* stencilled on the side in large blocky letters. He sighed as he got out of his car and approached the van. This wasn't looking good.

Inside the van were two men, both wearing matching white boiler suits and almost matching beards. Adams tapped on the window of the driver's side. The man inside looked at him through the glass and mouthed a word. *What*? In response, Adams made a circular motion with his hand to mime winding a window down. The driver did so, but with obvious reluctance, and he stopped when the window was open only a couple of inches.

"What is it?" the man behind the wheel said. "We're trying to keep the smell out."

"Have you found anything?" Adams replied. "I'm the medical advisor for the base. The boss has sent me down to see what's going on."

"They're still looking," the driver said, nodding in the

direction of the poo pond. As the window was wound back up, Adams saw two policeman at the edge of the lake with what looked like a long pole dipped into the gloop.

"Rather them than me," Adams muttered, walking back to his car. He climbed back into the driver's seat, set the air conditioning to recycle the air inside the car, and settled in to wait.

About ten minutes later, one of the policeman shouted something and raised his hand. The doors to the Mortuary Affairs van opened and the two men got out, walking over to where the policemen were. Adams stayed where he was. There were four of them for a start, and he didn't particularly want to go anywhere near the edge of the poo pond. He watched, fascinated, as the four men pulled on the pole. A few moments later, the unmistakable shape of a body was dragged out, covered in thick sludge. One of the policemen broke away from his companion and sank to his knees a few feet away before vomiting copiously on the ground not far from the radar installation.

Adams stayed in the car to watch and see what would happen next. The second policeman crossed to where his colleague was, said something to him, and then walked to his police car to use the radio. A sudden rapping on the passenger window of his car made Adams jump. He turned to see Delaney standing next to his car.

"Hop in," Adams said when he had reached across and opened the passenger door. He looked at Delaney, who was staring at the body next to the lake.

"That's him, isn't it?" he asked Adams. "My boss."

"I'm afraid to say that it probably is. What was his name again?"

"Rubenstein." Adams wasn't sure, but he thought he saw the ghost of a smile on the other man's face. "Jesus, what a way to go. I guess he couldn't swim."

Adams paused, momentarily lost for words. He knew people reacted in different ways to death, and that black humour was used by some as a coping mechanism, but he'd never seen it used by someone who wasn't dealing with it on a regular basis.

"Will you be happy to identify the body?" Adams asked. "Once it's been cleaned up a bit?"

"Yeah, I guess so," Delaney replied. Adams looked at him again. He was definitely smiling. Only just, but it was there. "What happens next, then?"

Adams wasn't sure what the answer to that question was, and was about to tell Delaney as much, when he heard a large engine rumbling behind him. He turned and looked over his shoulder as a large fire truck ground to a halt a few feet behind his car. A few seconds later, two firefighters approached the group at the edge of the pond. They all had a hurried conversation, and the firefighters walked back to their truck before returning. They were unspooling a hose pipe as they did so.

"They're going to hose him down," Delaney said with a grin. "This, I have to see." He opened the door and stepped outside. Adams frowned at the man's response and opened his own door to follow him to the group standing near the body.

"I don't think there's much you can do for this chap," one of the policemen said in a passable impression of an English accent as Adams approached. This was more the type of black humour that Adams was used to, but he didn't reply.

He watched as one of the firefighters turned a lever on the end of his hosepipe and a jet of water sprung out with a loud hiss.

"Not too strong, now," the other policeman said. "If you wash him back in there, you'll be going to get him." The firefighter adjusted the level until the water was not as torrential and guided the jet over the body.

The fire hose was surprisingly effective. It only took the firefighter a couple of moments to hose the body down. Adams took a step forward to look at it. Rubenstein was quite obese, wearing a pair of slacks and a shirt that had been blue at some point in the past, and was missing a shoe. That wasn't what bothered Adams, though. It was the expression on the man's face. Rubenstein's face was frozen in a rictus scream. If he'd been under the surface when he'd opened his mouth, then the last sensation he would have had was a torrent of human sludge, formed from urine and faeces, into his throat.

Unusually for him, Adams suddenly felt nauseated and was suddenly sympathetic for the policeman who had lost his breakfast. Even though he was a medic, there were some things that turned any stomach, and this was definitely one of them. Adams turned away from the scene in front of him and put his hand over his mouth. Behind him, he could hear one of the policemen asking Delaney a question.

"Is this him? The guy you reported missing?"

"Yes," Delaney replied. "That's Rubenstein."

The nurse in Adams wanted to say something to Delaney. To ask him if he was okay, comfort him perhaps. Despite his strange behaviour, Delaney had just seen the body of someone close to him. But Adams said nothing. He just walked back to his car so he could leave this awful scene and get some fresh air before he threw up as well.

Besides, he needed to brief the base commander on the discovery of a body.

66

Delaney tried to remember to look sad as he regarded Rubenstein's body. Inside though, he was buzzing.

"What do you think happened to him?" he asked the policeman. It was the one who had been behind the desk when Delaney had reported Rubenstein missing. Hopefully, Delaney had livened up his day a bit. This was way more exciting than reading a copy of *Guns 'n Ammo*, for sure.

"I guess he must have slipped here," the policeman replied, pointing at the edge of the lake where the scuff marks were still visible, "and then slid into the pond." He took a couple of steps towards the edge, careful not to get too close to it. "Once you're in there, it doesn't look like there's an easy way to get out. And at night? No chance. He wouldn't even have been able to see the edge of the pond."

The two firefighters who had sluiced Rubenstein down had rolled their hoses away and were about to leave. They exchanged a few words with the two men in boiler suits over by the fire truck and, a few seconds later, the large truck roared into life. One of the boiler-suited men walked over to Delaney and the policemen. Under one of his arms was a rolled-up piece of material that looked like a tarpaulin, and in the other hand was a box of latex gloves.

"Can you help us get him into the body bag?" he asked. Delaney wasn't sure if he was asking just the policemen, or him. He took a few steps back to distance himself from the group.

"I, er, I need to get going," Delaney said. "I'd love to help, obviously, but, um, you know. I'm grieving and all that?"

Ignoring the disbelieving looks of the policemen and the man in the boiler suit, Delaney turned on his heel to walk away. There was no way he was going to help them get the fat bastard into a body bag. Rubenstein's body might have been hosed down, but he was still covered in shit. One of them called something out after Delaney, but he ignored it and kept on walking.

TEN MINUTES LATER, he was back at the boardwalk. At least the air was fresher here, but Delaney still wanted a shower. He could feel the particulates of the poo pond clinging to him. As he walked past the coffee shop, intent on getting back to the accommodation block to get cleaned up, he saw a familiar couple of faces sitting at one of the benches outside it. It was Isobel, sitting with a large Canadian soldier. Delaney walked over to them, eager to speak to her.

"Hey, Isobel," he said as he approached. She looked up at him and smiled broadly. Delaney felt his stomach churn. She was pleased to see him. Her colleague, less so. The soldier with Isobel was just staring at him with a look of barely disguised hostility. She said something to him in French, and he shrugged his shoulders before getting to his feet and walking away without a single word to Delaney. Not that Delaney could care less. "Sorry, did I disturb you?"

"Not at all," Isobel replied. "He was about to go, anyway. He needs to be back at work." She glanced down at her watch. "So do I in a few moments, I'm afraid."

Delaney sat down opposite Isobel, occupying the seat that the soldier had been sitting at.

"I've not got long myself," he said. "I need to get a shower. Hey, listen. I've got some bad news."

"Oh," Isobel replied, her smile fading. "Is everything okay?"

"Not really." Delaney made a concerted effort to look sad. He wondered for a moment about trying to get his bottom lip trembling, but that would be taking it a bit too far. "Do you remember Rubenstein? My boss?"

"Yes, I remember him. Why? Has something happened?" He nodded his head and bit his lip instead of trying to wobble it.

"Yes, he's dead."

Isobel's mouth formed a perfect *O* shape and her eyebrows shot up. She whispered something in French before putting a hand over her mouth, disappointing Delaney who had been staring at the way her lips covered her teeth.

"What happened?" she asked, her voice almost a gasp. She was so surprised that she forgot to pronounce the *h* properly.

"He drowned," Delaney said, "in the poo pond." He

could feel the corners of his mouth twitching, and he had to focus on his expression. Delaney tore his eyes away from Isobel's face and stared at the table between them.

Isobel reached out and took Delaney's hands in her own. Her fingers were cool, just like he'd imagined they would be. She wrapped them around the back of his hands and squeezed gently.

"Mark, that must be awful for you. I am so sorry to hear that."

Delaney sat as still as he could, not wanting Isobel to move an inch. He frowned as he looked at her hands over his, trying to commit the sensation of her bare skin on his to his memory. It was the first time she had touched him, and that was important. It was the start of *them* together.

Eventually, to Delaney's disappointment, Isobel took her hands off his.

"I need to go back to work, Mark," she said. "I'm sorry, but I have to be back."

"What time do you finish?" he asked, looking at her with what he thought was a hopeful expression. "Only I don't really want to be on my own this evening. I was wondering if maybe we could meet up? I could show you my office, and the work I've been doing on the rocket system?" Delaney paused, forcing himself to slow his voice down. He knew it was a side effect of not taking his pills, talking too quickly, but Isobel didn't seem to notice.

She frowned and pursed her lips for a few seconds.

"I finish at six thirty," she said, "but I have to phone home at seven. Edouard is expecting me to phone him." Delaney was about to ask who Edouard was when Isobel continued. "Why don't we meet here at eight? We can have a coffee and talk. Then you won't be on your own."

Isobel smiled at him and got to her feet. She waved at

him, a gesture that was filled with suggestion. Delaney watched her walk away, swaying her hips at him as she did so even though she was wearing combats.

He grinned, looking forward to the evening already. If he wasn't meeting her directly after work, then she would be wearing civilian clothes. Delaney hadn't seen her in civilian clothes before, and he wondered if she would wear something special for their first time together.

Delaney bit his lip as he imagined her getting ready for him before he stood as well. He needed a shower.

67

Lizzie slammed the Ridgeback into gear and left two deep gouges in the sandy ground as the heavy vehicle leapt forward. She blinked a couple of times, determined not to cry, and made after the vehicle in front. Moving was much safer than sitting still, and cover wasn't that far away.

The lead vehicle rounded a corner ahead of her and dropped out of sight. It was backtracking, following the same route that they had taken to the rendezvous point, and Lizzie knew that they would probably reconvene just the other side of the bluff they'd been parked on. There was a dip in the ground where they would be out of line of sight of the village.

In her rear-view mirror, Lizzie could see Travis clinging on to the roll bar. His face was grim and his jaw clenched. She returned her attention to the road ahead, and she pulled the Ridgeback into a right-hand bend so hard that the large wheels struggled for purchase on the loose ground. Travis put his hand on her shoulder and squeezed it as he leant forward to shout in her ear.

"Lizzie, slow down, mate."

She eased up on the accelerator, not wanting to add a road traffic accident to her first patrol. Ahead of her, the other vehicles had pulled to a halt. Lizzie drove to join them, parking the Ridgeback with the nose facing down the hill and back toward the village. She turned to see Travis standing in the back of the vehicle, looking at the others. He mimed drawing his hand across his throat, the same gesture that the local in the village had made to her. This time, however, all it meant was that he wanted the other drivers to turn their engines off. The silence when they all did so was deafening.

"Vehicle commanders, on me!" Travis shouted, banging his fist on the top of his helmet as he did so. "The rest of you, do your fives and twenties and get into all round defence." Lizzie watched as several gunners started running toward her vehicle while the rest started scouring the ground in front of them out to five metres. Then they would do the same thing out to twenty metres. Then, and only if nothing out of the ordinary was seen, would they get into a defensive position.

As the gunners organised themselves into a loose circle around the front of her Ridgeback, Lizzie heard Travis talking to her.

"Lizzie, I'm going to take charge if that's okay?" His voice was low, and obviously he didn't want the others to hear what he was saying. Lizzie was a sergeant, whereas Travis was a corporal. Technically, with Ricky's death, Lizzie was the most senior person on the patrol in terms of rank.

"That's fine by me, Travis," Lizzie replied, her voice trembling. "I'm not a gunner, am I?" As Travis climbed down the side of the Ridgeback, Lizzie squeezed her way out of the hatch on the roof to join him.

"Right, listen in!" Travis turned to the assembled group in front of them. "Ricky's dead. He took one to the head. Even though he was right next to our medic when he got slotted, there was nothing that could have been done."

A couple of the gunners looked at Lizzie as Travis said this. Several of them frowned as they saw her, and she noticed a couple of them staring at her Kevlar helmet. She unfastened the strap and slipped it from her head, fairly sure that they were in enough cover for it to be safe. When she looked at the fabric covering of her headgear, she realised it was splattered with blood. Ricky's blood.

"This is the plan, gents," Travis said. His voice was commanding and authoritative, despite—or perhaps because of—their situation. "We're going to head back to Kandahar, but we'll take an alternate route. One that doesn't go through Lower Barbur. Jimmy?" He pointed at one of the younger gunners who was kneeling on the sand. "You're in the lead vehicle, so start planning a route."

"I reckon we should go back through that village," one of the other gunners said. Lizzie looked at him and saw that his face was contorted with anger. "Kick in every fucking door until we find that sniper and string the bastard up by his bollocks." The gunner then looked at Lizzie and his face changed to a more contrite expression. "Sorry, sarge," he said. "Excuse my language." If their situation hadn't been so desperate, it would have been amusing the way he immediately apologised.

"Shut up, Robson," Travis said sharply. "You're supposed to be a professional, so start acting like one."

Lizzie tuned Travis's voice out as he barked instructions to the others in the group. She took a deep breath, suddenly exhausted. She knew it was a combination of normal tiredness and the adrenaline of the last few moments leeching out of her, but all she wanted to do was to curl up and sleep. Lizzie closed her eyes, just for a few seconds.

"Lizzie?" She opened them again with a start. "You okay?" It was Travis. The rest of the group had dispersed, obviously having been given their instructions.

"Sorry, I'm fine," she said, reaching for her water bottle to moisten her mouth. To her surprise, Travis started laughing.

"That's pretty hard core, that is."

"What is?"

"We're in the middle of a contact, and you have a snooze." His smile broadened. "Legend."

Lizzie looked at him and couldn't help but return the smile, albeit briefly.

"I wasn't snoozing. I was resting my eyelids."

"Sure you were," Travis said, taking the bottle of water from her and swigging from it. "Never let the truth…"

"…get in the way of a good story, I know." Ignoring the blood spatters, Lizzie replaced her helmet on her head and fastened it. "We good to go?"

"Reckon so," Travis replied, standing on the passenger seat and twirling his hand in the air to tell the other drivers to start their engines.

A few moments later, once the clouds of black exhaust gasses from the armoured vehicles had dissipated, the convoy set off. Lizzie was clutching the steering wheel so hard that her forearms were aching, and she had to force herself to try to relax.

They were heading back to Kandahar. At least once they got there, Ricky could be looked after properly.

68

Adèle looked at the nursing staff gathered in front of her. Standing by her side, his arms crossed, was Major Laurent. They had spent the previous couple of hours going through the decontamination procedures, which although she had found earlier wouldn't be needed by the Mortuary Affairs team, had still been a useful exercise.

"Quelqu'un a-t-il des questions?" *Does anyone have questions?* All she received in response were blank faces, and it was obvious from their expressions they hadn't found the training session as useful as she had thought they might. It was, Adèle conceded to herself, tricky to see how it was useful to learn how to decontaminate a casualty with injuries from chemical weapons when they had rockets raining down on their heads. But, as she had mentioned to Laurent earlier, if they had been needed by the Mortuary Affairs team then at least they would have looked professional.

"Okay," Laurent said, taking over as Adèle knew he would. "Back to your stations. I know it's not that busy at the moment, so there can be no excuses for your areas not to be clean, tidy, and fully stocked." He paused, staring at them as if he was expecting a challenge. Adèle hid a smile. Behind all his front, Laurent was no more threatening than a puppy. "So, go. I will be checking your areas before the end of the shift."

As the nurses dispersed, several of them grumbling good-naturedly under their breath, Adèle called out. "Isobel, could you stay for a moment, please?"

Adèle waited until it was just her, Isobel, and Laurent in the emergency room.

"Have I done something wrong?" Isobel asked, her eyes flicking between Adèle's and Laurent's.

"No, not at all," Adèle replied. "We were just wondering what you'd heard about the body in the poo pond. One of the girls said you'd heard something about it?"

"Oh, yes," Isobel said, her eyes brightening. "I did. Do you remember me telling about Mark's boss? The fat man?"

"Who is Mark?" It was Laurent, still with his arms folded over his chest.

"He was a patient here," Adèle explained to the major. "He had a laceration on his hand that we stitched. A contractor."

"Yes, him," Isobel continued. "Well, it was the fat man in the pond. I saw Mark today, and he told me about it."

Adèle glanced at Laurent, but he didn't notice her looking at him.

"Are you seeing him again?" Adèle asked. "Mark?"

"Yes, this evening. I'm meeting him later. He doesn't want to be on his own so soon after losing his friend. Although I'm not sure how friendly they actually were."

Isobel frowned, her forehead creasing with a concerned look. "But even so."

"Thank you, Isobel," Adèle said. "That'll be all."

"Oh, okay. Thank you ma'am, sir."

Adèle remained silent while Isobel left the emergency room. When it was just her and Laurent, she crossed to the kettle in the corner of the room and turned it on. A coffee would be good, although she would have preferred a glass of ice cold wine. She watched the kettle as it came to the boil, her arms folded across her chest.

"What is it?" Adèle jumped. She'd not heard Laurent cross the room and stand behind her.

"What do you mean?" she replied, not looking at him. "There's nothing the matter."

"Adèle," Laurent said. "Don't bullshit me. We've known each other too long for that. Something's troubling you." It wasn't a question, and Adèle sighed in exasperation at Laurent's statement. She knew he wouldn't let it go.

"It's this Mark boy," Adèle said. She paused before continuing, wondering how much to tell him about her concerns. The conversation she and Isobel had wasn't one that could be repeated, but she wanted to talk to someone. "There's something a bit off about him, and I don't think Isobel sees it."

"How do you mean, off?"

"It's the way he looks at her. It's animalistic. I saw him watching her in the DFAC."

"Adèle," Laurent said, taking a deep breath. "Take my advice on this as a man. Isobel is a stunning young woman. The fact that this Mark has noticed that isn't unusual. I would be surprised if he didn't."

"She just doesn't realise that, Laurent," Adèle replied with a sigh. "That's the problem. She seems to exist in this bizarre world where everyone's lovely. But I don't think this Mark is. It was the way he was looking at her I didn't like."

"Like he wants to fuck her?"

Adèle recoiled at Laurent's words, even though she knew he had hit the nail on the head. Her hand reached for the gold cross around her neck.

"Laurent, please," she said. "There's no need to be vulgar."

"I'm not being vulgar, Adèle," he replied. "I'm being honest. There aren't many women in this dump, and ones like Isobel stand out."

"And I don't?" Adèle managed a smile.

"Adèle, you know for a fact that if I was straight, I would be absolutely desperate to be with someone like you."

"That is the best excuse I've ever heard for not making a play for someone," Adèle replied with a wry smile. "If I wasn't gay, I'd jump into bed with you in an instant." Laurent didn't advertise his sexuality. It was as much a part of him as the fact he was left-handed.

"What do you want me to do?" he asked her as the kettle reached the boil and flicked itself off. "That's why we're having this conversation, yes?"

"Can you keep an eye on her?" Adèle replied as she reached for the mugs and the jar of instant coffee on the table. "Discretely?"

"Of course I can," Laurent said, his expression hardening. "Leave it with me."

69

Adams declined the air commodore's offer of another coffee and sat in the same plastic chair he'd been sitting in earlier. When he'd knocked on the door, the response had been exactly the same as before. A few seconds pause before being invited in to see the boss standing behind his desk.

"So, Adams," the air commodore said, "you've got an update, I take it?"

"I have, sir, yes," Adams replied. "Not good news, I'm afraid. They've recovered a body from the poo pond."

"This Rubenstein bloke?"

"Yes, sir. His colleague confirmed it at the scene."

"Is he okay, the colleague?"

Adams thought back to the look on Delaney's face when he'd seen Rubenstein's body. He'd certainly looked okay to Adams. If anything, he was almost pleased.

"I think so. I'll keep an eye out for the lad."

"Good man," Maugham said. "Must have been a bit of a shock, and under those circumstances as well. Do the police know what happened?"

"They think he just slipped and fell in. The sides are really slippery, and there are no emergency ladders or anything."

"Hmm." Maugham took a sip of his coffee. "Maybe we should install some, or at least fence it off."

"He was only there because they were installing the new radar system. Most people wouldn't go near the place with a bargepole."

"True, true," Maugham replied. He opened his mouth to say something else when there was a knock at his door. Adams hid a smile as he wondered what the air commodore would do. Would he stay where he was in his armchair, or move so that he was standing behind his desk? To Adams's delight, it looked as if the boss was thinking the same thing.

"Enter," Maugham called out after obviously deciding to remain where he was. The door opened and Simpkins's head appeared.

"Sorry to disturb you, sir, but I need to brief you on something."

"If it's the body in the poo pond," Maugham replied, "Adams here has just been filling me in on that."

"No sir, it's not that," Simpkins said. "There's been a contact with the regiment. One dead, I'm afraid."

"Bloody hell," Maugham replied with a sigh. "It never rains, does it?"

"Any wounded?" Adams asked.

"Um," Simpkins paused for a few seconds. "No?" The way he answered Adams's question just made it obvious that he didn't have a clue. "They're on their way back and haven't requested the Trauma Response Team. Plus, they've got a medic on the patrols now." *Nice recovery,* Adams thought as he watched the air commodore.

"Right, keep me in the loop. Thank you." Simpkins's head disappeared, and he closed the door behind him. "The regiment's getting hammered at the moment. You know they lost two only the other day?"

"I read about that in the paper, yes," Adams replied.

"So, back to the poo pond issue. My main concern, apart from that poor man's family of course, is that the anti-rocket system gets up and running. Will his death affect that, I wonder?"

"I can try to find out if you want, sir?" Adams said. "I'll go and make sure that the other engineer is okay, and either ask him or get him to come and brief you?"

"Would you mind, Adams? I know it's a bit outside your area as the medical advisor, but at least I might get a sensible answer from you. If I sent Simpkins, who knows what the reply would be?"

"Leave it with me, sir," Adams said, getting to his feet.

A few moments later, in his office, Adams checked on the large crash map where Delaney's office was located. He couldn't be certain exactly where it was, but he knew it was in the middle of a sprawling complex of buildings not far away from where the rocket strike had been earlier in the week. After checking to make sure he had his car keys in his pocket, Adams left his office and made his way to the car.

70

Lizzie stood underneath the shower, turning the water as hot as she could stand it. Finally alone for the first time since she had left the base that morning almost twelve hours earlier, she finally let the tears run down her face, safe in the knowledge that no one could see her crying. She closed her eyes to wash her hair, and an image flashed in front of them. Ricky, standing in front of her, just before he'd been shot. The bullet that killed him could just as easily have hit her, or Travis. It was, all things being considered, about the worst possible start to her tour.

She washed as quickly but as thoroughly as she could. There was nothing worse than not having any hot water, and Lizzie didn't want to use it all up so that none of the other women in the block could shower. She patted herself dry in the confines of the small cubicle before wrapping the towel around herself and stepping out into the main changing area.

In the changing room was another woman who Lizzie hadn't seen before, also dressed in a towel. In fact, she'd hardly met any of the other women in the block. Lizzie wasn't that keen on meeting people without many clothes on, but as she nodded at the other woman, she said hello anyway.

"Ah, you're English?" the woman said with a thick French accent. Lizzie looked at her. She was very pretty and had long dark hair that was cascading down almost to the small of her back.

"I am, yes. Sorry, I'm Lizzie." Holding her towel with one hand, Lizzie extended her other hand for a handshake. "Are you French?"

"Canadian," the woman replied with a broad smile. "I'm Isobel. I work in the hospital."

"Oh, okay. I'm a paramedic, but I'm here with the RAF regiment. I'd rather be working in the hospital, though, to be honest."

"What is this regiment?" Isobel asked.

"They patrol around the base to keep the perimeter secure. I only got here yesterday and…" Lizzie's voice tailed away and she stopped talking, not wanting to break down in front of a woman she'd only just met. Especially when she was only wearing a towel. "Sorry, it's been a tough day."

Isobel regarded her with a sympathetic expression, but to Lizzie's relief, seemed to realise that she didn't want to talk about it.

"I've had a few of them myself," Isobel said before changing the subject. "You must come to the hospital one day, have a look around. We're quite proud of it."

"I'd like that," Lizzie replied. "I've heard good things about it. I worked out of the British hospital in Helmand last year. We dropped quite a few casualties up here, but I never got the chance to see inside it."

"What job were you doing in Helmand?"

"Trauma Response Team," Lizzie said. "Working in the back of Chinooks." Isobel eyebrows went up.

"I'd love to work out of a helicopter. That must have been really cool."

Lizzie looked at Isobel's face carefully, but there was no hint of anything other than genuine interest in her expression.

"I don't know if cool is the word I'd use to describe it," Lizzie said, subconsciously running her tongue around the inside of her mouth even though the scars from the metal plate in her face had long since healed. "It was pretty hair-raising sometimes."

"Sorry, hair-raising?" Isobel asked, dropping the *h* from the word hair. "What does this mean?"

"Oh, er, sorry." Lizzie tried to think of an alternative word that wasn't too dramatic. "Scary."

"Hair-raising," Isobel muttered with a frown. Lizzie almost laughed, realising the woman was trying to memorise the phrase. Maybe she could persuade the Canadian woman to teach her French? That way, at least Lizzie could get something out of the tour. "Sorry, my English is still not very good." Isobel's easy smile returned. "But I am having some lessons."

"You could teach me some French," Lizzie said, "and I could help you with your English? I don't know any French, though. Other than a few swear words."

"Sure, I can teach you to swear like a proper Canuck. But if you just go to a hockey game, you'll learn most of them there, anyway." Isobel laughed, and Lizzie joined in, feeling some of the stresses of the day start to fade away.

"So, I must shower. Pleased to meet you," Isobel said, turning and unfurling the towel before throwing it onto a hook on the wall. Lizzie looked away quickly in embarrassment, feeling frumpy in comparison.

"Pleased to meet you too, Isobel," Lizzie replied, her eyes fixed firmly on the floor before she chided herself for being daft. Isobel stepped into the shower and, a few seconds later, Lizzie heard her gasp and mutter something in French as the shower started up. By the time she had picked up her wash bag, Lizzie could see wisps of steam coming from the cubicle, so she knew there was still some hot water left for the poor woman.

A few moments later, Lizzie had dressed next to her bedspace. She was pleased to be wearing something more comfortable than combats. Her clothing from earlier, including the fabric cover of her Kevlar helmet, was stuffed into a bag ready to go to the laundry. Lizzie just wanted to check whether it could go in the normal machines, or if it needed to be washed separately as it was effectively contaminated with blood and God only knew what.

"What I need," she muttered to herself as she checked her face in a small compact mirror, "is a medical adviser who might know the answer to that question." Lizzie allowed herself a grin before she picked up her helmet and body armour and headed for the door.

It was time to find Adams.

71

"Oh my God, you are enormous!" Delaney smiled at the look on Isobel's face when she slid his hospital gown up. It was a mixture of shock and admiration, and when she touched him for the first time, it sent a shockwave right through him. He was kneeling on a hospital trolley with his legs either side of Isobel's abdomen. She was wearing a hospital gown as well, and he could see her nipples pressing against the thin fabric. He reached down and squeezed one of her breasts hard, enjoying the way she gasped in delight as he did so.

Delaney was in two minds as to what to do next. He could put himself in Isobel's mouth, or he could just *do her* the way she wanted him to. Deciding on the latter, he ripped the hospital gown from her slim frame and pushed her legs apart with his knees, leaving her in no doubt what was about to happen. She squealed with delight and raised her arms above her head to grab onto the railing of the trolley. Her squeal turned into a guttural moan when he entered her for the first time.

"Mark, you are so big," she said, looking at him with wide-open eyes. "Do it to me hard. As hard as you can." Both times, Isobel dropped the *h*, which thrilled Delaney.

He gradually built up a rhythm, every thrust accompanied by a moan from Isobel. Only moments later, her eyes rolled back in her head and her eyelids quivered as she orgasmed, her teeth grinding together as she came. He could feel her gripping him as the waves of pleasure overtook her. If he hadn't had his left hand firmly pressed over her mouth, she almost certainly would have screamed in ecstasy. Delaney could feel the familiar sensation in his groin and knew he wasn't far away from giving her what she wanted. He slid both hands to her neck and put his fingers on her throat.

"Yes, Mark," Isobel groaned. "Just like that. Harder, though."

Delaney increased the pressure on Isobel's neck as he continued thrusting. It wasn't going to be long now. He'd known the minute he'd laid eyes on Isobel that she was filthy and only wanted one thing. Which he was giving to her now with interest. He dug his fingers into her neck, hoping to time the moment of her unconsciousness with his release. Isobel's eyes widened, and she gasped for breath as he increased the pressure, staring at him as she started to black out but making no effort to stop him. Her knuckles were white as she held on to the railings of the trolley, and Delaney allowed a smile onto his face. Any. Second. Now.

The loud banging on the wall of Delaney's Corrimec was so hard that it almost knocked his lamp from the bedside table. He flicked his eyes open, staring at the ceiling of his accommodation.

"Dude," a male American voice shouted. It was

slightly muffled by the thin walls, but not so much that he couldn't hear it. "If you're going to rub one out, try to do it quietly." The voice was followed by several cat-calls and jeers from other occupants of his accommodation.

Delaney closed his eyes and tried to recreate the moment, but it was gone. He felt himself softening and knew that he wouldn't be able to finish.

"Bastards," Delaney muttered. He pulled at himself half-heartedly, trying to return to where he had been only seconds before, but it was no use. He couldn't even see Isobel anymore in his mind's eye. "Bastards."

Delaney swung round and sat on the edge of the bed, looking between his legs at his rapidly dwindling manhood. It wasn't fair, he told himself. He had been so close. But perhaps when *it* actually happened later that evening, it would be better. He might not last as long as he wanted to, but perhaps the release would be more powerful.

THIRTY MINUTES LATER, Delaney was sitting in his office drinking another of Rubenstein's sodas. It wasn't as if the fat bastard could complain, was it? He waited for his computer to finish booting up before checking that the feed from the radar down at the poo pond was working properly. He opened the software—which he had written—that summarised the activity in the air out to a radius of almost five miles.

According to his screen, there were four aircraft operating in the area. He had programmed in the profiles of most of the air platforms in use on the base so that the software would recognise them as friendlies. Their size, their speed. Angles of takeoff and landing. He'd entered pretty much every air platform he knew that flew out of the base into it.

There was a Black Hawk helicopter doing something a few miles to the south of the base. Delaney glanced at the map on the wall. The helicopter was over the range area, so it would be live firing. A smaller, much faster moving blob on the screen was identified as an F16 returning to base following a mission. A Hercules transport plane was being held several thousand feet above his head, no doubt waiting for confirmation from the tower to start its final approach. The only thing that the software didn't recognise was a small aircraft circling to the north.

Delaney hummed, clicking on the aircraft to get the software to bring up some more information on its movement. This was what he was good at, pills or no pills. In a matter of seconds, he had created a new profile for it. Judging by its size, speed, and the tight circles it was turning, it was an unmanned aerial vehicle of some sort. He nicknamed it *Drone 1* until he could identify exactly what it was. The military, perhaps unsurprisingly, hadn't released the profiles of all their air platforms. Maybe this was one of the new, supposedly top secret, ones. Isobel would be fascinated by it, he was sure.

He closed down the software before opening the browser and navigating to one of his favourite pornographic websites. Once he'd found a clip he liked, he started playing it and walked over to the storeroom at the back of the Portakabin. He had prepared it for Isobel's visit as best he could and tidied it up. Maybe he should just move in here? There were toilets and showers not that far away, and at least he wouldn't have any neighbours. He and Isobel could be as noisy as they wanted, whenever they wanted. Delaney realised that he should have come

Incoming Fire

here for his personal time, instead of in the accommodation. If it wasn't for the fact that he was supposed to be meeting her in an hour or so, he could have finished off what he had started back on his bed. But he didn't want to spoil the storeroom before he'd had a chance to spoil her in it.

Delaney walked back to the main office and had just sat down in his chair when there was a knock at the door. He got to his feet, pleased that he hadn't decided to use the storeroom after all, and crossed to the door.

"Hey, Delaney." It was Adams, the medical advisor. "Have you got a few minutes, mate?"

72

Adams looked at Delaney who was almost hiding behind the door of his Portakabin.

"Hi, Mr Adams," he said, not making any effort to open the door.

"Just Adams is fine. Do you have a few minutes?"

"Sure." With that, Delaney closed the door in Adams's face. With a chuckle, Adams was about to knock on the door again when Delaney reopened it and stepped back to let Adams into the office.

"Can I get you a drink?" Delaney asked. Adams paused before replying, taking the interior of the Portakabin. The walls were covered in maps, and every table had some sort of electronic gear piled on it. The air smelt musty, as if it hadn't been occupied for a while, despite the faint whirring of an ancient air-conditioning unit underneath the window.

"That'd be great, thank you."

Delaney grinned at him, almost inanely.

"What would you like?"

"I suppose a can of Stella's out of the question?"

Delaney laughed at Adams's question, overdoing it, in the medic's opinion. Adams had only been half joking, though. It was common knowledge that despite the entire base being completely dry, the contractors always seemed to find a way of smuggling alcohol in.

"Sorry," Delaney said. "Will Tango do you? It should be cold."

"Magic, thank you."

As Delaney crossed the room to a small fridge in the corner, Adams noticed a pill bottle on the table nearest him. He leaned forward, frowning when he saw the label. Whatever the pills were, they weren't ones he was familiar with, and he made a mental note to look them up later. Delaney returned with a can of Tango, and as he passed it to Adams, Adams realised that the musty smell in the Portakabin wasn't the air. It was Delaney himself.

Adams cracked open the can and took a drink.

"That's lovely, thank you."

"No problem," Delaney replied. "They were Rubenstein's, but he's not around to drink them anymore."

Adams looked at the contractor carefully. He was still smiling, but he was frowning at the same time. "That must have been a shock. Him dying like that?" he asked, watching Delaney closely.

"It was," Delaney replied, not meeting Adams's eyes. "A big shock."

"The contract monitoring team has let the company back in the UK know, anyway," Adams said.

"Have they?" Delaney said sharply, finally looking at Adams. His frown was deeper and his smile gone in a split second. "Why have they done that? I can cope fine without him."

"It's standard operating procedure," Adams replied.

"For a..." Adams paused, not sure how to phrase things. It wasn't exactly suspicious circumstances. "For an unexpected death. You can't imagine how much paperwork things like that generate." Adams tried a smile, but it wasn't reciprocated.

The two men sat in an awkward silence for a moment, Adams not sure what to say. He waited for a while to see if Delaney would offer anything, but he was just staring at his fingertips.

"I have got one question for you, Mark," Adams said. "The air commodore was wondering if Rubenstein's, er, death will impact the rocket defence system at all?"

"No!" Delaney barked back, almost shouting. It made Adams jump, and he nearly spilled his drink. "No, it won't. Who's saying it will?"

"Hey, it's okay, Mark," Adams said, going straight into his well-practised *calm the hell down* mode he used so often in the emergency department. "No one's saying that, no one at all."

"It's all calibrated and fully operational. I'll show you."

Delaney reached across the table and pressed a switch on one of the computer monitors. Adams was treated to a very short view of a young blonde woman doing something to an older man that her mother definitely wouldn't approve of. He pressed his lips together to hide his smile as Delaney gave him a nervous grin.

"Whoops," the contractor said, closing the window down. "Sorry about that."

"Don't worry about it," Adams replied with a chuckle. "I can't even look at the BBC website on my work computers, let alone that sort of thing."

"Yeah, well, I turned the firewall off now that Rubenstein's not around to nanny me anymore."

A moment later, Adams was looking at a complicated piece of computer software. Delaney did his best to explain it, but he was talking so rapidly that Adams lost track quickly. What he was able to understand was that the radar assembly was tracking everything in the air, which was what it was supposed to do.

"That's very clever," Adams said when he could get a word in edgeways. "The things people can do."

"Thank you," Delaney replied. "It wasn't easy, but I got there in the end."

"You wrote the software?"

"Yep."

"Blimey," Adams said with newfound respect for the man. "Okay, so I can tell the air commodore that everything's on track?"

"Yep."

"Okay, cool." Adams paused and looked at Delaney, whose attention was fixed on the screen in front of him. "Listen, Mark. If you need to chat to anyone about, well, about what's happened, you know where my office is, don't you?"

"I'll be fine," Delaney replied, "besides, if I'm going to talk to anyone, I'll talk to my girlfriend."

"Sure, but trying to chat on the phone or via e-mail isn't the same as being able to sit down with someone face to face."

"She works here as well."

"On the base?" Adams asked, trying to hide his surprise.

"Yeah, in the hospital. I'm seeing her in a bit for a coffee." Delaney replied. "Then we'll probably come back here for a bit of, well, you know." He gave Adams a knowing smirk.

Adams glanced around the office, wondering where Delaney was planning to have a bit of, well, you know, but he couldn't see any likely locations. Deciding against asking him about it, Adams got to his feet.

"Okay, I'd better leave you to it then, mate," he said. "Thanks again for the drink." Adams looked at Delaney, but he had reopened his browser window and was watching the young blonde woman who, as it turned out, was remarkably flexible. Unable to help himself, he watched for a few seconds before turning to leave. "I'll see myself out," Adams muttered as he stepped out into the heat.

73

Adams was sitting in his office on his sofa trying to get himself comfortable. In the corner, his radio was tuned to the British Forces Broadcasting Service channel who were playing a football commentary from back home. He wasn't even sure who was playing, but the familiar sound of the commentators' voices was somehow reassuring. Adams could, he thought, have a power nap before dinner. If he could get himself comfortable on the sofa.

A few moments later, having tossed and turned for a while, he had just accepted that a power nap wasn't going to be an option when there was a soft tap at his door.

"Hang on a sec," he called out, getting to his feet and picking up the pillow to hide it away in a drawer. Adams wondered for a moment whether he should take a couple of steps and stand behind his desk to greet his visitor. If it was the air commodore, and he was the only other person he'd seen in the TLS building, Adams was sure the senior officer would see the funny side of it. Adams grinned and did exactly that, putting his hands down on the desk just like Maugham. "Come in."

To Adams's delight, it was Air Commodore Maugham who opened the door. When he saw Adams standing in his own power pose, he threw back his head and guffawed with laughter.

"Very good, Adams," Maugham said, smiling broadly. "Very good indeed. Am I that obvious?" Adams didn't reply, but just grinned instead.

"Everything okay, sir?" Adams asked. He'd already briefed the base commander on his visit to Delaney, and the fact that as far as the contractor was concerned, his boss's death wasn't going to hold anything up.

"Yes, yes, absolutely fine." He glanced to his side for a second before continuing. "I've brought you a visitor. They weren't sure where you worked, but managed to find my office instead, so I offered to bring her here." Maugham looked at Adams with a fatherly smile. "I think I'll leave you to it." With that, he disappeared, leaving Adams wondering who was outside his door. He had just stepped out from behind his desk to see who it was when Lizzie walked through the door.

"No way!" Adams gasped, his jaw dropping. "What the hell are you doing here?"

"Well, that's nice," Lizzie replied, grinning and looking around the interior of his office. "I come all this way to see you, and that's the greeting I get. Your office is a bit shit, isn't it?"

Adams stepped forward and pulled Lizzie into a hug. He couldn't believe it! She hugged him back and then a few seconds later pulled away a few inches so that she could kiss him. It was, Adams thought as he kissed her back, quite possibly the most memorable kiss he'd ever had.

When they broke apart, mostly so that they could breathe, Adams looked at Lizzie to see that her eyes were moist with tears.

"Is that a pistol on your belt?" she asked, "or are you just pleased to see me?"

"Hey, you," he said, reaching up with a thumb to wipe one away from the corner of her eye before it rolled down her flushed cheek. "What are you crying for?"

"It's nothing," Lizzie replied, blinking. "I'm just pleased to see you, that's all. It's been a bit of a tough old day. But it's suddenly got a lot better."

"How come you're here?" Adams said, wanting to kiss her again but settling instead for her nuzzling her head into his shoulder.

"I'm here with the regiment," Lizzie replied, her voice muffled. She had her arms wrapped around him as if she never wanted to let him go. "Battle casualty replacement for Sergeant Miller. We only got here last night and have been out already."

"Why didn't you tell me you were coming? I'd have met you on the pan."

"No time," Lizzie said, looking up at him. "Besides, I wanted to surprise you."

"Well, you've managed that in spades. I can't believe you're here."

They hugged for a few more moments, Adams still not believing that Lizzie was here in his office. Eventually, reluctantly, they let go of each other.

"My God, Lizzie," Adams said as he watched her looking around his office. "This is amazing. I can't believe it."

"Would you stop saying that, Adams," she replied with a grin as she sat on his sofa. "I know it is. Bloody hell, this is uncomfortable." She bounced up and down on it a couple of times, and the springs in the well-worn cushions squeaked in protest. "Get your kit off, let's christen this bad boy."

Adams laughed in reply before reaching up for his belt buckle. "Oh my God, don't you dare!" she squealed, slapping his hands away from his belt. "Can you imagine it? We'd both be on the next plane home."

"We'd also be legends," Adams laughed in reply. "I can't think of a better way to crash and burn out of a tour than that."

"Yeah, well dream on, matey boy." Lizzie stood up and put her hands on his chest, stepping forward so that they were only inches apart. She tilted her head up toward him. "Much as I'd love to be shagged senseless on a rickety old sofa, this lady has standards."

Adams slid his hands around her hips and clasped them behind the small of her back before tunnelling under her top with his fingers so that his hands were touching her skin.

"Two things there, Lizzie, if I may?" he said in a low voice as someone scored an absolute screamer into the top corner on the radio.

"Go on," she replied, a smile playing across her face.

"One is your apparent desire to be shagged senseless," he said, "which brings me to my second point, which is that you consider yourself a lady." He pulled her toward him, digging his nails ever so slightly into the soft skin of her back. "A lady would not be shagged senseless. A lady would be made love to, gently and tenderly, until she was glowing with delight."

"Adams?" Lizzie replied. "Can I suggest that you are completely and utterly full of shit?"

"Guilty as charged, your lady," Adams said, pulling her towards him.

"Mmm, that feels familiar," Lizzie murmured. Adams remembered back to the pub in Thetford, when they'd been in a very similar situation. Except that this time, there was no hotel room for them to go to to release the tension. "Can I tell you something?"

"You can tell me anything."

She leaned in to his ear and whispered. Adams listened intently, as Lizzie told him two things. The first was that if he ever repeated what she was about to say, she would have to kill him. The second thing she said made him immensely proud and profoundly sad at the same time.

"Seriously?" he asked her, looking at the twin spots of colour on her cheeks. She nodded in reply. "Blimey."

"Adams?"

"Yes, Lizzie?"

"Can we maybe go and get a coffee or something? Only it's a bit warm in here."

"We could have sex on that sofa instead?" Adams replied with a half smile. "If we're really, really quiet? We could be, like, tantric?"

Lizzie smiled back at him, her cheeks flushed. She reached behind her back and pulled his hands away, taking a half step back and blowing her cheeks out.

"You are such a chancer, Paul Adams. Mine's a latte with two sugars please, mate," she said with a laugh, "and you're buying."

74

Delaney's jaw was aching, and he attempted to relax the muscles in the side of his face. He knew that it was just a temporary side effect of not taking his meds, and that it would wear off in a day or so. He thrust his jaw forward to make the muscles stop clenching and took a sip from his coffee.

He was sitting outside the coffee shop on the boardwalk, watching the world go by while he waited for Isobel. It wasn't long before he spotted her, walking toward him wearing a pair of white cotton slacks and a blouse that showed her curves off perfectly. He raised his hand and waved at her, pointing at the coffee on the table to show her he'd already bought her one.

"Hey, Mark," Isobel said brightly as she sat down opposite him. "How are you?"

"I'm good, thanks. How was your shift?"

"It was busy," she replied. "How's your hand?"

Delaney glanced down at his palm. He'd put a fresh plaster on it just before leaving to meet Isobel, not wanting her to think he wasn't taking good care of his stitches.

"It's fine," he said. "Hey, would you like to come to my office? I can show you how the software works?"

"Oh, Mark," Isobel said with a sigh. "Can we do it another time? I'm so tired." She made a show of yawning, but Delaney knew she was only doing it for effect. He smiled, but it was to hide his anger. He'd spent hours tidying up the place so it was ready for her.

"I can get my van? That way you wouldn't even have to walk."

"You have a van? I didn't know that."

"It was Rubenstein's, but he doesn't need it anymore." While he had been tidying the office earlier, Delaney had found the spare key to it. Seeing as the police hadn't returned the original one, it was probably right at the bottom of the poo pond. "Will I get it?"

"Seriously, Mark," Isobel replied before lapsing into French. "J'ai la langue à terre."

"What does that mean?"

"I'm really tired. But I promise, we will do it another time."

Delaney noticed how Isobel blinked at him twice in rapid succession when she said the words *do it*. Beneath the table, his fists were clenched so tight that he could feel his stitches pulling, but he forced a smile onto his face. She still wanted to *do it* with him, that much was for certain. Otherwise, she wouldn't have blinked like that, would she? He'd wanted it to be tonight, though. Not another time.

"Okay, no problem," Delaney said. "How are you getting on with the book? Did you bring it so we can talk about it?"

Isobel frowned and took a sip of her coffee. When she put it back down, she was still frowning.

"It's not a very nice book, Mark," she said. "I've decided not to read any more of it." Her face brightened as she continued. "But I have asked Edouard to order me some other books in English on the internet."

"Okay, cool," Delaney replied. "Who is this Edouard bloke? Is he your brother?"

"Oh, no," Isobel said, laughing. She tilted her head back as she did so and Delaney stared at her neck for a few seconds. "Il est mon chum," she said, her eyes drifting over his shoulder. "He's my boyfriend."

"Your boyfriend?" Delaney asked quietly. "You never said you had a boyfriend?" His jaw was starting to ache again, really badly this time. Isobel just stared at him, her eyebrows raised.

"Um," she said, "didn't I?"

"No, Isobel," he replied. "You didn't."

"I'm sorry, I didn't realise. I think you'd like him, though, if you ever met him."

Delaney tried to hide his anger by sipping his coffee. He looked at Isobel through half-closed eyes, imagining her spreading her thighs for someone else. *Doing it* with another man.

"Fucking slut," he murmured under his breath.

"I'm sorry?" Isobel replied. "I didn't catch that?"

"Nothing," Delaney said, taking a deep breath, holding it like his therapist back at home had told him to do when he felt the anger was about to take control, before releasing it slowly. He put his coffee down and placed his hands back on the table, knowing that if he put them back under the table, he would split his stitches. "I thought that maybe you wanted, er, you would like to, I mean..." His voice tailed away. *Do it. Do it hard.*

"To what?"

"Maybe, you know, be more than friends?"

"Oh, Mark," she replied, putting her hands on his and making him jump. "I never meant to give you that idea. I've been with Edouard for years. You're a lovely man, but we can only ever be friends."

Delaney looked down at Isobel's slender fingers, and an image of her using them to pump the unknown Edouard furiously flashed across his eyes. These fingers, which he'd thought to be so pure, had been used to pleasure another man, and now they were touching him. He snatched his hands away.

"Mark? Are you okay?" Isobel was looking at him with an expression of concern, but he knew it was false.

"I'm fine," he said through gritted teeth. "Absolutely fine, thank you for asking."

Isobel's expression turned into a frown.

"Are you sure?"

"Yes, honestly," Delaney replied. "Sorry, I'm a bit tired as well."

The way that Isobel shifted in her chair told Delaney that the slut was about to leave. Sure enough, a few seconds later, she yawned again. Delaney closed his eyes, not wanting to look at her mouth, knowing what she had used it for with someone else.

"Mark, I'm going to head back to my accommodation and get an early night," Isobel said. "I am exhausted, and you look stressed. Maybe you should do the same?"

"Yes, you're right. Sorry, I'm not really myself. What with everything that's happened over the last few days."

She looked at him with what he knew to be an absolutely fabricated attempt at concern.

"Okay, well, sleep well." She smiled, but he didn't return the gesture as she got to her feet. Isobel looked as if she was about to say something else to him, but she just walked away.

Delaney watched as Isobel walked down the boardwalk, swinging her hips to advertise herself to anyone who was watching. He could hear a high-pitched whistle in his ears, another side effect of coming down off his medication, but he shook his head to dispel it.

Perhaps, Delaney thought, this Edouard was fictitious? Was he a test that Isobel had invented to see how he would react? The more Delaney thought about it, the more convinced he became that this was the case. He knew that Isobel wanted him, and only him. She wanted him to be challenged, to think that there was another man vying for her. A competitor who didn't exist.

Delaney suddenly felt foolish for not realising this a few moments before. How had he missed those signs? It was her way of telling him that she wanted to *do it* with him, and only him. But he had seen through the test for what it was. She had shown him her neck, not because she was laughing, but to prove to him that it was his to wrap his hands around.

He got to his feet, threw his half-finished coffee into the nearest bin, and set off after Isobel.

75

Lizzie sipped her coffee and watched the couple who Adams had pointed out to her before he'd left to get their drinks.

"That didn't look good," she said to him over the top of her latte. "Are you sure they're an item?"

"Well, that's what he told me earlier," Adams replied, breaking a cookie in half and offering Lizzie the piece he'd not taken a bite from. "Your man Delaney said his girlfriend works in the hospital and that he was meeting her later. They were supposed to be going back to his office for some how's your father."

"How's your father?" Lizzie said, spluttering with laughter. "Did you actually just say that?"

"Well, you know what I mean," Adams replied, looking affronted.

"I think that phrase kind of disappeared about the same time colour televisions got invented."

"That must be the girlfriend, though. I didn't think it would be her. Isobel, her name is."

"She's very pretty," Lizzie said. "I was talking to her in the shower." As soon as she said this, she saw a smile appear on Adams's face. "Not *in* the shower, I mean in the ablution block. She was wearing a towel. And then she wasn't." Adams's smile broadened.

"Really? Please, continue."

"Adams, you are a pervert. You've only been here for a few days and already you're disgusting."

"Okay, okay." Adams held his hand up in supplication. "I'm sorry." He paused for a few seconds before continuing. "Do you think they've just had a barney then?"

"Without a doubt," Lizzie replied, watching as Delaney got to his feet and set off in the same direction as Isobel. "Trust me on that one. I think he's been given the good news, which for him probably isn't."

"Poor bastard," Adams replied. "First his boss dies, then his very fit girlfriend gives him the elbow."

"What do you mean, very fit?"

"Okay, a bit fit."

"No, you were right first time. I've seen her naked." Lizzie paused for effect, managing to shiver without laughing. "She is very fit, and she's invited me for a naked pillow fight later with her equally fit friends."

"Can I come?"

"If you come in drag, of course. But I'm doing your make-up."

"Sure, I'll bring a trowel in case you forgot yours," Adams replied. Lizzie laughed and grabbed his hand, almost knocking his coffee over. She held on to it, squeezing her fingers together, knowing that she was about to start crying.

"Lizzie?" Adams said in a whisper. "What's up?"

"Oh, for God's sake," she replied, "I don't want to be like this."

"Be like what?"

"Adams, I was showering earlier and there was blood swirling down the plughole. It was Ricky's."

"Who's Ricky?"

"He was the flight sergeant who died today. I was sitting in front of him, eating a sodding sausage roll, when he got shot in the head right in front of me." Lizzie could feel the tears rolling down her face but couldn't do anything about them. "I couldn't do anything."

"Jesus, Lizzie, why didn't you say? I didn't know you were there."

"I am saying. Day one out with the regiment, and my flight sergeant gets slotted." She took a deep breath. "And tomorrow morning, I've got to go back out there again like nothing's happened."

Lizzie knew that her voice was too loud, and was aware of other people in the coffee shop looking over at her, but she didn't care. Adams said nothing, but linked his fingers in hers and she loved him for it. They sat in silence for a few moments, Adams just staring at their hands. He seemed to have a knack for knowing when to speak, and when to not speak.

"Adams?" Lizzie said. He didn't respond. "Paul?"

"Yeah, I'm here." Adams looked at her with a half-smile. "I'm always here, Lizzie."

"Would you rather talk about the naked pillow fight?" Lizzie sniffed loudly before shooting a look at the couple sitting on the bench next to theirs when they gave her a look. Adams said nothing, but just squeezed her hands.

"I'm always here, mate," he said in a whisper. "You know that. I always have been."

"Shut up," Lizzie replied, "unless you want me to start blubbing again."

Lizzie reached out onto the table and grabbed one of the serviettes that Adams's cookie had been wrapped in. She blew her nose as loudly as she could, glancing at the couple on the adjacent table as she did so, and rolled it up into a ball when she had finished. She was tempted to throw the ball at them, but decided against it.

"Right then," Lizzie said. "That's that out of my system. Let's have a game of truth or dare."

"No."

"Why not?" she asked, attempting a smile.

"Because no one in this coffee shop wants to see me naked."

"Come on, it'll be fun."

"Nope."

"Aw," Lizzie said, now grinning at Adams. "You're no fun."

"When Harry met Sally?"

"You wouldn't."

"No, I wouldn't. But if I dared you, then you'd have to. Still want to play?"

"Maybe not," Lizzie grinned. Adams still had her hands in his, and he was rubbing his thumb over the back of her hand just like he had done in Cyprus. And just like in Cyprus, the effect was the same. She sighed. "Why can't it just be like this all the time?"

"How d'you mean?"

"It's just like we're here, you and me, in this little bubble where everything's fine. No-one's dying, it's just two people who like each other enjoying each other's company." Lizzie took a deep breath. "But any minute, a rocket could land on our heads, and that would be that."

"If that happened, Lizzie Jarman," Adams said, "I would die a happy man."

"Oh my word, I'm so sorry." Lizzie pretended to hiccough. "I just did a bit of a sick burp when you said that."

Adams looked at her, and she saw that his expression was deadly serious.

"Lizzie, we fit, you and me. I'm sorry if that's not what you want to hear, but it's true. It's just taken me a while to realise it."

"I think we're biologically designed to fit, Adams," Lizzie replied, trying to lighten the moment. "So there shouldn't be any surprises there. What we did was nothing more than millions of years of evolution."

They sat in silence for a few moments. Lizzie wasn't sure what to say, or even whether to say anything at all. Adams seemed distracted somehow.

"What are you thinking?" she asked, eventually. He just shook his head. "Paul, tell me?"

"Oil."

"What?"

"Oil. That's what I'm thinking."

"What are you talking about?"

"The springs in the couch in my office."

"What about them?"

"I've got some oil in the car." Adams looked at her mischievously. "Plus, I don't think there's anyone else in the building."

"For God's sake," Lizzie replied, frowning and crossing her arms over her chest.

"What?" he replied, looking wounded. "Did I say something wrong?"

"You could have told me that half an hour ago." Lizzie

got to her feet and pulled Adams to his. "Come on. As the shepherd said to the sheepdog, let's get the flock out of here."

76

"Que ce qu'il se passe?" Adèle said as the doors to the emergency room flew open and Major Laurent burst in. *What's happening?* With him was Isobel. He had one arm around her shoulder to support her, and her face was streaked with tears.

"She's been attacked," Laurent said, his face a mask of anger. The knuckles on his left hand, which was resting on Isobel's shoulder, were scraped and bleeding.

"Isobel?" Adèle said, ignoring Laurent. "Are you hurt? What's happened."

"I'm fine," Isobel replied, sobbing. "I'm not hurt. Please, I'm fine."

Adèle looked at her face before running a practised eye up and down her body. There were no injuries that she could see, but as she looked at Isobel's neck, she could see bruises starting to form. The top few buttons on her blouse were also missing, and Adèle reached up to pull the collars back together. Then she gently touched the bruises.

"What are these, then?" Adèle whispered, frowning at Laurent as she did so. "What are these if you're not hurt?"

"Nothing, it's nothing," Isobel sobbed.

"Laurent, go and make Isobel a cup of sweet tea."

"I'm not going anywhere," Laurent shot back. Adèle fixed him with an expression that she didn't use very often.

"Now, Major Laurent." He glared at her before acquiescing. Adèle waited until he had left before returning her attention to Isobel.

"Isobel, come and sit down." She guided her to a chair and sat opposite. "Look at me." Isobel raised her head to do as instructed. "Tell me what happened. All of it."

"Nothing happened, not really."

"Isobel?" Adèle kept her voice soft and stroked Isobel's hands. They sat in silence for a few moments, Adèle knowing that she would talk when she was ready.

"It was Mark. Mark Delaney," Isobel finally said with a sob.

"What did he do to you?" Adèle suddenly started thinking about forensics. She'd not had to do a rape examination in years, but they had the equipment somewhere.

"Nothing, not like that anyway," Isobel replied, as if she could read Adèle's mind. "We had a coffee, and I left to walk back to the accommodation. I was just walking past one of the new shelters when he came up behind me and pushed me into it." She gestured to her chest. "He grabbed me here and when I screamed, he put his hands around my neck."

"Then what?"

"Then I punched him in the face." It was Laurent, returning with three cups of tea balanced in his hands.

Adèle looked at his left hand and saw that he had cleaned his knuckles up, leaving just a few superficial scrapes. "I would have punched him again, but Isobel stopped me."

"You would have killed him, sir," Isobel replied. "I could see it in your eyes."

"There's still time," Laurent muttered.

"Laurent, go to your office and wait for me there, please," Adèle said sharply. His presence wasn't helping.

"Fine, I will. I need to call the police and let them know, anyway."

"No!" Isobel said. "I don't want them involved."

"It's not up to you, Isobel," Laurent shot back. "He was going to-"

"Laurent!" Adèle almost shouted at him, but managed to temper her voice at the last moment. "Just go to your office. Don't call anyone or go anywhere. Let me take care of Isobel, and then we'll talk." Laurent just stared at her, unflinching. "Major Laurent, go to your office and remain there until further notice. That is a direct order."

Laurent turned on his heel and left the emergency room. Adèle sighed. She would have to deal with his insubordination later. She returned her attention to Isobel and started to fuss over her.

"Isobel, my darling child," Adèle whispered. "None of this is your fault, do you understand?"

"But it is my fault," Isobel said, her tears starting up again. "I told him about Edouard, and Mark said something about how he wanted to be more than friends with me. That was what made him angry."

"That's still not your fault."

"I don't want anyone to know, ma'am."

"Isobel, I think under the circumstance you can call

me Adèle?" She smiled at the young woman and was rewarded with a watery smile in return.

THIRTY MINUTES LATER, having made sure that Isobel had been accompanied back to her accommodation by the largest two soldiers she could find in the hospital, Adèle went to find Laurent. Unsurprisingly, when she entered his office, he was still fuming.

"You can wipe that stupid look off your face, Laurent," Adèle said, standing in front of him with her hands on her hips. "If you ever speak to me like that again in front of a junior soldier, I will charge you for insubordination." He glared at her before obviously realising that she wasn't going to back down.

"I apologise, ma'am," he said contritely. "It won't happen again."

"No," Adèle replied, softening her voice. "I know it won't. You did the right thing, Laurent. I know all you want to do now is to go and find Delaney and continue where you left off. But that would be the wrong thing to do. Okay?" She looked at him and saw him nodding his head in agreement. Laurent wasn't a stupid man—far from it—but she could feel the anger coming off him in waves. Adèle walked behind him and placed her hands on his shoulders, massaging them. "Come on, relax," she said softly. "I know you're angry. So am I, but this isn't you."

"How is Isobel?" Laurent asked Adèle when she sat down a few moments later.

"She's fine," Adèle replied. "Shaken up, but not hurt. The poor little thing. She must have been terrified."

"She was. Lord only knows what would have happened if you hadn't told me to keep an eye on her."

Adèle touched the crucifix that hung around her neck. She noted that Laurent hadn't tried to take any credit for his intervention, but highlighted the fact that it was her who had asked him to watch out for Isobel.

"She's adamant about not involving the police, though," Adèle said. "She doesn't want anyone to know about what happened to her."

"I don't see why she should be like that."

"That's her call, Laurent. Not ours."

"But what about our responsibility as commanders?" Adèle thought for a moment before Laurent continued. "What if this man rapes someone? I think that was his intent with Isobel. We cannot do nothing."

"You're right," Adèle said with a sigh. "Leave it with me. I will make sure that the necessary action is taken."

77

"Morning, sleepyhead." Lizzie grimaced at Travis's bright and breezy voice. "Rough night?"

"Thanks, Travis," she replied. "You look like shit as well." It was far too early in the morning for banter, and Lizzie hadn't had a cup of coffee yet.

"Over there, mate," Travis said, nodding at a small table in the corner of their briefing tent. Lizzie looked to see a cup of coffee from the shop on the boardwalk. "Julie Andrews, just how you like it." Next to it was a paper bag.

"Please tell me that's a muffin in there?" Lizzie asked him.

"Of course it is," he replied with a wink. "You can't beat a good muffin first thing in the morning."

"If you say so," Lizzie grinned. "I wouldn't know what with me being a lady and all that." Travis just laughed as she made her way over to the table. "You're a diamond."

"It's your turn tomorrow. But I prefer blueberry."

"Got it." Lizzie opened the paper bag and sniffed deeply. "Oh my God, I think I've died and gone to heaven."

"You're not the first woman to say that to me in the morning, mate."

"Travis, would you just stop with the innuendos and let me have my brekkie?"

As she sunk her teeth into the muffin, Lizzie thought back to the previous evening. When she and Adams had gone back to the TLS building, the night shift in the operations office had dissuaded them from christening his couch, so they had just talked. For the first time in months, Lizzie could finally get so much off her chest. That was one of the things she liked so much about Adams. The fact that she could talk to him about anything, knowing that he would listen, and it was also one of her main concerns about being in a relationship with him. If, for any reason, the relationship didn't work out, she didn't think they could go back to being just friends.

"I don't think that's daft at all, Lizzie," Adams had said last night when she had told him this. "But don't try to predict the end of something that's only just begun. You never know, we could still be annoying each other in thirty years' time." She had smiled but not told him she liked the sound of that very much.

"I'd eat your muffin a bit quicker, mate," Travis said. "The Int O's here, and it's the fat lad." Lizzie managed to squeeze the last bit of her muffin into her mouth just as the door opened and the Intelligence Officer walked in. He was a captain, instantly recognisable by his green beret and enhanced waistline.

"You look like a hamster," Travis whispered in her ear, and Lizzie coughed with laughter, almost inhaling some crumbs.

"Ladies, gentlemen," the Int O said, wheezing as he spoke. "All set for this morning's briefing?"

Lizzie half-listened to the brief, knowing that Travis would have it all in his head. As the patrol medic, she didn't need to have an in-depth knowledge of what the regiment were doing as long as she was with them when they were doing it. This morning's mission was to go to a village some distance from Kandahar. It was outside the range for rockets, but it was on the flight path for planes approaching the air base, so it was an area of interest.

Twenty minutes later, having paid a last visit to the bathroom, Lizzie was sitting in the front seat of her Ridgeback. On the horizon to the west of the base, the sky was just beginning to lighten. She didn't bother looking at her watch, knowing that it would only annoy her, but she resolved to have an early night.

After about twenty minutes, as they traversed a bluff that looked down on the air base, Lizzie heard Travis shouting at her to stop the vehicle. Lizzie stamped on the brakes, wondering what was going on. She looked back at him to see him pointing at a spot a few hundred metres away where three smoke trails were rising into the air.

"Rockets!" Travis shouted over the noise of the idling engine. Lizzie watched the smoke trails, transfixed. There was something almost beautiful about them, despite their deadly cargo. She realised that she was holding her breath as she followed the smoke.

When the rockets reached the top of their arcs, the smoke trails died away within a few seconds of each other. No longer able to see where the rockets were, Lizzie fixed her attention on the base in the distance. She saw three clouds appearing not far from the perimeter fence, followed several seconds later by a low rumbling noise when the sound of the explosions reached them.

"Middle of nowhere, mate," Travis said with a smile. "Kandahar one, insurgents nil."

Ahead of them, the lead Mastiff had moved off, so Lizzie put the Ridgeback back into gear to follow them.

It took them longer than they had expected to reach the village, and when they drove through the centre of it, they were surrounded by children. It was a much different reception to the previous village they had visited, and Lizzie made a mental note to pick up a few bags of sweets from the shops back at Kandahar for their next trip.

"They look almost pleased to see us, Lizzie," Travis said as he climbed down into the passenger seat of the Ridgeback. This was supposed to be a reassurance visit for the locals, so him in the back waving a machine gun around wasn't thought to be the best approach.

"They're just kids, Travis," she replied. "Poor buggers, can you imagine growing up here?"

"Not really," he said, waving at a shy child who was hiding behind her mother's skirts. The child raised a tentative hand and waved back at them.

The lead vehicle turned around in a large clearing in the middle of the village. On the edges of the clearing, several people were setting up market stalls. Lizzie looked at the produce on them and could see everything from large bowls of what she thought were dried fruits, bright red pomegranates, and clusters of grapes as large as Travis's thumbs.

"We should have got some of them grapes," Travis said as they left the village behind them and entered a narrow dried-out culvert with high sides. "Set us up a little winery. Bit of Marmite, some grapes, and bingo. Before you know it, we've got some Pinot Grigio."

"Ew, yuck," Lizzie replied with a grimace. "That sounds disgusting. Can you really make wine out of Marmite?"

"I think so," Travis said.

"I can't stand the stuff."

"No way, Lizzie Jarman? You don't like Marmite? You are so dead to me now."

Lizzie laughed and was just about to reply when she caught sight of some movement on top of one of the walls of the culvert. Seconds later, a rocket-propelled grenade hit the front of her Ridgeback.

78

Delaney sat bolt upright in bed when the Giant Voice sprung into life. He hadn't been asleep when it sounded, but lying in bed thinking about what had happened over the last day or so.

There was a thump in the distance as a rocket impacted a few seconds later. It sounded as if it was some distance away, but Delaney knew that even if it was closer, it wouldn't hit him anyway. That wasn't how it was supposed to happen and, as the next impact sounded even further away than the first, that just reinforced it. If he had been outside, then he would have put his helmet and armour on anyway just to be seen to be doing the right thing.

Delaney grinned as he listened to the alarm warbling, imagining all the other occupants of the base scrambling into cover like ants. He needed to get to the office to see if Steel Sky had caught the trajectories of the rockets. If they had, then he would be able to get the rest of the system in place, and he was desperate to do that before Rubenstein was replaced. Delaney was in charge until that moment, so this was his opportunity.

He swung his legs over the edge of the bed and winced at the pain in the side of his face that the movement caused. When he looked at himself in the small mirror on his wall, he had a dark bruise on the side of his face that was starting to extend underneath his eye.

Delaney hadn't seen the blow coming until the very last second. The soldier who had hit him had come from nowhere. It was just as well that Isobel had stepped in to intervene, or Delaney might have killed him. Sure, he'd been on the ground with the soldier standing over him and about to hit him again, but Delaney would have been able to roll out of the way, spring to his feet, and teach him a lesson. It wouldn't have mattered that the soldier was much larger and stronger. Delaney knew how to fight.

As he dressed, Delaney thought back to the moments before the soldier had interrupted him and Isobel. The feeling of his hands on her breasts had been exquisite, and the look of delight on her face when he slid his hands to her neck was just proof of how much she wanted him. Delaney would have preferred their first time to not have been in a concrete air-raid shelter, but if that's what she wanted then that would have been fine by him. Until that bloody soldier spoiled their fun. In a sense, all he had achieved was heightening the anticipation of when he and Isobel would be together.

Delaney sat on the edge of the bed and closed his eyes for a moment, waiting for the all-clear to sound so he could get on with his day. He didn't have to wait for long.

With the all-clear tone still sounding, Delaney made his way to the van and started it up. He looked over his shoulder into the rear and at the mattress he'd put in it last night. One of the rooms in the accommodation block had been left with the door open, so he'd used the opportunity to procure the single mattress from the bed under the cover of darkness. As far as Delaney was concerned, it was another sign that he and Isobel hadn't meant to be in the air-raid shelter.

Deciding against stopping for a coffee, Delaney drove straight to the office and reversed the van so that the doors were as close to the Portakabin entrance as possible. Ignoring the pain in his face that the effort caused, he dragged the mattress out of the van and into the storeroom before parking the van in its usual spot. Then he fired up the computer to see what the radar array had captured.

When he saw the numbers scrolling down the screen, Delaney pumped his fist in the air.

"Yes!" he shouted. It was all there. Even though it was only the raw data, he could already see the patterns starting to form in his head. The point of origin, the speed, trajectory. It was all there, and all he needed to do was to pull it out so that it was presentable.

His fingers flew across the keyboard to set up the software to capture the data and crunch the numbers. It didn't take long, and a few moments later he was looking at an animation of the rocket attacks less than an hour before. He'd been right about the impact points. There had been three rockets altogether, all of which had impacted in a large open space on the far edge of the base. The nearest building was probably almost a kilometre away.

Delaney ran the simulation again, this time overlaying the real time processing of the data to identify the point at which the heavy machine guns could have intercepted the rockets. Even with the time it would take them to spin into position and the rounds to reach the incoming rockets, they still would have destroyed the projectiles before they had crossed the perimeter wire. There was no doubt in Delaney's mind. Steel Sky worked.

With Rubenstein out of the way, there was no need for Delaney to visit Darpak and his dingy little internet café. He saved a copy of the simulation as a video file and brought up his secure e-mail program before attaching the file and the raw data.

Here are the files from the rocket attack this morning. Delaney pressed send and listened for the whoosh that told him it had been successfully delivered. He got to his feet and grabbed a can of drink from the fridge before switching his browser to watch something more entertaining while he waited for a reply.

The reply to his e-mail was much quicker than he'd expected. He watched the rest of the scene, enjoying the way that the slim brunette appreciated what the two men on the screen were doing to her. When the clip came to its natural and impressively copious ending, he switched back to the e-mail programme.

Excellent Mark. Well done. Are you going to arm the system?

Delaney tutted with frustration. Of course he was going to arm the bloody system. What sort of fool did they take him for? He typed a terse one word response. *Yes.*

Delaney picked up the phone and ran his eyes down a list of numbers tacked to the wall. When he found the one he wanted, he dialled the number listed.

"Armoury?" a male voice with an American accent said.

"Yes, hello. It's Mark Delaney here from Aeolus."

"Oh, yeah. You after your machine guns?"

"Yes, please," Delaney said with a grin. "Can I get them installed today?"

"Sure thing, sir," the voice replied. "It'd be good to get them out of the way."

79

Lizzie heard someone screaming as the Ridgeback rose a couple of feet into the air. When it came back down to the ground, all the breath was knocked from her body and the screaming stopped. She hadn't even realised it was her.

"Fire!" Travis shouted. At first, Lizzie thought he was trying to get the rest of the patrol to open fire, but as she felt the wave of heat through the shattered windscreen, she realised that the front of their armoured vehicle was engulfed in flames.

"Shit, shit, shit," Lizzie muttered as her hand flew to her harness. She pressed down on the release button, but nothing happened. It was stuck, probably from the impact of the rocket-propelled grenade. Not only that, but the inside of the cabin was filling with dense black smoke. Lizzie blindly reached above her head to where an emergency tool was located. It had a sharp blade for slicing through seatbelts, but when her hand found the area it should have been in, it was gone. The blast must have dislodged it.

Travis had managed to get his harness off and had leaned across Lizzie to turn the engine off and flick the battery master switch off. He was desperately tugging at Lizzie's harness, but it was stuck fast.

"Relax, Lizzie!" he shouted. "The extinguishers will kick in any second." In the front of the Ridgeback was an automatic fire suppression system known as the Zero 360. It had six nozzles, all attached to a gas extinguisher bottle in a stowage box on the front left-hand wing. Right where the rocket-propelled grenade had hit them. Unknown to Lizzie or Travis, of the four nozzles in the engine compartment, only one of them was working, and the fire was far too intense for it to make any difference.

Lizzie tried her best to relax, but she could feel the panic rising in her chest. She gulped and inhaled a lungful of thick black smoke before coughing violently. At the back of her mind was the thought that perhaps, by the time the flames reached her, she would already be unconscious. Next to her, Travis started coughing.

"Just go, Travis!" Lizzie tried to scream, aware of the sound of gunfire outside the vehicle. She couldn't determine, nor did she care, whether it was incoming or return fire. She screwed her eyes tightly shut and tried to take shallow breaths, but already she could feel herself getting light-headed at the lack of oxygen. "Travis, please," she muttered. "Just go."

The next thing Lizzie knew, she was being violently shaken back and forth in her seat. She opened her eyes and looked down to see Travis sawing at her harness with the multitool he wore on his belt. It was working! The small blade was about a quarter of the way through the thick material, but even through the thick smoke, Lizzie could also see the flames creeping towards her legs. She didn't want to burn to death. Not here. Not today. Lizzie contemplated taking some deep breaths of the acrid smoke to bring the inevitable forward, but she didn't think she would need to. Her vision was already starting to grey out.

"Don't you fucking dare, Lizzie" Travis screamed in her ear. Lizzie flicked her eyes open as he wrenched her forward, freeing her from the harness. Strong hands lifted her up and back into the main body of the Ridgeback. The smoke was less dense, and she took some grateful breaths. Travis dragged her back to the rear of the vehicle and tried to open the doors at the back. She heard him swearing when he realised they wouldn't open, followed by several loud thumps as he kicked at them.

Lizzie tried to get to her feet, but she had no strength in her legs whatsoever. The only thing she managed to do was to roll onto her side and vomit. Everything was disappearing from her field of vision. She needed oxygen, and quickly, but there was no way she would be able to get the cylinder from the wall when she couldn't even stand.

The next sensation Lizzie felt was being pushed upward, hard and unceremoniously. Bright sunlight hit her face, and she blinked as she took in a deep breath of fresh air. The sound of gunfire had intensified, and she realised that she was on the roof of the Ridgeback. Travis was clambering out of the troop hatch on the top of the vehicle. She let him lower her down the side, unable to assist at all, and he dropped her the last few feet onto the sand before thumping down next to her. Then he bent over and picked her up, throwing her over his shoulder like a firefighter.

As Travis ran toward the vehicles in front of them with Lizzie draped over him, she vomited again, spraying the back of his legs with blackened bile. Then she felt more hands on her, dragging her into the Mastiff as its machine gun on the roof barked. As she was thrown into a seat, just before she passed out, she felt a mask being placed on her face and heard the welcoming hiss of oxygen.

80

Adams knocked on the door of the Portakabin and took a step back, careful not to tumble down the steel stairs that led to the entrance. He could hear someone shuffling around inside the prefabricated building.

"Hold on, I'm coming." It was Delaney. His voice was muffled through the closed door. A few seconds later, the door was thrown open. "Oh, it's you." Adams saw the grin that had been on Delaney's face when he opened the door disappear. He also saw the florid bruising by Delaney's right eye.

"Sorry if I'm disturbing you," Adams said, looking at Delaney's face. "What happened to you?"

"Oh, nothing," Delaney replied, his grin reappearing as he tentatively touched his cheek. "I fell down those stairs in the dark." He nodded at the metal staircase Adams was standing on.

"Okay," Adams said slowly, looking more closely at the bruising. There were no abrasions on his skin, which if he'd fallen onto the rocky ground at the bottom of the steps, there would have been. "Can I come in?"

"Sure." Delaney stepped back from the door and walked into his office.

Adams followed him inside, realising that it was even more dishevelled than the previous day. The musty smell was still there. If anything, it was worse.

"How's things, anyway?" he asked the contractor.

"Fine, fine," Delaney shot back, his voice clipped. "Just a bit busy, that's all."

Adams looked over at the computer screen, grateful that it wasn't showing pornography this time. On the screen was an animated image of what looked like rockets flying through the air. Delaney noticed him watching the animation.

"That looks pretty cool," Adams said, hoping to try to make some sort of connection with the man. "Did you do that?"

"I did, yeah," Delaney replied. "I crunched all the data from the rocket attack this morning. It should have taken days, but it only took me an hour or so. That's the animation of the attack."

Adams watched as the wireframe rockets on the screen exploded in a burst of pixels before the film looped back to the start again.

"Very impressive," he said to Delaney. "I wouldn't know where to start with all that."

In response, Delaney started telling him about how the calculations were arrived at, but he lost Adams within a few minutes. Adams waited as he continued, barely taking a breath between the hurried sentences. Delaney was talking so quickly that Adams struggled to understand him. Not in terms of the subject he was talking about—there was no way Adams was going to get his head round that—but in terms of the words themselves. Delaney was speaking so fast he was running them into each other.

Finally, he stopped and looked at Adams with an expectant expression.

"Like I said, Mark," Adams said, smiling, "very impressive." Delaney nodded his head twice in quick succession, stared at Adams for a couple of seconds, and then walked over to the other side of the Portakabin. "So, what's next?" Adams asked.

"Machine guns," Delaney replied, his attention fixed on a map on the wall. "Four big bastard machine guns. I thought that's who was at the door."

Adams stifled a laugh at the thought of four machine guns knocking on the door.

"Okay, I get it. Then the system will be fully up and running?" he asked.

"Yup," Delaney said. "Full coverage of the main part of the base. All the main buildings will be covered. Your office place, the hospital, most of the DFACs."

As Delaney mentioned the hospital, Adams's thoughts turned to seeing Delaney and the nurse at the coffee shop the night before. He looked over at him, wondering whether to bring the subject up, but the man was so jumpy already that he didn't want to make him worse if he had been dumped like Lizzie had said. Maybe that was why he was so tense?

"Excellent stuff," Adams said. "I'll let the base commander know. He'll be really pleased. Unless you'd like to tell him, of course? After all, it's your achievement."

"No, that's fine," Delaney replied, still engrossed in the

map on the wall. "You can let Sir Maugham know that I've got it covered."

Adams looked at him, wondering if he was making a self-deferential joke, but Delaney's face was like a stone as he traced his fingers over some contour lines. Adams took the opportunity to look around the office. It was much untidier that it had been. The bin in the corner of the room was overflowing with empty cans and coffee cups, and more were strewn on the tables. The whole place needed a good half hour with a large bin bag followed by an industrial vacuum cleaner.

"So, Mark," Adams said. "How is everything, mate?" Delaney didn't reply, so Adams tried again after a few seconds. "Is everything okay?"

"It's fine," Delaney snapped his head round at Adams. "I'm just busy." Although they were a few feet apart, Adams could see the muscles in the side of Delaney's jaw tensing. "Lots to do, see? Lots to do."

"Okay, sure," Adams replied, holding his hands out. "Sorry if I'm disturbing you."

"Well, you are." Delaney turned back to the map.

Adams thought for a moment about saying something else to the man, how if he ever wanted to talk he knew where he was, but he decided against it. He made his way to the door and looked back at Delaney, who was now scribbling furiously in a notebook.

"I'll see you around, yeah?" Adams said as he put his hand on the door handle.

Delaney didn't reply, but just kept scribbling.

81

Lizzie's eyes fluttered open, and she looked around the inside of the Mastiff. It was larger than her Ridgeback, and not configured as an ambulance as her own vehicle had been, but it was recognisable enough. It was moving quickly, and she was being jolted from side to side. Opposite her was Travis, who had his eyes closed.

She grinned briefly, remembering his words to her after Ricky's death. Maybe she wasn't the only one who was able to snooze on the job? It was only the two of them in the rear, but she could see two men in the front seats and hear the gun turret above her head being moved from side to side. There was no firing, and she knew that they would be exiting to a safe location to regroup and determine their next steps. Which hopefully was to go back to Kandahar. This had been a mistake. She should never have volunteered to come out to this Godforsaken place. Not after the last couple of days.

Lizzie reached up and pulled the oxygen mask from

her nose and mouth. Her mouth was dry from the medical gas and she looked around for a bottle of water. Across from her, Travis grunted in his sleep.

"Hey, Travis," Lizzie said, reaching out and touching his knee. He didn't respond. "Travis, wake up, you lazy bugger." When there was still no response, Lizzie started to get concerned. She undid her harness—at least this one wasn't buckled beyond repair—and stepped across the vehicle to sit next to him. The minute she sat down, Lizzie knew something was wrong. Travis was paler than she'd ever seen him. "Travis?" There was no response to her voice, nor to her shaking his shoulder.

Lizzie's hand instinctively flew to his wrist, and she struggled with the vibration of the vehicle to find his pulse. When she eventually found it, it was weak and thready.

"Help me!" Lizzie screamed at the top of her voice. In the front of the vehicle, the gunner in the passenger seat turned around. "Fucking well help me!" she screamed again, looking at the gunner with desperate eyes. She undid Travis's harness and was trying to manhandle him onto the floor of the Mastiff when the gunner arrived.

"What's going on?" Even though he was shouting, his Welsh accent was obvious.

"Help me get him on the floor, Taff!" Lizzie shouted back. "I think he's hurt." Between them, they managed to get Travis onto the floor of the vehicle. "Can we stop? I need some light as well."

Taff disappeared for a few seconds. Then the lights in the back of the Mastiff came on, but there was no obvious change in the Mastiff's speed. His face reappeared next to Lizzie.

"We'll be stopping in a moment. Just need to get to safety. What can I do?" he said, his concern obvious.

"What medical kit have you got?"

"Not much. Let me grab it."

"Get the oxygen as well." Lizzie undid Travis's helmet strap and eased it from his head. She could see that his lips had a faint bluish discolouration. When Taff handed her the oxygen cylinder, Lizzie checked the gauge on the top. It was almost half-full. She slipped the mask over Travis's mouth and nose and turned the dial up as far as it would go.

"Here you go, mate," Taff said as he put a camouflage bag with a Red Cross on the exterior next to Lizzie. She opened it, looked inside, and then upended the bag to tip the entire contents out. It wasn't much more than a first aid kit.

"Focus, Lizzie," she muttered as she looked at Travis's face. "No obvious catastrophic haemorrhage. Airway looks good. No need for an adjunct." She glanced at the contents of the medical bag. "Not that I've bloody got one." She watched for a few seconds as Travis took a couple of breaths, watching his chest and neck as he did so. "Resps are shallow, trachea looks central, but he's still cyanosed even with oxygen."

"What's going on, Lizzie?" Taff asked as the Mastiff started to slow down.

"Not now, Taff. Bit busy. Can you go and tell the driver to turn the engine off when we've stopped? We need a 9-line as well."

Lizzie's training gradually took over as the Mastiff stopped. She and Taff managed to get Travis's body armour off, and she undid his combats to get to his chest. She watched him take another couple of deep breaths.

"Air entry looks equal." She ran her eyes over his chest. "No obvious injuries, no bruising. Taff? Have you got any scissors?"

"I've got a knife." Taff handed her his own multitool, its blade extended, and Lizzie remembered Travis using his to free her harness just moments before. Her fingers were shaking as she used it to slice up the sleeves of Travis's combats. She took the opportunity to check his heart rate again. It was racing—well over a hundred beats a minute, probably more—but she could only just feel his pulse. Lizzie didn't need the exact rate to know that Travis was in trouble.

"I need to roll him over," Lizzie said as the engine of the Mastiff was turned off. The driver, a gunner who Lizzie didn't know, appeared a few seconds later. "Get his head," Lizzie barked at him. "Me and Taff are going to roll him. On three, Taff, right?"

Lizzie counted to three and, with the driver supporting Travis's head, they rolled him onto his side. After making sure that Taff had a good grip of Travis, she peeled his combats from his body to look at his back.

When she saw the small blackened hole just above Travis's shoulder blade, Lizzie felt her own heart start to race.

"Oh, fuck," she whispered before returning her voice to normal. "Okay, let's put him back down." They lay Travis back down on the floor of the armoured vehicle and Lizzie turned to the driver.

"Get on the Bowman and raise a 9-line. We've got a Cat A patient, haemodynamically compromised. We need the TRT and we need it now." She looked at the pathetic array of medical equipment she had available. There was nothing in it that she could use to help Travis.

"Haemo what?" the driver asked.

"Just get me a fucking helicopter with a medical team," Lizzie barked back at him, "before this man bleeds to death in front of us."

82

"Morning, Simpkins," Adams said to the operations officer. They were standing in an area known as the courtyard of the TLS building that served as an unofficial smoking area. Dappled sunshine was coming through a camouflage net that covered a large hole in the ceiling. The hole wasn't an original feature, but one made by a large unguided bomb that a lucky pilot had managed to put through the roof to say hello to the Taliban who had been inside at the time. "Another rude awakening this morning. Where did they come down?"

"Near the perimeter fence on the east side of the base," Simpkins replied, sipping his coffee. "The EOD lot are over there now, but there's nothing for them to do, apparently."

"Better there than here, I guess."

"Definitely. Much else going on?"

"Don't think so, mate, no," Simpkins replied, stubbing his cigarette out in an overflowing ashtray. Adams looked at the army officer, wondering whether to pick him up for calling him mate. Technically, Simpkins should have called him sir, but seeing as only a few days ago Adams was still a flight lieutenant, it didn't seem right. "I think there's a message for you in the ops room."

"Okay, cheers. I'll nip down there now."

"I need to get back, so I'll come with you."

Adams and Simpkins walked down the corridor of the building to the door of the ops room. At least with Simpkins, Adams wouldn't have to knock and wait like an errant schoolchild who had been sent to the headmaster. Simpkins entered the code into the Simplex lock on the door, and Adams followed him through into the room. He searched his desk for a moment until he found a small yellow sticky note, which he handed to Adams. On it were the words *Medical Advisor—call the hospital*. In one corner of the room, a lieutenant was sitting at a screen, staring intently at it.

"Simpkins, could you come and have a look at this, please?"

Adams followed Simpkins as he walked over to look at the screen. It was open to JChat, a chat room used across Afghanistan by pretty much everyone in uniform.

"What've we got?" Simpkins asked.

"There's a contact at this grid." The lieutenant stabbed at the screen. "That's not far away from the base." Adams felt his chest start to tighten as he thought about which troops would be in the area.

He leaned forward to read the report on the screen. There wasn't a great deal of information, but there generally wasn't. When people were under fire, they tended to be quite brief with the initial report. All Adams could see was a callsign, and the words *CONTACT—WAIT OUT*.

"Which callsign is that?" Adams asked the lieutenant.

"Regiment." Adams's chest tightened even further as the lieutenant continued. "That's the patrol that left at first light this morning." It was Lizzie's patrol.

In the opposite corner of the room, a phone rang loudly, making Adams start.

"9-line," Simpkins muttered under his breath as he crossed the room. Adams's mouth had gone dry, and he suddenly wanted to sit down. Lizzie was out on that patrol. He listened as Simpkins repeated the words that the caller was giving him, using the standard request for a medevac. The only line that Adams was interested in was the third line—the number and type of casualties.

"Line three," Simpkins said. "One Cat A."

Adams's stomach flipped over, and he rushed to the door of the ops room. He left without a word and hurried back to his office, wondering for a moment if he was going to be sick. What if it was Lizzie? His Lizzie? When he got to his office, he picked up a bottle of water and took a small sip from it before sitting on the sofa he and Lizzie had sat on the previous evening and put his head in his hands.

If the helicopter detachment wasn't at the other end of the base, a good fifteen minutes' drive away, he would have got in his car to go down there and demand to be let on the back of the Chinook, using his rank if necessary. He had the skills and experience to just slot into the existing Trauma Response Team. But he knew that by the time he got to the pan, the helicopter with them on board would have already left. There was nothing he could do. In Adams's hand was the yellow note that Simpkins had handed him earlier.

Adams got to his feet and left his office quickly. The only thing he could do was go to the hospital. At least then, if Lizzie was the casualty, he would be there for her.

A FEW MOMENTS LATER, Adams pulled up outside the hospital. When he had been a few hundred metres away from the main entrance, a Chinook had flashed over his head on its way toward the perimeter of the base, its downwash rocking his car. It could only be the TRT, and from the way it was being flown, the pilot was in a hurry. That suited Adams fine.

He parked his car and walked through the main entrance before making his way to the emergency room. When he opened the door, he saw Adèle coordinating some of the other nurses. She smiled at him and waved before holding up two fingers and mouthing the words two minutes. Adams watched her as she made sure her team was prepared for the incoming casualty. She was working methodically, quietly instructing the nurses. It was something he had done hundreds of times himself, and he hoped that the way he did it was as effective as the way she was.

"Adams," Adèle said a moment later, smiling warmly at him as she approached. "How are you?" When she reached the area he was standing in, her smile faded and was replaced by a frown. "What's wrong?"

"Nothing, nothing," he said, waving his hand dismissively.

"Well, I don't believe you," Adèle replied, her smile almost returning. "We've got a casualty coming in soon, but I did want to speak to you about something else at some point."

"What's the casualty?"

"We've not got much information, just that it's a Cat A with a gunshot wound to the shoulder and smoke inhalation." Adèle was looking at Adams curiously. He was desperate to ask if she knew if it was a male or female casualty, but he knew that it would be a really odd question that she wouldn't know the answer to, anyway.

"Do you need any help?" Adams asked. Adèle looked at the rest of the team in the emergency room before replying.

"Not unless you've suddenly become fluent in French."

"Oh, okay," Adams replied.

"You're welcome to hang around and observe, though. You look like you want to?"

Adams didn't know whether to be relieved that Adèle had offered, or annoyed with himself for being so obvious.

"If you don't mind, that would be great."

83

Adèle left Adams to his own devices and returned to her team.

"Tout le monde est prêt?" she asked them. *Is everyone ready?* She received some nervous nods in reply, but that was fine by her. Nervousness was fine. It kept people on their toes and stopped them from making stupid mistakes.

Adèle glanced across at Adams, who was worrying the skin around his fingers with his teeth. She needed to speak to him about the incident with Delaney, but couldn't do it now with a casualty inbound. Besides, he was distracted about something. He hadn't told her what, but Adèle was long enough in the tooth to read the man. That was the main reason she'd suggested he should stay in the emergency room. So that she could keep an eye on him, as well as everything else that was going on.

"Okay, people," Adèle called out in French. "We've got about fifteen to twenty minutes before the helicopter gets back. Now is the time to go for a pee if you've not been already."

Two of the nurses glanced at each other and disappeared, while the rest just milled about the trauma bay. Adèle cast her eyes over the equipment that they'd spent the last few moments preparing. They were ready for whatever was thrown at them.

"Adams, come with me," Adèle said. "We have a few minutes, and they're all set." She led him out into the empty corridor outside the emergency room. "What's wrong? And don't tell me nothing." She gave him a look intended to be half stern, half motherly.

"This casualty you have coming in," he said after regarding her for a few seconds, "it might be a good friend of mine. She's out on that patrol."

"She?" Adèle asked. "Are you sure? The patrols don't normally have female members."

"She's a paramedic, not a gunner," Adams replied. "She was out with the patrol yesterday that took the casualty from the sniper as well."

Adèle looked at him closely. She wanted to give the man a hug and tell him everything would be okay, even though they both would know it might not be, but her instincts told her that if she as much as put a hand on him, he would break down. Adèle knew without asking that whoever this woman was, she was more to Adams than a good friend.

"Okay, well you know that if she is hurt, she will be in the best hands."

"I know, I'm just worried, that's all." Adams took a deep breath and sighed. "What was it you wanted to speak to me about?"

"Of course you are," Adèle said with a wan smile. "That other thing can wait if you want?"

"No, let's chat about it now if you have time? It would be good to have something else to think about."

"Sure," Adèle said, "let's grab a coffee." She glanced toward the emergency room. "They're all set in there and, besides, we'll hear the helicopter."

The two of them walked slowly down the hospital corridor toward Adèle's office, talking as they did so.

"You know Isobel, the nurse you met the other day?" Adèle asked Adams.

"The pretty one?" Adams replied, making her laugh.

"What? The rest of us aren't? Yes, the pretty one," she said. "She was attacked last night." Adams stopped and stared at her.

"Is she okay?"

"She's fine, just a bit shaken up. One of my team was able to intervene before anything too serious happened." Adèle continued walking and Adams followed. "But she doesn't want anyone to know about it."

"Does she know who her attacker was?" Adams asked.

"Yes." Adèle stopped just outside her office door. "It was a contractor. Mark Delaney?"

"I've not long come from his office. The two of them were in the coffee shop last night," Adams said. "It did look like they'd had a bit of a barney, and when I saw him just now he had a black eye. That would be one of your team intervening, I take it?"

Despite still being annoyed with Laurent, Adèle smiled as she walked into her office, followed by Adams.

"Yes," she replied.

"I don't suppose you've got a BNF?" Adams asked. "I need to look something up."

"Sorry, BNF?"

"British National Formulary."

"Um, no. I have a Canadian version, but it's in French. You're welcome to use the computer though?"

Adams thanked her and crossed to the computer sitting in the corner of the room. Adèle watched as he navigated his way to the British National Formulary web page. She looked over his shoulder as he typed in the names of some drugs.

"When I was in his office yesterday, there were some medication bottles lying around," he said as he peered at the screen. "They were all prescribed to him, but I didn't recognise the drugs. This is one of them." He pointed at the screen, and Adèle read the text underneath the name of the drug.

"Wow, that's a pretty potent anti-psychotic," she whispered. Adams typed in the name of another drug.

"So's that one," he said. "I did think he was a bit jittery earlier. How on earth did he get out here when he's on that lot?"

"He's a contractor," Adèle replied with a sigh. "We've had quite a few in with things we don't see often in the military. Cardiac problems, diabetes. All sorts."

"How did he meet Isobel?"

"Delaney was a patient here a few days ago. He cut his hand." Adèle looked at Adams. "That's how he met her. They went for a coffee and it seems he misinterpreted it as her being somehow interested in him."

"Oh, that's not good. I take it she isn't?"

"Far from it. But it seems he didn't take it too well." Adèle opened her office door and led Adams inside, asking him what he wanted to drink before making her way to the kettle. "But even though Isobel doesn't want to do anything about it, I can't do nothing."

"Absolutely. So what do you want me to do?"

"Can you speak to the base commander? Just tell him about the attack, but not who was the victim."

"Of course. When you say she was attacked, can I ask what he did?"

"He touched her breasts and had his hands around her neck when my colleague intervened." Adèle started making them both a cup of tea. "It was one of the majors who works for me. I'd asked him to keep an eye on Isobel."

"Thank God you did," Adams replied with a frown. "Imagine if you hadn't."

"I'd rather not, Adams."

"That does sound like quite a serious sexual assault, though. Wouldn't the police be more appropriate?"

"She won't give a statement." She looked at him in exasperation. "Believe me, I've tried."

"What about the major? If he saw what happened then he could report it? They wouldn't even need to speak to Isobel, I wouldn't have thought."

Adèle paused for a moment, suddenly feeling foolish. Neither she nor Laurent had considered that approach. The only problem with it was that Laurent had hit the contractor, even though he was more than capable of stopping the assault without resorting to violence.

"It's an option," she said, "but Laurent struck this Delaney man quite hard. I wouldn't want him to get into trouble over it."

"You said Isobel won't talk to the police?"

"That's correct."

"So who's going to tell the police that your major hit Delaney? Maybe he fell down some steps or something?" Adams asked her. "It would just be the contractor's word against his. Who would they believe? A commissioned officer in the Canadian Armed Forces or a civilian contractor who's just been caught sexually assaulting a young woman?"

A slow smile crossed Adèle's face as she considered the approach.

"You know something, Adams?" she said as she handed him his mug of tea. "You're quite devious for a nurse, aren't you?"

In the distance, Adèle could hear a faint but very familiar noise. From the sudden look of anguish on Adams's face, he could obviously hear the same thing.

"Maybe we don't have time for a cup of coffee, after all?" Adèle muttered as she put her cup on the table and made her way to the door.

Adams was only a few inches behind her.

84

Lizzie almost fell from her seat in the back of the Chinook when it landed harder than she was expecting. She had spent the short flight struggling not to vomit, not helped by the medic's insistence on her wearing an oxygen mask throughout the flight. While the rest of the gunners were helping to load Travis onto a stretcher, she had been led to the front of the helicopter where an oxygen saturation monitor was placed on her finger. Lizzie had looked at the screen and could see that her heart was racing far quicker than it should have been, and that her oxygen saturations were low. But apart from the oxygen mask, she'd been given no other treatment or further assessed. This didn't bother her in the slightest. She would much prefer the team worked on Travis, anyway.

Lizzie watched the medical team as they gathered up their equipment and got ready to move the stretcher with Travis on. He was covered with a blanket and had a large monitor that trailed wires toward his body between his legs. One of the medical team shut off the two large-bore intravenous lines that the team had put in during the flight and placed the bags of fluid next to the monitor.

She could see through the wide opening at the back of the helicopter that there was an ambulance waiting at the edge of the landing pad with some medics making their way toward the ramp. They were crouched over as they approached, but were still being buffeted by the downwash from the rotor blades. Lizzie closed her eyes for a few seconds as the frame of the large helicopter settled from the landing. She wanted to get up and help, but didn't feel well enough to stand.

Shaking her head, Lizzie lurched to her feet. She was at least going to try. As soon as she stood, a wave of dizziness hit her and she sat back down in the canvas webbing seat with a thump, pulling the oxygen mask from her face as she did so. Lizzie watched Travis being carried out to the ambulance and, above her head, she heard the rotor blades slowing down. She closed her eyes again, realising that she was on the verge of passing out. And a few seconds later, that's exactly what happened.

WHEN SHE CAME to a few minutes later—although it could have been hours for all she knew—she was staring at the roof of the helicopter. The only sound she could hear was the faint metallic ticking of the enormous engines above her as they cooled down. She was lying on a stretcher with a large plastic box under her feet, raising them into the air.

"Hey, Sergeant Jarman," a male voice said. "You're back with us, I see?" Lizzie looked to see the medic who had led her into the helicopter smiling at her. She didn't recognise him, which was unusual. The medical services in the RAF were pretty small, and almost everyone knew everyone. She opened her mouth to speak, but only a croak came out. "Here," the medic said, passing her a bottle of water. "Have some of this. I'm Corporal Goodson, by the way." He looked young, early twenties at most, and Lizzie didn't think he could have been out of training for that long.

"Hi," Lizzie managed before she took a sip of the water. It was freezing and tasted of soot.

"Your blood pressure's a bit on the low side," the corporal said, taking the bottle from her and replacing her oxygen mask. "That's probably why you keeled over. The ambulance is just dropping your friend off at the hospital and then they're coming back for you."

Lizzie tried to sit up, but the corporal put his hand on her shoulder to stop her.

"Please, I need to see him," she said. "Let me get up."

"Nope," Corporal Goodson replied. "You're not going anywhere until that ambulance comes back." Lizzie lay back down, knowing that the young medic was right, but she was desperate to see Travis.

She closed her eyes again, opening them when she heard a commotion at the back of the helicopter. She lifted her head to see Adams picking his way through the medical equipment that was strewn all over the floor. As he reached her, she managed to sit up, this time unopposed by the corporal. Adams knelt down next to the stretcher and stared at Lizzie with a look of horror on his face. Then he wrapped his arms around her and hugged her tightly.

"Don't you ever," he said in her ear, "don't you ever do that to me again." Lizzie didn't reply, wanting to hold on to him for as long as she could.

"How's Travis?" she said a few seconds later. "Do you know how he's getting on?"

"I don't," Adams replied. "They took him into the emergency room and I came straight here." She disentangled her arms and looked at him.

"Did you run all the way down here?" Lizzie asked. "Only you've got a face like a tomato."

"I had to run the last few hundred metres," Adams said, an easy smile crinkling his face. "I didn't think the pilot would appreciate me screaming up and parking right behind his helicopter." He turned to the corporal, who was starting to tidy away the equipment and rubbish from the medical team's work on Travis. "Hey, corporal? Have you got any baby wipes or anything like that?"

Corporal Goodson opened one of the medical bags and pulled out a packet which he threw across to Adams. Lizzie watched as Adams opened the packet, his fingers trembling, and pulled out a wipe. He used it to mop Lizzie's forehead and, when he showed it to her, it was black with soot.

"What the hell happened to you, Lizzie?" he said as he pulled more wipes from the packet.

"We got hit with an RPG. I didn't see it until the last second. There was nothing I could do. Then the Ridgeback just went up in flames. It must have gone in under the armour." She took a deep breath, determined not to cry. "I was completely trapped. Travis got me out and at some point took a round to the shoulder. I don't think he even noticed."

"Bloody hell, Lizzie," Adams said, wiping her cheeks down. "I'm going to buy that man a pint as soon as I can. Maybe even two."

"I'm sure he'd appreciate that." Lizzie managed a weak

smile. "I could murder a glass of Pinot Grigio if you're buying?"

"That's more like it," Adams replied. "It's just a shame the nearest one's several thousand miles away from this dump."

They both looked toward the back of the helicopter at the sound of a vehicle. Lizzie could see an ambulance pulling up and, when it screeched to a halt, a female nurse in Canadian combats got out of the passenger's side. She stepped up onto the ramp of the helicopter and made her way toward them, whispering something to Corporal Goodson as she passed him. Lizzie's heart started racing as the British medic started walking back toward the ramp.

"Adèle?" Lizzie heard Adams whisper.

As the nurse knelt down by the stretcher, Lizzie looked at the older woman before bursting into tears. Lizzie knew what she was about to say.

"No, no, no," she sobbed as Adams put his arm around her shoulder.

"Ma cherie," the nurse said, "I'm afraid I have some awful news for you."

85

Delaney squinted at the screen in front of him, grinding his teeth and bouncing his hand on his leg. It was perfect. He was looking at a camera feed from the radar installation by the poo pond, and could see all four machine gun emplacements. He'd set the radar to track a drone that was flying over the range area several kilometres away, and he could see the guns making minute adjustments as the drone changed path.

On the screen in front of him, he could see a cargo plane on finals, so he switched the targeting to the plane as it lumbered its way toward the runway. Exactly as they were supposed to do, the machine guns tracked the plane as it flew past, swivelling round to keep themselves on target.

"Excellent," Delaney muttered, wishing that his jaw would stop aching. Maybe he should speak to Isobel, see if she could get him something to stop it from the hospital pharmacy? Of course she would. Isobel would do anything for Delaney, he knew that.

Delaney tapped a few commands into the computer to turn the tracking mode of the radar and its sentries into the mode he'd designed to track incoming rockets before arming the machine guns. Now anything that approached the base at a speed of over one thousand feet per second in an arc would be destroyed seconds after the radar had picked it up.

He closed down the radar software and opened up his secure e-mail client.

It's all fully operational. The reply came less than a minute later.

Excellent. Let it take out a few rockets and feed back the performance.

That was it. No thanks, no appreciation. Just a request for feedback. Delaney wasn't even going to dignify that with a reply. They didn't know who they were dealing with, that was the problem. He could tell them, but he thought they would probably be too stupid to understand. Delaney started giggling when he thought about how far he had come and in such a short space of time. Finally, he was beginning to see clearly exactly how much power he was wielding, and that was thanks to Isobel. She had opened his eyes and made him see.

Delaney opened and closed his mouth a couple of times to try to relieve the tension in his jaw muscles, but it didn't work. He got to his feet and crossed to the fridge, getting a can of soda to press against the side of his face. That had some effect, but he could hardly walk around with a can of soda strapped to both sides of his face, could he?

He was still laughing when he heard a knock at his office door. Delaney looked at his watch. Was it Isobel? If it was, she was early. He'd not instructed her to be here until after dark. Perhaps, when she had heard his message inside her head and realised that he could talk to her that way, she had been so excited that she'd decided to come straight away? He grinned as he realised that must be the case.

As Delaney crossed to the door to let her in, he checked himself quickly in the mirror. Apart from the bruise on his face where that pathetic soldier had hit him, he was looking good. He licked his index fingers and smoothed his eyebrows down, concentrating hard to see if he could hear Isobel messaging him in his head. There was nothing, but that was to be expected. She would need to be shown how to develop the ability to speak as well as hear. But Delaney could teach her how to do that, just like he'd taught himself.

There were two surprises when Delaney opened the door. The first was that it wasn't Isobel. The second was the punch he received to the abdomen from the soldier who was standing outside his office.

Delaney gasped, doubling over in agony, as a large pair of hands dragged him into his office and threw him into one of the chairs. The chair wobbled a couple of times, but it wasn't until the soldier brought his fist round in another punch—this time to the side of Delaney's head—that he fell out of it and onto the floor.

He curled himself up into a foetal position, certain that more blows were coming, but there were none. Shaking his head to dispel the ringing in his ears and struggling to take a breath, Delaney opened his eyes to see who his attacker was. At first, he thought it was the same soldier who'd interrupted him and Isobel in the shelter, but as his eyes focused on the other man, Delaney realised it was the one who had been sitting with Isobel in the coffee shop. The man looked at him with utter disdain and said something in French. He was large, far bigger than Delaney was, and very angry.

"Ow does it feel?" the soldier said in heavily accented English, not pronouncing the first *h* like Isobel often did. In contrast, there was nothing attractive about the way that this man did that. "To be," he continued, "without a defence?"

"Do you mean defenceless?" Delaney replied, forcing a laugh out of his mouth. "You stupid Canadian idiot." He was rewarded by the soldier following up his punch to Delaney's stomach, but this time with a boot.

Delaney closed his eyes as he fought to breathe through the pain and sent an urgent message to Isobel to come and get this brute away from him. He didn't mind the pain—it was only physical and wouldn't last—but what if this man was going to kill him? The next kick was much, much harder and aimed at Delaney's ribcage. He felt, rather than heard, a bone breaking. Perhaps more than one? The pain in his chest was instantaneous and agonising.

The next thing Delaney knew, the soldier was kneeling down next to him, dragging him up off the floor so he was in a sitting position. He put his face inches away from Delaney's, so close that when he spoke, flecks of spittle flew onto Delaney's cheeks.

"If you go within fifty metres of her ever again," the soldier said, pronouncing every word carefully and with venom, "I will kill you." He stared at Delaney, his eyes clear blue and burning with intensity. "Do you understand?"

Delaney paused before replying, taking a shallow breath that hurt like a knife. He wanted to tell this stupid

Canuck to fuck off, but knew that would only provoke him even more. Delaney nodded his head slowly.

"I understand," he said, trying to sound as sincere as he could. This man wouldn't know about the connection that he and Isobel had.

The soldier pulled his head back and Delaney thought he was about to stand. Then he drove it forward and into Delaney's face, his forehead impacting with Delaney's nose and causing a blinding flash of light.

As everything faded to black, Delaney quite clearly heard Isobel's voice in his head.

"Mark?" she was saying. "Are you there?"

86

Adams jumped as the telephone on his desk rang, and he dropped the barrel of his pistol onto his desk. It was the first time since he had arrived that anyone had called him, and he hadn't been expecting the phone to be as loud as it was.

"Squadron Leader Adams?" he said as he picked up the receiver. Adams almost used his previous rank, but caught himself just in time.

"Hello, sir." It was Simpkins, the operations officer. "Could you pop down to the main briefing room, please? The boss wants his command team all in there for a brief."

"Sure, I'm on my way." He took a moment to reassemble his pistol before sliding the magazine back into place with a satisfying click and placing it in his holster. He had almost finished cleaning it anyway when the phone had rung.

Adams got to his feet and put his hands to the small of his back to stretch. He was exhausted and could happily have slept, perhaps even on the sofa in his office. Adams knew that it was a comedown from the adrenaline that had been coursing through him before he'd found out that Lizzie was okay. Or at least, if not okay, not badly injured. When he walked out of his office into the corridor, he almost walked into Air Commodore Maugham.

"Ah, Adams," Maugham said. "Quick word in your office?" Adams turned and walked back in, followed by the air commodore. "I hear you were at the hospital just now. What can you tell me about the casualties?"

"Um, two casualties from the incident, sir," Adams replied. "One died in the emergency room, the other one's doing okay. She's inhaled a lot of smoke but should be fine."

"She?"

"Sergeant Lizzie Jarman, sir," Adams said. "You met her the other day."

"Oh my Lord, well thank goodness your friend's okay. Did you know the chap who died?"

"No, sir. I know his name—Corporal Perkins—but I'd not met him."

"Have you spoken to your friend, Sergeant Jarman?"

"I have, sir, yes."

"Did she say what happened? The initial reports from the scene were a bit confusing. Or Simpkins was a bit confused. Probably both. I know I'm about to be briefed, but I'd like to hear what you know if that's okay?"

Adams was thrown by being asked by a senior officer if it was okay for him to speak. He thought back to what Lizzie had told him in the hospital before Adèle had shooed him away, telling Adams that Lizzie needed to rest.

"They got hit with an RPG. It must have got through the armour somehow and it started a fire in the engine. Lizzie only just managed to get out. Her harness was buckled, but Corporal Perkins managed to free her and carry her to the Mastiff."

"Good lad," Maugham said, nodding for Adams to continue. Knowing the air commodore was talking about Corporal Perkins and not him, Adams did just that.

"He must have taken a round in the shoulder while he was carrying Lizzie. One of the nurses told me that the entry point was just by his shoulder blade and there was no exit wound." Maugham frowned in response. "The bullet could have gone anywhere in his thoracic cavity, or even further."

"Good grief," Maugham said. "How awful. So unsurvivable, then?"

"I'm afraid so, sir."

"Right, thank you."

"Sir, can I grab five minutes of your time at some point later?" Adams asked the base commander. He needed to talk to him about Delaney and what had happened between the contractor and Isobel.

"Of course, is after the brief okay?" Adams nodded in reply.

Maugham turned and left Adams's office. Adams hurried after him as he strode down the corridor. When he reached the briefing room, the base commander threw the door open. Inside the room, several people braced up at his arrival with one or two trying to stand.

"As you were," Maugham barked, marching to the front of the room. "Right, Simpkins. Sitrep, please?"

Adams took one of the few spare seats at the back of the briefing room and listened while Simpkins gave a hesitant but reasonably comprehensive brief on the events of the day.

"Well, ladies and gentlemen," Maugham said when

Simpkins had finished speaking. "I've spoken with PJHQ back in the UK about this, and it's gone all the way up to the ministers. Losses like the ones over the last few days just aren't sustainable, and the Prime Minister's getting a right old kicking in the media. The death today is only going to make that worse. So I've made the decision to discontinue patrols around the perimeter."

There was a silence in the room as the occupants processed this information. Adams was relieved by the news, not just for Lizzie, although it wasn't clear whether she would be going back out on patrol or straight back home as a battle casualty. He desperately wanted it to be the latter, but had no influence over the decision.

"Are you sure that's wise, sir?" A female officer sitting near the front of the room asked.

"No, Hayley," Maugham replied, "I'm not. But I have no choice. Since they've started patrolling, the only real effect that the regiment has had is on the medical evacuation chain."

"How long for, sir?" It was the same officer who'd asked the previous question.

"We'll re-evaluate it in a week or so," Maugham said. "By then, we should have a good idea of how well this Steel Sky system works. At the moment, if I understand correctly and someone please correct me if I have this wrong, about five square kilometres of our most valuable assets are protected. If it's as good as it's supposed to be, then I've got authorisation to buy a further six systems for coverage of the entire base."

The air commodore concluded the brief a few moments later, striding out of the room, and everyone in the room started talking as soon as he had left. Adams got to his feet and made his way to the air commodore's office to tell him about Delaney.

"That's all I bloody well need," Maugham muttered when Adams had briefed him on this incident. He picked up the phone on his desk and jabbed at the buttons on it. "Hayley? My office, please." Maugham looked at Adams as he put the phone down. "Hayley's my chief engineering officer," he explained. Adams frowned, not understanding what an engineer could do about the situation.

A few moments later, there was a tap at the door. Maugham glanced at Adams with a brief smile as he took up his standard position behind his desk.

"Enter," Maugham barked. The door opened, and the woman from the briefing walked in. She looked to Adams to be in her mid-forties and was wearing a lieutenant colonel rank slide on her combats. "Hayley, meet Adams. He's my medical advisor. Adams, this is Hayley."

"Ma'am," Adams said with a nod in the engineer's direction. She didn't even look at him, let alone acknowledge him.

"Hayley, this Steel Sky system?"

"Yes, sir?"

"Can you maintain and run it?"

"We've got contractors for that, sir," she replied.

"We've got one contractor left for that, and he's about to be arrested. So can you run it until they send a replacement?"

Adams saw a smile spread across Hayley's face as she replied.

"I'd love to, sir," she replied.

"Very good. Adams? Go and find my chief rozzer. He'll be lounging around the smoking area in the courtyard pretending he's really busy, but don't worry if you can't find him. I'll catch him in morning prayers first thing tomorrow."

Adams glanced at the chief engineer, who was still ignoring him before turning to walk toward the office door.

"Yes, sir," Adams replied. "Leave it with me."

87

"How are you feeling, Sergeant Jarman?" Adèle asked as she walked into the ward area of the hospital. In Adèle's hands were some pieces of paper with an almost indecipherable series of words and numbers.

"Not too bad, ma'am, thank you." Lizzie's voice was husky, and from the way she winced when she talked, Adèle could tell that her throat was painful.

"Please," Adèle replied. "It's Adèle. Now, I have some good news and some bad news." She held up the papers in her hand. "Do you want the bad news first?" Adèle smiled as she said this to try to reassure the young woman in front of her that the bad news wasn't really that bad.

"Okay."

"So, your chest x-ray is clear, but your blood results are not so good. I have your arterial blood gas results." Adèle squinted at the paper in front of her while Lizzie fiddled with a small square of gauze taped to the inside of her wrist. "You have a degree of arterial hypoxameia and reduced oxyhaemoglobin saturation."

"Okay, what does that mean? I'm a paramedic, not a nurse, don't forget." Adèle saw a faint smile on her face as she said this.

"You don't have enough oxygen in your blood. You'll need some more chest x-rays and blood gasses over the next few days, but we're worried about inhalation injury."

"Great," Lizzie replied, smiling at Adèle. "More blood gasses. Is that the bad news?"

"Not really, no," Adèle replied. "The problem with an inhalation injury like yours is that it could get worse. It could, potentially, get quite a bit worse, but that's rare. If it does happen though, a field hospital in Afghanistan is not the place to be. Which is the good news."

"Sorry, I'm not following?"

"You're going home, Lizzie. There's a medical team on their way from Cyprus to get you. They'll be here later today. This evening, I think."

"Seriously?" Lizzie said, her eyebrows raised. "But I've only been here for a few days."

"That doesn't matter," Adèle replied. "You're going home. No arguments."

Adèle wasn't surprised that the look on Lizzie's face was one of pure relief. The poor girl had been through so much over the last couple of days based on what Adams had told her. More than most people experienced in an entire career, let alone a single tour of duty. She wasn't going to tell Lizzie, but Adèle had pushed the British doctor back in the United Kingdom as hard as she could to make sure that he made the right decision for her.

"They're on their way now?" Lizzie asked.

"Yes, they left an hour or so ago, apparently. Your friend, the one who died? He will be on the same plane with you."

"Travis?" Lizzie whispered.

"That was his name?" Adèle reached forward and took Lizzie's hand.

"Yes, kind of. It's, it was, his nickname. His last name was Perkins. So, Travis Perkins."

"I don't understand."

"It's a shop back home. It's a military thing. Like if your last name's *Bell* then you're known as *Dinger*, whatever your real first name is."

"Oh, I see. What was his actual name?" Adèle watched as tears welled up in Lizzie's eyes. She squeezed her hand reassuringly.

"I don't know," Lizzie replied in a whisper. "I only ever knew him as Travis." Adèle looked at Lizzie and her heart went out to her. "Do you know what time the flight is?"

"Not exactly, no. But it will be this evening. It's quite full as one of your regiments is in the middle of a, um, I'm not sure what the correct word is in English."

"Roulement?"

"Vous parlez français?" Adèle said with a laugh. *You speak French?*

"No, er, I mean, non." Lizzie managed a wan smile. "Will I be able to see Adams before I go?"

"Of course you will," Adèle replied. "I will make sure of it."

A FEW HOURS LATER, Adèle was sitting in her office finishing some paperwork from the day shift when there was a tap at her thin plywood door. A few seconds later, Major Laurent's head appeared around it.

"Adèle?" he said. "Vous avez un visiteur." *You have a visitor.* He stepped back to let Adams walk into the office.

"Hey, Adèle," he said as he entered. "I hope I'm not disturbing you?"

"Not at all," Adèle replied, putting down her pen. "Laurent was just about to make some coffee, weren't you?" With a frown, Laurent crossed over to the kettle and flicked it on with an irritated glance in her direction.

"I got a bit of a garbled message from the ops room in the TLS," Adams said, sitting down in one of the chairs. "I know there was a message from earlier, but the ops officer wasn't sure if it was a new message or another copy of the old message."

"It was a separate one," Adèle replied with a laugh. "I wanted to let you know that your friend, Lizzie, is going to be flying back to the United Kingdom this evening."

"Oh, thank goodness for that," Adams said, breathing a sigh of relief. "The thought of her going back out there was really preying on my mind." Adèle frowned, trying to understand what he had just said. Her hand touched the crucifix around her neck. Was it that sort of praying or had she misunderstood him? "Is she on the regular trooper flight?"

"I think so, yes. It's very busy, I understand, but they've made room for her."

"They always will make room for casualties. No one minds being delayed if they've been bumped for someone with a medical team. Can I see her?"

"Of course," Adèle said. "I'll take you down there in a few moments."

"How do you take your coffee, Adams?" Laurent asked as he spooned instant coffee into three mugs.

"Julie Andrews, please."

"I'm sorry?" Laurent replied with a quizzical expression.

"White, with no sugar. White, none." Adèle watched as Laurent's frown deepened. "White nun? The Sound of Music?"

Adèle started laughing as she realised that Laurent had absolutely no idea what Adams was talking about. She switched to French and explained the joke, but Laurent didn't seem to see the funny side of it.

"I spoke to Air Commodore Maugham earlier about what happened to Isobel," Adams said before thanking Laurent as he passed him his coffee.

"What did he say?" Adèle asked.

"He was furious. He sent me to look for his Chief of Police, but I couldn't find the man anywhere. Bloody scuffers." In the past, military police officers had dragged soldiers who had fainted from parade grounds, making sure that as they did so, they scuffed the soldier's highly bulled shoes. Even though this was a long time ago, the nickname had stuck.

Adams took a sip of his drink. "This coffee's lovely. I'll be coming here more often. How is Isobel doing, anyway?"

"I've not seen her today. Laurent? Have you?"

Laurent glanced at his watch before replying.

"She's on the night shift so she'll be here in few hours. I'll check on her then."

Adèle got to her feet and walked over to collect her coffee, noting with irritation that Laurent hadn't brought it to her. He could be really petulant at times, but she decided against saying anything to him in front of Adams.

"Come on Adams, bring your coffee with you," Adèle said. "I'll take you down to the ward to speak to Lizzie."

88

Delaney winced as he touched his fingers to the bridge of his nose. The slightest touch sent a white-hot shard of pain into what felt like the centre of his brain. He knew it wasn't actually in his brain, but it certainly felt like it.

He didn't think his nose was actually broken. From what he could tell it was still straight. It was just bloody painful and he couldn't breathe through his nostrils any more. Not that the second part was a problem. He could only take shallow breaths, anyway. Any more than that caused a similar pain in his chest, but that pain went into his heart, not into his brain.

That soldier had been lucky, Delaney thought as he dabbed tenderly at his nostrils with a tissue. Bloody lucky. If Delaney had wanted to, he could have easily killed him. But he hadn't and was the better man for it. Besides, Delaney could wait. At some point, the soldier would wish he'd never been born. Him and all his mates. It didn't matter what nationality they were. Anyone in a military uniform—apart, of course, from his Isobel—was now one hundred percent on the other side, and that was not a good place to be.

He rolled the tissue in his fingers to find a bit with no blood on it and was about to dab again at his nose when his computer pinged with an incoming e-mail. Delaney wiggled the mouse to turn the screensaver off.

The e-mail was from back home. More specifically, it was from his old boss. From the man who ran the company that Delaney had been fired from. Except he hadn't actually been fired. It was just made to look that way so that Delaney could get the job at Aeolus.

That data packet you sent was perfect. We've used the full trajectory information to calibrate, and our system is now fully functional. There's no need for any more data, so we don't need to wait. Delaney tried to snort with derision and was rewarded with a blinding dagger in his nose, which caused tears to stream down his face. Delaney swore under his breath and reached for a clean packet of tissues.

"Your system?" he said as he ripped open the packet. "It's not your system, it's my system." The e-mail was referring to his old company's version of the Steel Sky system. The one he'd built with his own hands. The one that was significantly better than Steel Sky, but unfortunately almost twice as expensive. That was why the military had chosen Steel Sky over their system.

Okay, so what now? Delaney typed. He sent the e-mail, knowing that the reply would be quick. He closed his eyes for a second to see if Isobel was trying to reach him, but he couldn't hear her. The only thing he heard was another ping.

Steel Sky has to fail and fail badly. Then they won't have a choice but to buy ours, and you'll already be in place to install it.

Delaney thought for a few moments before composing a reply.

What about when the new engineer gets here? He got to his feet to get a drink from the fridge. As he opened it, the Portakabin shook as a large transport plane flew overhead. A few seconds later, Delaney heard a screech as the plane touched down on the runway. As the plane rumbled away into the distance, his computer pinged again.

He's been in a car accident so won't be coming. They're trying to get a replacement, so whatever you do, it needs to be soon. Make Steel Sky fail badly enough that the military seniors won't dare try to use it again.

Delaney sipped his drink and thought for a few moments. The simplest way for it to fail was for it to just not work. If it let several salvos of rockets through and just sat there idly while they exploded, then that would be a major failure. But would it be bad enough? He closed his eyes again.

"I've got an idea?" It was Isobel! It sounded like she was standing right next to him, but when Delaney flicked his eyes open, she was nowhere to be seen. He closed them again tightly. "Can you hear me?"

"Yes," Delaney messaged her back, pressing his lips together to make sure that he thought the message and didn't actually say it. "I can hear you!"

When Isobel told him her idea, Delaney started chuckling.

"What is it?" she said. "What's funny?"

"Nothing's funny, my darling. Your idea is brilliant. Absolutely bloody perfect."

"I thought it up just for you, Mark, to make you happy."

"That makes me very happy."

"Are you going to do it?" Isobel asked, and Delaney grinned before she continued. "Are we going to *do it* afterwards?"

He closed his eyes as tight as he could and tried sending her a mental image. It was a composite of a photograph he'd found on the internet, but in his head he had replaced the man's face with his, and the woman's with Isobel's. There were two very different releases imminent in the photograph. The man's was primal while the woman's was far more meaningful. On the web page where Delaney had found the image, the photograph was titled 'La petite mort'.

"Do you want to *do it* like that?" he asked her. She laughed in reply, and her voice started fading away. She would get better at communicating this way with practice, Delaney knew.

"Come and get me, Mark," Isobel said as her voice receded into the distance. "I'm waiting for you to come and get me."

With a contented smile, Delaney finished his can of soda. He crushed it and threw it in the direction of the waste bin in the corner of the room, but it missed. As he got to his feet, Delaney realised he could smell something. Something horrible. Something faecal.

Ignoring the pain in his head that the sudden movement caused, Delaney's head jerked from side to side. For an awful second, he thought Rubenstein had come back for him, dripping in human sludge and slurry. But there was no-one else in the Portakabin but him. It was just him and that horrendous smell.

. . .

Later that evening, almost ten o'clock by his watch, Delaney was sitting in the front seat of his van and looking out over the poo pond. As usual for that time of the night, there was a low-lying fog over the surface and immediate perimeter. He knew it was radiation fog, caused by water droplets from the pond being suspended in the air. Once the sun had gone down and the ground started to cool, the air lost the ability to hold the moisture as vapour. He idly wondered if the smell within the grey veil was worse than in the surrounding air, but he had no intention of finding out.

Around fifty feet in front of the van was Steel Sky. The plinths it was mounted on were hidden under the fog, and the radar array and four heavy machine guns looked as if they were floating. As he watched, all four of the guns whirred as the motorised gimbals they were mounted on made a synchronised tiny adjustment. Delaney grinned, knowing that they were doing exactly what he had programmed them to do. Watch and shoot. Watch and shoot.

While he waited, Delaney thought back over the events of the day. It had taken him a while to programme the system to do what Isobel wanted it to do, but he had gone over his numbers three or four times to be sure they were correct. He was doing it for her, after all.

Delaney closed his eyes and thought about Isobel. She was back in the Portakabin, waiting for him. When he'd picked her up earlier, she'd been delighted to see him. He closed his eyes tighter and sent her a message.

"Is everything okay?"

"Perfect," she replied. "I'm here, waiting for you. Hurry back."

89

Lizzie sat up in her bed when she heard the distinctive sound of a Hercules transport plane overhead. She glanced at her watch—it was bang on time for once—and then looked at the chair by the side of her bed. In it, Adams was snoozing using his hand as a pillow. She looked at him as he slept. That was the worst part about being sent home. She wouldn't see him for months. But at least she would see him. If she stayed out here, that was far from certain. He looked absolutely exhausted, and she didn't really want to wake him up, but she didn't have long.

Adams mumbled something in his sleep and adjusted his position in the chair.

"You awake, sleepyhead?" Lizzie said. Then she felt her stomach lurching when she remembered that Travis used to call her that. Adams just mumbled something in reply. "Adams, you lazy bastard," Lizzie said, much louder. "Wake up!"

"What?" Adams's eyes flicked open, and he looked

around as if he didn't know where he was. "What's going on?"

"My Fat Albert's just arrived, so the medical team will be here soon to collect me," Lizzie replied. "You know what they're like about timings."

"Yeah," Adams said, running his hand over his chin. Lizzie heard the scraping noise of his stubble. "That's only so they don't get left behind here while their plane disappears into the night without them."

"Do you blame them?"

"Not in the slightest. You got everything?"

"I think so."

Lizzie looked down on the floor next to Adams's chair. Her large black rucksack was there, complete with its dusty yellow and green ribbon, as well as her carry-on bag. Not that the Hercules had a hold, though. Her rucksack would just be thrown in the plane with the other freight. Like the odd coffin.

She knew Travis would be right at the front of the plane, hidden from the sight of the other passengers by a curtain. The plane would land at Brize Norton to decamp all the passengers and their bags and then disappear for a couple of hours before returning with just him on board. His final flight.

"If you have left anything behind, just let me know and I'll send it on to you. It's Birmingham you're going to, isn't it?"

"Yep, at least to start with. Hopefully, I won't be in for long and I can get back home."

"That reminds me," Adams said, leaning forward and reaching into his pocket. He pulled out a set of keys. "Here you go."

"What are they?"

"They're the keys to my flat. It's empty, so you might as well use it if you wanted to get away from Honington."

"Are you sure?"

"Of course I'm sure," Adams replied with a grin. "But there are a few rules."

"Okay." Lizzie started smiling.

"Don't annoy Mrs Higgins, my neighbour. Don't be putting the toilet seat down all the time. Leave it up until it's needed. Don't adjust the temperature in the shower. It took me months to set it properly."

"Yes, that's all good. I can do that."

"Under no circumstances are you to watch any of the DVDs on the bottom shelf of the bookcase in the lounge. That's my Frankie Vaughan collection."

"He was a singer, wasn't he? I didn't know he did films as well."

"It's rhyming slang, Lizzie."

"Frankie Vaughan?" Lizzie replied, thinking. "Oh. Porn."

"Yeah, so they're off limits."

"Why? That's not fair!" Lizzie said, trying to keep a straight face. "Have you got any good stuff?"

"What sort of good stuff?"

"I don't know, dwarf porn maybe?"

"Um, there's a few films with Bridget the Midget in, I think." Lizzie couldn't stop herself from cackling with laughter at Adams's response, but her laughter soon turned into a rasping cough. "That one's in between 'Womb Raider' and 'Shaving Ryan's Privates' if I remember correctly."

When she had stopped trying to cough and laugh at the same time, Lizzie thanked Adams for the keys.

"Don't worry, I'll look after your flat if I do use it," she said, "and your porn collection."

"It's no problem. I like the thought of you being there," Adams replied. "Seriously. I do like the idea of that."

"Me sleeping and farting in your bed?"

"Maybe not the farting bit," Adams said with a smile as he put on a stupid foreign accent that wasn't from anywhere in particular, "but the thought of you being in my bed gives me a funny feeling in my trousers."

"Adams, come here and give me a hug, would you?" Lizzie said. He stood and did just that, wrapping his arms around her and holding her tightly.

"I'll see you soon, yeah?" he whispered in her ear, and Lizzie could tell he was trying not to cry.

"You big soft lump," Lizzie whispered back. "I'll see you in Cyprus for your R&R. I know which hotel we'll be staying at already. Do you want me to bring any DVDs?" She didn't want Adams to start blubbing because she would be only seconds behind him.

"There isn't any porn in my flat, Lizzie," Adams replied, managing to chuckle. "Sorry to disappoint you."

"There might be by the time you get back," Lizzie replied. Adams's chuckle turned into a laugh and he was just about to say something when a loud female voice rang around the inside of the ward.

"Well, no wonder the bloody woman can't breathe properly!"

Lizzie looked up to see a squadron leader marching across the ward toward them, a broad smile on her face. It was one of the nurses from the aeromedical evacuation squadron at RAF Brize Norton. Lizzie didn't know her, but knew she had a fearsome reputation.

"Hey, Cassie," Adams said as the woman approached. She was about five foot five, slightly overweight, and had her blonde hair tied up into a fierce-looking bun. Lizzie looked at her green flight suit with various badges and patches on it. "I thought you were a nurse?" Adams asked her.

"I am a nurse, Adams," Cassie replied with a smile in Adams's direction. "A proper one too, not like you emergency department divas."

"So why are you dressed like a pilot?"

"Very funny," Cassie said. "Now piss off and let me introduce myself to my patient." She turned her attention to Lizzie, and Lizzie saw Adams raise a hand in her direction before turning to leave. Before he left, she caught the glint of a tear in his eye, but he brushed it away as soon as it had appeared.

"So," Cassie said, "I'm guessing you're Lizzie Jarman?"

"That'll be me," Lizzie replied.

"So far, so good then." Cassie smiled. It was a genuine smile, and despite her reputation, Lizzie warmed to the woman. "Now, we've got about ten minutes before we have to get to the pan. Do you need a last minute wee? Only the toilets in the back of a Hercules weren't really designed for ladies?"

90

"Que voulez-vous dire, manquante?" Adèle said to Laurent as he burst into her office. *What do you mean, missing?*

"Isobel's missing, Adèle," Laurent replied, his voice trembling. "She didn't turn up for her night shift, and she's not in her accommodation."

"Merde," Adèle replied. *Shit.*

"What should we do? That's not like her at all."

"No, you're right. It's not." Adèle thought for a few seconds, wondering what the best course of action would be. There weren't that many other places she could be. "Have we checked anywhere else? The gym? The boardwalk?"

"No, not yet," Laurent replied. "I sent a runner to the accommodation block when we realised she'd not arrived for her shift, but that was it."

Adèle was just about to reply when there was a tap at her door. She looked up sharply, irritated at the interruption.

"What is it?" she barked, switching to English when she saw who it was. It was Adams, the medical advisor. "Now's not the best time, Adams, to be honest."

"Oh, okay, I'm sorry." He made to leave but something in his expression softened Adèle's response.

"No wait," she said, "it's me who should be apologising. I'm sorry I snapped at you."

"I just wanted to let you know that Lizzie—Sergeant Jarman—had been collected by the aeromed team, that was all."

"Okay, excellent," Adèle replied, managing a smile. "Thank you for letting us know."

"Also, I wanted to thank you for looking after her." He glanced at Laurent as he said this, and Adèle saw Adams frown. "What's going on?"

"One of our nurses hasn't turned up for her night shift, that's all," Laurent replied. "She's probably just forgotten."

"Is it Isobel?" Adams asked.

"Yes, it is," Adèle said. "Laurent is about to send some people out to look for her, make sure she's okay."

"Are you going to send someone to Delaney's office?" Adams asked.

"You think he might have done something to her?" Laurent replied, crossing the office to stand right in front of Adams. It was an almost threatening gesture, but Adèle didn't think it bothered Adams in the slightest.

"I went to see him earlier," Adams replied. "He was really, I don't know, tense."

"Go on?" Adèle replied, suddenly curious. "How do you mean?"

"I don't think he's very well, and I'm not sure he's been taking his medication. The bottles didn't look any emptier today than they were yesterday."

"What medication?" Laurent asked.

"His anti-psychotics."

Laurent swore loudly in French, and Adèle recoiled.

"Laurent, please," she said in English.

"If he's done something to her," he replied, also in English, "I will-"

"Laurent, enough," Adèle said firmly. The last thing she needed was him going off on an ill-advised crusade.

"Do you want me to go to his office and see if he's there?" Adams asked.

"I'll come with you," Laurent said.

"No, Laurent, I need you here. Would you mind going, Adams?" Adèle replied. Adams nodded his head.

"Sure, no problem. I can tell him I'm just making sure he's okay, having just lost his boss and everything."

"Thanks, Adams," Adèle said. "I'd appreciate that." He turned to leave, telling them he'd call if there was anything to report before he did so. She waited for the door to close before returning her attention to Laurent.

"Laurent, what on earth has got into you? First there was that nonsense the other day, and now this." She kept her tone measured and friendly, but at the same time wanted to make sure that Laurent knew she wasn't going to be fobbed off. "What's going on?"

"Nothing, Adèle," Laurent replied. She looked at him carefully, knowing that he wasn't being truthful but unsure how hard to push him. "Honestly, everything's fine."

"Laurent, look at me." Adèle got to her feet and crossed to where Laurent was standing with his arms tightly crossed over his chest. "Relax your arms." He did so, and she took his hands in hers. "As a friend, a close friend I hope, I think there's something going on that's affecting your work. So talk to me as a friend before I have to discuss it with you as your boss."

Laurent let out a deep sigh before replying.

"There's just some stuff going on at home, that's all."

"What kind of stuff?"

"It's Patrice."

"He's your partner?"

"At the moment." Laurent looked deflated as he looked at Adèle with sad eyes. "I'm not sure he will be when I get back."

"Oh, I see," Adèle said. "I'm sorry to hear that, Laurent, I really am. And of course being here means you can't deal with it properly, the way you want to." Laurent just nodded. "But don't let it colour your judgement, that's all I would say." Adèle nodded in the direction of the door. "Those boys and girls out there, they look up to you as a good leader and a good man. Don't let them down."

She watched as he nodded, and she could see some of the resolve she knew he had in spades come back into his eyes.

"Thanks, Adèle," Laurent said. "I didn't want to burden you with it when I know you've got so much else on your plate."

"Then you're a fool," Adèle replied with a kindly smile, "if you think that's a burden to me. So, what shall we do about Isobel? It is quite out of character for her not to come in to work."

"Well, hopefully she's just not realised that she's supposed to be working. I'll send some of the team to the places you mentioned. The gym, the boardwalk."

"And if she's not there?"

"I guess we'll have to get the police involved. She'll be

missing, after all. I just hope she's not with this Delaney. That worries me a lot."

"Yes, I think you're right there," Adèle said with a sigh. "It worries me too."

91

When Adams parked his car outside Delaney's Portakabin, he could tell straight away that it was deserted. There were no lights on at either of the windows and, as he approached the air conditioning unit that was underneath one of them, he could see it wasn't on. Adams stepped up to the door and rapped on it anyway, but there was no response.

Adams returned to his car and opened the boot to get to his medical grab-bag. He opened it up to look for the torch he knew was in there. When he found it—a green standard issue torch that was a lot more powerful than it looked—he flicked the switch to make sure it was working before making his way back to the Portakabin.

Standing on tip-toes, Adams was just about able to see in through the window. He used the torch to illuminate what he could inside the building, which wasn't much. He needed something to stand on so he could see inside properly, but he couldn't find anything. Adams returned to his car, got in it, and drove it forward a few feet so that he would be able to stand on the bonnet.

When he finally could see inside the Portakabin, he started to get concerned. It looked as if Delaney had been burgled. The interior had been completely trashed. The maps on the walls had been ripped down and screwed up into large balls, several of the tables had been tipped over, and the large computer monitor that he'd seen Delaney working at was smashed. In the centre was an impact mark with a spider's web of fine white cracks surrounding it.

Adams angled the torch to see what else was inside the Portakabin, and his feet slipped on the bonnet of his car. Swearing, he managed to grab the window frame before he slipped off the car completely. As he did so, the torch illuminated something that caught his attention inside the building. On the floor, next to the overturned fridge, were several rolled up balls of tissue paper. It wasn't the paper that bothered Adams, though. It was the fact that they were covered in blood.

He got down from the car and returned to the door of the Portakabin, trying the handle to see if was locked. It was, so he wiggled the handle to see how solid the door was. Delaney could, potentially, be inside and injured. If he was struggling with his mental health, he may have self-harmed which would explain the blood-soaked tissues Adams had just seen. Adams took a step back and looked at the door. He raised his leg and kicked the door as hard as he could just above the lock. To Adams's surprise, it flew open. He stifled a grin as he stepped through. Adams had always wanted to kick a door in, but never had the opportunity before.

"Delaney?" Adams called out. "Are you in here, mate?" He shone the torch round to find the light switch next to the door and flicked it on.

When the fluorescent lights flickered into life, Adams could see that the damage to the inside of the Portakabin was worse than he had thought. Almost everything that was breakable inside the building was broken. Phones were strewn on the floor, ripped from their cables. The floor was littered with detritus and torn up paper, and the only sound apart from the lights humming above his head was a computer fan whirring in a case with a large dent in the side. There was no sign of Delaney.

Adams saw another door at the back of the Portakabin. He crossed to it and tried the handle, but it was locked as well. When he repeated the same movement as he had done with the other door, he could tell that it was a lot more robust. As he stopped rattling the door to consider what he was going to do next, he heard something from the other side. Whatever it was, it sounded muffled.

"Hello? Is that you, Delaney? It's Adams." He stopped to listen and heard a definite thud. "I've come to make sure you're okay, Delaney. Can you let me in?" He was rewarded with three thuds. It must be Delaney. Perhaps he had been burgled, after all, and then locked into this room? "Stand back from the door, Delaney," Adams called out. "I'm going to kick it open."

It took Adams four solid kicks before the door even looked as if it was going to open. When he saw it give a little at the edge, he tried a shoulder barge, but all that did was hurt his shoulder. Gritting his teeth, he put everything he had into one more kick and the door finally flew open before rebounding straight back into the jamb.

Adams pushed the door open, turning his torch back on to illuminate the interior of the room. He saw the mattress on the floor that the door had bounced back from, and then he saw Isobel. Adams was so shocked at the sight of the woman that he almost dropped the torch. She was lying on her side on the mattress, her arms and legs folded behind her. As he flashed the torch over her face, Adams could see that she was gagged as well as tied up.

His hand flew to the multi-tool on his belt and he whipped it out, his fingers trembling. Adams opened the sharpest knife in the tool and knelt down next to Isobel.

"It's okay, Isobel," he told her as he reached behind her head to untie her gag. "It's okay, I've got you." The second he loosened the gag, Isobel spluttered and started shouting.

"You must hurry!" she said, tears streaming down her face. "Leave me here! You must hurry!" Adams made a shushing sound as he bent over the young woman to look at her hands and feet. She had been hog-tied with black plastic cable ties. There was a set around her wrists and another set around her ankles. A third set ran between the other two, pulling her arms and legs back into what must have been an excruciating position. Adams started sawing at the cable tie that joined her arms and legs together, noting blood around Isobel's wrists and ankles where she must have struggled to escape. "Adams, you must go!" Isobel shouted again as he sawed at the thick plastic. When his knife cut through the cable ties, Isobel screamed as her arms and legs were released.

Adams made short work of the ties securing her wrists and ankles, and helped Isobel get into a sitting position on the filthy mattress. She was sobbing as he did so, murmuring something in French.

"Isobel, what's happened?" Adams asked.

"It's Delaney," she replied, looking at him through her

tears. "I was walking to work, and he bundled me into his van and brought me here. But you must find him!"

"Are you hurt?"

"No, he just tied me up. But you must hurry!"

"Why?"

"That anti-rocket system he's in charge of. It's got machine guns attached to it."

"I don't understand, Isobel," Adams said, thoroughly confused. "Is he going to do something with the machine guns?"

"Yes!" Isobel replied, almost screaming at Adams. "He's going to use them to shoot down a plane!"

92

Lizzie tried to make herself as comfortable as possible on the stretcher and ignore the curious stares of the soldiers who were settling themselves in around her. She'd not been on a Hercules since she was taken home from Afghanistan after her previous tour, and she couldn't remember much about that trip at all.

"Are you comfortable, sweetheart?" Cassie asked her. "Can I get you anything?"

"A privacy curtain would be nice," Lizzie said. In response, Cassie turned and stared down the darkened interior of the transport plane. Lizzie saw several soldiers catch her eyes and turn away.

"Sorry, Lizzie," Cassie replied as she fussed around her. "We're already using it."

Lizzie turned and looked toward the front of the plane. There was an olive green curtain that extended from the ceiling to the floor. Behind it, Lizzie knew, was Travis. Attached to the curtain was a taped piece of paper with the words *URINAL U/S* in large capital letters. The only reason that any of the other passengers would have to go to the front of the plane was because there was a urinal up there. By declaring it as unserviceable, none of them would realise there was a coffin secreted behind the curtain.

"How long until we take off?" Lizzie asked.

"Not long now," Cassie replied. "They're just closing the ramp. A few moments, I'd imagine."

"Can you keep a secret?"

"Of course I can." Cassie smiled conspiratorially at Lizzie and leant over so that her ear was close to her mouth. "I love a good secret, me."

"I don't really like flying," Lizzie said. Cassie laughed in response.

"You chose the wrong service to join if you don't like flying."

"It's more the takeoff and landing bit that I don't really like," Lizzie replied. "I mean, if something's going to go wrong, that's most likely when it'll happen, isn't it?"

"Lizzie, these Fat Alberts are safe as houses. When was the last time one of these old boys had a problem on a routine mission like this one?"

Lizzie thought for a moment. Cassie was right. There had been some problems with Hercules transport planes over the years, but it had always been on operational sorties, not routine flights. She settled back in the stretcher and tried to relax. Around her was a hubbub of noise. Her fellow passengers, all soldiers returning home at the end of their tour, were in good spirits and talking excitedly. Lizzie caught fragments of their conversations, smiling when she overheard one of them telling another about how much he was looking forward to his first beer in three months. Another couple were talking about football and Arsenal's chances in the FA cup. Their voices faded away as the engines started spinning into life.

"It's a busy flight," Lizzie said to Cassie, opening her eyes.

"Full house, I reckon," Cassie replied. "I was talking to the loadie on the way over and he said they had seventy pax including us. Do you want these?" Lizzie looked to see Cassie holding up a large green pair of ear defenders with a band across the top. "Or I've got some of the little orange squishy ones if you'd prefer. I don't know about you, but I can't sleep with these on. They make my ears sweat."

"I'll have the squishy ones if that's okay."

Cassie handed Lizzie a small packet, and she opened it, rolling the small lozenge shaped bits of foam in her fingers. As she put them in her ears, the background noise of the engines and the soldiers talking faded into the background.

Lizzie closed her eyes again. It wouldn't be long now, and they would be on their way home. She felt, rather than heard, the engines as they reached full power and a moment later, the aircraft lurched as it started to taxi out to the runway.

93

Delaney grinned as he heard the engines of the Hercules starting up in the distance. He got out of the van and walked over to the radar array, the mist swirling around his feet as he did so. The smell wasn't any worse in the fog, but nor was it any better. He raised a hand and ran it over the top of the radar sensors as if it were a pet dog. Which it was, in a sense. It was his pet. His creation. His idea.

He looked at the four machine guns as he recalled the first time they had tested the system. It had worked perfectly. No thanks to that fat fuck, Rubenstein. It was only Delaney's brilliance with the software that had meant the trial had worked and Aeolus had won the contract. No one else thought that, of course, but Delaney knew it was the truth.

The guns themselves were L1A1 12.7 mm heavy machine guns. The bastard children of the Browning M2 fifty calibre machine gun, widely recognised as one of the finest heavy machine guns ever developed. Their belt feeds were adapted so they could deliver several thousand rounds from their ammunition boxes through a disintegrating belt mechanism.

Delaney had even adapted the guns so that the software in the radar array monitored the temperature of the guns. If they looked like they could be overheating, the software would automatically turn two of them off and keep the other two operating, switching them over according to the temperature. The worst-case scenario was that following an initial sustained period of fire, only two out of the four guns would be operational, each one spitting out over ten rounds a second in the direction of whatever they were configured to attack and bring out of the sky. Which, in this case, was a Hercules C130J transport plane.

Delaney watched as the four sentinels jerked in unison, moving themselves to align with the Hercules. He smiled, knowing that the plane was on the move, and closed his eyes to message Isobel.

"It's started!" he told her in his mind.

"Fantastic," she replied almost instantly. "I'm watching through your eyes. I can't wait to see this!"

Part of Delaney wished that Isobel was here next to him to properly witness what was about to happen instead of watching it via him. But she hadn't wanted that. When he'd picked her up earlier in the van, she had asked him to secure her so that she felt safe, telling him exactly how she wanted to be restrained without physically speaking a word.

Delaney had been only too happy to do as she wanted. Tying her up this way would, she had told him, just increase the pleasure they would have when he returned. He had tenderly wrapped a piece of cloth around her mouth, just as she had asked him to, to help her focus on communicating with him just using her mind.

In the distance, Delaney could hear the pitch of the engines of the Hercules change. The droning got louder and higher as the pilots got ready to take off. In front of him, the heavy machine guns quivered in anticipation, ready to deliver the contents of their ammunition boxes the moment the plane reached five hundred feet. It was too high for the pilots to recover, and that was assuming that the full fuel tanks in the wings hadn't exploded, which was the exact part that the guns were aimed at. Two fuel tanks. Two wings. Two guns each.

That was the bit Delaney was looking forward to most.

94

Adams jabbed at the brakes of his car, sending the vehicle into a sharp skid. Before it had stopped moving, he had already thrown the driver's door open and leapt out. He skidded on the damp ground, regaining his footing and sprinting toward the Steel Sky array. He could see a solitary figure standing in the centre of the machine guns next to the radar assembly. It was Delaney.

When he got closer to Steel Sky, Adams started shouting.

"Stop it, Delaney! Fucking make it stop." Adams skidded to a halt a few yards in front of the contractor. When Delaney turned to look at him, even in the dim light Adams could tell the man had taken a kicking. "Turn it off!" Adams screamed.

Behind them, the noise of the Hercules's engines got louder as the plane approached them. Adams looked at the machine guns jerking. Isobel had been right. They were tracking the plane as it made its way down the runway toward them.

Adams watched as Delaney closed his eyes tightly for a second before opening them again.

"She says no," he replied, his voice low and even. "This is supposed to happen."

"Who says no?" Adams shouted.

"Isobel."

"No, she fucking doesn't. I just found her, tied up in your office."

"She. Says. No."

"Delaney," Adams said, taking a deep breath and trying to keep his voice calm and measured. If Delaney was having a psychotic episode, then shouting and screaming at him wasn't going to have any effect. No matter how high the odds were. "Delaney, listen. You don't have to do this. There are people on board that plane." People like Lizzie.

"It's too late," Delaney replied, his voice soft. "There's nothing I can do, no matter how much you want me to."

"Delaney, turn them off!" Adams said, watching as the machine guns adjusted to keep themselves targeted on the Hercules.

"I can't." In the distance, Adams heard the change in the sound of the aircraft as it left the ground. The next part of their flight path would see the Hercules going into a steep climb to gain altitude and safety. "The minute that plane gets to five hundred feet, my four guard dogs here will start barking. And there's nothing you can do about it."

Adams thought frantically about his options, knowing that he only had seconds to stop Delaney. He pulled the Browning pistol from his holster and brought it up into the aim, pointing it directly at Delaney's face. Delaney took a step backwards in response.

"Turn it off, Delaney."

"I said, I can't." Delaney was looking at Adams with a faint smile on his face. "I destroyed the computer back in the office so even if I wanted to, I couldn't change Steel Sky." He started laughing. "Put that down and let's watch the show."

Adams thought back to the night he had spent with Lizzie and the look on her face as she had clung to him as they moved in unison, her eyes closed and a look of intense concentration on her face. Then she had opened them and looked at him, and at that moment, just at the moment of his release, Adams had realised how much in love with her he was. And she was about to die.

"Last chance, Delaney," Adams said through gritted teeth.

"There is no last chance, Adams. There is only this." Beside them, the four machine guns made a clicking sound as the belts started feeding rounds toward the firing mechanism and Adams knew that it was too late. He knew then that he would happily die for Lizzie Jarman. And he would also kill for her.

He tightened his grip on the Browning pistol, looked down the sights at Delaney as the contractor took another step backward and raised his hands in the air.

Adams closed one eye before pulling the trigger. Then he pulled it again, and again, until finally he was firing on an empty magazine.

95

Lizzie jumped as the aircraft lurched in the air. She had heard some sort of awful wrenching noise, metal on metal, and the plane was now juddering violently. She reached out her hands and grabbed the sides of her stretcher, her heart suddenly racing.

"What's going on?" Lizzie shouted, forgetting about the hearing protection she had in her ears. "Cassie?" Around her, the plane was shaking violently and Lizzie could see the other passengers looking at each other with concerned expressions. Lizzie reached her hands up to her head and pulled the small foam lozenges from her ears. She could hear a metallic screeching that almost drowned out the noise of the engines.

"Blimey, you weren't joking when you said you didn't like flying, were you?" It was Cassie, and she was leaning over the stretcher with a smile on her face.

"What's happening?" Lizzie said, trying not to let her terror show.

"Nothing," Cassie replied, putting her hands on

Lizzie's. "Nothing's happening. Just relax. Or I'll give you a needle that'll relax you for me."

The juddering started to subside, and Lizzie could hear relieved laughter from the other passengers in the plane.

"What was that?" Lizzie asked, her heart subsiding.

"It was just the flaps being retracted," Cassie replied. "The same thing happened when we took off from Cyprus. The loadie said they were a bit sticky, that's all." Lizzie could feel the plane start to settle down in its flight path as the screeching noise receded. "Okay?"

"Sorry," Lizzie said, feeling foolish for being so dramatic. "Just gave me a bit of a fright, that's all."

"Don't you worry about it, Lizzie," Cassie said with a smile. "Like I said, safe as houses, these Fat Alberts are."

96

Adams's ears were ringing from the sound of an entire magazine being emptied less than two feet from his ears. When he'd fired the pistol previously, it had always been with the benefit of hearing protection.

He looked at the smoking remains of the Steel Sky radar array in front of him. Every single one of the thirteen rounds in his pistol had hit home and riddled the honeycomb box that had been on top of the pole. Smoke was pouring from the ruined radar array. It was the only thing he could think of to do as the machine guns had clicked into action. For a second, Adams regretted not saving the last round in the magazine for Delaney. Unlucky for some, and it certainly would have been unlucky for Delaney, but Adams's only focus when he'd been squeezing the trigger as quickly as he could was to destroy the control mechanism for the machine guns.

Adams listened to the retreating sound of the Hercules's engine as it disappeared into the inky black sky above his head. He didn't think any rounds had been fired

Incoming Fire

from the machine guns in the end, but he still needed to deal with Delaney. Adams re-holstered the pistol and squinted in the direction of the last place he'd seen the man. He was gone. Adams was just thinking that the contractor had run when he'd started firing, when he heard a splashing noise.

"Delaney?" Adams called out. "Are you there?" There was no response. Adams took a few tentative steps toward where he knew the edge of the poo pond would be and listened carefully. There was another faint splash. "Delaney?"

Adams looked at the mist that was floating above the poo pond and noticed an area where it was swirling in a whirlpool effect. There was another splashing sound, this one much fainter than before. Adams paused for a moment, wondering what to do. He couldn't see Delaney, he didn't know where the ground ended and the poo pond begun because of the mist. Adams tilted his head to the side and listened carefully, but the only sound he heard was a bubbling noise.

97

Air Commodore Maugham settled back into his sofa and lifted the coffee to his lips before taking a small sip. In front of him, a television was showing a live feed from the BBC News channel. On the screen was a static shot of the rear of a Hercules transport plane. Maugham recognised the RAF station the plane was sitting in without having to refer to the ticker-tape feed at the bottom of the screen. It was RAF Brize Norton, a base he knew well but had never had the privilege of commanding. Maybe one day he would?

As he watched, the BBC commentator's voice cut in.

"We're live at RAF Brize Norton, where the latest casualty from the conflict in Afghanistan is being repatriated. Corporal Ryan Perkins, aged twenty-four, was killed in action just outside Kandahar air base." The commentator at last had the good grace to shut up as there was some movement on the screen in front of Maugham.

Maugham had spent most of the afternoon crafting a citation for Corporal Perkins. He had managed to speak to several members of the patrol that had come under attack, and to a man they had all told him how Perkins had managed, under concentrated enemy fire, to rescue one of their team from a horrible demise in a burning vehicle. Maugham was hopeful for a Military Cross at the least. Perhaps even higher.

At the end of the day, the air commodore didn't care what Corporal Perkins received, as long as the young man was recognised for his bravery. If Her Majesty the Queen agreed with Maugham, then Corporal Perkins's family would be the recipients of a very special medal with a crimson ribbon. But, Maugham thought as he sipped his coffee, that would be entirely up to Her Majesty.

Maugham sat up straighter in his chair as the scene in front of him started to unfold. The commentator started talking and Maugham reached for the remote control to mute him, preferring to concentrate on what was happening on the screen. The camera zoomed in on the rear of the Hercules C130J, and Maugham saw the feet of the pall bearers appear.

The first pall bearer to appear fully on the screen was a sergeant. Maugham could see from the embroidered badges on her lapels that she was a medic. Opposite her was a young regiment corporal, selected no doubt because he was the same height as the sergeant.

Maugham got to his feet as he watched the party carry the flag covered coffin to the waiting hearse, the male pallbearer at the rear mouthing silent instructions. Maugham snapped a salute up, holding it until the party had manoeuvred the coffin into the vehicle. Then he let his arm fall to his side, and he felt every year of his service weighing upon him.

"Corporal Perkins," Maugham muttered under his breath as he looked at the closeup of Sergeant Jarman's tear-streaked face on the screen in front of him. "I salute you."

AUTHOR'S NOTE

Hi. Nathan Burrows here,

Thanks for getting this far - I hope you enjoyed reading *Incoming Fire* as much as I enjoyed writing it. Adams and Lizzie will be back soon...

If you did enjoy the book, perhaps you would consider leaving a review to help other readers find it? But if you didn't enjoy, perhaps you could let me know instead?

Either way, by all means drop me a line at nathan@nathanburrows.com and let me know what you thought. I'll always reply!

Speak soon,

Nathan Burrows

nathanburrows.com

ALSO BY NATHAN BURROWS

THE GARETH DAWSON SERIES

Blind Justice - Gareth Dawson Series Book 1

An innocent man sent to prison for life. A lawyer gives him a second chance. Can they overcome an unfair system to clear his name?

Gareth Dawson is innocent. He's not a murderer. His main problem is that the British justice system doesn't agree with him. He might be a reformed thief guilty of many things in his past, but not murder. In the space of a few short months, Gareth has gone from being married to the woman of his dreams to facing a life sentence.

Inside Her Majesty's Prison Whitemoor, a Category A prison in Cambridgeshire, Gareth's got all the time in the world to go over the events that led to the guilty verdict. The guilty verdict which cost him everything in the world that he loved. His dignity. His freedom. His wife.

Gareth is approached by a lawyer, Paul Dewar, who claims to have information that will vindicate him. But is it enough to set him free? As threats against Gareth increase on the inside, Paul Dewar's challenge, and Gareth's fight for freedom, begins.

Blind Justice is available on Amazon

~

Finding Milly - Gareth Dawson Series Book 2

Jimmy Tucker is dying. There's only one person he wants to tell. His daughter—Milly. But when he gets home from the hospital, she's vanished without a trace.

The inoperable brain aneurysm deep within Jimmy's head could burst at any time—a cough, a sneeze, or a blow to the head could kill him instantly. With the police not interested in Milly's disappearance, Jimmy takes things into his own hands and begins to look for his only daughter. But it doesn't take him long to realise that his daughter is not the woman he thinks she is.

As he gradually discovers Milly's shocking private life, Jimmy enlists the help of Gareth Dawson, an ex-crook with a big heart. But Gareth can only help Jimmy up to a point.

As the pressure mounts, can Jimmy uncover the truth about Milly's disappearance before it's too late—for either of them?

Finding Milly is available on Amazon

∽

Single Handed - Gareth Dawson Series Book 3

When a dismembered hand is discovered in a lobster pot off the North Norfolk coast, it's one less missing person for the police to look for. Until something much darker emerges...a blackmail note.

Gareth Dawson, a reformed criminal whose gruff exterior hides a kind heart, is trying to deal with the aftermath of his brother-in-law's death. But if the extortionist reveals the shameful secret that Gareth's brother-in-law has been hiding, the truth will destroy both his memory and the lives of those mourning him. As well as those who aren't.

With his sister refusing to go to the police, Gareth realises that he will have to deal with the situation—alone and single handed. But who is telling the truth? And who is lying?

Can Gareth identify the blackmailer and uncover the truth about his step-father? Or are some family secrets best left hidden...?

Single Handed is available on Amazon

∽

The first three books in the series are also available as an eBox Set which is available on Kindle Unlimited.

The Gareth Dawson Series (Books 1-3) eBox Set is available on Amazon

Printed in Great Britain
by Amazon